Praise for

THE INVISIBLE

"An alpha female heroine, along with an engaging plot loaded with realism, makes for a captivating historical thriller. Even better, it's all drawn from the life of a real American hero."

—Steve Berry, *New York Times* bestselling author of *The Warsaw Protocol*

"An extraordinary profile of the immense courage and daring of Virginia Hall and an intimate look at the cost of war. . . . Emotionally charged, compulsively readable, richly detailed, and meticulously researched, Robuck's novel brings a forgotten World War II heroine to life and thrusts the reader into a dangerous world of espionage. An unforgettable book!"

—Chanel Cleeton, *New York Times* bestselling author of *The Last Train to Key West*

"*The* book for current times. The bigger-than-life heroine, Virginia Hall, and her band of Resistance fighters are ripped from the history books and put into glorious Technicolor by talented author Erika Robuck. . . . With gripping prose that brings the terror of war onto the pages and highlights the selflessness of ordinary people fighting together for a cause, *The Invisible Woman* should be required reading for everyone today."

—Karen White, *New York Times* bestselling author of *The Last Night in London*

"Erika Robuck shows us exactly how biographical fiction should be written: with respect for the historical record, a deep understanding of the subject, and the empathy to allow the character at the heart of the novel to shine through. Virginia Hall was a true hero, and she comes to extraordinary life in this book. I loved everything about it. . . . If you only read one World War II book this year, make it this one."

—Natasha Lester, *New York Times* bestselling author of *The Paris Secret*

"In this captivating, page-turning read, the talented Erika Robuck plunges her readers deep into the little-known critical espionage undertaken by the brilliant and brave spy Virginia Hall during World War II. *The Invisible Woman* shines a light on this courageous historical woman, whose pioneering work as an agent deserves recognition."

—Marie Benedict, *New York Times* bestselling author of
Lady Clementine

"Erika Robuck has given readers a precious gift. . . . [She] combines meticulous historical research with stunning prose and unforgettable characters to offer a book that is breathtakingly beautiful, and readers will not be able to put it down."

—Allison Pataki, *New York Times* bestselling author of *The Queen's Fortune*

"Robuck has mastered the balance of weaving fact with imagination to bring history's intriguing and underappreciated female figures to life. The harrowing exploits of World War II secret agent Virginia Hall are told with such nail-biting detail, there were times I had to close the book and wait for my pulse to drop. Absolutely riveting."

—Lee Woodruff, journalist and *New York Times* bestselling author of
Those We Love Most

"If you love historical fiction with a huge-hearted juggernaut of a heroine, *The Invisible Woman* is for you. This tense and vivid novel stands out. . . . When you like a character, and then admire her, and then want to meet her, you know the author has made her come uniquely alive. I read this book in a blur—that's how compelling it was."

—Stephen P. Kiernan, author of *Universe of Two* and *The Baker's Secret*

"Simply extraordinary. Beautifully written and intensely gripping—readers will be inspired by this tale of Virginia Hall and her unrelenting courage, conviction, and resilience during the darkest days of the war. Profound and riveting, this novel is a must-read."

—Kristin Beck, author of *Courage, My Love*

THE
INVISIBLE
WOMAN

Erika Robuck

Berkley
New York

BERKLEY
An imprint of Penguin Random House LLC
penguinrandomhouse.com

Copyright © 2021 by Erika Robuck
Readers Guide copyright © 2021 by Erika Robuck
Penguin Random House supports copyright. Copyright fuels creativity, encourages diverse
voices, promotes free speech, and creates a vibrant culture. Thank you for buying an authorized
edition of this book and for complying with copyright laws by not reproducing, scanning, or
distributing any part of it in any form without permission. You are supporting writers and
allowing Penguin Random House to continue to publish books for every reader.

BERKLEY and the BERKLEY & B colophon are registered trademarks of
Penguin Random House LLC.

Library of Congress Cataloging-in-Publication Data

Names: Robuck, Erika, author.
Title: The invisible woman / Erika Robuck.
Description: First edition. | New York: Berkley, 2021.
Identifiers: LCCN 2020032235 (print) | LCCN 2020032236 (ebook) |
ISBN 9780593102145 (trade paperback) | ISBN 9780593102152 (ebook)
Subjects: LCSH: Goillot, Virginia, 1906–1982—Fiction. | GSAFD: Biographical fiction.
Classification: LCC PS3618.O338 I58 2021 (print) |
LCC PS3618.O338 (ebook) | DDC 813/.6—dc23
LC record available at https://lccn.loc.gov/2020032235
LC ebook record available at https://lccn.loc.gov/2020032236

First Edition: February 2021

Printed in the United States of America
1 3 5 7 9 10 8 6 4 2

Cover images: front © Susan Fox / Trevillion;
spine © Rekha Garton / Trevillion
Cover design by Emily Osborne
Book design by Alison Cnockaert
Interior art: map of France by Peter Hermes Furian / Shutterstock

This book is a work of fiction. References to real people, events, establishments,
organizations, or locales are intended only to provide a sense of authenticity, and are
used fictitiously. All other characters and all incidents and dialogue are drawn
from the author's imagination and are not to be construed as real.

For Virginia Hall
a.k.a.
Artemis, Diane, Germaine, Marie, Camille,
Philomene, Brigitte, Louise, Anna . . .

The Special Operations Executive, or SOE, was a British World War II organization, formed in 1940. Their espionage, sabotage, and aid to Resistance groups made life hell for Nazis behind enemy lines. The Office of Strategic Services, or OSS, established in 1942, was its United States counterpart. When they were charged with their overall mission, Winston Churchill reportedly told them to "set Europe ablaze."

THE
INVISIBLE
WOMAN

Prologue

Summer 1926
PARIS

A S THE LAST full summer moon rises, an American walks arm in arm along the avenue with her new Parisian friend. They've just seen Josephine Baker at the Folies Bergère and can't say whether they're giddier from the champagne or from watching Baker's bare-breasted performance in a skirt made entirely of bananas.

The girls have rooms at a pension not far from the École Libre des Sciences Politiques, where the American will study in the fall, and where the Parisian is already a student. They dawdle on the way back, taking their time enjoying the City of Light, stopping to admire the Louvre and the Arc de Triomphe du Carrousel.

"I can imagine my first letter home to Daddy and Mother," says Virginia, the American. "'Although classes have not yet begun, I'm receiving quite an education.'"

The French girl giggles.

The silver case from Virginia's handbag flashes in the light of the streetlamp. She places two cigarettes in her mouth, lights them, and hands one to her friend.

"'The culture is entirely new,'" she continues, after exhaling. "'It's . . .'"

"Bananas!"

Their laughter echoes off the buildings on a side street, where a co-

coon of wealth and silence subdues them. In the shadows of the looming pale-stone residences, Virginia feels the hairs on her arms rise, and leads her friend back to the more populated streets. Once they've returned to the bustle, the French girl speaks.

"Josephine Baker has had a thousand marriage proposals. I'm just hoping for three or four before settling."

"Two thousand," says Virginia.

"You want two thousand proposals?"

"No, silly. Baker has had two thousand. If I ever decide to get married, I'll do the proposing, though Mother would be mortified to hear me say that."

"If you want to land a Frenchman, you'll need to work on your accent. It's terrible."

"Oh! How dare you!" Virginia tickles her friend until she apologizes.

Soon they arrive back at the pension, a cream-colored corner building with black wrought iron balconies. Over the entrance, a bas-relief grotesque griffin with a grumpy, judgmental face keeps watch. Virginia has named him Johnnie, after her older brother. Music spills from the windows of a top-floor apartment, and the lights inside reveal figures dancing.

"A party," Virginia says. "Let's go."

"I'm so tired."

"We're twenty years old! There's no *tired*."

"My feet are killing me."

"Johnnie would approve of your wish to turn in," Virginia says, pointing up at the griffin. "So, I do not. Come!"

Her friend throws up her arms in surrender. Virginia takes the French girl's hand and pulls her into the building. Gold-beaded fringe from her hem tickles the backs of her long legs as she skips steps all the way to the fourth floor. When the young women reach the gathering, Virginia straightens her dress, smooths her hair, and leads her friend into the room, where they fold into the mass of revelers.

Heartbeat pulsing in time to the music, Virginia joins the dancers by the open window. The portable gramophone runs down every two or three songs, and each time the record slows, the group finds it increasingly hilarious to freeze—like spent windup dolls—until someone cranks the player back to life.

The hours fall away at double speed. The more she drinks, the more Virginia wants to trap time in her hands, but it slips through her fingers like champagne. The slurred French around her becomes difficult to understand, and her brain aches from trying to find the right words. Suddenly she's aware of how hot it is in the fourth-floor apartment.

Her friend reclines on a couch, nodding off, where the erudite boarder—the one who sits in the common room making a show of reading French philosophers—kisses the girl every time she starts to drift. Virginia crosses the room and, the next time he goes in, spreads her hand over his entire face and pushes him so he falls over on the couch. He comes up straightening his glasses and apologizing, and scurries to join the tide of young men and women pouring out to the balcony to watch the sun rise. Virginia helps her friend up and they recede, slipping into the hallway shadows.

After her friend is safely tucked in bed, Virginia creeps on bare feet down to her own room on the second floor, where she slides the lock chain, leans her head back against the door, and closes her eyes. Once the room stops spinning, she drops her heels on the carpet and pads over to the balcony, stepping outside to inhale the fresh, dewy air. Two floors above, she can hear voices from the party.

"You have a cut between your eyes, under your glasses."

"It's from the American. She pushed me."

"Were you trying to kiss her?"

"No, her friend."

"Idiot!"

The reprimand brings a smile to her face and, as she takes in the skyline before her, she can't help but laugh at the magnificent, absurd, surreal dream of being in Paris.

It's her father she has to thank for this. He was the one who'd taken the family to France when she was a small girl, and Paris had made its first indelible impression. He'd awoken her before her mother and brother got up, and carried her in his strong arms over to the balcony of their hotel suite so he could show her the magic of the Paris sunrise. She could still smell his pipe smoke and see the dimple in his handsome face as he grinned at her while she took in the city bathed in early-morning light. It was the same conspiratorial smile he later gave when—in spite of her mother's protests—he approved her wish to study here. He approved of everything she wanted, especially if it was out of the ordinary mold her mother so desperately wished for her. Her eyes had been set at the horizon ever since.

I know what I'll write to Daddy, she thinks. *I'll write, "Thank you."*

Thank you for allowing me to travel here, to the city of my heart. To receive an education. To watch the shadow of the skyline at dawn. To hear the bells of Notre-Dame ringing the Sunday call to worship. To feel the warmth of sunrise, nudging the city awake, turning the Seine into a river of gold beneath the fresh blue sky.

"It has brought me to life," she says.

PART ONE

Artemis

Chapter 1

S EAS ARE ROUGH and mortally cold and, though she surely approaches her death, Virginia Hall can't row fast enough. France is within sight.

The warnings of her superiors echo in her mind.

"As a wireless operator in fully occupied France, you'll have six weeks to live."

Good, she'd thought. *Six weeks. Forty-two days.*

One day for each of those brave men and women she'd abandoned during her first mission in Lyon. If they're still alive, they surely languish in prisons and concentration camps, yet she escaped. The thought nearly chokes her, as it has every day for the last eighteen months, but she shoves it aside. She *will* go on.

In spite of the frigid night, Virginia sweats. The British gunboat only took the agents so far. They have to use a dinghy the rest of the way. She can feel the sting of blisters forming, and her partner Aramis—they are trained to use only code names—is too tired to continue. At sixty-two, he's old for a secret agent. As much as Virginia hates traveling with another, it will only be for a little while. His mission is confined to setting up safe houses and gathering intelligence in Paris, while Virginia's will take her to the outskirts of the city and then on to the mountain region of the

Haute-Loire. She'll coordinate supply drops to help arm and organize Resistance forces, the Maquis, to prepare them to rise up and fight when the Allies finally land. Any reporting she can do on Nazi activity won't go amiss, either, and Virginia is itching to help rain terror on their heads.

Still, the Haute-Loire seems remote, unimportant, and far from action, but Vera Atkins, a high-ranking intelligence officer with the SOE, is adamant that Virginia covers it. One thing is sure: Remote or not, Virginia will never again abandon France. Even if it means defying orders. This time she will stay until the liberation.

Hoping to discourage her from returning to France, Vera gave Virginia the grim details of the fates of all the wireless operators they'd lost in recent months.

"You can't bring them back by going and getting yourself killed," Vera had said.

"No, but I can help win the war."

"A noble motivation," Vera said. "Are you sure that's the only reason you want to return?"

It isn't. But Virginia didn't share that with Vera.

"You're a superwoman, just as the rumors said," says Aramis. "If your prosthetic leg weren't such a topic of conversation, I'd never have guessed. What's it they say you named it? Herbert?"

Cuthbert, she thinks, clenching her teeth.

Because the Gestapo took to calling her "the Limping Lady" when they started hunting her in Lyon, what she had once kept secret was exposed. As if she needed another reason to hate the Nazis. She's weary of people making a fuss about her leg, and most of all she's weary of this man. He has been talking since they met less than twenty-four hours ago, including telling her his real name, his day job, and details about his actual family. Most secret agents sneaking into Nazi-infested France might stay a little quieter, but Aramis is undeterred.

"With any luck, we can get you a stiff drink once we land," he continues. "Maybe the safe house will have a wine cellar they'll be happy to share for a small fee."

When he reaches across the dinghy to pat the concealed money bags at Virginia's hips, she drops the right oar, grabs his arm, and twists it.

"Never touch me again."

His eyes grow wide behind his spectacles. After a moment, she releases his arm and returns her hand to the oar. During the mere seconds she wasn't rowing, the dinghy turned, and a swell knocked the thirty-pound wireless suitcase into her good leg. Cursing her temper, she struggles to turn the vessel to cut the waves head-on instead of running parallel to them. Aramis picks up his set of oars to help her. They're soon on track, and in the silence between them, Virginia can no longer ignore the throbbing in her jaw.

Just last week, she'd sat in recovery from the sadistic dentist who had replaced her American fillings with gold, in the French way. Secret agents had to become their parts down to the last painful details. Vera had stood over her in the recovery room.

"Your first mission was a tea party compared to what now awaits you," Vera said.

Vera helped recruit Virginia for the SOE early in the war, before the US had been involved, when Virginia could use her cover as an American journalist to travel freely. Vera had formed and tested her, and continued to do so at every opportunity, even now that Virginia transferred to the OSS under American general William J. Donovan. With a price on Virginia's head, Vera didn't think it wise for Virginia to return to France. "Wild Bill" Donovan had overridden Vera, however—the grin he'd given Virginia reminiscent of the one her father gave when overriding her mother—and Vera never missed an opportunity to remind Virginia of the danger she faced.

"The new collaborator militia of thugs, the Milice," said Vera, her eyes intense on Virginia's, "are just as dangerous as the Nazis. In fact, more so. As native French, they understand dialect, know who's an outsider, and take delight in hunting the Resistance."

Virginia's mouth went dry. On her first mission, a year and half earlier, she didn't have to worry about her American accent. Now, since the US was in the war, and the Gestapo had plastered wanted posters of Virginia's face all over France, she knew she'd have to go undercover, but it hadn't yet dawned on her that she would need to be so careful when speaking.

"Finding the Maquis and getting them to trust you will be a challenge," said Vera. "But you must if we are to unleash hell on the Nazis once Operation Overlord begins."

"D-Day," Virginia said.

"D-Day. Which will just be the beginning."

"The beginning of the end."

"We hope," said Vera. "After D-Day, if you've had success finding Maquis groups, we'll drop in officers to take command in your wake as you move toward the Haute-Loire."

"Do you have the official date?"

"That's not yet for you to know," said Vera. "You must await the signal."

The poem. Verlaine's "Chanson d'automne." Autumn song. She had to memorize it. The broadcast of the first stanza by the BBC will signal invasion is imminent. The second stanza will announce its commencement.

"Once I get the Maquis armed," Virginia said, "holding back men and women who've been waiting to avenge their losses will be like trying to stop a dam from breaking."

"But you must," said Vera. "Once D-Day comes, and the fighting is in the open, you know how the Nazis will respond."

No. None of them knew. But they could all imagine how a rabid beast would strike back once cornered.

Vera had pulled out a small brass container from her jacket pocket engraved with an *L*. Lethal pill. In case of capture.

"Do you want it this time?" Vera asked.

"You know the answer to that question."

Vera stared at Virginia a long moment before sliding the container back into her jacket, and, after checking Virginia's pockets to make sure there weren't any London bus ticket stubs or American playing cards, Vera grasped Virginia's coat lapels and looked into her eyes. Her face softened. She became the old Vera, before all the war losses.

"Don't put yourself in unnecessary danger. Change safe houses frequently. Don't get attached. When this is all over, I want to toast our success, not fly to the states to give your mother the bad news."

"At least she'd be gratified to know she told me so."

Vera frowned.

"This war has made us all so cold," Vera said, almost to herself before adding one more thing. "In your final region, there's a remote village at its heart: Le Chambon-sur-Lignon. Protecting it must be your highest priority."

"Why is it so important?"

At that, Vera had released Virginia's lapels and returned to her rigid posture.

The shore is now upon Virginia and Aramis. The fog conceals the rocks, and they sharply navigate a turn so they don't crash. The edge of the dinghy is clipped, and while Virginia is able to steady herself, Aramis goes overboard. He sputters, trying to stand while the surf pounds him. Virginia beaches the dinghy, disembarks, pulls the boat farther ashore to ensure it doesn't wash away before they can empty it, and turns to take in the view.

France.

If she were still able to cry, she would. She inhales the air, filling her lungs. Unbidden, the memory rises of her father whispering her awake and carrying her through the darkness to watch the Paris sunrise, but she pushes it aside. She knows that—like her father—that version of France is gone. As much as she would love to savor this moment, the clock is ticking. She turns her attention back to Aramis, who moans in the sand.

"My knee."

She swears under her breath and shushes him for his complaints. Working quickly, she lifts their bags from the rubber dinghy, uses her knife to slice holes in it, and heaves a small boulder inside the boat to sink it. Once she's sure the vessel is fully submerged, she returns to Aramis. She pulls his strappy valise over her shoulders, gives him her lighter clothing suitcase, and carries the wireless suitcase in her other hand.

They spot the path that will lead to the farm where they'll spend the night. An icy rain falls, and by the time they arrive at the barn an hour later, they're both shivering, exhausted, and starving, with only an hour to sleep before they have to catch their train. Aramis snores within minutes, but Virginia cannot. As it has every night since Lyon, the image of a pair of cold blue eyes and a sinister smile plays in her mind as she stares through the dark.

Six weeks to live, they told her. She has much to accomplish in that time.

Chapter 2

A S SUNRISE BREAKS over the frosty March morning, shafts come in the barn through holes, reminding Virginia of her childhood farm in Baltimore, the place her late father taught her to hunt and hike and row and skin a rabbit. The last time she was at Box Horn Farm, seven years ago, she'd taken her six-year-old niece, Lorna, sledding. Up and down the hill behind the barn, over and over. Each time they got to the bottom, Lorna shouted, "Again, Aunt Dindy! Again!" No matter how badly her knee stump ached, Virginia would climb the hill with the child and sled back down until the night forced them to stop.

Again. Keep going.

In spite of what lies ahead, and what drags heavy behind her, these memories give her the strength to rise.

Virginia paints gray dye on her auburn hair, uses icy water from the pump outside to wash the dye through, and combs her wet hair into a severe bun. Then she smudges kohl under her brown eyes, draws wrinkles on her forehead and cheeks, plumps her slender frame with layers of old-woman's clothing, and puts on a pair of fake eyeglasses. When she awakens Aramis, he's shocked at the transformation that has aged her several decades beyond her thirty-seven years. Without speaking, she passes him a packet of biscuits from her stash, sits next to him on the dirt while he eats, and stitches the tear in his pants. When she finishes, he stares at her with gratitude.

"Come, husband," she says in French. "We have a train to catch."

Frustrating as it is for her, Aramis must accompany her to Crozant, where her first contact will provide her safe lodging for wireless transmission. His escort is necessary so he knows Virginia's place in the circuit, and so he can talk for them if they're stopped. Her French is plagued with the American accent she can't shake—a reality that tortures her. If she and Aramis make it, she needs to check in with HQ as soon as possible to get their pins on the map of agents. If she doesn't make contact within two weeks, she will be assumed captured or killed, and another wireless operator will have to be sent in her place.

At the busy hub of a train station, Nazis swarm. They shove batons in her chest, demand papers, push her and Aramis roughly along from one checkpoint to the next. *Identity card. Proof of residence. Travel permit. Ration book.* She and Aramis produce the forged documents with their fake identities, certain that each stop will be the one that catches them. Virginia hadn't fully appreciated what her superiors told her to expect in France. She didn't comprehend the potency of full Nazi occupation, how it pollutes the air and poisons those who breathe it.

They make it through, but as she climbs aboard the train behind Aramis, Virginia stumbles on the step. A young woman with red hair and green eyes is at her arm, giving her assistance. Virginia can't help but wonder if the young woman is one of the Resistance or a collaborator—everyone must choose. Virginia gives a curt nod of thanks before continuing.

She and Aramis struggle to find seats in the heartbreaking crush of hungry, hollow-eyed, weary people. When they find a spot, the young woman squeezes in next to her at the window. Heat emanates from the woman like a flame, bringing the exotic scent of her perfume to Virginia's nose.

Guerlain's Vol de Nuit. Night flight.

It was the perfume Virginia's fiancé, Emil, had given her, a lifetime ago, when she was whole and alive.

Flinging all thought of Emil away with a shake of her head, she threads her arm through Aramis's. When the whistle finally blows, she jumps in her seat. This distresses her because she has never been jumpy. Jumpiness makes one a target. Perhaps Vera was right to worry that Virginia had no business returning.

The young woman touches her arm and offers a smile of reassurance. Ignoring her and calling upon her training, Virginia stares out at the station clock to regulate her breathing by the second hand. She'd been instructed at a series of manor houses throughout Britain in everything from hand-to-hand combat, to sabotage, to interrogation. Psychological evaluations were a critical part of the process. Virginia always received the highest marks in her ability to keep cool. But now, something she sees nearly undoes her.

It's a sketch of her own face staring back at her.

Her wanted poster.

LA DAME QUI BOITE—The Lady Who Limps, Most Dangerous of Allied Spies.

The drawing is alarmingly good. The high forehead, the angle of her jaw, and the sharpness of her stare.

She peels her eyes from the notice to the man of impressive stature who appears to have hung it. An officer in the Feldgendarmerie—the German military police—slides a roll of adhesive tape into the pocket of his overcoat. In charge of security in travel, the MPs stand out because of the half-moon metal plate necklaces they wear. When he turns, the silver of it catches the light.

She stops breathing. Her hands turn to ice.

High cheekbones. Thin skin. Blue veins visible along his temples.

Anton Haas.

Informer and henchman of Gestapo head Klaus Barbie, the Butcher of Lyon.

Why is Haas here, so far from Lyon? Has he been tipped off that she's back in France? That couldn't be possible. Could it? If he notices her, will her disguise be enough?

As the train slowly chugs to life, he approaches and walks alongside it. She tries to make herself small, but she can see his gaze stop at her compartment. Before he's out of sight, he points his gloved finger at the car as if to say, "I see you."

It takes miles for her shoulders to relax, and the release is more from the devastation of seeing her beloved France so broken than from relief. In the eighteen months she's been gone, the deterioration of the landscape is astonishing. Bombed-out buildings. Gestapo-infested streets and stations. Swastikas taunting from every flagpole and government building. Trees bare in spite of the arrival of the equinox. It's as if even nature can't bring itself to life under occupation.

The stretches of brown countryside and Aramis's rambling chatter begin to hypnotize her and, in spite of trying to stay awake, she soon dozes. It seems only a moment has passed when the barking of vicious dogs awakens Virginia with a jolt. The doors open to the Montparnasse station in Paris, where they'll transfer trains, and a group of Nazi soldiers pushes their way aboard.

Haas, Virginia thinks. *He recognized me.*

Her heart pounds, and she feels a stab of regret for refusing the lethal pill Vera offered her. As the Nazis and their dogs get closer, the people around her stare at one another, terrified, unsure about getting off. Each passenger car leading to theirs has its doors thrown open. The shared heat between her and the woman at the window could combust their compartment.

As the barking grows louder, Virginia realizes her arm is still wrapped around Aramis's. She pulls away and folds her arms across her chest. If she's going down, she won't bring another agent with her.

The woman at her side clears her throat to get Virginia's attention, and points to her forehead. She reaches up to wipe it and is horrified to see a streak of gray dye on her hand. She folds her arms back across her chest, rubbing her stained hand on her jacket, desperately hoping more dye isn't running down her face.

Their door slides open. The soldiers are upon them. She can smell the dog's breath. Sees its teeth bared, saliva dripping from its muzzle. She's rigid as marble. They point in her direction.

In terrifying situations, time slows. The scene expands, stretching like a canvas picture over a frame that's too wide.

But I thought I had six weeks to live, she thinks. *I haven't even gotten started.*

In a moment, her side is cold and she's again alert. It's the red-haired woman they drag from the compartment. It takes every ounce of strength Virginia has in her to keep her arms folded instead of pulling on the woman's legs, trying to keep her from being taken.

Her memories from Lyon come alive, and she can almost see the good doctor, one of her closest confidants, being dragged away by the Gestapo. Hear the Morse code order home. Feel her best recruit grasping her arms, insisting she leave. Fleeing as the men and women around her fell like dominoes.

Once the woman is gone, the collective breath of those around her releases, but Virginia's does not. If it's not you they drag away, it's someone else like you. Maybe someone you love. Someone loved by others. Why isn't it you? When is it your turn? You almost want it to be your turn so you can breathe again, so the guilt no longer holds your neck in its grip.

As they transfer trains, Virginia reminds herself not to move quickly, not to disguise her limp and to even use it to fit her old-woman identity. Soon, she will no longer have to remind herself to play the part. This war has aged her beyond her years, the train ride alone a decade. Once they've made it safely onto the next train and become settled, Aramis breathes a sigh of relief. She can't relax, not after the scene she has just witnessed and imagining what horrors await that young woman. Aramis stares at her for a moment before nudging her with his shoulder.

"Come on, give a little smile," he says.

She thinks she might murder him. At the next station. Behind a building. Swift as lightning. Her first wireless message to London could simply begin, "Aramis eliminated." The thought cheers her. Still, she refuses to indulge this ridiculous man with a smile.

"A little levity goes a long way," he continues. "I know we're at war, but if we wallow, life will be miserable. 'I'm in France!' I tell myself. There's no place I'd rather be."

There's a dear old man in the compartment with them who has lines like deep tire grooves in his gaunt face. His eyes have lost their color. Is it cataracts or the war that has snuffed their light? He watches Aramis with narrowed eyes. *An ally*, Virginia thinks.

"Silence," she grumbles, playing the part of the long-suffering wife.

The old man's eyes twinkle at her. For him, she has a little smile.

Though remote, the station at Crozant is also crawling with Nazis. There are fewer travelers here, less places to get lost, a closer space for observation. She's desperate for the open air of the farm that awaits her. Desperate to be free of Aramis. Desperate to communicate with London to assure them of her safety. *If* she stays safe.

Holding Aramis back, she gestures to the old man to allow him to exit first. He bows to her before putting on his black beret, picking up his small satchel, and exiting. As she and Aramis step off the train, the Nazi soldiers push the old man roughly through each checkpoint. She and Aramis, too, are shoved, interrogated about their papers, and harassed along the way. When they reach the last checkpoint, the young MP there stops them. The hair peeking from his helmet is an unnatural shade of yellow that matches his stained teeth. He attempts to make his narrow shoulders appear larger with rigid posture. He keeps his brown eyes on them. He smiles, but it isn't kind.

This is a lowly man, Virginia thinks. A physically un-ideal Nazi in every way. One who might bleach his hair to appear more Aryan, one without rank or power who wants to prove himself. There is no Nazi more dangerous.

"What kind of man allows his wife to carry the heavy suitcases?" the MP asks in slow, strange French.

"One with a sprained knee," Aramis says. "I'm ashamed to say."

"You should be," the MP replies. "Maybe I could lighten the load."

Virginia makes a slight adjustment in posture, tipping her balance as if the clothing suitcase is the heavier of the two. The MP grabs it from her, opens the latches, and empties it on the floor. He kicks through the clothing with his boot, unearthing a brassiere.

"Here, bitch," he says to Aramis. "Wear this. Show them what kind of man you are."

Aramis whimpers when the undergarment is draped over him, and keeps his eyes to the ground.

"Clean it up, *Hexe*," he says to Virginia.

Hag. The last word spit in German—one of the languages in which she's fluent—gives her morbid pleasure. He believes she's an old woman. She places the other suitcase on the ground and crouches to reload the clothing into the first. The MP makes a move to open the wireless suitcase. If he does, they're finished. With all the components, there's no way to disguise what's inside. She tenses, eyeing the gun in his holster. She'll take it and kill him and as many Nazis as possible before she goes down. The moment he touches the clasp, his commander shouts to him in German.

"Why are you wasting time, Dummkopf?"

A commotion at the station door draws her eyes to where the commander speaks with three men in blue jackets and blue berets. The Milice.

She works slowly, willing herself not to rush or to draw attention. When she finishes, she stands and edges Aramis in the opposite direction of the Milice, careful not to meet their eyes but alert to their conversation. She's able to pick out only bits and pieces.

Farmer. Stolen petrol. Resistance.

Once they're out on the road, Aramis stops and places his hand over his heart, where he still wears the brassiere. He collapses on a bench.

"I don't know if I can go on," he says.

"What happened to 'a little levity goes a long way'?"

"It's too much. I didn't know it would be like this. My heart hurts. My knee aches."

"A lot worse will hurt if they catch you."

She pulls the bra off him, shoves it in her clothing suitcase, and offers her arm. He doesn't take it.

The Milice come out of the station with the Nazi MPs. One of them lets his eyes linger on Virginia and Aramis before joining the group. Her relief is profound when they head in the opposite direction.

Again. Keep going.

She takes a deep breath.

"You will not lie down for them," she says.

She reaches for his arm and pulls him to standing.

THE FARMHOUSE OF their destination is several kilometers from the station at Crozant, and when they arrive at the crude stone dwelling, Aramis is in agony. Virginia is relieved to see the small farmer, leaning on an ax and wiping his face, matching the description of one Eugène Lopinat. He looks to be in his early fifties and in need of a good meal. An old woman stares out the window at them through thick spectacles. A quick scan of the surrounding property disappoints Virginia; there's no barn in sight. Where is she supposed to transmit? She nearly thinks they stopped at the wrong place until the farmer gives the correct reply to her scripted question.

"How long since you've had a farmhand?" she asks.

"It has been a long time," the man says.

He gestures with his head for them to follow him. The smell of chicken droppings and cow dung hangs in the air, and craggy, bare trees lead to a dilapidated toolshed. Several scrawny hens scatter off the path, one taking flight to rest atop the ancient well. A fire smolders in a pit.

"Do you have a place I can sit?" Aramis says. "I sprained my knee."

The man looks at Aramis and back at Virginia in disgust, clearly disappointed by the agents he was sent. She can't blame him. But soon he'll see; she will prove herself. Once in the back door of the house, Aramis settles heavily into a wooden chair.

"Do you have anything for the pain?" Aramis asks.

The farmer shakes his head in the negative, but the old woman from the window joins them and produces a flask from the folds of her skirt. Aramis takes it with gratitude.

"Forgive my son's bad manners," she says. "No wonder Eugène can't find a wife."

The man waves her off and abandons them to return to the yard to chop wood. The old woman turns to Virginia.

"We were told only the woman would stay."

"Yes," says Virginia. "He returns to the station after he rests."

"The *boches* took our plow, our horse, and our cart, so you'll have to walk back."

Boche. It's the French's slur for the Germans, from the word *caboche*. Thick-skulled, dim-witted, block-headed thug.

Aramis groans.

"Rest fast," the old woman says, patting him briskly on the shoulder. "The wolves are circling. The Resistance here managed to slash the tires and steal petrol from a convoy. The Kommandant disciplined his lazy soldiers, but now they want French blood. You didn't pick a good day to arrive."

Leaving Aramis with the suitcases, Virginia follows Madame Lopinat out the back of the house. There's a cane by the door she uses to poke along in front of her as they go.

"My eyes are no good," Madame Lopinat says. "Eugène needs help. In addition to what you do, can you be of assistance around the farm? Cooking, taking the cows to pasture, that sort of thing."

"Yes," Virginia says.

Taking cows to pasture is the perfect cover for a secret agent in need of fields for airplane supply drops. While she's here in Crozant, she needs to coordinate at least one drop before moving on. A month ago, the closest Maquis group, one hundred kilometers south, was hunted and executed, and morale in the region is low. The area is thick with Nazi activity, and the small number of peasants in the region brave enough to resist are afraid. They need to know they aren't forgotten.

Virginia looks at the feisty old woman and feels a surge of admiration for her. How many has she lost to the war? Yet she's still standing as tall as she's able, doing what she can to fight evil, even if it's only allowing a boarder to stay for a short time. This woman has surely lost so much more than Virginia has. She inspires Virginia to keep going.

Virginia opens a rusty gate for Madame and takes her arm to help her up the hill. Once they reach the top, Madame is breathless, so they pause to take in the fields. In spite of the brown grass and the barren trees and the broken fences and the chill still in the air, Virginia feels her chest open. Far down the lane, past where the cows wander, she sees an old barn. Relief fills her.

"Curious," Madame says. "For a woman of your age, you aren't winded."

Some remarks need no reply. Instead, Virginia points to the barn.

"Is that where I'll stay?" she asks.

The woman peers at her for a moment before answering.

"No," she says. "Over the hill is a lane leading to a cottage with a loft. My husband built it when we were first married. If he were alive, he'd be proud to have you here."

ONCE ARAMIS LEAVES, with promises to find a trusted courier as a go-between for them, Virginia heads to the cottage. It's tiny, has stale air, no running water, no electricity, and no indoor toilet. It smells of mice droppings and mildew, and the stove looks too small to properly heat it. Five years ago, she would have been horrified by it, but for someone who has slept in barns and ambulances, with strangers in a frozen cabin in the wasteland of the Pyrenees, and on the roach-infested floor of a Spanish prison, it's heaven.

In spite of her exhaustion, she hauls the heavy wireless up the ladder, hiding the suitcase deep under the cot in the loft. As much as she wants to wire headquarters to let them know she's arrived at her first stop, tonight is not the time to do so, not with agitated Nazis on the hunt for the Resistance. After filling a pitcher with water from the pump, using it to wash herself and her stump sock, and removing her prosthetic, Virginia collapses into the bed on the ground floor, hoping to fall asleep without a downer. Though her body is worn-out, her mind won't stop racing back to the past.

As war in Europe loomed, Virginia had been desperate to do something. She'd been officially rejected by the US Foreign Service because of her leg, and the British army because she was American, but found the French ambulance service welcomed her with open arms, sending her straight to the front.

She falls asleep thinking of those early days of the war in 1940, before France fell to the Germans, and drops into a familiar nightmare.

ON HER LAST ambulance trip, fifty yards from the convent hospital, Virginia and her partner run out of gas. The wounded soldier has to be carried the rest of the way. Blood from the blisters on Virginia's knee stump soaks her sock. She can smell it through the soldier's gore and her own stink. Blood falls from the man's blasted leg like water from an open faucet. It bleeds the way her foot bled from her own accident. She carries him the way her friends carried her.

Once they get him to the hospital, she helps a nun hold the soldier down while the doctor saws. The screams go through her. There's no anesthesia.

When it's over, she limps to sit on a stone wall outside the hospital, and soon the nun joins her, wrapping her in a coat. It smells of tobacco and sweat. Another aroma reaches her: lily of the valley, threaded through her bootlaces. Little beauties in the horror. Virginia pulls out a stalk and brings the flowers to her nose.

"Mary's tears," the nun says.

She lights a stub of a cigarette, a tiny torch in the night. She must have found it in the soldier's jacket. She holds the cigarette out to Virginia, but she declines.

"Another name for the flower," the nun says. "Legend has it that when the Virgin wept at her crucified son's feet, these bloomed. No wonder our fields are thick with them."

"This is hell," says Virginia.

"Hell?" says the nun, a dark laugh escaping her. "You are not old enough to remember the Great War. My dear, we are only at the gate."

Chapter 3

VIRGINIA SNAPS AWAKE in the early hours of the morning and doesn't try to go back to sleep. When her eyes adjust to the darkness, she crawls out of bed, attaches her prosthetic, dresses, and climbs up the ladder to the loft. There's a cot where she can sit, and a small bedside table, just wide enough to accommodate all the components of her transmitter.

She pulls the suitcase out from under the cot, opens it, and runs her hands over the Type 3 Mark II radio transceiver. This strange device, known as a B2 in the field, will be her lifeline between France and England. On her first mission, Virginia wasn't trained as a wireless operator—a "pianist," as they're known—which made her dependent on others and lacking the degree of control she needed. When her pianists in Lyon were arrested, even though they hadn't given her name under torture, incriminating papers showed Virginia's code name heading the circuit. And it was a double agent—who'd ingratiated himself, pretended to be one of their own—who'd gone to the Nazi MP, Haas, to help zero the target in on Virginia.

She clenches her teeth at the thought of the vile man who infiltrated her network, rendered her useless, and effectively wrote death sentences for the brave men and women at her side. Without Vera's eyes on her,

Virginia finally admits to herself that the desire to hunt him down is the other—perhaps less noble—reason for her return. She was betrayed by someone she allowed in her circle, and who he was—what he is—makes his sin greater than any other kind of betrayal. Still, she won't allow it to take her off task.

Not yet.

Knowing the Nazis are thick on the ground here, certainly searching for any signal, Virginia will need to make this transmission as short as possible. Fortunately, the loft has a window with a tree within reach. She unrolls the antenna, threads it through the highest branches possible, and attaches it to the device. She pulls the curtains closed tightly, using a clothespin to hold them shut around the wire, and lights a candle. She plugs in the battery, attaches the Morse code transmitter, and pulls on the headphones. Taking a deep breath, she notes the time on the wall clock she can see from the loft, turns on the radio, and adjusts the dial to find the right frequency. Once she has it, she taps the poem she chose for her call sign and security check. Then she turns the knob to "receive" to await the reply.

As the minutes tick by, she begins to doubt herself. What if she set up the wireless incorrectly? What if her Morse code message was jumbled? What if the Nazis have caught her signal and are approaching the cottage right now? If there are any homing vehicles in the area, they can zero in on her transmission site within twenty minutes.

Virginia's hands are like ice and her head is tight with a coming headache, but a sudden sound reaches her. A flurry of dots and dashes squeaks through the headphones like little fairy voices. A single word comes through with an exclamation. Her code name, the one she'd chosen to spite the Nazis, who'd christened her Artemis, among other, less flattering names.

—Diane!

She grins and exhales.

—Did you make it to Stop 1? HQ types.

—Yes. Aramis also in place.

```
—Good. When find good DZ, wire for date/time.
```

DZ. Drop zone. Fields for receiving airplane-parachute drops. With rolling farmland as far as the eye can see, she won't have a problem finding one. Finding people to help her receive the drops, however, will be another story.

```
—Copied.
—Any requests?
—English tea.
—Crossword puzzles?
```

Virginia smiles. She can almost see Vera dictating over the shoulder of some young woman at HQ, dribbling cigarette ash all over the poor girl.

```
—Yes.
—GB. BC.
```

Good-bye. Bonne chance.

Excellent. Five minutes.

While Virginia packs up her wireless and stores it back under the cot, a fond memory comes to her mind, stirred by the mention of crossword puzzles. She can almost see the latticed London café windows filtering the January light, dust motes playing in the rare sunshine, that day in 1941 when Vera Atkins began recruiting her for the SOE.

Virginia recalls spotting Vera by her trademark perfectly arranged, glossy black hair, sitting in a corner booth, smoking, moving her gaze between the newspaper in front of her and the café. Her eyes lit up when she saw Virginia.

"If we were in France, you'd no longer be allowed to smoke," Virginia said, sliding in the booth.

"And why is that?" Vera asked.

"Rations. They seem to think only men need tobacco."

"Perhaps they're right. Women can endure anything."

Vera had held out a pink container of Passing Clouds cigarettes to Virginia.

"No, thanks," said Virginia. "I can't be dependent upon anything if I ever want to get back to France."

"How do you plan to do that?"

"I'm working on it."

Vera stared at Virginia a moment before stubbing out her cigarette in the near-overflowing ashtray. She turned her attention to her handbag, where she searched a bit before finding a folding knife. It was rough and well used, military issue. Vera opened it and ran the blade along the pencil tip, slicing away wood and making a sharp point, curled shavings littering the tablecloth. A waiter joined them.

"The usual?" he said to Vera.

"Thank you."

"And you, miss?"

Virginia peeled her stare from the knife, glanced over the menu, and ordered the watercress soup.

"Feel free to order the roast and potatoes," said Vera. "I'm treating, and I have extra ration coupons."

"I can't remember the last time I had meat. Roast and potatoes, it is."

When the waiter left, Virginia leaned in. "How did you come by those?"

Vera gave a coy smile, folded up her knife, dropped it back in her purse, and began the newspaper crossword puzzle.

"I understand you volunteered for the French ambulance service at the beginning of the war, before coming to London after the fall of France," Vera said. "Why did you volunteer?"

Virginia found it odd that Vera worked on a crossword while at lunch with her, asking personal questions, but sensed there was nothing the woman did without intent.

"In spite of my immaculate record at embassies across the world," Virginia said, "the US rejected me for Foreign Service. France was happy to use me."

"Were you rejected because of your leg?"

Virginia was taken aback that Vera knew. Virginia didn't speak about her prosthetic with anyone, especially because it seemed to be such a roadblock to employment.

"Cuthbert?" Virginia said.

Vera lifted her eyes to Virginia's. "You call your prosthetic leg Cuthbert?"

"Yes. It's a joke. Saint Cuthbert is the patron of birds. Since I was hunting them when I shot off my foot, the name seemed fitting. And, to answer your question, yes, that's ultimately why I was rejected."

Vera turned her attention back to the puzzle.

"When you were stationed at Metz in the ambulance service," Vera said, "did *Cuthbert* get in the way?"

Virginia never mentioned where she was stationed. Vera clearly already knew the answers to some of the questions she was asking. Still, Virginia decided to play along. She had nothing to lose.

"No, though he complains and tries to be troublesome, Cuthbert is stubbornly operative."

Still not looking at her, Vera raised her eyebrows.

"What did your training for the French ambulance service entail?" Vera asked.

"Basic first aid," Virginia said. "Automobile repair and operation. Physical fitness."

"Good. I hear you're a linguist. Which languages do you speak?"

"French, Italian, Spanish, and German, fluently. Passable Russian."

If Vera was impressed, she didn't show it.

"Tell me about war," Vera continued. "What has surprised you?"

"Human capacity for evil."

"What about yourself?"

"Endurance."

As Vera completed the puzzle, the waiter arrived, placing two steaming, gravy-soaked plates of roast and potatoes before them. Conversation ceased while they ate. Virginia savored bite after bite of the tender meat and made quick work of devouring the feast.

"You eat with the fork in your left hand, tines down," said Vera.

"I picked up the habit in France. It's more efficient than switching hands after the meat is cut with your right hand, wouldn't you agree?"

The waiter returned and whispered in Vera's ear. She reached in her

handbag, placed the ration cards on the table—which he whisked away—
and began erasing random letters on the crossword. When she finished,
she dropped the pencil in her handbag.

"Forgive me," Vera said. "I must go. I have enjoyed this thoroughly,
and hope we meet again soon."

Virginia hardly knew if she could say she enjoyed the experience, but
it was interesting, and the food was a treat.

"Thank you," said Virginia. "I haven't eaten this well in months. I hope
I can repay you someday."

Vera nodded and left her. Virginia watched her go, noting the pointed
glance she gave the waiter. *What a strange woman*, she thought. Vera
wanted something from Virginia, and she didn't know if she gave it. There
were many heavy things in the air that seemed unsaid between them.
They existed like missing notes in a symphony. Like missing letters.

In a crossword.

Virginia sat up straight and glanced around the room, where she saw
the waiter staring at her. He turned his attention to the table nearest him
as if he were not. Her eyes returned to the crossword puzzle. She reached
out, slid it so it faced her, and began to scan the words, noting the letters
Vera erased.

N. O. R. T. H.

North. North what?

U. M. B. E. R. L. A. N. D.

The Northumberland Hotel in Charing Cross was a setting used in
The Hound of the Baskervilles. Did Vera mean the Hotel Victoria on Northumberland Avenue, where members of the War Office often congre-
gated in the pub? Her heart quickened. She searched the puzzle but could
find no further clues as to when she should go there. While she thought,
the waiter returned, placed the ticket on the table, and cleared the dishes.

Vera already paid.

Virginia's heart continued to pound as she scanned the scribbled handwriting on the lunch ticket.

Tea 1.10. Roast and potatoes, 2 × 7.00.

January 10. Fourteen hundred hours.

When the tenth arrived, at the appointed time, Virginia had shown up at the Victoria, had asked for Vera at the pub on the first floor, and was led to the hotel upstairs. When the door to room 238 opened, Vera had beamed at her from behind a veil of smoke.

"I knew you'd come," Vera said.

"It was simple to figure out," Virginia said.

"For you. You'd be surprised how many have failed that exact test. And that just gets you in the door."

The room wasn't a hotel room at all, but a dingy, smoky, paper-filled office. Heavy blackout curtains framed boarded windows. Virginia scanned a long table littered with ashtrays, pencils, and dirty teacups. A photograph of her own face stared up from a thick file folder. She felt both flattered and violated.

"Who are you, really?" asked Virginia. "And what do you want from me?"

Vera motioned for Virginia to sit across from her while closing Virginia's file.

"As you have deduced, I do not work for the War Office. Not exactly," Vera said. "In July of last year, Churchill found out about a network of clandestine, nonmilitary groups across Europe who had been gathering intelligence and sabotaging Nazi efforts at advancement by any possible means. He organized the forces and set the wheels in motion for them to grow, officially creating the SOE."

"SOE?"

"Special Operations Executive. In charge of coordinating and supplying local Resistance groups and engaging in espionage and sabotage in enemy territory. I am with F Section, for France. We work with the RF—de Gaulle's Free French forces—to undermine and make the Nazis in France as miserable as possible. We also provide safe houses along escape lines for downed pilots, wanted Resistance members, and Jews. I am recruiting you to join us."

After years of treading water at American embassies, banging her head against a secretary's typewriter, desperate for someone to give her a chance to make a real difference in the world, Virginia felt as if a weight crushing her chest were released.

"I see your elation," Vera had said, "but you must understand the magnitude of what I'm asking and know that nothing after today will be simple again. Only twenty-five percent of recruits make it through training. You will be expected to take orders without question or explanation. You must become a link in a chain, only aware of those immediately around you, doing work you might not understand but that somehow connects a vital network. It's also best if you sever personal relationships."

Already done, she'd thought.

Her beloved father, dead from a cardiac arrest brought on by the Depression. A mother who had never understood her. A brother with a life and family of his own, half a world away. A niece and a nephew too young to remember her if she never returned. A broken engagement with Emil, a Polish junior officer from her time at the Warsaw embassy, just before her accident. For all intents and purposes, she was unmoored.

"You will receive no praise or accolades for your service," Vera continued. "Without military uniform, if captured, you will not fall under Geneva protection. As a woman, you will be doubted and resented, even by some men within our ranks. You'll be lonely—far more so than you can imagine—and in constant danger. We are the smallest organization of war services with the highest casualty rate."

Still, Virginia was certain. As she was about to accept, Vera pushed a pile of folders across the desk.

"Open these. Look at the faces."

Virginia opened each file, looked at the man or woman, noted the stamp.

KIA. MIA. KIA. KIA. MIA.

"That's only a sample, and it's just the beginning," Vera said. "Their relatives have vague letters of lies. There will be no parades in their honor. If they are lucky, their deaths came swiftly—a bullet to the head. If not, they were raped, tortured, hung from a tree near a town square as a warning."

Virginia could imagine the knock at her mother's door, Mother opening it, receiving the news with stoicism—her unease betrayed only by her hands fluttering along her pearl strand. Her mother would say to her brother, "I told Dindy. I knew it. Why couldn't she stay home like a good girl?" But Virginia knew her mother would crack in the night. She would sob in bed all through the dark hours, the way she sometimes did when the facade became too much.

Nauseated, Virginia stood and walked to a window with no view. The air was thick with cigarette smoke. Half the lights in the room weren't working. She had the sudden certainty she was being watched. Her eyes settled on the closet door.

"Paranoia," Vera continued. "Malnutrition, exhaustion. Also, you can expect Nazi retaliation on innocent civilians for every act of sabotage you incite. Cruel, brutal retaliation. Guilt will be your constant companion. But if we in the SOE are to 'set Europe ablaze,' as Churchill directed, these are the necessary casualties of war."

There was still no question in Virginia's mind. She was convinced everything she had experienced in her life—everything she had suffered—was preparing her for that moment. She hadn't felt this alive since she'd watched the sun rise over Paris, all those years ago. Virginia glanced once more at the closet and turned to look Vera in the eye.

"I accept," she said.

"Then welcome," said Vera, "to the Ministry of Ungentlemanly Warfare."

Chapter 4

AFTER TAKING THE cows to pasture, and finding a good field for a drop, Virginia returns to the farmhouse to begin the work of recruiting. This is the hard part: trust. Building it and practicing it. Especially with a ticking clock. But she has managed before, and she'll manage now.

In Lyon, a doctor was her first recruit. Though he was only seven years older than she, he seemed more so because he was bald, wore glasses, and had a wise, kindly air about him. On their first meeting, she'd walked along the bookshelves of his cozy study, reading the spines, stopping to run her fingers over the words of a thick, brown book lettered in gold.

La vie et les aventures surprenantes de Robinson Crusoé.

"A favorite of mine," the doctor had said.

"It was also my father's favorite."

"Is he where you get your courage from?"

"Yes," she said.

"And from your mother?"

"My strong opinions."

She can hear his laughter in the echoes of her memory, and it both lifts and crushes her spirits. Will she ever see him again?

Virginia soon spots Eugène. After scanning the surrounding fields and road to ensure they're alone, Virginia joins him in the backyard.

"Monsieur Lopinat, a word."

He either doesn't hear her or chooses not to.

The SOE courier for this region had to escape, and when he returned to London, he warned HQ that Eugène, a distant cousin of his, was a tough nut to crack, made worse by the feeling that the region had been abandoned. The courier assured them, however, of Eugène's absolute reliability. Skepticism and caution are traits Virginia prizes in her contacts. She's found that the friendlier the person, the more dangerous they tend to be.

The betrayer of her Lyon network had been friendly. He knew all the right things to say. And yet she'd had a gut feeling that something was off. She'd disregarded it because HQ vetted him, and because of who he was—the regret she feels burns sharp and painful. Never again will she ignore her instincts.

"Please, I need to speak with you," she says.

Eugène stabs a bale with his pitchfork and spreads the hay over the mud, still crispy from the morning's frost. His breath comes hard, encircling his head like locomotive steam.

"I need a name," she says. "One person willing to help me. I'll take it from there."

He mumbles something.

"What's that?" she asks.

"I said, what kind of organization uses old women to do their dirty work?"

"A desperate one," she says.

He wipes the sweat from his forehead with a handkerchief and resumes working. She picks up a rake and helps him. After a long while, he again speaks.

"What kind of help do you need?"

"An Allied plane is going to parachute a container of supplies for the Resistance here. I need a group to help receive it, and a barn to store it. It's a dangerous job. Those who do it must stay up all night crouching in a cold field, break down the container, and scatter supplies in wagons."

"We've been promised drops from your people before, but they've never delivered."

"I know. But that's about to change. All we need are moonlight and manpower. The container is packed and ready with food, medical supplies, weapons to defend the power plant here the Nazis will no doubt try to destroy on retreat, and explosive kits strong enough to demo the bridges leading to the plant."

A bitter laugh escapes his mouth.

"You must have the wrong place," he says.

"I assure you, I do not. The invasion is approaching. The Allies will make it here. And when they do, we need you to be ready."

"Invasion—bah! We've heard about that for years and it hasn't happened."

He stabs the hay bale and walks away from her.

"Do you want to live this way forever?" she says, following him. "In fear? Watching the Nazis steal food from your mouth? From your mother's?"

"Of course not. My brother was killed at Dunkirk. My father died after France surrendered because we no longer had access to insulin. Thirty thousand diabetics dead in two weeks because of a simple shot they couldn't get." Eugène's voice catches, and it takes him a moment to recover. "I'm only able to stay on here because I farm, so the boches can use me. Otherwise, I'd be in a work camp in God knows where."

His shoulders slump. She notices the rope holding up the pants that are too large for him—pants that might have been tight before the war started. She feels a pang in her heart. No matter how much she loves France, she knows she can only understand a fraction of what he's been through. This is his home, and, unlike her, he has no choice but to be here.

"The injustice is agonizing," she says. "I know. Believe me. But soon you'll see."

His posture softens, but he still doesn't agree.

"I can get things for you, personally," she says. "If you help. A small reward. Something just for you in the container."

"Like what?"

"Anything. Ask for it."

He pauses, looking around at the sad farm, the scrawny chickens, and the ancient toolshed.

"A wife."

"How about something that fits in a metal canister packed with ammunition."

"Steak," he says.

She frowns, looking at the cattle.

"The boches have my cows tagged and numbered," he explains. "When they want beef, I have to butcher under military guard. All day long I look at meat and can't have it."

"I'll get it for you."

Eugène smiles. How could she not have thought about first appealing to a man's stomach? She's been out of the fray for too long.

"I won't give you names, though," he says. "I'll ask my friends. If they want to help, they'll show up. If not, you're on your own."

"Fair enough. Tell them to listen to the BBC tonight. Before the end of the broadcast, when they read personal messages, I'll have headquarters get this one through: 'The cow is medium rare.' When they hear that, have them meet me at your southernmost field with flashlights and a cart."

"A medium-rare cow? That's ridiculous."

"Haven't you heard the crazy messages read over the BBC each night?"

"Yes."

"They're put there by agents communicating with the Resistance. They're memorable and unique, and the Germans have no idea what they mean."

Eugène is skeptical, but he'll soon see.

"Once I get the supplies for you," she says, "do you have a storage place for it and men who will actually use it?"

"You just deliver and let me worry about distribution."

She's about to protest but thinks better of it once she realizes she's gotten further with him sooner than she thought she would.

That afternoon, she transmits her strange phrase and requests to headquarters. That night, she follows Eugène to the barn. Along the way she recites the D-Day poem in her mind, embedding its lines within her, wondering if tonight will be the night.

Les sanglots longs / Des violons / De l'automne. When a sighing begins in the violins of the autumn song.

She thinks each line all the way to the end, to the ones that will light the fires of the Resistance all over France.

Blessent mon coeur / D'une langueur / Monotone. My heart is drowned in the slow sound, languorous and long.

When the Allied armies invade from the north, Resistance fighters will need to rise from the south and the east and the west. The cost of life will be high, but it will be worth it if they're able to drive out the Nazis. The alternative is unthinkable.

They cross the road and climb the fields to the barn. Once inside, Eugène kicks hay off the floorboards, lifting them to reveal a radio and an old car battery. She watches as he connects it to the device. In moments, a welcome sound reaches their ears: the opening notes of Beethoven's Fifth. These broadcasts—*The French Speaking to the French*—are the lifeblood of the French people. The Nazis control Radio Paris, spewing lies and intimidation, but the BBC gives hope. It reassures. It allows them dispatches from General de Gaulle, inspiring those brave enough to risk listening.

When the news concludes, personal messages begin. On and on the phrases and codes go, with no mention of medium-rare cows. Eugène paces. Virginia feels a trickle of sweat on the back of her neck. She isn't a praying woman but finds herself imploring whatever powers that be to help her.

"And that concludes our broadcast," the announcer says.

Damn.

Eugène swears and crosses the barn to switch off and hide the radio. But then, the announcer's voice returns.

"I'm sorry," the announcer says. "Hope you're all still listening. One more bit from a breathless messenger in the hallway. 'The cow is medium rare.'"

Eugène looks at her with his mouth open wide. She grins at him, giddy with relief.

"Come," she says. "Your steak awaits."

HER RECEPTION SQUAD is less than ideal.

Joining her and Eugène in the dark are a stout woman with apple-round cheeks, a bald man with slanted eyes and a large nose, and an old man slowly bringing up the rear. When she sees the deep grooves in his gaunt, smiling face and the twinkle in his pale eyes, she returns the smile of the man from the train. He removes his black beret and bows to her.

Eugène introduces her as Diane, but the peasants don't offer their names.

The three sad, poor little musketeers, she thinks.

She tries to imagine them wiring bridges with explosives, and defending power plants with guns, but she can't. She hopes there are younger, more able-bodied resistors in hiding who didn't want to risk themselves for a drop they didn't believe would happen. Still, this team is better than nothing.

The night is crisp and clear, dazzling with stars and celestial light. In another life, Virginia would have run barefoot through the dewy grass, but tonight she's terrified. This is her first drop attempt, and she's heard horror stories of planes shot down and Nazis waiting in ambush. Every cracking stick makes her sweat, and the shadows seem to be alive.

Taking a bracing breath and plunging ahead, she leads them to the hedge bordering the field, where the plane is scheduled to drop its loot. *If the plane arrives, that is.* She can't bear to think of the loss of credibility she'll suffer if she doesn't deliver.

The bald one starts to light a cigarette, but she shakes a finger at him. They can't draw attention to themselves. He grumbles, puts it away, and folds his arms across his chest, rocking back and forth to keep his blood moving. The woman takes out a flask and passes it around, improving the collective mood considerably. The sweet scent of cognac reaches Virginia's nostrils and burns off after a long draw that lights a fire in her. The old man thanks the woman, then turns to Virginia.

"How will the plane find us?" he whispers. There's no malice or disbelief in his voice, only genuine curiosity.

"The Lysander is a scrappy little flier," she says, leaning close to him. "They fly low and slow, using the reflection of the moon on rivers to navigate to drop zones. When we hear the drone of its engine, we'll form a diamond and hold our flashlights to the sky. The pilot will drop the container in the center of our formation, and then off he'll go into the night."

"*Fantastique,*" he says.

Seeing the outline of the old man's beret against the sky brings a sudden smile to her face, reminding her of her best recruit from her Lyon mission.

As a member of the Sûreté, or French National Police, her recruit was quite a coup—a man bold, courageous, and reckless enough to work as a double agent for the Allies. From inside the police station, he'd helped her with intelligence, mock interrogations, and prison breaks. After he was forced to escape France, Virginia sheltered him in a safe house in Madrid—where she was stationed for her second mission—and helped arrange his passage to London for official SOE training. Since his return to London, the few times she and her recruit had been able to meet on weekends in pubs, Louis—as he was now code-named—would wear a beret, which he'd make a show of removing and holding to his heart when he'd see her. Louis is due to be dropped back in the field any day now—maybe even tonight—and she can't wait to see his bright, young face.

"How long does it take them to get here?" says Eugène, scowling. They convened at eleven, and it's now almost twelve thirty.

"Three to five hours," she says. "Depending upon wind conditions and avoidance of antiaircraft units."

"Humph," Eugène says.

They continue to wait, huddling together for warmth, watching the surrounding areas for movement. Listening. One o'clock comes and goes. The bald one unrolls his cigarette and chews the tobacco inside, spitting at intervals. The cognac has been drunk. The stout woman dozes. Two o'clock arrives.

"I'm out," says Eugène.

As Virginia is about to protest, she hears a droning sound.

Elated yet unable to believe their ears, they stand and look to the sky. In the moonlight, as the droning gets louder, she can see the tracks of tears on the faces of her drop team. Eugène turns his gaze on her, and it's filled with gratitude. She smiles and bows her head to him.

I told you, she thinks. *You are not forgotten.*

She directs the group to assume their positions, and they spring to action. In spite of the low temperature, as soon as their flashlights shine toward the sky, she's soaked through with sweat. The noise, the signals— they can wake sleeping beasts.

She soon makes out the form of the Lysander as it flies low over the countryside. Once it draws near, she flashes her light four times. After a few moments, she sees the flicker of the pilot's light in the cockpit, followed by the dark form that drops from the plane, parachute slowing its descent. They switch off their flashlights and converge upon the container, staying back until it lands with a slam, right on target.

Over the next hour, they pry open the cylinder and work to unload and hide three hundred pounds of supplies in the hay cart. There are biscuit tins, canned fruit, Spam, aspirin, guns, ammo, and the promised bridge explosive kits with French-language instruction books. Virginia sees how her helpers' demeanor has changed, how energized they are, how full of purpose. They seem younger and stronger than they were when the night began.

"Diane," whispers the old man. "This is for you."

He tosses her a book with her name written on it.

Crossword puzzles, in French.

She smiles, tucks it in her pocket, and removes the last item—a black military canteen, brutally cold to the touch. She hands it to Eugène, who takes it like it's the Holy Grail. The others drag the parachute and empty container to a hole Virginia dug earlier that day. They cover it and disguise the fresh dirt with leaves and small rocks before returning to the cart. The sound of a breaking twig by the hedge causes them to crouch low. A scan of the area reveals nothing. They soon rise, and she grabs one of the poles of the cart.

"We'll take it from here," her old friend whispers, waving her off.

"Let me help."

"An *old* woman like you should rest," he says with a twinkle in his eye.

"All right, but be careful," she says.

Before they go, Eugène clears his throat. He stares into the canteen, from which the frosty steam of dry ice pours, and whispers like one enchanted.

"*Mes amies.* Come to my house—at midnight—and you will have your reward."

Chapter 5

THE RUMBLING MAKES her teacup tremble on the table. She pushes back from her chair, climbs the ladder to the loft, and looks out the window toward the horizon, where a line of SS panzers crawls along the high road. Though she knows her cottage is well hidden, she can't shake the dread.

Keyed up from the overnight drop, and with only an hour before her morning farm chores, Virginia set up her radio to transmit the drop's success to HQ and ask if she should make another before moving on. They weren't receiving a clear signal, and she'd adjusted the antenna to no avail. The weather was fair, so the next likely reason was interference by Nazi RDFs: radio direction finders. Virginia broke down the wireless and stored it as quickly as possible. She won't bring extra danger to the people risking so much to board her.

Try as she might to suppress it, Virginia feels a surge of affection for her drop team. Eugène and the three musketeers are the nameless and faceless in this war, the anonymous armies of common folks doing the work of secret agents. When they have success, the total transformation it brings can't be described in words. Virginia doesn't know how Eugène knows them or why they agreed to such a dangerous activity, but it doesn't matter. Even if only for a night, their small success is balm, easing her guilt. But her presence puts them in danger, and she's needed in other places. She expects a courier from Aramis any day now, updating her on his progress securing safe houses. She'll make one last transmission, then—if HQ approves it—she'll move on to her next stop.

There are five tanks and three lorries headed east. She'll report the numbers to HQ in her next transmission, along with how many troops are left in Crozant and the morale of both the Nazis and the French. With rumors of invasion, perhaps the Nazis are corralling troops to guard the larger cities. Could they be heading to Lyon?

Lyon. It's only a train ride away.

She can hear the words in her ear as if the devil on her shoulder whispers them.

You're disguised, it says. *You can check and see if any are left from your network.*

Though she tries to ignore the temptation, the thoughts continue.

Paris is closer. You can check in with old contacts. And while you're there, you can hunt the betrayer.

No. Winning the war is more important than winning a personal battle. For now.

She clutches the windowsill, taking deep breaths until the anger passes and the convoy is out of view. Once she's composed, she makes her way to the farm.

Madame Lopinat is in the yard when Virginia arrives, directing an unusually bright version of her son to fetch an aged wheel of cheese from the shed. When Eugène spots Virginia, he lifts his hat.

"Bonjour!"

Madame looks from him to Virginia with suspicion.

Virginia nods and follows them to the kitchen, where Eugène whistles all the way.

"What's this?" says Madame. "What are you two up to?"

"You'll know soon enough," Eugène says, kissing his mother and leaving them.

The pungent smell of cheese fills the room.

"Fourme d'Ambert," says Madame. "Eugène said to take it out for a feast. I won't argue with that, though I've no idea where the rest of this feast will come from."

An idea occurs to Virginia.

"Is this all the cheese you have?" she asks.

"No. There's a little more."

"May I sell it?"

"To whom? Every self-respecting farmer in France knows how to make cheese."

"Nazi soldiers."

"I don't want the boches' filthy money."

"No, but if I sell it to them, they have things of value I can take from them."

"Like what?"

"Secrets."

"What kind?"

"The kind that help end wars."

Madame's milky stare bores into Virginia. After a few moments she seems to make up her mind about something.

"You're free to sell it," she says. "If you can make Eugène whistle, you must be able to make miracles happen."

Before Virginia can thank Madame, a noise draws Virginia's attention to the road. What she sees out the window fills her with rage.

"Bonjour!" calls Aramis from a bicycle.

Virginia storms out of the house toward him, grabbing his handlebars when he stops.

"You fool," she says. "We shouldn't be seen together. You're putting us all in danger."

His smile dissolves.

"You were supposed to find a courier as a go-between," she says.

"I was busy finding safe houses—of which I've managed to add four."

"At least come around back."

An icy rain starts. Once they're tucked behind the house, Aramis speaks.

"I know you have quite the reputation around headquarters," he says, "but superwoman or not, I'm tired of your abuse. Ever since our landing, you've been unnecessarily cold, critical, and harsh."

"You've no idea the restraint I've used with you. You should be thanking me."

"Well, I won't be intimidated by you any longer. I'll do things the way I see fit."

"You do whatever you like, but don't do it anywhere near me. Ever again. Now, tell me the safe-house addresses and their code phrases and get the hell out of here. You're risking the lives of good people."

He grumbles, fumbling through his pockets before producing a torn shred of paper. He thrusts it at her. She feels as if an explosion goes off in her head.

"You wrote it down?" she says.

"You expect me to memorize all that?"

Virginia's head aches as she grits out, "You never write anything down unless you're able to burn it. And you never, ever carry it on you. Now go. You're a danger."

"I need to rest. And eat. The trip exhausted me. My knee is still—"

"Now." Virginia can hardly control the rage bubbling up inside her. "Or my next message will include notice of your elimination."

He jerks backward as if he's been slapped. Mumbling under his breath, he climbs back on his bicycle.

Her heart doesn't stop pounding until he's out of sight. She decides she'll cut him off when she moves on by not disclosing her next location. He'll need to find another pianist.

NOT ONE, BUT two fat steaks to divide among the six of them. Rich, tangy, decadent fourme d'Ambert. Three bottles of Cabernet Franc that had been hidden and saved for a special occasion. She planned on only drinking one serving, but the glass seems to refill itself, and it brings down her blood pressure.

She learns the three musketeers are on the parish council. The stout woman is married to the bald man. Their son was one of the Maquis killed south of the region. The old man is her father, a widower. Even though they've only been in one another's acquaintance for a short time, Virginia has a fierce longing to protect them and restore their world to right order.

"My stomach might regret this," the old man says. "But it's worth it."

"*Oui*," says Eugène.

"Will you be with us long?" asks the woman.

"She means," says her husband, "can we expect to eat like this on a regular basis?"

The woman giggles and pushes him.

"Probably not," Virginia says. "I hope we can arrange another drop. But if not, you're well stocked and you have your marching orders."

"Thanks to you," says the old man.

"The others wanted us to pass along their thanks," says Eugène. "They regret they are not able to meet you but hope to thank you in person after the liberation."

Virginia bows her head to him and takes a drink, reveling in the blissful feeling of relaxation that follows. She doesn't tell Eugène that odds are she'll be dead long before then.

Madame Lopinat dozes in her chair, a smile on her lips, hands crossed over her stomach. Much to the amusement of the group, she starts to snore. The woman touches her arm.

"Go to bed," she says. "We'll clean up."

"Thank you," Madame says, retiring to her room.

Once she's gone, the old man turns to Virginia.

"May I ask," he says, "what has brought you here, doing what you do?"

"All the way from America," says the woman.

The reminder of Virginia's accent sobers her. She starts stacking the dishes around her.

"I'm sorry," says the woman. "I can see I upset you. Please, I have only admiration."

"To know the world cares," her husband says. "You can't know what that does for us."

"We've lost so much," says Eugène. "Fathers, brothers."

"Sons," says the bald man, his voice cracking.

"I speak for all of us," says the old man, "when I say helping you gave us a reason to hope again. And we'll do it as many times as you need us."

Those from her Lyon network said the same thing. An old couple had opened their doors to the hunted, faked heart attacks in busy places while sliding stealthy fingers into the pockets of collaborators, pilfering ration cards and money for the cause. There has been no word on Monsieur, but Madame is at Ravensbrück, along with a brothel madam who—in addition to providing safe houses, food, and intelligence gathering from her girls' Nazi clients—had become a dear friend.

A wave of distress washes over Virginia, and she looks down at the table, trying not to break.

"Go," the woman says. "We'll take care of this."

Virginia doesn't argue. The room has become claustrophobic. As the woman begins to clear the dishes, and Virginia starts to leave, Eugène stops her.

"If I had any doubts about resistance," he says, "they're gone."

"Worth dying for," says the woman.

"It's true," says the old man.

"Absolutely," says the bald one.

Their words are like cold water thrown over her.

"Do you mean it?" Virginia says. "Because as you all know, that's a very real outcome."

All of her people in Lyon had said the same thing—the cause was worth dying for. She has said it countless times herself. But do they really mean it? Does she?

"Take your imagination to the worst place it can go," she says. "The Nazis go further. When you go home tonight, I want you to think of the worst punishments you've heard for resistors. Imagine they're inflicted on you. After that, if you still think this is worth dying for, maybe I'll see you for another drop."

Chapter 6

GERMANS DO NOT respect personal space. Virginia doesn't know if it's an intimidation technique or a cultural difference from Americans, but each soldier she encounters at the market stands close enough for her to smell the musky, virile cologne they wear, even over the cheese she peddles. It sickens her that, while French men and women are rationing soap and starving in their own country, these Nazis are clean and well fed. They plunder French goods like pirates and treat their occupation like a holiday.

One day, they'll pay.

"Did you get to sample the goods while you were on leave?" one soldier asks another.

"*Ja*. And I had her wear the perfume I bought for my wife, so I can remember Paris when I go home."

Their vulgar laughter is revolting.

She's more grateful than ever for her disguise. One of the perks of being in the OSS is their appreciation for a good trick. Vera and the SOE look down their noses at such tactics, but Wild Bill knows a costume not only lets one hide a true identity, it allows one to take on a persona, to separate action in the field from real life. She can retreat into the old

Frenchwoman she's supposed to be to help her endure and, ultimately, to enact the morally objectionable tasks that might be necessary to win the war.

How she wishes she could crush and sprinkle a lethal pill over the cheese these men intend to buy. She wouldn't need her disguise to carry out that task.

"Dieses ist gut," one soldier says to another.

Virginia pretends not to understand their debate over the merits and shortcomings of stinky cheese.

"Wie viel?" he says to her in German.

How much?

After a breath she reminds herself, *I'm a French peasant woman. I don't understand what this Nazi says.* She lets her eyes wander away from him, staring along the road toward the church. Quaint, ivy-covered buildings give way on either side to a low stone wall topped with spikes of wrought iron.

"In French, idiot," says the other soldier in German.

"It's always good to test them. Spies have been caught for such a simple misstep."

"Spies? This old hag?"

"There's at least one in this region."

"How do you know?"

"The Gürtelpeiler detected a signal. It's just a matter of time before we find the rat."

"I hope I'm there when they do."

Their laughter pierces every nerve in her body. She swallows, but there's no saliva. As they continue to chat, the market falls away and it's as if she's back at a café in Lyon, with her beloved friends, the first time she met the betrayer.

They were celebrating Virginia's birthday at a black market restaurant, where the owner always kept a table in a private room for resistors. HQ had alerted Virginia through her pianist that a new contact from Paris was supposed to join them, but he hadn't shown—not unusual in the circumstances. It had become late, and the doctor, the prostitute, Louis, and Virginia had grown drunk and silly on wine and cake.

Knowing Virginia's love of Josephine Baker, Louis had managed to get his hands on a personalized, autographed picture of her through an underground contact. Virginia was in ecstasy to receive it, especially knowing Baker was a fellow resistor, using her touring to gather intelligence for the Allies, smuggling vital information via invisible ink on sheet music.

"It's the best present I've ever received," Virginia had said.

"Then I think a kiss for the gift giver is in order," said Louis.

Virginia had held Louis's face in her hands, leaned in toward his puckered mouth, but quickly pivoted, smashing her painted red lips on his cheeks and forehead. With the group in hysterics, and Louis shouting at her and tickling her to attempt to fend off the lipstick attack, they didn't hear the quiet code knock at the door. Virginia was mortified to see the owner of the café step in on their antics, a stranger in his wake. As all heads whipped to face them, Louis stood up from his chair and touched the gun hidden in his pants, managing to look menacing in spite of his kiss-covered face.

"He says he's supposed to meet Marie," said the café owner, before ducking out.

Marie. Her false identity.

The man stepped forward and removed the hat that had been covering his eyes. They were piercing, icy blue, and they found hers immediately. He addressed her.

"Chez Nous sent me."

Chez Nous. Code for London HQ.

It felt as if sparks went off in her head with every word he spoke in his German-accented French, introducing himself by his code name. She felt suddenly, deadly sober.

"Come," said the kindly doctor. "Join us."

"No," Virginia said, trying to control her voice. "I'll see him at a table in the café."

She didn't want him to get a good look at her people.

She gave the doctor a glance, followed by one to Louis. Then she left the group and walked out to the main dining area of the restaurant, the man following close enough behind her for her to feel his breath on her neck. She took a seat at the wall, facing out, grateful for the late hour and the thin crowd, and waited for him to speak.

"I have a list of points of the boches' current coastal defenses for Chez Nous. Our pianist was taken, so please give it to yours."

He placed a pen on the table—presumably containing the rolled-up map—but she didn't take it. He glanced over his shoulder and then leaned closer.

"I see I make you ill at ease," he said. "You can trust me."

Trustworthy people rarely said such a thing. Still, she reminded herself that HQ vetted him, and he knew the right code phrases. But she couldn't relax.

"Is it my accent?" he asked.

She nodded.

"Apologies," he continued. "Naturally, that worries people. Especially one as sharp as you, Marie. I should have said I was born in Luxembourg."

Suddenly, she feels a flick on her forehead. She blinks her eyes, disoriented, staring around her at the market in Crozant.

"I asked how much?" the German soldier says in French.

"Um," she stutters. "Ten francs."

That memory had come alive, removing her entirely from the present. How can she guard against such a thing in the future?

He reaches in his pocket and tosses the money on the table before grabbing a wheel of cheese and leaving her. Once the soldiers are out of sight, she packs up with trembling hands and starts back for the Lopinat farm, pausing along the way to read the departures board at the train station.

The time to move on has come.

Back at her cottage, it doesn't take Virginia long to pack the suitcase of her personal effects. She hides the gray hair dye in a dentures case Madame gave her from her late husband. Virginia pulls the money bags HQ provided for funding Resistance operations out from under a floorboard, sets aside a good sum for the Lopinats, and stuffs the rest in sacks at her hips, under her skirt. Then she tidies the cottage, leaving her sheets in a pile on the straw mattress.

I won't miss this, she thinks, climbing the ladder to the loft one final time.

Acutely aware of the danger, she takes time scanning the surrounding roads as far as the eye can see. She debates whether to alert HQ of her plans before leaving, or once she arrives at her next stop, and determines this is the best time. She might not make it to her next stop, and, if she does, it could be some time before she's able to transmit.

After she's set up, she takes a deep breath, notes the time, and sends her check code. Within moments her signal is received, and communication starts. She lets them know the area is hot, and she'll leave for her next region on the night train. This time, though, only a few minutes pass before HQ tells her the connection is bad. She stands and looks up and down the lane again, seeing nothing but fog and cows. She tells them it's the bad weather but signs off quickly.

As she begins to break down the B2, a rumbling calls her attention to the road. It's the sound of an engine. She jumps up and is horrified to see an SS Opel Blitz truck barreling down the lane. She reaches out the window, yanking the aerial antenna. It gets stuck on a branch, and she has to lean halfway out the window to disentangle it. Without taking care to wind it up, she dumps the wire and the components into the suitcase as quickly as possible, pushes them deep under the cot, and pulls the bedside table over on its side in front of the cot, blocking the view.

She can hear the truck turning onto the driveway leading to the cottage. She hurries down the loft ladder, slipping on the last rungs and gasping from the pain of her knee stump smashing into her prosthetic leg on the landing. She drags the ladder away from the loft and drops it in a dark corner of the room.

The squeak of brakes alerts her that they are just outside.

She quickly spreads the sheets over the bed, and opens her suitcase, stuffing her clothes back in the wardrobe and standing her suitcase beside it.

The doors to the truck slam, and German voices approach. In seconds the soldiers bang on her door.

Sweating and out of breath, she hobbles to the door and opens it to reveal a Hitler-mustached SS officer and the soldiers she met at the market.

"May I help you?" she says.

The man looks over her shoulder, taking in the small cottage with his stare. His eyes dart this way and that, until they find the loft.

"Come out here," he says.

She obeys, stepping onto the walkway as he gestures with his head to the soldiers to search the house. They knock against her on their way into the cottage.

"What do you do here?" he says to her.

"I help on the farm. Take the cows to pasture. Cook. That sort of thing."

She forces herself not to flinch as she hears banging, tables overturned, cabinets rummaged.

"Why are you so winded?" he says.

"I'm an old woman. I was napping when you arrived."

He narrows his eyes at her, then pulls three posters from a satchel he carries.

"Have you seen any of these people?" he asks, unrolling the posters one at a time.

The first is of a stout woman of middle age, with apple-round cheeks.

The second, a bald man with slanted eyes and a large nose.

The third, an old man with deep grooves in his gaunt face, pale eyes, and a beret.

Your heart is ice, she thinks. She imagines enclosing it in a shield of ice, keeping it from banging, from pumping the blood through her body.

"No," she says, proud of how smooth she keeps her voice.

One soldier yells in German, "There's a loft!"

"What's in the loft?" he asks her in French.

She's able to force out a bitter laugh. "If only I were young enough to climb up and tell you."

There's more scraping and pounding about inside.

"Eine leiter!" one shouts.

A ladder.

This is it, she thinks.

She takes quick stock of her surroundings. Running isn't an option. She'll be shot in the back. The officer has the keys to the lorry in his hand. She could spring for those and steal the vehicle, but she'd get only so far. The dagger hanging from his belt is the best choice. She'll slit his throat, find his Luger, and shoot the soldiers. Or die trying.

There are layers of shouting inside the cottage. She tenses, ready to spring, as one of the soldiers comes out holding something. She's so sure he'll have the wireless suitcase that it takes her a moment to register what's in his hands: a basket. As he presents his findings to the officer, the other soldier follows.

"I knew you were hiding something," he says. "How do you think the Reich would feel to know you're hoarding cheese?"

"She sells it at the market," says one of the soldiers.

She looks down at the ground, pretending to be ashamed.

"We'll take this off your hands," he says. "We're watching these farms all the time. Don't think you can hide anything larger than a wheel of cheese."

After they pile into the lorry and leave her, she staggers back into the cottage, closing the door behind her and collapsing in a chair. Her heart bursts free from the ice she'd forced around it, making her feel hot and dizzy. She looks up at the loft.

Dear God, how close she'd come. She almost didn't break down the suitcase in time. Would that have been worth her life and that of her hosts?

And the three musketeers. On wanted posters! Her acquaintance is pure poison.

Once she's sure the Nazis are gone, she repacks her things, and pulls on her coat.

At the farmhouse, Madame stands watching at the window. Eugène repairs his plow. Virginia nods for him to follow her inside, and Madame joins them in the kitchen.

"I need to leave," Virginia says. "They're onto me. I want to thank you for the risks you've taken to host me."

"It was our honor," says Eugène.

"A very small thing to do for the Resistance," says Madame.

"Nothing done for the Resistance is small."

Virginia places a bundle of francs on the table. Their eyes grow wide.

"Another thing," she says. "The Nazis just showed up at my door with wanted posters bearing the faces of our drop committee."

Eugène exhales a curse.

"Your faces weren't on them," she says. "Yet. Can you get word to your friends? They must flee. Immediately."

She tells them two safe-house addresses in Paris.

"Memorize these. I know these people and can vouch for them. If they don't have space, they'll find it for you."

"Thank you," says Madame, while Eugène says the addresses over and over.

"I beg you to tread carefully," says Virginia. "You can't be seen with them. Under any circumstances."

They're all silent, each letting the weight of the words and situation settle fully over them.

"It's still worth it," says Madame. "Dying for."

"I thought you were asleep when I gave my speech," says Virginia.

Madame smiles and reaches for Virginia's hands. Caught with a sudden rise of emotion, Virginia gives Madame a squeeze, nods at Eugène, and leaves them.

AN HOUR LATER, Virginia arrives at the railway station in town. It's usually busy in the evening, so Virginia is alarmed to see empty stalls and streets. There's no line at the counter, and the man working is pale, his hand shaking as he passes her the ticket and tells her the train will leave an hour late, but doesn't elaborate.

Something is wrong.

She glances from the man to the MPs at the platform. They're restless—wild eyes alert—like a pack of wolves just returned from the hunt.

When the transaction is complete, she scans the station for a safe place to sit while she waits. On her way to a shadowed bench in the corner, an MP blocks her path. His lips are red and chapped, and a dark energy coming from him causes her to recoil. If she weren't in disguise as an old woman, she'd be afraid he'd drag her behind the station and rape her.

She's still afraid.

"Where are you going?" he says, face inches from hers.

"Cosne," she says, lowering her voice, crone-like. "To see my cousin."

"Why would you want to leave a sweet town like this? It's almost free from all the rot that dirties it."

The laughter of the others reaches her. She doesn't know how to answer him.

He grabs the ticket from her hand and demands her papers. She produces them, as steadily as she's able, and waits for his sentence. He looks through everything before staring at her a long moment and thrusting the pile back at her chest. When he returns to the soldiers along the platform, she decides she'll wait on a bench outside the station, away from them. She takes the door farthest from them and creeps along the empty walkway, looking into town, searching for a clue as to what's going on.

A movement down the lane calls her attention toward the church. The priest—bent as Christ himself on the climb to Golgotha—pulls a cart behind him. When he gets to the stone wall topped in wrought iron and looks up at it, he vomits.

Her eyes find what sickens him.

She can't look away. She tries, but even the dirt is thick and black with blood. She's immobilized, unable to move toward it or away, even when the MPs cross the road to the priest, harassing him, beating him for working slowly, laughing at him as he wraps his arms around the legs of the corpses, pushing up, trying to take down the members of his parish council who have been impaled on fence spikes.

Three of them. With wanted posters nailed to their chests.

A stout woman with apple-round cheeks.

A bald man with slanted eyes and a large nose.

And an old man with deep grooves in his gaunt face. Pale eyes staring at nothing. Black beret on the ground at his feet.

Chapter 7

S HE CAN'T REMEMBER how she made her legs walk her back into the station, slip her into the shadows for the agonizing wait for the late train, and take her to a seat. It's only when she's been riding an hour, and the landscape is hidden under the veil of night, that her mind is able to form a coherent thought.

My people, she thinks. *My musketeers.*

A strangled groan escapes her, though she's unable to produce tears. The woman across from her averts her eyes. It isn't unusual to see people in distress in France, but no one wants to look on the grief of another. Virginia covers her mouth with a shaking hand and breathes deeply into it until she's able to steady herself. Slowly, slowly, she again forces the ice around her heart, trapping it in a small cage where it can only beat enough to keep her alert but not alive enough to feel.

Can I continue these missions of madness? Is it worth it for good people to lose their lives?

Her responsibility to those from her first mission urged her return to France, but now she's added to the list of names and faces that need to be redeemed and avenged. How could she think she'd be equal to such a task? Who would be?

She looks at her hands—calloused and dirty from just days of farm-work, still shaking from what she saw. An old woman's hands.

But I'm not an old woman, she thinks.

She closes her fingers into fists, and her heart again bursts to life. Rage fills her.

She should have lunged at the Nazis back at the station. She would have scared them, forcing them to shoot her. It would have been over with quickly. But no. The three musketeers didn't have the luxury of a quick death. Were they shot before they were hung, or were they forced to die slowly? Did they beg and plead, or did they bear their deaths with dignity?

No. No one could maintain dignity dying on a fence spike.

As the hours pass, as the cities spread out and the valleys grow to hills, as the train stations grow fewer and farther between, her mind runs on a wheel.

Is humanity doomed? Is it even redeemable at this point? What's the use of doing any small act of good when evil seems to overpower it? The darkness seems to blot out all the light.

And did the peasants really mean it? Was resisting worth dying for? Madame Lopinat's assertion came without her knowing the fate her friends met, so it offers Virginia no absolution. Will the Lopinats meet a similar fate for helping? There were no wanted posters with their faces, but Crozant is so small, it's likely only a matter of time before they're revealed.

Guilt will be your constant companion.

It's so heavy, so potent, it could use its own seat.

Cold though it is, she forces herself to tuck the men and women of Crozant away in a file folder in her mind. If she's to continue on, there's no other way. She imagines stamping the folder KIA, closing it, and handing it to Vera.

Winds buffet the train. Splatters of rain hiss against the glass. Travel-ing alone has its risks because of her accent, but she has no choice.

As the dawn breaks, she turns her thoughts to the future, imagining the map of France dotted with stops on her circuit. The main region of her new network is located throughout the Massif Central—the highlands of central and southern France. It is remote and mountainous, and only the locals have a clear understanding of the geography. She had argued with Vera about stationing her in a mountain region.

"Send me back to Lyon," Virginia had said.

"If you want to be a kamikaze, enlist with the Japanese."

"Then anywhere else, but not mountains. I can't face that again."

"Then that's precisely why you must."

Mountains. It's impossible to articulate what they represent to her. The terror of the crossing in winter—with a prosthetic leg—was bad enough, but add the guilt over abandoning her people, the Gestapo breathing down her neck, and the knowledge the betrayer was still at large, and it crushed her. She had never experienced a terror like she felt on every level during that crossing, but even then, she hadn't seen with her own eyes the murder of her people.

Until today.

The air feels as thin as it did in the Pyrenees. It takes her miles to catch her breath. Once she does, she forces her thoughts to her new contacts, a husband-and-wife team, code names Lavilette and Mimi. She knows these people can be trusted. Mimi is the sister of Louis—her dear Lyon recruit. Lavilette is a gendarme—a local French police officer—also working for the Resistance. Louis said if there are Maquis in the region, Lavilette will know about them. If she can find him and get him to trust her, her mission can truly begin.

"When you're introduced to my brother-in-law," Louis had said, "tell him you're the answer to his prayers."

"That's quite a thing to say to a new contact."

"Trust me. The joke's on me. I once said it to a girl in a bar, and my brother-in-law was there to hear me get rejected. He's never stopped harassing me for it. It'll make him trust you."

Thoughts of Louis lift her spirits. He always knows how to lighten her mood. She recalls one harrowing day in Lyon with him, when they'd gotten word a group of arrested agents were being deported. Louis had used his police car and travel permit to race to one of the stations where the train was scheduled for a stop. Virginia had gone with him and watched from over a newspaper at the station café, holding her breath as Louis didn't hesitate to flash his badge at an MP, climb aboard the train, and stride through two compartments of Nazi soldiers to the cattle car holding the agents. While making a show of chastising his fellow countrymen for rebellion, he had slipped a file through the bars in a last-ditch effort to help them escape. Then he hopped off the train and winked at her as he walked by, and when she met him across the street at the agreed-upon time, she found a middle-aged barmaid giggling and blushing over him. She can still see the grin Louis had flashed at her. It would do her good to see it again.

When the train pulls into the station at Cosne-sur-Loire, she's surprised by the absence of MPs. There are only young soldiers here, and the baby-faced, wide-eyed, polite junior lieutenant checking papers looks like he's just out of Hitler Youth. He scarcely gives her papers a glance before sending her through and wishing her a good day. She doesn't respond—silence for the enemy is the rule among the French under occupation—but she thinks it's interesting to find a human among those she considers inhuman. Boys like him are in a special kind of hell.

Cosne is a humble town—rows of simple houses, cramped streets, old women at doorsteps and benches. It hardly appears to be the kind of place harboring secret armies ready to rise, but she trusts Louis and she knows how appearances can be deceiving. She relies upon it.

The map of Cosne she studied is carved in her mind. She makes the left and right turns, following a twisty maze of ever-tightening streets until she sees the house of her destination. It's dark brown with pale green louvered shutters. There's a small window in the peak of the roof—an attic—a good place to transmit. She glances up and down the street one last time before approaching the door and knocking. In a moment, a dark-haired, clear-eyed woman bearing a resemblance to Louis opens it, and a young boy—who could *be* Louis at about ten years old—wearing a dagger on a strap, stands in front of her.

"How long since you've had a housekeeper?" Virginia asks.

"It has been a long time," says the woman.

Louis's nephew steps toward Virginia when the door is closed.

"Diane?" he says. "You're not what we expected."

His mother pushes him on the shoulder, shushing him.

"Colonel Lavilette?" Virginia says, looking down at the boy. "You're not what I expected, either."

His laugh, joined by his mother's, is so sharp—so sudden—it blasts her like a beam of light emerging from black clouds.

FROM THE BACK alleys of town, to the side streets, to the open fields, Virginia follows Mimi and her son. The terrain has been moving upward and, while Virginia can barely catch her breath, the mother and son show no signs of slowing. It's hard to be a young woman whose acting as an old woman is starting to feel real.

As they continue, the air begins to feel impossibly thin; it's becoming a noose. A vision flashes before her eyes. The Pyrenees.

Virginia is aware her memories are trying to come alive—like they did at the market—and she doesn't know how to stop them. Disoriented, she panics, stumbling and falling on a mound of earth. There's a small face in hers.

"Are you all right?" the boy says. "Did you see something bad?"

"Give her space," says Mimi.

"*Maman*, she's scared."

The boy is coming more clearly into view.

"You're safe here," he says.

"I know," says Virginia, finding her voice. "I'm having a bad memory."

"Oh," the boy says. "Like a nightmare."

"A little. But I'm awake."

"What's the nightmare?"

"Boy, give her space," says Mimi, kneeling. "You know how it is for people in war."

You know how it is for people in war.

It's such a simple sentiment, yet it slips something in Virginia's splintered mind into place. Head clearing, Virginia pulls herself to standing. While the boy appraises her, Mimi simply waits for her nod, and they continue toward the forest.

Virginia thinks back to the psychologist's questioning before this mission. The OSS wanted to see if she was mentally fit to return.

Do you have nightmares?

No.

Trouble breathing?

No.

Sudden, unexplained rage?

No.

Times when you seem lost in the past?

No, she'd lied. Lies for a living. Every day, a lie. If only she could lie to herself.

The trees ahead are large and heavy with the damp air, their tops obscured by fog. The scent of pine is rich around them. Virginia keeps close to Mimi and her son; they follow no path, and she would never be able to find her way if she lost sight of them. On and on they walk until the trees and underbrush thicken to walls around them. At the mossy banks of a stream, Mimi stops and makes a high-pitched whistling sound, like that of a gray wagtail. Soon, a strapping man appears from behind a fir tree, a broad smile on his face. He leaps across the stream and pulls Mimi into him. She wraps her arms around his neck and kisses him. The boy joins them, throwing his arms around his parents.

Virginia stands in awe. Or is it envy? Or terror? With such an abundance of love, there is much to lose.

Mimi pulls away from the kiss and whispers in the man's ear. He turns his attention to Virginia, looks her up and down, and frowns. After a long moment, he whistles across the stream. A slim man of about thirty years of age appears with a board, which he uses to make a bridge for the group to cross. They go even deeper into the woods until a clearing appears.

It takes Virginia a moment to spot them. They are filthy, slim, and feral, standing on rocks and between trees, camouflaged in dark clothing. The whites of their eyes give them away one by one. With each new man she sets her gaze on, her heartbeat quickens a little faster, her hope rises a little higher.

She has found them.

The Maquis.

PART TWO

Diane

Chapter 8

COSNE-SUR-LOIRE, FRANCE

A T VIRGINIA'S CHILDHOOD summer home, Box Horn Farm, the Little Gunpowder Falls meanders through her family's property. Virginia and her brother, John, would lug their canoe as far as they could carry it, drop it in the stream, and give it a good start before pulling in the oars and letting it carry them where it would. They'd thrill when they'd knock against a boulder or a fallen tree that would spin them in the wrong direction, and they'd have to trust the current to carry them backward to the next obstacle that would right them.

Though he isn't smiling, the man before her has a dimple in his right cheek, just like her father's and her brother's. This forest could be the one at Box Horn. The stream she's just crossed could be the Little Gunpowder Falls. The pressure in her chest releases.

"Colonel Lavilette," the man says, extending his hand.

"Diane," she says, giving him a firm shake. "The answer to your prayers."

The dimple deepens from his grin.

"So, you do know Louis," he says.

"I do."

"Call me Lavi."

He nods for her to follow him and begins to lead her around the crude camp.

She can see the Maquis have been living like dogs. Ten men to each of the hole-filled tents meant for three. A pit for empty sardine cans and refuse, hidden by pine branches. A gully for a latrine covered with a splintered board. They can't even have a fire for fear of getting noticed. It doesn't take long to see the whole of the camp, and to understand how vulnerable they are.

"How many men do you have?" she says.

"We're a hundred strong," says Lavi. "But we're starving. For food and arms."

"You'll have both."

"When?"

"As soon as I can find a field and wire headquarters to arrange a drop."

The hundred men have drawn closer. Lavi's grin is gone. He has his arms crossed over his chest, and he eyes her wearing a dubious expression. She knows she doesn't look like one who could prepare and arm men for battle, but she'll soon show them.

"How many sections have you formed in your company?" she says.

"We're only one large group."

"Then how are you training them?"

"We're just trying to survive. It's hard to train them without weapons."

Virginia had hoped for more organization but takes his point. At least they have numbers of able-bodied soldiers, and, if they prove worthy, they can be joined to others.

The three musketeers rise in her mind. She pushes them down.

"I'll have arms for them soon," she says. "But we need to start preparing them for D-Day."

"Ah, the fabled day."

"It's just on the horizon, Lavi. Why do you think they're dropping so many of us?"

"I don't see so many. I see one old woman."

"If you'd like me to move on and find another Maquis group, I'll do so. But tell me now so I don't go to the trouble of unpacking my bags."

That silences him.

"As I was saying," Virginia continues, "break the hundred men into four sections of twenty-five men each. Start making targets. They have daggers, yes?"

The boy pulls his from his holster, brandishing it. "Of course!"

"Good," she says, her fingers itching to ruffle his hair, but she holds herself back. "We can start with hand-to-hand instruction while we await arms. I'll also begin briefings on how to rig up railroad explosives."

Lavi continues to glare at her. Mimi touches his arm and gives him a long look. Lavi softens under his wife's touch but again goes stiff when he turns to Virginia.

She looks over the Maquis, meeting their scowling faces one by one, committing them to memory. These men have lost everything. They've been told for years of a pending Allied invasion that has yet to come to fruition. They're sitting ducks. Until their bellies and hands are full, they won't have the hope and courage necessary to fight.

She had wanted to wait for a supply drop to build confidence, but the pressure of a hundred men calls for immediate action. She slips into an empty tent and pulls a fat stack of fifty-franc notes from her hip pouch. It can at least get Lavi and his men started on black market provisions, which Frenchmen consider patriotic because it deprives Nazis of goods and supplies. When she emerges, she hands the money to Lavi.

As he flips through the bills, his eyes open wide. He looks up at her as if he might be willing to hope that she's the answer to their prayers after all.

LONG AFTER DINNER has been eaten, the rich aroma of Mimi's lentil stew hangs in the rafters of the attic where Virginia has been installed. She forgot to ask Mimi what time transmission would be best, so she climbs back down the stairs and walks along the hallway, following the sound of the woman's and her son's voices, praying. She doesn't want to intrude upon the moment, but she can't stop herself from staring around the door frame to where Mimi tucks Louis's nephew into bed. A candle burns in a holder, illuminating the boy's arsenal of real and pretend weaponry, his rocking horse, and his maps.

Nephew.

That's what Virginia called Louis in Lyon, and he called her Auntie. Though only five years older than Louis, she'd felt an instant, protective bond with him. She'd schooled him on the caution so foreign to his nature but that was necessary for clandestine work, and he provided her intelligence and support within the national police and prison system. More important, he always seemed to sense when loneliness threatened to engulf Virginia, and would show up at her apartment with treats, jokes, card games, or alcohol.

"Sainte Marie," whisper Mimi and the boy, "Mère de Dieu, priez pour nous pauvres pécheurs, maintenant et à l'heure de notre mort."

Holy Mary, Mother of God, pray for us sinners, now and at the hour of our death.

"Amen."

They each make the sign of the cross, ending with their foreheads together. Mimi plants a waterfall of kisses over the boy's face and hugs him for a long time.

The image of the three peasants on fence spikes assaults Virginia. Their faces become Mimi's and the boy's, but the pain is worse because they're family to Louis. She feels a sudden rush of anger at this woman for putting her son in danger, and at Louis for giving her the contact names at all. She turns to leave, but the boy spots her.

"Bonsoir, Diane," he says, thawing the ice in her veins.

"Bonsoir," she says.

Mimi leaves her boy and follows Virginia down the hallway. Virginia can't meet the woman's eyes.

"What is it?" Mimi asks.

"I wanted to ask when it's safe to transmit, but it isn't safe. Not with a boy in this house."

"You're free to transmit anytime. You will not get found here."

"I don't believe it."

"As the head of the gendarme in the region, my husband has danced on the head of a pin, yet he's kept the worst from here since the war began."

"There are soldiers at the station. Presumably there's a barracks nearby."

"On the other side of town."

Virginia throws up her hands.

"They think we are a nothing town of sleepy peasants," Mimi says.

"The place I just came from was a nothing town of sleepy peasants. Do you know what happened to them?"

"You think I don't know the risks?" Mimi says, narrowing her eyes and crossing her arms over her chest. "My whole family resists. That's why we work well together. We have trust."

"Yes, even down to the child. But aren't you afraid of what could happen to him?"

"Yes. But I'm more terrified of what could happen to him growing up in a world where his mother and father and uncle and cousins didn't do everything in their power to stop evil. Terrified of losing the respect of the young man God gave me to mold and shape and bring light to the world. If every one of us are slaughtered in this war, it will be worth it to stand proud before God and watch the gates of heaven open before us."

"I can't take comfort from that. I don't have faith in God."

"It doesn't matter," Mimi says. "God has faith in you."

Virginia shakes her head and looks down at her feet. Mimi places her hands on Virginia's face and raises it to hers.

"And so do we," Mimi says. "Now go. Send your transmission. Be the answer to our prayers."

Chapter 9

*D*ON'T GET ATTACHED.

Virginia doesn't want to warm to Louis's sister and nephew. In another life, she knows they would have been fast friends, but in war it's too dangerous. Hadn't she learned that lesson in Lyon? She'd let her network into her heart, and now it's broken.

She tries to discipline herself by imagining the suffering these people could face for harboring her. She's brusque, answers questions as briefly as possible, and asks few in return. But Mimi keeps Virginia so busy searching for drop fields and getting the lay of the land, and the boy reminds her so much of a little Louis, the combination of sheer industry and human contact begins to thaw her. She's even been sleeping better and hasn't had a memory episode since her arrival here.

Lavi remains distant with her. The conditions have not yet been right for a drop, and she refuses to lug her B2 to the forest to show the men she truly is communicating with London. This weekend, however, is Easter, and Lavi promised Mimi and the boy that he'll stay with them instead of at the camp. Virginia will use the opportunity to show Lavi the B2.

When Lavi arrives, they're thrilled to see he found a small ham on the black market. He thanks Virginia and assures her the men are enjoying their own Easter feast. He surprises his son with chocolate eggs, which the boy puts at each setting. When the adults move the eggs to surround his plate, he's overjoyed.

Virginia is also thrumming with excitement, and barely able to keep her secret. Last night, HQ let her know that Louis and his team were dropped safely, and he plans to rendezvous with his family on Easter Sunday before proceeding to his assigned region. If Louis were a cat, he'd have used seven or eight lives by now. He, too, had to make the Pyrenees crossing and survive Spanish prisons, and he hasn't seen his family or beloved France in ages. It will do them all good to reunite.

Virginia doesn't want to tell Mimi in case anything goes wrong, but she decides to bring Lavi into her confidence with the hopes it will make a bridge between them. While Mimi checks the ham, Virginia motions for Lavi to follow her to the attic.

After taking a few moments to check the streets from the window, Virginia pulls the wireless suitcase out from the trunk where she stores it under a pile of quilts. Lavi watches with interest as she shows him the aerial antenna, the headphones, and the switches.

"And you can receive messages instantly?" Lavi says.

"Once I turn the knob, yes."

"Is the signal detectable?"

"It is. It takes twenty minutes for a Nazi RDF to zero in on transmission."

Lavi looks down the staircase, where he hears Mimi and his son talking.

"I never go longer than ten minutes," she says. "But I've been asking Mimi for another safe house in the region. It's not good for me to stay here long term. Maybe you can persuade her."

He nods.

"Has London given you a drop date yet?" he asks.

"The full moon was last night," she says, packing up the equipment. "Though you'd never know it from the cloud cover. It can happen anytime in the next few days, if the weather cooperates."

"The weather." He rubs his eyes.

It has been awful: rainy, foggy misery.

"What phrase should I transmit to the BBC so your drop team knows to be ready?" she says.

"I get to choose?"

"Maybe then you'll believe that I really am working with London on your behalf."

He thinks for a moment. "How about 'The fool's prayers are answered'?"

"Excellent."

Once the wireless is back at the bottom of the trunk, Virginia looks down the stairs, and, when she's sure Mimi can't hear them and the boy isn't spying, she leans close to Lavi.

"Speaking of prayers being answered, I have more news," she whispers.

"Invasion?" he says, eyes lighting.

"No, not yet."

His face again darkens.

"News that will make Mimi happy, that is," she says. "Louis had a safe landing. He'll stop here on the way to his region."

Lavi's shadowed face breaks into a grin, and for a moment Virginia is startled by the image of him outside of war.

"I didn't want to tell Mimi in case of any trouble," Virginia says. "But I wanted you to know."

"Merci! Can we at least tease her a little?"

"How?"

"Tell her you need an extra place setting for an agent passing through who might need a meal. That way, if he doesn't show up, no harm."

"Good idea."

For the first time since they've known each other, Lavi doesn't have a frown for her. He stares at Virginia a long moment, looking from her hair, to her face, to her old-woman's clothing. It seems to be dawning on him that there's more to her than meets the eye. Before he has time to study her further, she heads downstairs. Once in the dining room, she calls to Mimi.

"Where are the plates? I just remembered we need an extra setting."

"In the lower left cupboard cabinet," Mimi says, appearing in the door, wiping her hands on a towel. She looks from her husband to Virginia. "Who's joining us?"

"I hate to impose," Virginia says, "but HQ said an agent might be coming through. I know he'll be hungry if he makes it. I'll gladly share my portion."

"Nonsense. There's plenty, if only for today."

After Virginia sets Louis's place, she stands at the window and watches the street. The church soon rings the noon bells, and a swell of people emerges from the great wood doors. And there in the crowd—a shadow amid the parade of old women in white Easter dresses—she spots him.

Louis.

He's square shouldered and wiry. He struts like a rooster, lifting his hat at every woman he passes. Has she taught him nothing about invisibility? She shakes her head but can't help but smile.

Virginia gets Lavi's attention, motioning toward the window. He stands from where he and the boy play with Dinky trucks, and when he spots Louis, he beams. He taps his son on the head and points out the window. When the boy sees, he cheers.

"Shhh," says Lavi. "You get the door and bring him to Maman in the kitchen so she won't alert the whole neighborhood."

"Oui, Papa."

Virginia withdraws into the shadows of the hallway to watch them: the boy opening the door and being picked up and swung around by Louis. Lavi bear-hugging his brother-in-law. Father and son leading Louis to Mimi in the kitchen, and the whoop of joy that follows. They kiss and hug and talk over one another. Virginia struggles to contain her emotion, and ducks into the toilet to check her face in the mirror.

The last time Louis saw her she had coiffed hair and a sleek suit, and wore red lipstick. The face that looks back at her now is drawn and haggard, a badly aged version of her former self. How she longs to free the real woman.

"Diane," says Mimi. "Where are you, my friend? My prayer answerer."

Virginia takes a deep breath and steps out of the bathroom. Mimi clasps her hands and leads her into the dining room. When Louis sees Virginia, his mouth drops open and he shakes his head. He lets out a low whistle.

"Auntie," he says. "The months have not been kind."

He crosses the room and scoops her into an embrace, swinging her around and kissing her cheek, while she swats at him.

"Put me down, Nephew!" she says. "You smell like a barn!"

"Which is exactly where I slept last night."

"Put her down," says Mimi. "You'll break her!"

"Bah," he says. "This old-lady disguise is as bad as her French accent."

Virginia slaps him on the shoulder.

"I knew it!" says the boy.

"Please," says Virginia. "A little discretion."

They laugh around her. Mimi urges them into the sitting room to catch up. As they file in, Louis touches Virginia's arm and passes her something from his pocket.

"From Vera," he says. "Happy birthday. A few days late. She says to put it on when you're ready to come out of hiding."

It's a tube of lipstick. Lou Lou. Red.

The lump in Virginia's throat prevents her from answering. She hadn't even remembered her birthday passed three days ago. April 6. If you'd have told her back in 1940 that the war would still be going on to see her turn thirty-eight, she wouldn't have believed it. She might have even gone home to her mother.

ONCE THEY'VE EATEN dinner, the boy has had his chocolate, and Mimi puts him to bed, they file up to the attic, bringing the radio and waiting for the BBC broadcast. Soft music plays, a jazzy waltz one could imagine in any Parisian club. Virginia closes her eyes for a moment, savoring the sound, imagining a smoky, prewar, left-bank café.

Louis flops on Virginia's bed, falls backward, and rubs his eyes. While she feels so much older than her thirty-eight years, Louis seems more boyish than his thirty-three.

"Don't get too comfortable," Virginia says. "I don't want my bed to smell like goats."

"Oh, come now," Louis says. "Then you can dream of me."

Virginia laughs and rolls her eyes.

"Nonsense," says Mimi. "We have a cot for you downstairs."

"Where are the others in your team?" asks Lavi.

"Scattered in safe houses. We meet tomorrow before we start making our way."

"Where are you heading?" says Mimi.

As Louis opens his mouth to answer, Virginia hushes him.

"Please," she says. "You know better. The less we all know, the less danger there is."

"She's right, *chérie*," Lavi says, touching Mimi's arm.

Though Mimi bristles, Lavi pulls his wife into him. He wraps his arms around her and dances her through the attic to the waltz.

The room falls away, and Virginia is back in 1932, at a party in Poland. She worked at the American embassy in Warsaw and found her duty of entertaining members of the Polish Junior Army a highlight. Virginia and her embassy friend had stared over at the young, square-faced, clear-eyed, blond man Virginia had seen in the halls but hadn't yet had the pleasure of meeting.

"Who's that fair one over there?" Virginia said. "The one who keeps pretending not to look at me?"

"Emil," her friend said with a sigh. "We thought he wasn't interested in women."

"Why?"

"All us girls have been trying to get his attention for months, but he seems to only have eyes for the boots of the man marching before him."

"He certainly has eyes for me tonight," said Virginia, passing off her cocktail with a wink. "Hold this, would you?"

Virginia flashed a grin at Emil, before turning her attention to a stack of records on a nearby table. She smiled when she saw the name: Josephine Baker, "J'ai deux amours." Two loves: my country and Paris. My heart ravished between the two. Virginia pulled the record from the sleeve, placed it with care on the turntable, and lifted the needle, relishing the crispy sound of the blank space on the record. That sound was the curtain fluttering, the intake of breath before the first note was played. The foreplay. And then, Josephine.

Virginia closed her eyes, letting the music take her back to her university days. She told herself she wouldn't open them until Emil was in front of her.

"Jesteś nowym urzędnikiem?"

Voilà. Virginia opened her eyes, and the fair man was before her. She gave him her most dazzling smile.

"No Polish. Not yet," she said, shaking her head. "English?"

"Angielski?"

She nodded.

"Nie."

"French?" said Virginia, knowing she was showing off.

He shook his head no, clearly disappointed.

"German? Sprichst du Deutsch?" she said brightly.

Emil's face transformed. He took her hand and guided her to the tile in the hall the guests were using as a dance floor. His hand was cool on her hot fingers.

"Ja," he'd said.

"Diane."

She startles and finds herself back in the attic, Mimi, Lavi, and Louis staring at her. Heat creeps up her neck.

"The broadcast is over," says Mimi, breaking the awkwardness. "No violins."

"On a bright note," Louis says, "I want you all to be the first to know. I'm in love."

"You're always in love," says Lavi.

"With whom?" Mimi says.

"A pianist. Like Diane. I met her in training. She's due here any day now."

Virginia frowns at him. When will he ever learn?

"I see your disapproval, Auntie," Louis says, looking at her. "But you'd understand if you saw her. That black hair and those red lips and red nails. Her passion and fire."

"You're ridiculous," says Virginia.

"I know. She said we should wait until the war is over, but I told her, why should anyone wait for love?"

"Why, indeed," says Mimi. "And what is the name of this woman of passion and fire? In case we come across her."

"*Code* name," says Virginia.

"Sophie," Louis says. "Code name Sophie."

Virginia's head feels tight, and she's suddenly desperate for all of them to leave her small space. Memories of Emil always weigh her down. She shouldn't have indulged them.

She and Emil had a lightning-fast romance. In just months, they were engaged. Neither of their parents approved. Her mother's reaction was predictable and could be dismissed, and she knew she could bring Daddy around. But Emil's mother was devastated that her son fell in love with an American. She was convinced he would move away and leave her alone. In spite of Virginia's and Emil's passion, and many rows, Emil would not go against his mother's wishes.

And what if they had married? The Nazis killed all Polish officers. Virginia would be a widow—perhaps with children—stuck in what was left of Poland.

Lavi and Mimi file out, but Louis remains.

"Are you all right?" he says. "You don't look well."

"I'm tired, starving, and covered in old-lady makeup."

"HQ is proud of you," he says, not sensing her need for him to go.

"Especially Vera. She brags constantly. Even if she wants you back in London. I told her—of any of us—you are the one no one needs to worry about."

Virginia manages a small smile.

"There she is," says Louis.

He steps toward her and wraps his arms around her. Her stiff hug causes him to pull away quickly. He looks at her again with a question in his eyes.

How can she explain how rough these twenty days have been? These twenty months? How tired she is? The accumulated weight of the losses? She can't say it, but she can give him a warning.

"Everything is different now," she says.

"It is different, because the boches know they're about to get sent back to hell."

"Yes. And they'll drag as many people with them as they can."

"But not us. Not today, anyway."

She stares at him a long moment. His face remains open and energized. He's hopeful in a way she hasn't been in as long as she can remember. She won't steal that from him. Not tonight.

"No," she concedes. "Not today."

Chapter 10

O N   T H E   T H I R D night after the full moon, Virginia waits in the
field with Lavi, Mimi, and four Maquis. As hope was wavering,
they had finally heard the words on the BBC—"The fool's prayers are
answered"—and the drop was in progress. The men keep looking from
her to the sky, eyes wide, thoughts readable.

*Can it be? Will we really receive our first drop? Will we no longer be sitting
ducks?*

She wishes she could feel as excited as they do. The dread over the
dangers the drop could bring still eclipses her excitement, especially after
what happened to the three musketeers.

Louis is not with them. He slipped away before sunrise, the day after
Easter, and is bound for who knows where to do who knows what. She
hopes he stays focused on his mission instead of on his love life. Vera
would have an aneurism if she knew agents were dallying with one another. Yet Virginia could foresee this problem. The SOE and OSS were
rushing to get agents out the door as quickly as possible in advance of
D-Day. Cutting corners in training was a dangerous business. But if her
superiors could make peace with it, why couldn't she?

The last night of her own training, before Virginia's first mission,
comes to mind, giving her a shiver at its remembrance. She was on the

English Channel at Beaulieu Estate—one of the dozens requisitioned for the war effort—for SOE finishing school. Weeks of gritty, intense physical exercises in Scotland came to a rather shocking halt, as recruits were now expected to behave civilly and normally, fully taking on their new identities. Virginia found that game of pretend far more strenuous than the gauntlet she'd already run. On that last night, Virginia was awoken from a sound sleep by a prick at her throat.

"Your name!" the assailant shouted in German-accented English.

Virginia had sucked in her breath but didn't reply as they forced her at knifepoint out of bed. She'd stumbled, trying to regain her balance on one leg. Cuthbert stood, indifferent, below the window. Cold, sickening fear had gripped her until one of them called her a cripple in German.

"Hitler would gas you," another said in English.

All fear was replaced with anger, steeling her. Her temper had its perks. They'd dragged her out the door, while she hopped on her good leg to keep up. She was taken all the way to the basement, thrown in a chair, her hands tied behind her, the rope tearing the skin of her wrists. A light was thrown on her face, shadowing her interrogators—one in front of her, one behind—leaving her exposed and vulnerable.

For hours, they'd questioned her. Just when she was sure it was a test, they would dump a bucket of ice water over her, and she thought it wasn't. Then, as suddenly as it all began, the interrogators turned off the light and locked her in the dark basement. Rodents squeaked along the walls, and her teeth chattered from the ice baths. She didn't know how much time passed, but, maybe an hour or two later, she heard a key in the lock. She sat up straight, trying to control her shaking. In the light from the hall she saw a welcome silhouette: her instructor. He had cut her loose, wrapped a blanket around her shoulders, and helped her all the way back to her room. She felt as if she'd collapse, and couldn't wait to sleep off the traumas of the night.

"Meet in the yard in ten minutes," he said.

With a groan, she draped her soaked nightgown over her desk chair, strapped on her prosthetic, changed into her pants and boots, and slid a knife in its holder. Her clock read five thirty in the morning. In the yard, she found a team of five assembled in the dark—all the recruits that were left from the original thirty. She was given a raid map and a destination. A quick scan revealed the trail was almost six kilometers. As they set out, hints of dawn lay on the horizon, but the great, glowing moon remained.

The hike was brutal. She was bruised, parched, injured, and exhausted beyond comprehension. Yet as they dodged and killed mock enemies, advanced toward their goal—as the sun rose with its brilliance—Virginia felt a superhuman strength building in her. At the top of the final climb, after they'd slashed the tires on the vehicles and laced the escape routes with faux explosives, they ambushed the group of men in German uniforms who ran from the cottage, firing on them with blank shells, and engaging in hand-to-hand combat. When the mock raid was complete and successful, Vera had emerged from the forest, as smoothly as if they were meeting at a dinner party.

"Congratulations. You have not only completed a training program most people wouldn't have hopes of surviving a fifth of, you've done so with courage and flying colors."

Vera gazed down the line and, letting her stare rest on Virginia, gave her a nod.

"Now, let's set Europe ablaze."

Virginia had wanted more physical training before this mission, but there hadn't been the time or resources. They were all stretched thin as frayed rope.

"Bonsoir," says a voice.

The group jumps in surprise, and Virginia draws her knife, lunging toward the figure. She's intercepted by Lavi just in time. Wild-eyed in the dark, the boy stares at the blade in terror. Lavi slaps his son and whispers a tirade of curses and reprimands, while Mimi tries to calm him. Virginia falls to sitting on the ground, trying to catch her breath.

Then comes the sound: the low drone. They stop and look heavenward for the answer to their prayers.

Climbing to standing, Virginia puts her knife away with a shaking hand

and pulls out her flashlight. Mimi moves to take the boy, but Virginia grasps his hand and pulls him along with her. He wipes his tears and runs to keep up with her as she strides to the top of the field. The others fan out around her and, once Virginia places her flashlight in the boy's hands and flicks it on, the others follow—points of light reaching to the heavens. She wraps her hands around his to flick the dash, dot, dot. Morse code, *D*, for Diane. The plane returns the signal, and soon three parachutes drift toward the ground. Lights off, the Maquis fetch the horse and cart from the barn at the edge of the field, and the group rushes to unpack, sort, and bury the containers.

Each discovery gives joy to the men around her, and she has trouble keeping them quiet. Cigarettes, canned meat, astringent, gauze, tape. It's the weapons that bring them to near ecstasy. Sten guns—lightweight and easy to assemble—grenades, pistols, explosive kits—dozens of them. Once the supplies are loaded into the cart and they hurry alongside it to the barn, the Maquis on either side of Virginia lift her, bearing her like a queen all the way. When she insists they put her down, Lavi catches her, wrapping her in an embrace that swallows her up. She gives him a stiff pat and pulls away as quickly as she's able.

"Diane," he says. "Forgive me. For doubting you. I just didn't think a . . ."

"I knew she could," says Mimi, kissing her friend on both cheeks.

Next, the boy creeps toward her.

"I'm sorry, too. I . . ." His voice trails off.

Virginia kneels down to his eye level.

"I accept your apology," she says. "But if you want to help, you must first get approval from your superiors. Is that clear?"

"Oui, Madame."

She stands, keeping her face serious as she looks at the Maquis. They stare at her with a mixture of disbelief and adoration, clearly awaiting a speech or some words of encouragement. But in her mind, their faces become those of the three musketeers. Then those of her Lyon network.

Don't get attached.

She crosses her arms over her chest and leaves them.

Chapter 11

VIRGINIA CAN'T STAY with these people.

She's halfway through her life expectancy in the field. She's managed two successful drops. But the memories that yank her out of time keep coming, and the carnage left in her wake from Lyon and Crozant continually plays out in her nightmares. She cannot—will not—have Mimi and her family meet the same fate.

Early in the morning of her twenty-fifth day, Virginia freshens her disguise makeup, packs her clothing suitcase, and finds Mimi in the kitchen to insist she find another safe house.

"Please," says Mimi. "The boy knows he was wrong to sneak up on us at the drop. It won't happen again."

"I almost killed him."

What she has barely admitted to herself is that, in that moment, she saw the face of the betrayer. She's a liability to this family.

"But you didn't," says Mimi. "He's fine. We're all fine."

"We're all fine until we aren't. I need a new safe house."

"No, please."

"*Another* safe house," Virginia continues. "A second place to wire HQ. Even if it's a barn. It's not yet time for me to leave—we need at least one more drop for the Maquis here—but I can't keep transmitting from this house."

"I will discipline my son better."

"No, it isn't his fault. Or yours. It's the nature of the work. I can't be around children. And I can't always control my temper."

"None of us are perfect."

Exasperated, Virginia runs her hands down her face.

"Please," says Mimi, reaching out and holding Virginia's arms. "With Lavi in the forest, I feel safer having someone like you here."

"That's an illusion," says Virginia.

Mimi stares at her until a knock at the door startles them. Its quick staccato has urgency. Virginia goes to the dining room to look out the window while Mimi checks the peephole and opens the door. Though the young woman's eyes have dark circles underneath them and her skin is pale, she's a beauty.

"How long since you've had a housekeeper?" the woman asks.

"It has been a long time," says Mimi, closing the door.

The young woman has black hair, red lips, and red nails. Virginia can see why Louis is enamored.

"Sophie?" says Virginia, stepping from the shadows.

"Oui," the woman says. "Louis has been here?"

"Yes," says Mimi. "He'll be so glad to know you've arrived safely."

"Thank God," Sophie says.

"Come, have a seat," says Mimi. "I'll get you some water."

Virginia follows Sophie to the sitting room but doesn't join her. She stands, facing the front of the house, keeping an eye on the street in case this conspicuous young woman was followed. Mimi soon returns with a glass of water and a slice of bread, which Sophie devours.

"I'm sorry," Sophie says. "It's been a hard couple of days."

"No apologies," says Mimi. "How can we help you?"

After a long drink of water, Sophie takes a deep breath. Virginia notices she doesn't carry a wireless suitcase. Louis said Sophie was a pianist.

"Where's your B2?" Virginia says.

"I failed to make contact on my first transmission, so the section leader, Hector, dismissed me for another pianist. He kept the B2."

The wireless is not easy to operate, but the fact that Sophie wasn't successful with it doesn't speak well for her.

"My training was rushed," Sophie continues, as if answering Virginia's thoughts. "I told Vera—"

"Stop," says Virginia. "Keep names and networks to yourself. You need to return to HQ. I can connect you to an escape circuit through the Pyrenees, but it will take some time to arrange."

"No." Sophie stands. "I'm not going back."

"I don't have time to train you further as a pianist, and you have no equipment. As it is, my own is running low on batteries."

"I can do something else. Run weapons, help with drops—anything. Use me!"

In spite of herself, Virginia is impressed with Sophie's courage, but she's still skeptical.

"We do need a courier," says Mimi. "Desperately."

She's right. Since Virginia abandoned Aramis and all hopes of a courier through him, she could use one here. She typically doesn't like couriers to be as noticeable as Sophie, but sometimes one has to use what one is given.

"Do you have a safe house in the region?" Virginia asks.

"Yes."

"A courier needs to be inconspicuous," says Virginia.

"I can be that," Sophie says. She reaches in her pocket for a handkerchief and rubs off her lipstick. Then she arranges her face as sternly as possible.

"I see why my brother likes you," says Mimi.

Sophie hugs Mimi, her face aglow, forming another crack in Virginia's ice-encased heart. Sophie's eagerness, her enthusiasm, the way she can't hear the word *no* remind her of someone.

She reminds Virginia of her old self.

SINCE MIMI STILL hasn't delivered on a second safe house, Virginia takes matters into her own hands. She finds an abandoned barn on a hillside, several kilometers from Cosne. The signal is terrible—the barn loft is rotten and unusable—forcing her transmission time to run longer from the need to repeat messages, but she still religiously signs off at the nineteen-minute mark.

She alerts HQ that Sophie will be their new courier. Virginia's consolation is that the girl is vetted and at their disposal. With D-Day surely looming, they have little time to hesitate. Also, Virginia knows it will make Louis happy, and that pleases her.

In an attempt to make Sophie less conspicuous, they poke out the broken lenses of a pair of old glasses, dress her in drab clothing, and tousle her hair, but their efforts are futile. Sophie's beauty is like a deep red rose. Even if there's dirt on the petals, it's evident.

Virginia sits with Sophie day after day, feeding her names, addresses, messages, and code phrases the girl writes over and over until impressed upon her memory, which is remarkable. Afterward, they burn the papers and send her out. On trains, on bicycle, on foot. To Hector's network, to the Maquis, to Paris.

As much as Virginia hates to admit it, Sophie is a breath of fresh air. She works tirelessly. She never complains. She just wants more: more ways to help, more trips, more messages. Mimi is the same, ceaselessly moving, taking care of her house, her family, the network, and the villagers. The three of them have become quite a team.

Though her affection grows by the day, Virginia keeps her feelings close. These people must see her as a cold, burned-out bulb in a string of vibrant lights, but this is how it must be. She continues to push Mimi to find her another safe house.

"I'm working on it," says Mimi. "But it must be equal to your excellence. A place you'll feel comfortable and will benefit you. My question, if you'll answer, is where you'll go next. If I know, I can find a contact who can be a bridge between Cosne and the next place, someone of discretion and knowledge, a traveling companion who won't annoy you."

Virginia is pleased with the amount of thought Mimi has put into this. She had assumed her request was being ignored. Why does she make everyone an adversary? She must stop thinking the worst about people—these good people who are on her side.

Mimi stares at her, waiting. Virginia doesn't want to reveal the place of her final destination, but she doesn't have much choice. In spite of Mimi's perfect trust of her network, there's a carelessness to it. A bravado. They would never knowingly betray her, but they are so open and over-confident, mistakes can be made.

"I see you worrying about us," says Mimi. "But if we aren't worried about ourselves, why are you taking it on?"

These words—they're almost exactly what she said to Vera over and over about sending her back to France. Mimi means them, but she needs to know what can happen.

"At my last stop," says Virginia, "those who helped me ended up dead. On fence spikes. In a town square. Out for all to see. I can't live if that happens to you or the boy."

Mimi takes Virginia's hands in hers.

"Diane, I need you to hear me. And I mean this. If my boy and I end up on fence spikes for this cause, it will not be your fault. We're fighting evil itself. If we die doing so, we will be saints in heaven. Mighty saints, like those who have died before us. Like you, if you die."

"I'm no saint," says Virginia.

"Maybe not yet. But we are all saints in training, whether we know it or not. Now, tell me. Where is your next stop?"

Virginia swallows. Still holding on to Mimi's hands, she takes a deep breath.

"My final destination is the mountain region of the Haute-Loire. Specifically, the village of Le Chambon-sur-Lignon."

Mimi stares at Virginia a moment before a smile touches her lips. Virginia's heartbeat quickens. Can Mimi tell her more than Vera would share?

"I see what the name does to you," says Virginia. "Will you tell me why? What's so special about a place most people have never heard of? I thought I might be getting demoted."

"My friend," says Mimi, giving Virginia's hands a squeeze. "That certainly isn't the case. You will find out soon enough. This information helps me greatly."

Chapter 12

CALLING FAREWELL TO Mimi, Virginia pulls on her shawl to go and meet the Maquis for explosives training. The boy intercepts her.

"Uncle's coming!"

Virginia smiles, curious about why Louis has returned but glad to know he's well. But as Louis strides into the room holding Sophie's hand, Virginia's happiness turns to fury.

"Look who I found on the road," Louis says. "I demanded her papers and gave a thorough search of her person."

Sophie laughs and kisses Louis. As Mimi enters the room and looks from the pair to Virginia, she loses her smile. Virginia clenches her hands into fists.

"I have a present for you," says Louis, holding up a biscuit tin.

She stares at the tin but doesn't take it. Instead she pushes past them, slams the door, and heads to the forest.

The farther Virginia gets from town, the more her blood pressure drops. Almost an hour later, as she enters the woods, she can think clearly.

Louis and Sophie have put them all in danger, and he, above all, should know better. Agents should not be seen frequently together—especially three of them in one location. Louis was there to see her Lyon network disintegrate. They both ended up having to escape—her first, him follow-ing months later—with Nazis on the hunt for them, and both were lucky to survive Spanish prisons. She's always allowed Louis to keep her heart light, but this is not a game, and he can no longer treat it as such. If he won't follow protocol, she'll cut him and Sophie off.

When she arrives at the Maquis camp, they now greet her with warm shouts and waves. She looks around at them and thinks maybe she'll move out here. Their clearing has become a tent village. They've desig-nated medical and food storage tents, have dug a bunker covered with boards and branches for their arsenal, and have even set up a chalkboard area for instruction, where an explosive kit rests for her lesson. She knows men, however. As much respect as she has earned from them, they do not see her as one of them. But she's spent her whole life dealing with that, one way or another, and it's not going to stop her now.

When she spots Lavi, she whistles across the camp. He greets her with a smile, but his face becomes serious when he sees hers.

"What is it?" he says.

"Louis arrived."

"He's all right?"

"Yes."

"Then what's the problem?"

"He arrived with Sophie."

Lavi's eyes go dark. He rubs his hand across the stubble on his chin.

"I don't have to explain the danger it puts everyone in," she says. "They both know agents shouldn't be running around together."

"I'll talk to them when we finish here."

"Please do. They refuse to listen to me."

He nods, and then motions for the men to join them. Before she starts instruction, she takes stock of the men before her. Though still rough and slightly feral, their faces have filled out and their eyes are brighter. They look less like prey and more like predators. They give her their full, rapt attention.

"D-Day is coming," she says.

A cheer goes up around her.

"When?" they ask.

"HQ won't even tell me, but it's imminent. When that day comes, the Allied forces need you to rise."

There's more cheering.

"And not just in battle with guns and grenades. Strong as you are, one hundred men do not match the forces of their armies. Your value behind and within enemy lines is destroying it from the inside out. Specifically, the railways. Your sabotage will force the Nazis to use slower transport means, cutting them off from much-needed supplies and manpower."

While there are still shouts of affirmation, some of their faces grow dark, the stark realization of what they must do beginning to dawn on them.

"I know this will be painful," she says. "But if we do our job well, we can avoid civilian casualties. Most of the men who work the rails are resistors. With their help, we'll know who's riding, what's being transported, and where to make the cuts."

"My God," says one. "We're destroying our country."

"No," she says. "Your country is destroyed. It's a dead man on a stretcher. Tell me, does a medic worry about breaking the ribs of a soldier who isn't breathing when doing chest compressions, or does he do them, hoping to bring the man back to life?"

"He does them."

"You'll need to break a few ribs. More than a few. But that can all be fixed after the war. And if you don't do it, there will be no 'after the war.'"

She stares at them a moment longer, and when she sees they've received the message, opens the explosive pack and sets out each component—a block of claylike material, detonators, wire, and timed fuses.

"Plastic explosives. Simple to assemble, not especially sensitive, naturally adhesive, highly effective."

She scans the group for an assistant, one she can mark to become the expert. Seeking to elevate the weaker among the ranks, she looks through row after row until she settles on a small maquisard in the back. He's so meek he's made no impression upon her until this moment. When she nods her head for him to join her, his look is so grateful it warms her. She instructs him to cut three kilograms from the block for the demonstration. She shows him how to soften the material by rubbing it between her hands and forms the claylike substance into a circle. She attaches the detonator to the fuse and passes it to him to bury it deep within the explosive. His small, dirty hands are nimble and sure.

"Follow me," she says.

The group files behind her as she leads them to a dead tree about fifty yards from camp, where she sticks the explosive to it. She sends the men a safe, observable distance away, instructs the small maquisard to light the fuse, and they hurry to join the rest of the group. The flame burns like a little firework all the way to the plastic. In a moment, there's a blast. When the sound dissolves, they lift their heads. Once the smoke clears, they see the dead tree split in half down the middle, folded out like a great, curly V.

"Victory," says the maquisard.

The group cheers and slaps their new explosives expert on the back. Then each maquisard raises his hands in the subversive V gesture Churchill encourages among Allies and resistors.

She looks around at all of them, with their hands held high. All at once, victory feels as if it might be on the horizon.

LAVI TELLS VIRGINIA to give him a head start back to the house. She stays with the men, going over explosive techniques, amounts of charge necessary for each level of destruction, and practice with timers. After an hour, she leaves them. The boy meets her along the way pulling a small red wagon. He is uncharacteristically quiet, looking back and forth from the wagon to Virginia.

"What is it?" she says.

"Nothing."

His reply is quick and strained. They walk in silence, the wheels rusty and squeaking. He starts and stops himself from speaking a dozen times, but she remains silent. Finally, just before they get to town, she looks down at him. He bursts forth, near tears but strangely elated.

"I did it," he says.

"You did what?"

"Maman said I shouldn't tell you because you'll be angry."

"Then why are you telling me?"

"I can't stop myself."

"If your maman said not to, you shouldn't."

"But I think you might be proud."

"It's best for the Resistance to keep their duties secret, especially if their superiors command it."

"But—"

"No buts. Did your mother tell you to keep a secret from me?"

"Oui."

"Then it must be vital to the Resistance for you to do so."

He purses his lips and screws up his forehead.

"Do you know why you must keep this secret?" she says.

"Because the Ten Commandments say to honor our fathers and mothers."

"Do you know why—as a resistor—you must keep this secret?"

"No."

"Because if I learn it, and the Nazis catch me and torture me, they could make me tell the secret. That would put you, your mother, and anyone else who knows it in danger. Then, the Nazis could catch you and your mother, and torture you to find out more secrets. Now, do you still want to tell me?"

He shakes his head in the negative.

"I will be a good son," he says. "And a good resistor."

"Good," Virginia says. "Now, we shouldn't be seen together. Go."

He leaves her, running ahead with the squeaky wagon trailing behind him. She allows herself to smile when she's sure he doesn't see.

When Virginia arrives at the house, Sophie is gone, and the group is sober. Mimi nods at Virginia and leads her son upstairs while he whispers all the way. Lavi smokes by the fireplace. From where he sits on the couch, Louis gives Virginia a contrite look.

"I'm sorry," he says, gazing up at her. "I forgot myself and put everyone in danger. Please forgive me."

"I'm not worried about myself, so it isn't my forgiveness you need to seek."

"I've apologized to my family. Sophie has, too. We won't appear together here again."

"Here? Louis, I should hope you mean everywhere."

"Well, it will be hard to stay away, seeing that we're engaged."

Virginia feels her face warm, and a rising panic gives way to anger.

"Engaged?"

Lavi stubs out his cigarette and leaves them.

"Hard to stay away?" she continues. "Have I taught you nothing about invisibility? After all we've seen—all we've lost. Instead of hearing 'invisibility,' you've mistaken it for 'invincibility'!"

Louis stands, and crosses the room to meet her.

"I was there, too, you know," he says. "You're letting them win by being this way."

"What way is that?"

"Cold as the Pyrenees."

"How dare you."

"You have to move on from Lyon," he says. "You don't know our people are dead."

"I saw the doctor get dragged away. I saw one of our girls." Her voice catches.

"Yes, one of our girls with her face ravaged, but was she dead?"

Virginia shakes her head, both to concede and to rid her mind of the image of the Lyon prostitute tortured by Klaus Barbie.

"No," says Louis. "She wasn't dead. And I don't believe the doctor is, either. And the nun. And the old couple. Have faith in your people. You helped make us, Diane! Do you doubt yourself?"

I helped make you, she thinks, *but I let a betrayer destroy you.*

"Imagine the Gestapo capture you," he continues. "How long were we trained to remain silent under interrogation?"

"Forty-eight hours," she mumbles.

"That's right. Enough time to let your people get away. You trained them all to do that. Now imagine they put you on a cattle car to a concentration camp. How long do you see yourself lasting?"

"Until the liberation."

"Exactly. You wouldn't have come back here if you thought you'd die."

"You're wrong about that."

"Maybe I am. Maybe you're on a suicide mission. Maybe you will die. But that won't be my fault. Or Vera's. Or Wild Bill's. Will it?"

"No."

"And if you do die, you'll do so heroically, with honor. In the name of goodness and freedom. The same as any of us."

She stares into his eyes, desperate for his vitality to fill her, willing his words to satisfy her emptiness. The hunting accident that took her foot happened shortly after her split with Emil, and she hasn't allowed herself any intimacy since. Is it the shame of feeling physically incomplete? Or is it because of the war? Her heart so often feels like a stone in her chest. Another prosthetic. Will it ever come back to life?

Louis reaches out to pull her into his arms. She can't resist, and returns the embrace, allowing a wave of his warmth to crash over her.

"I'm sorry, but I'm sick over the betrayer," she says. "I shouldn't have ignored my gut, and now he haunts me. When I'm awake. In my nightmares."

"It's the same for me."

She pulls back and stares at him.

"I have nightmares, too," he continues. "Sometimes I'm not even asleep when I have them."

It's an enormous relief to hear this—that she's not going crazy. At least not alone.

"Sometimes I think hunting him would help," Louis says.

"That has crossed my mind. But I can't think of it right now."

"Then I'll find him."

"No, you absolutely cannot lose focus any more than you already have."

"What, you don't think I can manage it? Have you taught me nothing?"

"Not this. Not now. We have bigger battles to fight."

Mimi, Lavi, and the boy file into the room, ending their discussion.

Louis crouches down in front of his nephew, adjusting the boy's dagger strap.

"Keep them safe," Louis tells the boy.

"I will," he replies in a solemn voice.

"Don't do anything foolish."

"Like you."

The group laughs, releasing the tension. Louis swats the boy on the shoulder before standing and then kisses him on the head. He hugs his family and Virginia once more. Then, after giving them a long look, he slips out the back door and disappears into the shadows.

Chapter 13

THE BISCUIT TIN Louis brought contained a treasure: a new thirty-hour battery Virginia desperately needed for her B2. HQ is pleased with the number of Maquis in the region, and promises more supplies on the next drop, which—weather permitting—will be best if it's done in a week and a half, during the next full moon. If Virginia lasts until then, she'll have survived more than six weeks in France. She hardly dares to imagine it and the morale boost that will follow.

Now that two regions have supplies, and Lavi's Maquis are partially armed, each night she listens to the BBC, hoping for the words—the violins of autumn. She holds her breath over and over, but still, she's unsatisfied. When will D-Day come?

The high from the first drop is short-lived, and the men are again growing restless. They're less enthusiastic now when Virginia visits. They argue and fight among themselves. They miss their loved ones. Hiding is a prison unlike any other. It's preferable to forced labor in German camps, but it's its own kind of hell, especially when many don't have contact with their families. It's safer if their women and children don't know where they are.

We need more weapons, they say. *When can we wire the railways? When can we kill Nazis?*

Wait, she tells them. If you do it now, you'll only bring hell on innocent people. If the Nazis aren't occupied fighting the Allies, they'll occupy themselves with revenge.

Virginia passes on a few of the more egregious reprisal stories—including the fates of the three musketeers—to deter the men from acting on their anger, but that will hold them back for only so long. Lavi tries to defuse the tension, but the chorus of their voices is louder than his. It's at her ear when she leaves them. It plagues her through the nights. It stabs deeper every time the poem isn't said over the broadcast.

Tension also boils with Sophie. Virginia wasn't able to unload on Sophie when she'd reprimanded Louis, so she's constantly doing so in her mind. She's aggravated to see Sophie is once again adorned with her red lipstick and styled hair, but refuses to remind her of such dangers any longer. If they had more time, she'd find another courier, but they don't. Deep down Virginia knows what really bothers her about the young woman is how much she reminds Virginia of herself before the war losses. In fact, Virginia is disgusted to realize she could be her own mother chastising her young self for falling so hard and so quickly for Emil.

One rainy morning, when the boy is at school and Mimi is at the market, Sophie brings news. Virginia lets her in and returns to her place at the dining table, where she works out coordinates on maps of the surrounding areas for the next drop.

"We were in Paris on Tuesday," says Sophie, "so I was able to connect with Aramis."

"'We?'" Virginia says, looking up at Sophie.

So, she and Louis do continue to see each other. At least they're not meeting in Cosne, but it still stokes the fire of Virginia's anger.

Sophie blanches from the slip, and quickly sidesteps the question.

"Aside from a near miss with the Milice, Aramis is well established. He has three new safe houses, two of which are occupied by Allied airmen on escape."

"Let me guess. You wrote them down?"

"No," says Sophie. "I would never do anything so foolish."

Her voice trails off, and the word and its implication sit between them. Sophie looks away, and a tense, heavy silence falls. After a few minutes, Sophie clears her throat.

"When you're ready, I'll tell you," Sophie says.

Virginia sighs with impatience and grabs a piece of paper. She has developed a shorthand and will hide the note in the fireplace until her next transmission. Sophie recites the addresses and code phrases while Virginia scribbles.

"Aramis wanted me to apologize to you on his behalf," Sophie says quietly. "He realizes coming in place of a courier put you and your hosts in unnecessary danger."

"Anything else?" Virginia says.

Sophie continues to stand before her, eyes wide. She knows Sophie is trying to build a bridge, but frankly Virginia's in no mood, especially because she has no doubt Sophie will continue to see Louis against her advice.

"Is that all?" Virginia says.

Sophie's shoulders fall. She pulls on her kerchief to prepare to leave, but when her hand is on the doorknob, she turns back to Virginia. It seems to take her great courage to muster her words.

"You know, Diane. All of us—we aren't the enemy. Does it help you to be so angry all the time? So cold?"

Virginia feels her temperature rising. This girl needs to leave.

"Even Louis says you're different," Sophie continues. "He says you aren't the same woman he used to know."

Virginia flinches. That hurts, especially because—in spite of his nightmares—Louis's personality hasn't changed. He's the same bright young man with the same joie de vivre, yet she's as old and hollow as the identity she has taken. Regardless, Sophie needs to respect Virginia's authority.

"What do you want from me?" Virginia asks.

"Kindness," Sophie says. "And maybe a bit of gratitude or praise."

"Why do you seek my approval?"

"It isn't about approval. It's about simple human courtesy."

"Really? Well, you know what I value? Discretion. A lack of excitability. Extreme care for the lives and safety of those who harbor agents like us."

"I care about all those things."

Unable to contain herself any longer, Virginia slams her fist on the dining table.

"You don't!"

Virginia feels outside herself, watching, like an angel on one shoulder losing to the devil on the other. She knows her anger indulges a darkness that shouldn't be given release, but she's so tired, so tightly wound, so frustrated that she has no more control over her own temper than she has over the woman in front of her, she can't help it.

"You parade around war zones like a schoolgirl on her way to meet her sweetheart on holiday," Virginia says. "You gossip about me with other agents. You meet with Louis, endangering all of us over and over again. You have no self-control. No discipline."

"No discipline? How dare you—you've no idea what I go without to travel all hours of the day and night. The danger I put myself in. The sleep I lose to keep you connected."

"You aren't special. That's all of us. But all of us aren't indulging in wartime romances while men atrophy in the woods, alone, like caged animals."

At that, Sophie at least has the decency to look guilty. She turns her gaze to her feet. Virginia steps toward her.

"A ten-year-old boy and his mother—the nephew and sister of your fiancé—live in this house," says Virginia. "Do you know what the Gestapo do to those who harbor resistors?"

Sophie begins to cry.

"Do you know what the Gestapo do to women?" Virginia continues, unable to stop herself. "They torture and rape them for sport. My own contact, a prostitute, suffered in such a way. One of her girls had a bottle shoved in her mouth until her face split open around it. Do you know why?"

Virginia grabs Sophie by the arms. The girl sobs.

"Do you know why?" Virginia says. "Because she had been spying on her Nazi clients and feeding me information on them, and she wouldn't tell them where I was."

Sick, Virginia drops Sophie's arms and walks away from her. Virginia presses her fists to her forehead.

"I'm sorry," says Sophie, reaching for Virginia.

Virginia slaps Sophie's arm away from her.

"Get out," Virginia says. "Now."

She hears Sophie's ragged breathing. After a moment, the door opens, allowing in the aroma of rain and a rush of wind before quietly closing. Virginia staggers to the dining table. She leans on it, watching Sophie—shoulders slumped—pedal away in the rain. With a groan, Virginia sweeps the maps to the floor.

"Diane."

She turns to see Mimi in the doorway. Overcome with shame and remorse, Virginia buries her face in her hands. Her friend walks to her and pulls her into her arms.

IN THE LOW light of the lantern, while they wait for the night's broadcast, they share the wine Mimi pulled from her secret stash. The women take turns swigging from the bottle.

"Tell me about your friend," Mimi says. "The prostitute from Lyon."

When the bottle comes to Virginia, she looks at it and pauses. Simultaneously, a pain like a spike and the memory of the girl's torn face go through her head. She squeezes her eyes shut and takes a long drink.

"I don't know if I can," she says.

"What comes to mind? Anything. How about this? Is she alive?"

"I don't know. Word is she's at a work camp for women in the Resistance. Ravensbrück."

Mimi shivers.

Virginia recalls the day she met her friend, the head of a Lyon brothel.

Édith Piaf was playing on the gramophone. Silks and paintings hung on the walls. Real coffee with cream and sugar was served. Virginia had thought the woman was a society wife. How surprised she'd been to learn the truth.

"Do you know who was one of our closest allies in Lyon?" Virginia continues, feeling something loosen inside her.

"Who?" says Mimi.

"A nun."

Mimi laughs. "Now, that doesn't surprise me. We're all women, after all."

Virginia feels good speaking about her people. It lightens the weight of carrying them with her.

"The prostitute told me, 'In war we are the same,'" Virginia continues. "She thought I'd be offended, but I knew she spoke the truth. We both create illusion. We both aim to do a little good in bad situations."

"Isn't that the goal for all of us? Mothers and fathers. Nuns and prostitutes."

"But is it for nothing? The bad seems so much stronger than the good these days."

"Of course it's worth it. If there were one innocent man or woman on earth, it would be worth it to protect that goodness. It's all the Lord asks of each of us. Each day. Each hour. Each minute. Do the next good thing."

Virginia ponders that while thinking of Sophie. She was so hard on her. She must remember that she can't be as hard on others as she is on herself. She's had years to build up her armor. Others might not have had to do so.

The broadcast runs on, but it ends without the poem.

Mimi takes the last swig of the bottle.

"I have a confession to make," Mimi says.

"I thought I was the sinner here."

"We're all sinners," Mimi says. "So here goes: While I'm eager to hear the poem, I also dread it."

"Why dread D-Day? It's the beginning of the end."

"Because it will get worse before it gets better," says Mimi. "*If* it gets better. And then, even if it ends, think of all the people emerging from the rubble. Think of the women and children. All the empty places at dinner tables. The resentments between those who collaborated and those who resisted. The remorse for the things we've done that we thought were justified by the ends. We will all be called to account."

Chapter 14

THE NEXT DAY, after adding more gray to her hair and taking extra care with her old-woman makeup, Virginia asks Mimi to borrow her bicycle with the basket and several bags of lentils.

"Spy mission?" says Mimi.

"More like diplomacy. I know this is unlike me, but I need Sophie's safe-house address."

Mimi is glad to provide it, and soon Virginia sets out through the cloudy afternoon on her journey. Playing the part of the old woman, she pedals more slowly than she would like, taking time to rest often at stops along the way. She sees few soldiers—only at stations or government buildings—and is glad when the towns give way to sprawling fields. She notes several in her head for possible drop sites. Two hours later she sees the farm with the small row of well-spaced tenant huts of Mimi's description. The last in the row is nestled in a small grove of sweet chestnut trees. After she's locked her bicycle to one of them, she approaches the cottage. Muffled music comes through the door. She knocks softly, but there's no response. It occurs to her that Sophie and Louis might be inside together, but she has come too far to give up now. She knocks again, louder, and before she finishes, Sophie opens the door.

"Would you like to buy some lentils?" Virginia says.

The look Sophie gives her suggests she might like to throw a bag of lentils in her face. Virginia gives Sophie a small smile that seems to soften her. Sophie steps aside, motioning Virginia into the hut and closing the door behind her.

Josephine Baker's voice, along with sprays of fresh flowers in milk jugs and the rich scent of perfume, fills the room. A bottle of red nail polish is open on the table, its lid upside down with its brush facing the ceiling. Sophie holds out her hands, waving them, and crosses the room to turn off the music.

"No, leave it," says Virginia. "I saw Josephine Baker in Paris many years ago. It was another lifetime."

Sophie shrugs, and returns to the table where the bottle of nail polish rests. She puts the brush into the container and twists the top.

"I know all this must seem silly to you," Sophie says, gesturing toward the polish and the player. "But it keeps me sane. Normalcy."

"It doesn't seem silly," says Virginia. "Maybe I should try it."

Sophie looks at her as if she doesn't know whether or not she's being teased. Virginia places the lentils on the table, and opens one of the bags, sifting through the legumes until she finds the tube of lipstick Vera sent her through Louis. She hands it to Sophie.

"Here," says Virginia. "Louis brought it for me from Vera, but it doesn't really go with my outfit."

Sophie hesitates a moment before taking it.

"Thank you," she says. "I was running out. I thought you'd be pleased to see me looking less conspicuous."

"I'm not going to try to control you anymore. We each have our talents."

Sophie doesn't respond, nor does she ask Virginia to sit. Her fatigue from the ride compels her to take a seat anyway. Sophie walks across the room to the small bed. On her end table is a photograph of a handsome, dark-haired man—who is not Louis—lying on a picnic blanket.

"My husband," Sophie says.

Virginia's eyes widen.

"RAF pilot. He died in '42. Injuries from a training crash."

The man looks like he could be a Frenchman, so having his face nearby is no danger. It probably goes with Sophie's cover story.

Virginia realizes this young woman she has judged so harshly has lived a lot of life. It also occurs to Virginia that Sophie has suffered terrible loss but her light has not gone out. Virginia has a lot to learn from her.

"Louis knows all about my sweet Dennis," Sophie continues. "My guardian angel."

"Ah," says Virginia. "My father is mine."

"I didn't know you believed in such things."

"I wouldn't if I hadn't seen him with my own eyes."

"Truly?" Sophie sits forward, seeming to forget her anger.

"Yes. He died ten years ago, shortly before I had the hunting accident that took my foot."

Sophie's eyes flick down to Virginia's leg and back. They hold no surprise.

"You know about my prosthetic?" Virginia says.

"Most of us agents know about Dilbert."

"Cuthbert," Virginia says. "Anyway, after the infection and the amputation, I got pretty bad in my head. My father's spirit came to me in the hospital and told me to soldier on."

"It's good you listened to him," Sophie says.

"I guess. But I don't know if he'd be proud of what I've become."

Sophie stares at her a long moment. The song ends, leaving only the crackling sound of the needle on the record. Virginia stands to go. When she reaches the door, Sophie's voice stops her.

"Dennis was a boxer," she says.

Virginia turns back and sees Sophie holding the framed photograph of her husband.

"He used to tell me, 'It's not the fists alone that win the fight.'"

Virginia looks down at her hands. She thinks she is a fist, or at least a brain that tells the fists what to do. She looks back up at Sophie— surrounded in flowers, aglow with life and love. Sophie is a heart.

Virginia turns to leave, but Sophie's voice again stops her.

"Your father would be proud of you."

WHEN VIRGINIA ARRIVES back in Cosne, the sun is setting. The clouds have given way to a glorious pink sky, and the last light is rich and warm, making even the crudest old farmhouses glow with beauty. Virginia's knee stump aches from pedaling, but her heart is quiet—even content—if only for this moment.

On the outskirts of town, she spots the little figure of the boy pulling his wagon down a hill, toward the pilings of the bridge the Nazis bombed at the beginning of the war. The one they constructed in its place is farther down the river. Their ugly lorries drive over it like large black beetles.

She's about to call to him, when she notices a dinghy in the shadows of the old bridge. A mustached man of about fifty paddles it. She watches, ready to spring to help, but the boy moves with ease and surety. He pulls his wagon to the pilings, removes a small fishing pole, and leaves the wagon behind, proceeding to cast his line. While he fishes, the man in the shadows empties the contents of the wagon into his boat and paddles away.

Fear nearly choking her, she looks between the Nazi bridge and the old one. The man in the dinghy moves in the opposite direction of the Nazis, but, if they have a scout who observed the transaction, they could be here in no time.

She continues to keep watch the long minutes the boy waits. After a while, he pulls in his line, places the pole back in his wagon, and drags it up the hill and toward home. She follows him at a safe distance all the way and doesn't breathe properly until he's in the house.

Chapter 15

VIRGINIA KNOWS SHE'S having a nightmare because she's watching herself that December day in Smyrna, in 1933, the day of the accident. Her transfer to the Turkish embassy hadn't done anything to alleviate her pain over the breakup with Emil. Hungover from a night of drowning her sorrows, she almost hadn't gone hunting. If only she had stayed home.

The sun had warmed the little hunting party of consulate workers and their Turkish guide, so they were able to remove their coats and recline on blankets in the dead grass. They'd been getting to know one another, discussing their backgrounds.

"Virginia's grandfather was a pirate," her friend Elena had said.

"Hardly," said Virginia. "He was a sailor. Stowed away on his father's ship until he could buy his own."

"When he was *nine*," said Elena. "Can you imagine, a little boy on adventures like that? That must be where you get it."

"Get what?"

"Your fearlessness."

"No one's fearless," said Elena's husband, Todd. "We all have something that steals the breath from our lungs."

"Yes," said Elena. "And Todd's *something* is a snake."

"Is nothing sacred between us, woman?" he said.

"Snakes?" said Virginia. "I used to wear them to school around my wrist to scare the teachers."

"No," said Todd.

"Ask anyone. I spent all the summers of my youth on a farm, for Pete's sake. I can handle a canoe against the current, de-scent a skunk, and skin a rabbit. But, do you know the one thing I have never been able to master?"

"What?"

"I can't milk a damned cow."

The group laughed.

"Nothing makes me angrier," she continued. "My father gave hours of his life trying to teach me. I gave hours of mine trying to learn. And still—to this day—I cannot. It torments me."

"That's funny, but it's not a fear," said Elena. "My fear is rats. They're smart, you know?"

Shudders went through the group.

"How about you?" said Virginia to their handsome guide, Murat. "What do you fear?"

"*Ölüm*," he said. "Death. It is unknown what lies on the other side, but we will all find out."

They became silent. A breeze ran along on the yellow grass, waving it like fingers.

"You never admitted your fear, Virginia," said Todd.

"That's because I don't have any," she said, hoping her airy tone didn't betray the lie.

Loss, she thought, the faces of her father and Emil in her mind. *I'm afraid of losing those I love. So maybe I'll just stop loving.*

"You must pick something," said Elena. "Otherwise, we'll think you cold."

Cold. When Emil had made his final pronouncement, she'd forced a layer of ice around her heart. She hated the feeling, but it was the only way she could keep her dignity and move forward. She still hadn't fully thawed, but these things couldn't be spoken aloud, not to such new acquaintances.

"I know," Virginia said. "I'm afraid I'll never be able to milk a cow."

The laughter of the group rose around them like birds. The snipe began to call.

"Enough," said Virginia. "Let's hunt."

The Virginia watching this nightmare screams, trying to get her old careless, cocky self's attention. She watches—helpless, soundless—as that Virginia runs her hand along the fence that's too high to hop, loaded shotgun hanging from a strap, pointing down, banging against her thigh. Her friends scale the fence one by one.

"You first," says Murat. "I'll help you."

"I don't need help," she says.

With the shotgun still pointing down, the other Virginia hoists her right leg onto the fence. As she does so, her foot on the ground slips in the mud. The gun goes off, and the hunting party begins yelling. That Virginia doesn't understand why until she looks down.

Time stops.

My boot, she thinks, strangely. *Ruined.*

But then the pain arrives, uniting both Virginias. The scene becomes bright white, like staring at the sun.

The last thing she remembers is looking at Murat, and uttering, "Help."

SHE'S JERKED AWAKE, and it takes her a moment to realize she in Mimi's attic. Sophie's distraught face is in hers.

"What is it?" Virginia says, sitting up.

"Louis," cries Sophie. "He's been arrested!"

"No," Virginia whispers.

She reaches for her prosthetic and straps it on. She drops to the ground, pulls her wireless suitcase from under the bed, and starts setting it up.

"Where?" she says.

"In Paris," says Mimi. Her face is pale in the night, wet with tears.

"He was stealing plans for the German base his group was assigned to blow up before D-Day," says Sophie.

"How'd you find out?" Virginia says.

"Another agent," says Sophie. "She just missed being picked up with them."

"Them?"

"Yes, all three in Louis's team. They thought the driver they found was trustworthy, but he drove them straight to prison."

Virginia's hands shake while she positions the antenna, but by the time she starts to wire headquarters, they're steady. The women wait, staring at the machine, desperate for contact. Soon the sounds come through, her check is cleared, and she transmits what has happened. Their worst fears are realized when HQ confirms the report. A pianist in Hector's network already told them.

—Where taken? Virginia types, speaking aloud so the women know the conversation.

—Cherche-Midi.

Virginia's mouth goes dry. Mimi and Sophie gasp. The Paris prison is a vermin-infested torture chamber. An absolute fortress.

"I'll go and break the gates myself," says Sophie.

"No, you won't," says Virginia. "Not unless you have a death wish."

"We have to do something," Sophie cries.

Virginia holds up her hand, silencing the girl, trying to hear the Morse code. She listens, taking it all in, shaking her head with resignation.

"What?" says Sophie.

Virginia finishes her transmission and packs away the equipment.

"What did they say?" Sophie cries.

When Virginia is finished, she looks at Sophie.

"We need to separate and relocate. Immediately."

ONCE VIRGINIA IS able to calm Mimi and Sophie, she asks Sophie if she has another safe house at her disposal. She does, and tells Virginia

the address, which Virginia carefully files in her mind. Mimi will take her
son to Lavi for a few days, at least, and will then return to the house when
it's safe. In the meantime, Mimi will start warning all of her contacts that
the network is compromised.

Virginia's conversation with Louis comes to her mind.

"How long were we trained to remain silent under interrogation?"
Louis had asked.

"Forty-eight hours."

"That's right. Enough time to let your people get away."

Once Sophie leaves, Mimi gives Virginia the information for her new
safe house.

"The place you'll go is in Sury-près-Léré," says Mimi. "Cross the Loire
River and follow it ten kilometers north. You will see signs for the village.
The farm is on the outskirts, on the western side, second one out with
the blue door. The woman who lives there, Estelle—she refuses a code
name—is a widow of the 1940 fighting. She's a school friend of mine, and
a resistor. If the red flowerpot is in the front window, it's safe for you to
knock."

"If not?"

"About a kilometer from the house, there's a barn with a loft. You
must wait there until she fetches you. But tread carefully. The barn is
never empty. Many use it on their escape. If you must go to it, knock four
times and announce yourself by saying, 'Where did I leave my milking
stool?'"

"Thank you."

"Diane," says Mimi, taking Virginia's hands. "Estelle is your link to
Chambon."

A feeling of warmth and anticipation spreads over Virginia. She brings
it in check.

"I'm not leaving for the mountains yet," Virginia says. "This is only to
set up separate lodgings. There are more drops to take for your Maquis,
and I have experience with prison breaks from my first mission, not to

mention Louis's own experience. We'll try everything we can to get Louis out."

"If he doesn't get himself out first."

The women reach for each other, grasping hands and putting their foreheads together before they separate.

Chapter 16

HOURS LATER VIRGINIA arrives at the farm, her wireless suitcase feeling as if it holds a boulder. She limps from her knee stump's raw, rubbed skin. When will a good callous start forming?

The tall stone house looks like it was once a grand place but has fallen into disrepair. The facade is covered in the dormant vines of climbing roses and has a large, blue, arched door. The red flowerpot is in the window. The sight of it and the tulips pushing forth from the dirt lifts her spirits, but only a little. She's sick with terror for Louis and her people.

Goats surround her, greeting her with their calls. She pats their heads and picks a handful of grass to feed them. When she looks up, a woman with steely eyes and salt-and-pepper hair pulled into a loose bun stands at the door with her arms crossed. She's a little older than Virginia's true age but looks sturdy. Formidable.

"How long since you've had a farmhand?" says Virginia.

"It has been a long time," says Estelle.

The woman's posture relaxes. Virginia picks up her suitcases and walks into the house. Once she's in the foyer, she hears an old man shouting from an upstairs room. Estelle looks at the ceiling and sighs.

"My father. He thinks you're a German spy."

"Why?"

"He thinks that about all foreigners."

"Then I better find a way to sweeten him up."

"Impossible," Estelle says. "Steer clear of him. He never turned over his rifle from the Great War. It's always loaded."

Virginia listens to him continue to curse about her arrival.

"Is my room near his?" she asks.

"No. You'll be in the garret. I'll keep him well away from you. Come."

The stair ahead is wide at the bottom and narrows as it rises to a landing where it splits, leading to different sides of the house. Virginia is glad to take the staircase that leads to the right, away from the yelling man. On the second floor, dark wood beams and molding contrast with pale, faded wallpaper. Though the hall is shadowed, Virginia is able to make out the lush design of foliage teeming with birds.

"Can you remember a world so frivolous one could buy such wallpaper for an upstairs hallway?" says Estelle, a note of bitterness in her voice.

"Barely," says Virginia. "But this helps."

"Then I guess it's a good thing."

Estelle walks to a small door at the end of the hallway and unlocks it. Virginia follows the woman up the narrow staircase to the garret. There's a double bed and a desk near a window, a faded carpet on the floor, and a corner with a tiny table and chairs. The table is laid out for tea, and there's no dust in the cups. There are no cobwebs or dust anywhere, and the window looks as if it has been recently wiped clean. The air smells of other people, as if someone just walked out of the room.

"I hope no one was displaced for me," Virginia says.

"It was time for them to move on."

Virginia places her suitcases on the floor and crosses the room. Just outside the window, there's an ancient oak with new leaves whose branch tips skirt but don't obstruct the view of the surrounding area and the road leading to the house. She's high up, so transmission should be strong. It's a great relief to be here.

"Mimi says you need a traveling companion and a link to Chambon," says Estelle. "I'm glad to be both of those things, but I'm busy with my

own work. I'll need a day's notice if you want me to accompany you anywhere, and so I can have my young cousin come to take care of Father.
She'll stay out of your way."

"I appreciate your help more than I can say. As I'm sure you hear, my
French reveals my accent."

"Yes, you shouldn't take the railways alone."

Virginia tries not to bristle.

"If I get approval, I want to go to Paris tomorrow," Virginia says.

"All right. The bus makes daily trips to the train station in Briare,
where we can catch a connector to Paris. If we have to stay overnight, I
have an apartment at my disposal."

"Thank you."

Estelle waves her off, as if providing shelter and escort in Nazi-infested
France is nothing.

"I know you need to come and go at will," says Estelle. "You may use
either of the two bicycles in the shed at any time, but guard them with
your life. They're all we have to get around. And here is a master key to
the house. But please, only use it on the front door and in your door—no
others. It's an old house with many rooms, and we sometimes have . . .
ghosts."

IN HER TRANSMISSION that night, Virginia tells HQ Sophie's
safe house and her own new safe house, and that it's an easy bicycle ride
from here to Cosne and her Maquis. They agree on a field for a drop and a
date, just after the full moon. Then, she sends them a request.

—Permission to go to Paris. Intel on Louis's
prison break. Cherche-Midi.

Since Virginia learned of Louis's arrest, the nightmares have been
coming with more frequency, the memories of her time in the Spanish
prison fearing for her men and women circling again and again in her
mind. She might not be able to do anything for them now, but Louis is a

train ride away. She needs to do what she can, even if that's only letting him know he isn't forgotten.

—Declined.

Damn.

She knew the request was a long shot, but it doesn't make the answer any less frustrating. She can't bear to think of Louis in that place. Prisons like Cherche-Midi can break men, even men who seem unbreakable. Virginia is confident Louis can endure starvation; they have all mastered hunger in one way or another—but it's the solitary confinement that can make a social, loving man like Louis lose his way. Even when she was arrested and taken to the Spanish prison, she had a cellmate who kept her going. She asks again.

—One day. Tomorrow. With escort.

In the pause, while she waits for a response, a dark thing deep inside Virginia stirs. Thoughts begin to rise. Motives that are outside of a rescue mission. Virginia suffocates them, keeping oxygen from flaming that fire to life.

—Declined.

Virginia breathes deeply, trying to quell her rising desperation. Each minute in that prison is an hour. Each hour, a day. Each day, a week.

—Three agents imprisoned. Entire networks compromised. Experienced in prison breaks.

She was a part of several in Lyon, with Louis's help. There's a good chance she'll be able to get the men out, especially with all the bribe money to which she has access. There's silence for a long time—so long she wonders if her transmission has been interrupted. As she's about to try again, the dots and dashes come through.

—Permission granted, per Wild Bill.

Virginia grins. *Thank you, General Donovan.*

Oh, how Vera must rage. Virginia feels guilty for her triumph. There's nothing more frustrating than being overridden by one with higher rank, especially a man. Especially—to Vera—an American man.

—I won't disappoint you. Travel May 1. Briare to
Paris line.

—We'll get word to RAF.

The Royal Air Force. If they know the lines agents travel, they won't
bomb them.

Not for the first time since arriving, Virginia experiences a rush of
gratitude for her links to HQ. It would have taken days to get this information to them through another pianist, and she might not have had
success.

—Good. Prison contact?

—Alley outside café across street. Use rat.

The rat. SOE training included trapping, killing, and gutting rats as
foul little letterboxes. They're safe communication devices because no one
would pick up a dead rat. One does have to watch for cats, though. Dous-
ing the rat in pepper water usually keeps cats away. At least this rat has
already been killed and prepared.

After she packs up the wireless and stores it in the wall behind several
boards she's loosened, she removes her prosthetic and climbs into bed.
She reaches down to massage her aching knee stump. The wind picks up
and taps an oak branch against the glass.

She breaks into a cold sweat, suddenly remembering the tree outside
the window in the Turkish hospital where she had burned with infection.
She soon falls into an uneasy sleep, and the nightmare drops her right
there, into the hospital bed.

THE SHOTGUN PELLETS had shattered her foot. Thick mud seeped
into her cuts. Gangrene had set in before the moon rose. The doctor had
stared at her over his flimsy cotton mask and asked, "Your life or your leg?"

She hadn't answered at first. It was nearly impossible to attend to
anything—especially a decision of that magnitude—when the white-hot
agony of her pain so wholly consumed her. It was a terrible, humbling

thing to behold, to live. To burn with torture from foot to fevered head. This fire would not take long to make ash of her.

But just outside her window, winter had winked at Virginia in the glint of moonlight on an ice-encased tree limb. The branch was knobby and dormant and cold. Deliciously cold. She tried to swallow, wishing to suck the ice off the wood to relieve the fire in her. The limb tapped the glass.

I will reawaken, the tree seemed to say.

She was able to manage a word.

"Leg."

All became black, and waking on the other side of the amputation brought no relief.

She soon learned that phantom pain—the hurt of a lost limb—was as real as the actual pain on the stump. It traveled next to it, a second horse dragging an unwilling rider with no carriage over a rocky road. She came to understand that she was no longer whole. Her strong, shapely, lovely leg—one that had been stroked and kissed and relied upon without ever being properly thought of or thanked—was in a trash can. An actual part of her body thrown out with the rubbish.

"You're lucky," the doctor had said, while Virginia stared at the pills on the tray the nurse brought to her. "We were able to save the knee. Your exact measurements have been taken for a prosthetic."

She imagined the doctor using a measuring tape on her severed leg before tossing it in the wastebasket. Would he think her mad if she asked him to fish it out and cut a bone from it for her? Or maybe something smaller, like a toe. A talisman to carry. A rabbit's foot.

She couldn't help but laugh.

The doctor and nurse had given each other troubled looks.

That's right, she thought. *I'm losing it. I'm lost. And I will not continue this way.*

It was obvious to Virginia: She couldn't live without her leg. She would not live with pity. Oh, the pity! Her friends tried to hide their shock at her gaunt face, her vacant stare. Tried to hide how they wished to flee the sterile room where she lay, missing a piece of herself.

The nurse watched Virginia wash down the pills with water but didn't notice one remained tucked in Virginia's clammy, curled pinkie, the sweat allowing it to stick to her skin. She didn't notice Virginia slide her hand under the blankets and tuck the pill under her hip, adding it to a little pile. As the nurse crossed the room to shut the window, Virginia told her to leave it open.

"You'll catch your death."

"Promise?"

The nurse stared at her a moment. On her way out of the room, she turned off the light.

Virginia had glared through the darkness at the tree outside her window. Each day she watched the sun melt the ice, while the evening froze the drips into little icicles, and the night fully encased it. All while the limb tapped her window, mocking her with its indecipherable Morse code.

"Traitor," she said.

Tap. Tap. Tap.

If she could stand, she could break the branch and throw it in the snow far below. But she would never stand again.

The night air smelled of spices and winter, as it did the night she'd stood on her balcony, cursing Emil, drinking gin. What she wouldn't give to go back in time. If only she'd had just one more drink, the hangover would have been too much. She would have backed out of the hunting outing. She wouldn't have made the careless mistake that had cost her so dearly.

Dizzy with pain, she'd reached for the pills, collected them, and lifted her hand. Ten tiny white poisons glowed in the moonlight. Each on its own could do no harm; together they would end her. She closed her eyes and brought her hand to her mouth.

"Dindy."

Her eyes snapped open. Startled, she dropped the pills on her blanket.

The room smelled of her father's pipe smoke. He was somehow there, glowing blue in the moonlight. But no! Impossible. He was dead.

She squeezed her eyes closed and open again, wondering if she was hallucinating. Though his mouth didn't move, his voice was in her ear.

Don't, Dindy. It's not who you are.

"But I can't live like this," she whispered.

You'd break your mother's heart.

"I'm broken."

Then put yourself back together.

"No."

Keep fighting.

Tap. Tap. Tap.

Keep fighting.

HER EYES JERK open, and the branch outside the window keeps tapping.

She checks the time. Four in the morning. The next day. May 1. No sense trying to sleep any longer.

Hauling herself out of bed and strapping on her prosthetic, she reflects that she's come a long way from that hospital bed, but still has much further to go.

As she readies herself, she goes over the plan once more, her mind racing with stations and streets, names and faces, dates and times. The date is May 1. She keeps coming back to it. Why does it feel so important? She wonders if it's prophecy, if May 1 will bring the D-Day announcement.

She gives her disguise a final check before leaving the garret. When she reaches the landing of the split staircase and sees the first hint of dawn on the horizon, she suddenly realizes why May 1 is significant.

The date marks six weeks since she landed in France.

Chapter 17

THE WOMEN RIDE the dawn bus to the train station in silence. They don't need to speak; they've gone over the mission in detail.

Arrive. Rendezvous. Hide. Rendezvous. Depart.

If they're able to make contact, and Louis and his team are alive, they need to find the location of the three cells, the time the prisoners are taken to the courtyard for exercises, and how much bribe money it will cost to smuggle each out.

Sunup to sundown. Just another day in the field.

Six weeks, she tries not to think.

Estelle handles purchasing tickets and enduring communication at the checkpoints. It's a relief when the women finally find seats, and they settle as far from the front of the train as possible. Though safe from RAF bombings, rogue Maquis groups are a worry. If they've wired the tracks to explode, the farther from the locomotive the women sit, the better.

The trip should take two hours, but the stops and delays from over-zealous MPs make it take four. Every bang and slam brings a fresh layer of sweat to her clothing, and by the time they arrive in Paris, Virginia could use a drink. They disembark arm in arm—two gray, invisible women—each carrying only a handbag. Virginia's exhaustion is profound but, because cars and taxis are for Nazis and the metro is heavily patrolled, walking is the best option.

Seeing the deterioration of Paris gives Virginia fresh heartbreak. Swastikas defile every view. Queues of starving people wrap around the food shops. Theaters are desecrated with Nazi Imperial Eagles. Racist propaganda is everywhere. When they reach the boulevard Raspail, the sight that greets them chills Virginia. Along the street are hundreds of wanted posters of men and women, the majority of them labeled with the word EXÉCUTÉ.

Executed.

Estelle doesn't flinch or falter. She continues on, cool and serene. Virginia matches Estelle's pace, and decides to pull her eyes away from the posters. She doesn't want to risk disturbing her focus by seeing her own face.

The prison looms—impenetrable—two hundred tiny windows marking each of its solitary-confinement cells. Above its huge, arched door are the words PRISON MILITAIRE DE PARIS. The women veer toward the café across the street and, while Estelle goes in to get them a table, Virginia walks into the alley, where she spots the upturned rat. She slips her hand into her pocket, removes the sliver of paper, and tucks it into the belly of the rodent. She then drops the rat across the alley to the side visible to the duplicitous guard in the employ of HQ and returns to the café.

When she and Estelle finish their drinks, they leave, walking along the prison wall to get to Estelle's apartment. As they pass by, they hear a dreadful sound: the call to fire, the blast of guns.

The women hold each other a little tighter but continue steady on, hoping they aren't too late.

THE APARTMENT AT Estelle's disposal is a long walk from the café, and by the time they turn on the street, Virginia is so dizzy from hunger and pain in her knee stump, she almost doesn't notice where they are. When she catches sight of the bas-relief grotesque of the griffin on the cream-colored building, where four floors of balconies face the Seine, she stops short.

"Johnnie," she whispers.

Her old pension. From her university days.

The fourth-floor window where she saw the figures dancing all those years ago is shut tight, but the balcony that used to be hers is full of flower-pots bursting with blooms. She clasps her hands to her chest as if in prayer and takes a deep breath.

"You're shaking," says Estelle. "Come."

Estelle's place is across the way. Virginia allows Estelle to lead her into it but keeps looking over her shoulder at her old apartment and stumbles up the step into the building. Estelle catches her and continues to escort Virginia up the stairs to the third floor. When they enter the tiny flat, Virginia sees that her old place is in view. She sits in the window seat, staring at the bas-relief in wonder, only coming into the present moment when Estelle shoves a crust of bread in her hand.

"Who is this Johnnie?" asks Estelle, her face serious.

Virginia smiles.

"It's no one," she says. "I mean, it's the griffin on the building. I named it Johnnie, when I lived there, many moons ago, as a university student."

Virginia doesn't mention it's also her brother's name.

"Ah," says Estelle, sitting on the other side of the window seat.

Virginia takes a bite of bread but has a hard time swallowing. Estelle passes her a glass of water, and Virginia finishes it in three greedy gulps.

"I'm sorry," Virginia says. "I'm so stunned by this old life of mine before me, I lost the ability to think."

"You don't have to explain that feeling to me. I used to stay here with my husband. It was his brother's place. Now there's no brother. No husband. But it feels like they're just in the other room."

Virginia can't say a single thing to reflect how sorry she is for this woman's losses. She turns her gaze to Estelle, and it strikes Virginia how naturally she has fallen in with her. She knows part of it is due to the care Mimi took in choosing Estelle as a contact, and part is because of Estelle's warm, capable, straightforward nature. But the last part is because Virginia has allowed it. An urge rises in her to keep herself closed off, but that takes more work than simply reaching for Estelle's hand and giving in to the moment. Estelle smiles sadly, and the women return their attention to the building across the street.

"See the balcony with the flowers?" Virginia says. "That was mine. I watched a hundred sunrises from there. Kissed a hundred boys. You wouldn't believe what I was like before all this."

"Maybe you'll be like that again someday."

Virginia laughs and shakes her head. "No, that girl has died a hundred deaths since then. She has disappeared."

"I don't know. Doesn't it seem like a sign? In this whole city, this is where my apartment is, right across the street from your old place. And on a whole building of empty balconies, flowers spill off the one where you used to watch the sunrise."

"I suppose one can hope," says Virginia.

"My friend, that's all we have left."

THEY REST FOR an hour, before setting back out for the café. It's hard for Virginia to tear herself away, but she must. The clock is ticking.

When they arrive, it's one o'clock in the afternoon. The rat is in place, a hand-rolled cigarette in its belly. Virginia removes it, slides it in her pocket, and joins Estelle for a cup of foul café nationale, the ersatz acorn-and-chickpea concoction that's supposed to pass as coffee. After drinking half of it, she excuses herself to go to the toilet and, once locked in, unrolls the cigarette. Inside are two messages. The first is from the guard.

Transferring later this week. Need new liaison.

Damn. The timing is terrible. She'll have to search her contacts to see who might be granted entrance to the prison.

On the second paper, her spirits lift briefly when she sees Louis's handwriting, but plunge when she reads the words.

There are eight of us, not three.

Breaking out three prisoners would have been hard enough. But eight? Nearly impossible. She's about to flush the papers but sees Louis has written on the other side of it. The words are like a blast of icy wind.

> *Found him. Home: 16th A. Rue Spontini. Work: Saint-Maur-des-Fossés.*

She's unable to keep up with the waves of emotions she feels. Anger at Louis for pursuing the betrayer. Tenderness that he did it for her. Pride that they found him. Horror that the man is still operational. A dark desire to hunt.

No, not today.

She crumbles the paper in a ball and throws it and the cigarette down the toilet. It takes time to master her emotions while washing her hands. Looking in the mirror, she sees her eyes and posture are weary enough to match the age of her disguise.

When Virginia returns to the table, Estelle sees Virginia's exhaustion and takes strong hold of her arm. Virginia doesn't know how she'll summon the strength to make the return journey, but as they step onto the street and pass the prison, she hears a hoarse voice begin to call out, increasing in volume with each utterance.

"Not today!" he shouts, over and over.

Louis.

She takes a deep breath and stands up straighter. Resolved.

No. Not today.

AT THE STATION at Briare, waiting for the evening bus to Sury-près-Léré, there's an adolescent girl wearing a polka-dot kerchief on her dark hair. She fidgets with her coat and shifts from foot to foot. Her dark-circled eyes dart around the crowd until they find Estelle and Virginia. She's still for a moment and, once Estelle nods, the girl picks up her small suitcase and follows them onto the bus, where she moves past them to sit in the last row. Estelle leads Virginia to the seat in front of the girl.

"How long since you've had a farmhand?" the girl whispers in a shaking voice.

"It has been a long time," Estelle says.

Virginia looks from Estelle to the girl. Is this one of Estelle's ghosts?

Estelle's posture is strong, her chin held high, her hands cool and steady. Providing sanctuary and escape, she's one of the nameless throng—the anonymous, untrained men and women doing everything they can to help win the war. Yet Virginia is sure no one in the outside world will ever learn their names. When the war is over, people like Estelle, Mimi, and the Lopinats, or like Virginia's Lyon contacts—the doctor, the nun, the prostitute, the old couple—deserve statues, but all that will remain are gravestones in lonely churchyards.

Her thoughts turn to Louis. He's no longer the cat with nine lives, but a mouse, trapped. One of eight, not three. She wishes she'd been kinder to Louis before he left, and thinks of the meetings with him she'd taken for granted, never really believing he'd get caught.

Let D-Day come, she thinks. Once the Allies arrive, the war will start being won in the open. If only Louis can hang on.

As they near the small bus stop in town, Estelle leans back and whispers to the girl.

"Leave your suitcase. Take the main boulevard to the churchyard. Enter the cemetery, pause at a grave, and pray. Then make the sign of the cross over yourself. Do you know how to do that?"

"Yes," the girl whispers.

"Good," says Estelle. "Then take the path through the woods behind the cemetery. Follow it along the stream about a kilometer until you reach the barn. Knock four times and say, 'Where did I leave my milking stool?' I'll bring your things later."

"I'm afraid of the woods," the girl whispers, trying not to cry.

"Courage," Estelle whispers. "You've come this far. But you have a long way to go."

As directed, the girl leaves them at the stop, casting Estelle a quick, terrified look before she hurries away from them. Estelle sighs and mumbles a prayer.

The women make it home without incident. When the door opens to the foyer, the old man screams from upstairs about the German spy.

"Will I ever get the pleasure of meeting your father?" asks Virginia. "I do actually have a way with old men. I think I could win him over."

Her heart feels a stab of pain as she recalls the little, bereted peasant from Crozant.

"Probably not," says Estelle. "Getting around is hard for him. He takes his meals upstairs in his room. He talks to the ghosts of those we've lost as if they're sitting around the table with him, drinking imaginary port."

"Imaginary."

"Yes. We haven't been able to get him his beloved Barros Porto since the war began. I wish you could have known him when he was younger. He was a war hero. A mayor. He loved my husband so much. When he was killed in '40, my father mourned him as deeply as I did. His health started slipping after that. The Nazis have taken so much from us. I will work until my dying breath to take back what I can."

Estelle suddenly stops speaking, as if ashamed she's revealed too much.

"If you'll excuse me," says Estelle. "I need to check on . . ."

"Of course."

Before Estelle leaves her, Virginia reaches for her.

"I can't thank you enough," she says. "You've taken great risk for me, and I won't forget it."

"Think nothing of it," says Estelle.

Virginia nods and watches Estelle go, a wave of fondness washing over her.

That night, Virginia wires HQ. They're thrilled she made it safely back from Paris but sad to hear not only that they're losing their contact at

Cherche-Midi but that Louis is one of eight agents who have been rounded up. And Virginia isn't the only one with a tough report. HQ delivers the terrible news that Hector, the leader of the nearest circuit, who had dismissed Sophie, has been captured.

The small flame of hope that had been growing in Virginia is snuffed. She feels hollow, scooped out like a melon shell.

—How?

—Missed warning signal in pianist's window.

—So, the pianist is also?

—Captured.

Did he last six weeks? she thinks.

With shaking hands, Virginia confirms the drop date, adds a request, and signs off before the twenty-minute mark. Once her equipment is stored, Virginia climbs into bed and tries to sleep, but it's futile. She should have asked for more downers—exhaustion leads to mistakes.

Hector must have been exhausted. The way she is. It makes her sick to think a moment's carelessness can lead to the destruction of an entire network.

Chapter 18

I T HAS BEEN a week since Virginia should have died. She's living on borrowed time.

She feels a grim instinct toward pride at beating the odds, but the reality gives her no pleasure. If anything, it heightens the guilt she bears for surviving when so many have not, especially now that Louis has been arrested.

Further plaguing her is the address Louis has given her. Fighting the temptation to hunt the betrayer is an hourly battle in her heart, and having this information weakens her resolve. Instead, through Sophie, Virginia begins to spread the definitive word: Avoid this man at all costs. Courier to courier, network to network, news of betrayers travels like lightning through communication lines. It won't take long for the tables to turn, for the predator to become prey. The trick is holding off assassination to find more enemies, gain intelligence from the other side, and use the betrayer to supply false information.

Virginia has alerted HQ. Their continued reluctance to accept the fact that he's a double agent boils her blood, but she knows why. He's good. Convincing to the highest degree. He has leveraged his position perfectly.

It's hardest to avoid dark thoughts when Estelle makes her trips, leaving Virginia alone to brood. Estelle left the day before with the girl with the polka-dot kerchief. While she's gone, Estelle's young cousin—a dark-haired, dark-eyed wisp of a teenager—cares for Estelle's father. She acts as if she doesn't see Virginia when she passes her on the stairs. Like Estelle, she's the very picture of discretion, another of the nameless throng of heroes.

On her way out one morning, after seeing to the old man's breakfast and dressing, Estelle's cousin slips a paper into Virginia's hand and whispers, "From Mimi." It reads:

> *We're safe. Network on alert. My cousin, a doctor, can get prison access. There's still hope. See you at the drop.*

Virginia's spirits lift, giving her the strength to push on. With renewed energy, she heads out to the stalls to tend to the goats and listen for Estelle's return.

Farm life is an oasis in wartime, and Estelle's reminds her so much of Box Horn Farm. Though her family is one of some means and had a tenant farmer to do the actual work, Virginia always felt more comfortable in the barns and fields than in her mother's parlor, better with simple animals than complicated human beings. Mother had permanently moved from their townhouse in Baltimore City to the summer farm after Daddy died. It was there Virginia returned for her rehabilitation after the hunting accident.

AFTER YEARS OF total freedom, traveling abroad in embassies and consulates, Virginia nearly suffocated returning to her mother's home. Mother's continuous offering of a wheelchair Virginia didn't want, Mother's friends at tea, and meals between meals between meals exasperated Virginia and added to a troubling undercurrent of rage she couldn't shake. She knew her mother was lonely while she was gone and wanted only to help, but Virginia still found it hard to accept.

One spring day, voices of her mother's friends had drifted up the staircase. The women were eager, curious, and hopeful they would see crippled Virginia Hall to take their gossip back to this guild and that club. Virginia had sat on her bed, staring out the window, thinking back to Turkey, to Poland, to Paris. To Emil. She thought coming home would be a comfort, but the walls had grown too small. She couldn't live life ticking the time away on teas and socials.

It's not who you are, came her father's voice.

She had felt his loss more acutely at the farm. The place was haunted with him.

Resting in the corner of her room was the shotgun that took her foot. Shooting targets with Daddy's gun every day allowed her to make peace with it, to acknowledge it was her lack of respect for its power that resulted in her loss. She slung the unloaded shotgun over her chest, held her crutches in one hand, and grasped the rail with the other while she clomped down the staircase. She could hardly wait for the day her prosthetic would arrive, but until then she had to continue with those godforsaken crutches.

The women's voices below grew quiet. Virginia's hair was in a messy braid, she wore no makeup, and her stump hung below where she'd cut her trousers. She was sweating by the time she was on the ground floor. As she passed the parlor, her mother stared at her with quickly masked distaste, and stood to introduce Virginia to her guests. They were a flock of fat hens in floral garb, ridiculous doilies on hair set in parlors, painted fingernails on smooth hands. A sudden, irrational hatred of those women rose in her.

"Getting dressed up takes so much effort," said Mother.

Was she apologizing to her guests for Virginia's appearance?

Her mother babbled on about Virginia's stubbornness and refusal to rest, and the guests regarded Virginia with curiosity and pity. It was the pity that made her burn. Rude though it was, she left without a word. She couldn't trust herself to speak. She allowed the door to slam and, as she stumbled on the lowest porch stair, cursed loud enough for the women to hear through the open window. It gave her a thrill to imagine their discomfort.

It's not who you are.

Was her father now chiding her? She groaned and cursed her way to the forest, where she decided to go for living targets. Squirrels, ground-hogs, deer. She'd kill anything that got in her path. But on her way past the barn, a cow's mooing stopped her.

I'm afraid I'll never be able to milk a cow.

She'd said those words as a joke a lifetime ago, which was actually just months, but now they had taken on an unreasonable weight. Learning how to milk a cow suddenly became a hurdle she needed to cross to get better. She couldn't explain why, but she was compelled to conquer something—everything—that she had never been able to do.

She'd entered the barn, leaned her gun and crutches against the wall, and hopped to the nearest Holstein. The massive creature lifted her head from her trough and looked at Virginia with a challenge in her eyes. A calf chewed hay in the corner. Virginia plopped onto the milking stool. She pulled a bucket under the cow and reached for its udders. She squeezed, but nothing came out. Her fury nearly blinded her.

"Damn it!"

Any old farmhand could make the milk come. For her father and her brother, it was effortless. She was the most educated member of the family with the most iron, stubborn will of them all, but she couldn't get milk from the teat of a cow visibly bursting with it. She squeezed again, harder. The cow shifted on its feet, flicking its tail at her as if she were a fly.

Virginia couldn't take it. She stood up on her good foot, picked up the stool, and hurled it at the wall with all her strength, leaving a hole. Satisfaction at seeing the physical result of her anger was quickly replaced with shame. She cursed again, and hopped toward her crutches, stumbling and trying not to cry. As she turned to leave, she saw the calf walk to its mother and rub its head against her. The cow stopped eating and became still, almost pensive. Virginia watched until the calf began to drink, the milk letting down with ease.

When the calf was full and wandered away, Virginia fetched the stool and placed it next to the cow. She again pulled the bucket over and took a deep breath. Before trying to milk it, she rubbed the cow, running her hand along its side and its udders, until she felt a change in the animal, a stillness. Virginia pinched a teat near its base and began to squeeze. Milk shot out on her pants. She'd cried out with laughter.

She lifted her other hand to another teat, aimed into the bucket, and felt glorious success with each squirt. After Virginia finished her task, she stood, wiped her tears, and fetched her crutches.

WHO KNEW THE skill would come in so handy?

Virginia makes her way back from the goat stalls to Estelle's house, but the smile on her face at her memories quickly dissolves. She hadn't heard the Nazi Henschel truck arrive.

As the soldiers walk toward her, she catches snippets of their conversation in German.

"The house is large."

"Good place to billet."

"We'll have to exterminate the rats first."

Their laughter is chilling.

"Madame," the officer says in French. "We're searching for places for our men to convalesce. Surely you'll be happy to have us look over the property and see if it's suitable for our needs."

She squeezes her hands into fists. Strange though it is, when Nazis pretend to be gentlemen, it enrages her more than when they're cruel. There can be no diplomacy, especially at this point in the war. Struggling to swallow the venom rising in her, she's careful with her words and her tone.

"The owner is visiting family, so I can't say," she says. "I work with the goats."

"A little old for a milkmaid, aren't you?"

"What else would you have me do?"

He frowns. She should have held her tongue.

While he looks her over, she glances at the other soldiers. The men look tired and unkempt. Haunted around the eyes. She'll be glad to report on this sorry group to HQ.

"You aren't a Jew, are you?" he says. "We've heard things."

"No Jews here. Also, no running water. No electricity. Just goats. And an old man upstairs who's losing his mind."

"Give me your papers."

She reaches into her pocket and passes them to the officer. He scrutinizes them, running his thumb over her picture. Goose bumps rise over her skin as if he's actually touching her. She sees the wanted poster stark in her mind and feels exposed, certain they'll see "Artemis" staring back at them. After a few moments, he gives them back. He nods his head at the soldiers and points to the house. She feels her blood pressure rising with every step they take.

She knows she has hidden her wireless well and is nearly certain there aren't any ghosts in the house, but the thought of the old man's loaded gun brings fear to her heart. All weapons have to be turned over to the Nazis. As if on cue, she sees his face appear low at the window. He bangs the glass and shouts. When the soldiers open the door to the house, his voice travels to the yard.

My God, if they get to his room first and find that gun, they'll shoot him without hesitation.

"May I see to the old man?" she asks.

"My men will take care of him if he's a problem."

She swallows, but her mouth is dry.

"Sir," she says. "Have pity. Have you no father or grandfather?"

His right eye twitches.

"He's a veteran of the Great War," she says. "Surely, you'll give him the respect of a fellow soldier, no matter which side he's on. Let me calm him."

She doesn't know if appealing to the humanity of one she deems inhuman will work, but it's all she's got before trying to kill him. And killing him would only get her so far; she's grossly outnumbered, and the reprisals would bring hell on Estelle.

He looks up at the old man banging on the window. With the door open, she can hear bursts of words.

"She's a Nazi spy!"

She forces out a laugh.

"See," she says. "He thinks I work for you. He thinks we're on the moon. He thinks we're trying to poison him. A new mania every day."

The officer looks her up and down and laughs. When he gestures that she may proceed, it takes all her strength not to rush into the house and up the stairs to get to the old man before the soldiers do. When they enter the foyer, the officer shouts in German for the soldiers to leave the old man to her and continue searching the rest of the house. As she climbs to the second floor, her fear of the Nazis is now replaced with a fear of getting shot by the old man she's trying to protect.

Of all days for Estelle not to be here.

The old man's voice has grown hoarse and savage. Is his gun loaded and pointing at the door? She feels a phantom pain slice through the foot she no longer has. Getting shot nearly destroyed her once; she can't allow it to happen again, not this way.

When she arrives at his room, she places her hand on the knob. Taking a deep breath and standing off to the side, she opens the door several inches. She's glad to see a bureau mirror where his reflection reveals he sits at the window in his wheelchair, the steel of the gun shining in his lap.

A movement in the hallway catches her eye. A soldier kicks in the first door on this side of staircase. The old man hears and turns, wheeling toward the door with startling quickness. She darts out of view, and when she hears him approach, she lunges forward, grabs the gun from his lap, and rushes to the bureau. As she tucks it deep under a pile of clothes, the soldier arrives at the room.

"A spy! She's a German spy!" says Estelle's father.

She can see by the soldier's surprised reaction that he understands French, at least enough to hear the words *German spy*. Virginia turns slowly, holding a blanket she's pulled from the bureau.

"Monsieur," she says, consoling. "Please, go back to bed. You need your rest."

"She stole my gun," the old man yells. "She will kill me."

The soldier looks from her to the old man, scrutinizing the pair. She moves away from the bureau and approaches the old man as if he were a dangerous animal.

"Please," she says. "Let me help you back to bed. Then I'll get your gun, and your port, and some steak, and a nice dark chocolate cake for dessert. What do you think?"

She winks at the soldier as if conspiring with him over this absurd list of things the old man can't have.

Estelle's father is subdued. He doesn't look confused. He stares at her with an eagle eye. The soldier doesn't seem to know what to do, whom to believe.

"Help me get him in the bed," she says, taking the tone of the old woman over the young man. "Then you may search."

"Move him yourself," says the soldier. He proceeds forward, starting with the closet, moving to the bathroom, back out to the dressers and bookshelves, and finally walks to the bureau. Virginia's heart pounds all the way up to her ears. This could be it.

There's a sudden commotion in the hallway, the officer's voice rising over that of another's—a woman's. Estelle appears in the doorway, flushed, breathless, and terrified. When she sees Virginia, her eyes dart between her, her father, and the soldier, who has turned to face her. Estelle rushes toward her father and falls to her knees at his feet.

"Papa! You must not yell."

"But the boches," he says, pointing at the Nazi soldiers.

"Ah, ah," she says, chastising him for the slur. "They only need to make sure everything is all right here."

"Her," he says, pointing at Virginia.

"Yes, my farm helper. She's all right."

The officer directs the soldier to leave the room. He looks long at each of them before striding away toward the other end of the house. Virginia and Estelle stand still and silent, listening to his footsteps grow quieter. When the boots thunder down the stairs to the foyer, the two women exhale.

Estelle looks at Virginia and mouths, "The gun?"

Virginia nods her head toward the open door of the bureau. Estelle's eyes grow wide.

"How did you . . . ?" Estelle whispers.

"I'll tell you later."

Estelle crosses herself and turns her attention back to her father. The old man looks frail and small. Virginia had thought he was feeble of mind, but his sharp stare reveals that's not necessarily the case. As Virginia passes them to leave the room, the old man reaches out for her.

"You," he says. His grip is strong, his gnarled fingers like a claw around her wrist. "You saved my life."

THE SOLDIERS LEAVE them with warnings they might return, and instructions to organize and collect anything that might be medically useful to them. As they walk away, Virginia hears their conversation in German.

"It was clear. False tip."

"The Milice are getting jumpy."

"We'll check the outbuildings before we go."

Virginia tells Estelle what they said and is relieved to hear the barn is empty.

"I don't think they'll be back," says Virginia. "They were just saying so in case you were harboring anyone. Still, we must be vigilant."

Estelle breathes a sigh of relief. She had behaved admirably throughout the ordeal: stoic but cooperative. It's now, after the soldiers leave, that her exhaustion comes through.

"You could have been shot," Estelle says, struggling to control her emotions.

"I've survived that before," says Virginia.

The women share a laugh. Estelle knows all about the hunting accident.

"Just in case, do you know of another nearby safe house?" Virginia asks. She needs at least one more house in her loop if she's going to evade signal interception.

"Yes. In Sury-ès-Bois. A vacant, one-room shack on my cousins' farm. It's a short bicycle ride from here. You may have one of ours. Take the one with the rack on the back so you can stack up your suitcases."

"Excellent. Thank you. Now, are you sure you want to be on the drop committee? I don't have to tell you how dangerous it is. And it will be a big operation. I'm expecting many containers of supplies for Lavilette's Maquis, so it will take a long time to break down."

"I wouldn't miss it."

Sury-ès-Bois is about an hour's ride from Estelle's farm, and it's dusk when Virginia arrives, noting with pride that she isn't winded and her knee stump isn't raw. This lifestyle is putting her in as good a shape as she's ever been. In fact, she's growing so taut and lean she has to use more padding in her old-woman's disguise.

The shack is tiny, but it has a straw mattress on the floor, a drawer full of candles, a well with a bucket, and a small root cellar where she can hide her wireless suitcase. That night, she's able to stack old crates from the yard to hoist herself on the roof to attach the antenna to the rusty weather vane at its peak. The view of the surrounding roads isn't ideal, but she affixes the antenna wire loosely and runs it through the window so a swift pull will bring it down in a flash.

She wires HQ of all the developments and asks for another battery and a stash of downers. They reply in the affirmative and are glad to hear her report of the haggard German soldiers. Since her wireless training back in London, the black propaganda division of the OSS has been waging a specific battle on the psychological health of Nazis, infusing broadcasts, parlor gossip, and pamphlets with stories of venereal disease outbreaks among French brothels, bombings of German cities, Nazi officers having orgies with lesser-ranked soldiers' wives, and evidence of human excrement in barrack food. The devious minds in the black propaganda division are the kind you want on your side, and it appears their message is being heard.

Before she signs off, HQ lets her know her mother has been writing the War Office, worrying over the lack of contact from her daughter. Virginia is strangely moved to hear it. Mrs. Hall was told Virginia worked for the First Experimental Detachment of the United States Army, an organization that gathers documents for future historical war accounts, which is really a front for the OSS. But it's likely Mrs. Hall is shrewd enough to know that's not true. Though Virginia isn't a mother, she observes they seem to have a sixth sense for their children's well-being.

HQ says Vera's secretary will write back, assuring her of their frequent contact with Virginia and her safety, and does she want them to pass along a personal message?

—Tell her I miss her, the family, and the farm, and I promise to visit once we've won.

—Will do. GB. BC.

As Virginia packs up her equipment, she thinks back to the day when she learned to milk a cow and of when she'd returned to the farmhouse with the nearly full bucket. The milk had sloshed over on her pants the whole way back, but she was too happy to care. She had planned to leave the bucket as a peace offering, but when she returned to the house, her mother was waiting for her, wringing her hands, a contrite look on her face.

"You did it?" said Mother.

"I did."

Mother beamed at her. Then she walked slowly down the stairs, took the bucket, and placed it on the ground. In spite of how smelly and dirty Virginia was, Mother opened her arms and wrapped Virginia in a warm embrace. In the cloud of Mother's lily perfume, Virginia felt herself soften wholly for the first time since the accident.

Chapter 19

RACING THROUGH THE moonlight, wind in their hair, Virginia and Estelle ride bicycles to the drop field outside Cosne. It's the first time Virginia has ever looked forward to a drop. She trusts her well-trained team, and, if all goes well, the Maquis in the region will be fully armed, allowing her to start preparing for her next stop. They couldn't ask for better weather or clearer skies, and they make good time. When Mimi, Lavi, the boy, and the team of Maquis meet them, there's a flurry of hushed embraces and handshakes.

Virginia pulls off her rucksack and passes out flashlights. She reminds the group of formation and checks to make sure they brought the largest donkey cart they could find. Then they crouch in the moonlight, watching the heavens for their deliverance.

In the quiet, Louis creeps into Virginia's mind. Virginia leans to Mimi and whispers his name like a question.

"My cousin, the doctor, says he and his men are doing okay physically," says Mimi. "Several are beginning to decay mentally, but not Louis."

Hold on, Virginia thinks.

"I think he's going to make it," says Mimi.

"If the invasion would only come," says Virginia. "What about Sophie?"

"She's doing what she can with her Paris contacts, but hasn't had any luck."

"Sophie needs to think about leaving for London."

"I told her. She won't hear of it."

Virginia understands. At this point, there's nothing that could persuade her to leave.

Calling their attention back to the sky, the droning sound starts, first far away, then moving closer. They all separate and form the diamond, Virginia at the top. When the plane is in sight, Virginia flicks on her flashlight and the others follow. She and the pilot exchange signals. Then four containers parachute down to the field, landing with thumps in the thick grasses.

The group descends upon each container, opening them, unloading them onto the cart, and burying them in the pre-dug holes with skill and ease. These are fit, able-bodied men and women in good number. Working in concert, their movements are as fluid and seamless as a symphony. Their sense for the others in the group is sharp and alert. No words need to be exchanged. Only the soft exclamations of gratitude for the weapons, medical supplies, food, cigarettes, and forged ration cards can be heard. In the last container, Lavi finds a heavy, padded package wrapped tight and labeled "Diane." He tosses it to her, and she grins, eager to open it so she can give Estelle the Barros Porto that Virginia requested from HQ for Estelle's father. When their work is done, Virginia pulls them close together, holding hands in a circle.

"If the invasion comes before we're able to receive another drop," she whispers, "and I don't see you for a while, know that you are equipped and ready."

A quiet cheer goes up in the group. They raise their hands together, shaking them.

"Shhh," she says, smiling. "Listen. After D-Day, the war really begins. The Allies will start dropping teams of soldiers—Jedburghs, they're called— with at least one French officer in each group. They'll command you, and you'll be able to fall in with the Allied armies, like the soldiers you are."

"No longer terrorists," says a maquisard, his voice breaking.

Lavi pulls the man into a hug and looks over the maquisard's shoulder at Virginia with stark gratitude. The moonlight illuminates the tears on Lavi's face. They look like the rivers that pilots follow in the dark. Seeing his emotion releases a shard of ice in her heart. The group falls together in a clumsy sort of hug.

"All right, now," Virginia says. "That's enough."

Then they all disperse, allowing the night to shelter them.

SEVERAL MORNINGS LATER, Virginia nearly leaps from the bicycle while it's in motion. She leans it against a tree in front of Estelle's place and rushes to the farm stalls, peeking in each until she finds her friend. When she does, she stops short in the doorway, surprised to see three children with Estelle. They kneel in the hay, watching baby goats attempt to take their first wobbly steps. Estelle turns her head when Virginia's shadow falls over them. Two small girls cower into the side of an adolescent boy who has a patch of white in his brown hair.

"It's all right," says Estelle. She stands and wipes her hands on her bloody apron. "I'll be back in a moment."

Virginia steps outside and looks up and down the road for Nazi vehicles, relieved to see they are alone.

"What is it, my friend?" says Estelle.

"D-Day is coming."

Estelle breaks out into a wide smile and lifts her eyes to heaven.

"How do you know?" Estelle says. "There's been nothing about the violins of autumn on the broadcasts."

"In my last transmission, HQ said, 'Autumn is coming.' They want troop movement reports as soon as possible."

"Oh," breathes Estelle.

"I know," says Virginia. "I need to let the others know. We should all be listening together each night, if possible."

"Tell Mimi and her family to come stay with me. Lavi, too, if he'd like. There aren't as many troops here as in town at Cosne."

"All right," says Virginia. "One more thing. I need to make first contact with Chambon as soon as possible to find the leader of the Maquis. They need to start securing safe houses for me when I move on, and HQ needs numbers of men."

"I'll get to work on that immediately," says Estelle. "I have a trip coming up."

She notices Estelle's eyes flick toward the goat stalls and back to Virginia. She wants to ask Estelle if Chambon is haunted and, if so, how many ghosts it has, but she restrains herself. She'll know soon enough.

WHEN VIRGINIA ARRIVES in the forest, she's glad to see an even more organized camp of well-fed men in good spirits, ready to begin railway sabotage at a moment's notice.

"HQ will be pleased at how you've used your resources," she says.

"You'll let them know how grateful we are?" says Lavi.

"I will."

He's amenable to the plan to stay at Estelle's until the signal. There's nothing more he can do for the men now but pace with them in their prison. He'd rather have the time to rest with his family before the fighting starts. Neither of them has to say aloud what he really means, that he wants the time with Mimi and his son in case he doesn't survive.

He hands her a paper.

"I've had the men copying notices to hang throughout the entire department, once we hear the violins of autumn."

She takes it and reads.

THE HOUR WE HAVE LONG AWAITED HAS ARRIVED.

The words go on to rally French citizens to join forces with the Allies to bring about the liberation.

"I can barely contain myself," he says.

"I know," she says. "Me, too."

After returning to her cottage to pack her wireless suitcase and a small bag of necessities, she goes to Estelle's place. Lavi's family is already there, and she's scarcely had time to stow her things in the garret before the boy pulls her by the hand down the staircase.

"Come, see," he says, pushing open the great doors to the formal dining room and standing aside to admit her.

What was once a dark, dusty cavern of sheet-filled furniture is now a glittering gem. The heavy wood furniture has been scrubbed, the drapes beaten, the chandelier polished and lit, its candlelight amplified by its reflection along the ornate wall mirrors and the gleaming place settings. Cheeses and breads adorn the serving dishes. Seeing the spread elicits a loud growl from Virginia's stomach, much to the amusement of the group.

Estelle's father beams from his wheelchair at the head of the table, the bottle of Barros Porto next to his goblet. He rolls himself over to her, places his hand over his heart, and bows as much as he's able.

"Will you accept my deepest apologies and gratitude?" he asks.

She kneels to his eye level and takes his hands.

"You don't have to apologize for being a vigilant, careful soldier."

He kisses her hands.

She returns to standing and looks again at all of them, her affection for them punctured by the remembrance of her feast with the Lopinats and the three musketeers. She tries not to panic, not to think this is the beginning of the end for them, but she can't help it. Estelle sees her struggling and saves her by instructing everyone to take their seats.

The chatter around her is warm and lively, but she feels apart from it. She can't help but think of all the people who should be around this table and tables like it—of Louis, of Estelle's late husband, of the three musketeers, the members of her Lyon network. Her distress at not being able to fully enjoy this moment is acute, especially when the awful memory flashes before her so clearly, she could be standing on the main street in Crozant where the peasants are impaled on fence spikes. A little touch on her arm brings her back.

"Are you having one of your awake nightmares?" the boy asks.

She concentrates on the weight and comfort of his warm, steady hand.

"Yes," she says.

"Do you see the mountain?"

"No, not this time."

"Something worse?"

"Yes," she says. "But you helped wake me up again. Thank you."

He smiles at her and shoves a slice of cheese in his mouth.

She forces down a bite of bread. The tightness in her throat makes it difficult to swallow, but washing it down with a sip of the port Estelle's father insisted on sharing helps. As she finishes the glass, a word from Sophie gets her attention.

"Louis," Sophie says. "He and the others have been moved to Fresnes, just outside the city. There are reports of dozens of agents who've been rounded up and sent there. I'm working on a contact now."

Virginia's heart sinks. Fresnes is another solitary-confinement prison, infested with bugs and disease. Few agents have escaped it. Many haven't survived. The worst part: Fresnes is a holding place before deportation. He's going to be shipped out to a concentration camp. Her only consolation is that he isn't at Montluc. On the outskirts of Lyon, it's a prison of brutality and torture, and it's under the command of Klaus Barbie. If Barbie found out Louis was back, he might guess that she also returned. Virginia doesn't think Louis would ever break under torture, but either way Barbie would take his time destroying Louis.

"I'm encouraged by early leads," says Sophie. "And the location is better than Cherche-Midi's. It has to be easier to spring a man from farther outside the capital than deeper in it. Don't you think so, Diane?"

They all turn to her, eyes full of hope and expectation. She's able to muster a small nod. Sophie beams. Estelle and Mimi exchange a look before returning their attention to their meals.

After every morsel is eaten, and they work together to clean, Lavi carries Estelle's father up the stairs, while Mimi and Estelle take the wheelchair. The rest of them follow, gathering in the old man's room to listen to the BBC. The group is full of laughter and hope, sure the announcer's voice sounds different, more ebullient. When the personal messages begin, they all hold their breath, waiting for the words *Les sanglots longs des violons de l'automne.*

But the broadcast ends without them.

Chapter 20

THE NEXT NIGHT'S broadcast also ends without the words. And the next night.

And the next.

By May 30, Lavi is in a state. They all are, stuck in limbo, waiting for invasion. The weather has been awful—rain and wind every day. Estelle has been holding off on her trip to Chambon. Sophie hasn't worked on a contact at Fresnes. They're getting short-tempered with one another. They look at Virginia with side-glances. After another silent breakfast over stale bread and the last of Virginia's English tea, Lavi pushes back from the table, and throws his napkin on his plate.

"I can't stand this any longer."

"Darling, please," says Mimi.

"I'm leaving."

"Don't go," says Mimi.

"This is torture," he says, staring at Virginia like a bull in a pen. "Sipping British tea in luxury, while my men live like animals."

I'm as disappointed as you are, Virginia wants to say, but deep down she knows that can't be true. Her position as an American is different from theirs. Her sorrows can't compare. She shouldn't have shared HQ's message. Her own dashed hope is pressure enough. The added weight of theirs is crushing.

"At least come back at night," Mimi says. "We all have to listen together."

"I won't make any promises."

"Your men don't need you until the invasion."

"If there is one!" he shouts.

Sensing the roof about to blow, Sophie takes the boy out to the goat stalls.

"I at least need to be there to talk the men out of what they want to do," Lavi continues. "They want to start with sabotage now. I've been holding them off, but I might not any longer."

"That would be suicide," says Virginia.

She stands and crosses the room to the window, staring out at the rain.

"Really?" he says.

He strides over to her. She turns to him, meeting his stare.

"You know what's suicide?" he says. "Suicide is sitting in the woods rotting, while visions of Nazis sleeping in your beds, and eating your food in your kitchens, and raping your daughters, and killing your brothers assault you."

"Stop!" says Mimi, crossing the room and grasping Lavi's arm.

"We sit there with cold weapons in pits," he continues. "Every day three trains travel on the line to the north, and do you know what's on them? Our friends. Our neighbors. Our brothers being shipped to who knows where, while we sit here on a pile of explosives that could stop them. Think about it. If you knew Louis was traveling tomorrow, wouldn't you want to blow up the line that would stop them?"

"Don't put it that way, Lavi," says Virginia. "Don't dare act like I wouldn't strap a bundle of dynamite to myself to stop them from taking Louis. Until the Allies land, there's no distraction from reprisals. You sabotage now, the boches will have time to hunt and kill you. And your family. If you want to change the momentum of this war, you have to wait until you have the support you need, until you can join the light of your torch with the flames of armies."

"What armies? Where are they? They aren't coming!"

"You're wrong," says Virginia. "And if you die before that day, you won't be here to enjoy blowing the Nazis back to hell with us."

Lavi breathes heavily. After a moment, he leaves them, slamming the door on his way out.

"I'm sorry for his outburst," says Mimi.

"Don't be. I have to give myself that speech a dozen times a day."

"Do you think he'll come back tonight?" says Estelle.

"It's hard to say," says Mimi. "I don't have to tell you how stubborn he is."

Exasperated, Mimi leaves them to find her son and Sophie.

"Will you be all right if I go for the night?" says Estelle. "I need to get my ghosts on their way."

"Of course," says Virginia. "I'll look after your father."

"Thank you."

"I should never have shared what HQ said. I've made this worse."

"No," says Estelle. "We'd be in this place either way."

"You're kind to say so."

"When I come back, I'll have a contact for you."

"Good."

Her friend pulls on her coat and wraps her head in a black covering, giving her the appearance of a nun. The image of Virginia's friend, the sister from Lyon, comes to mind. Estelle suddenly looks very small and defeated. Vulnerable. A terrible feeling rises in Virginia.

"Be careful," she says.

"Always."

Virginia stays to clean up after breakfast. From the kitchen window, a movement catches her eye. It's Estelle, leaving the house with her suitcase, crossing the field to the barn. Her form grows smaller and smaller until the rain and fog erase her.

LAVI DOESN'T RETURN that night.

The broadcast has no violins.

Sophie leaves the next day.

In between sitting with Estelle's father and her farm chores, Virginia watches the lane, desperate for Estelle's return.

Morning becomes afternoon. Afternoon rushes terribly toward evening. The rain continues.

"She will come back today, oui?" says Estelle's father. Virginia plumps his pillows and helps him resettle in the large bed.

"I think so. She said one night," says Virginia, working to keep her voice light.

"Good. So, anytime now. I'm so afraid for her when she travels."

"Estelle is strong and capable. I have confidence in her."

A lie. War consumes the strong and capable every day.

After she finishes helping him with his soup, Virginia pours him a small glass of port and leaves him to take her supper with Mimi and her son. They silently agree the dining room is too large—too much a reminder of all those not at the table—and choose to eat in the kitchen. All they can hear is the rain pelting the windows, and the clinks of their spoons on their bowls. Even the boy—normally an unflappable chatterbox—is quiet. They all strain their ears, praying to hear the door open and close, but it doesn't. By the time they've finished eating and cleaning, night has fallen.

"The weather probably keeps them away," says Mimi.

The boy smiles, accepting his mother's words without question. Virginia wants to do the same, but the truth is, she's already trying to process what will happen if Estelle never returns. She's trying to imagine what that possibility means to this household, to her mission, and to herself. If she plans for the worst, she'll be able to carry on. That's what she tells herself.

Radio reception is poor that night. The broadcast, short. Do they imagine tension in the voice of the announcer? Do they miss notice of the violins of autumn?

When the program concludes, Mimi and her son leave Virginia in silence to stow the radio away and see to Estelle's father. He sits at the window in his wheelchair, holding his gun, refusing to go to bed.

"I'll watch for her," he says.

"Monsieur," says Virginia, "Estelle would want you warm in bed. She can take care of herself. She'll be home tomorrow."

"She said she'd be home today. She has never not come when she said she would."

"The weather is bad."

"Then she'll be cold when she arrives. I'll stay up for her and keep the fire going."

It's clear he won't listen to her. She brings him a blanket, lays it across his lap, and walks to the door. Before heading for the garret, she turns back and looks at him. He's so small and frail against the large window. She won't be able to sleep while he stays up all night struggling to add logs to the fire. With a sigh, she returns to the room and closes the door. She pulls a chair to sit with him at the window, keeping watch.

THE WORST THING about staying up all night is the torment of old memories from which one cannot awaken. All the worries and regrets and guilt she's able to suppress in the industrious hours of daylight grow from the night's shadows, overwhelming her with their darkness.

It's as if she's back at the doctor's office in Lyon, when she'd agreed to meet the betrayer to give him funding for the Paris circuit. In spite of HQ continuing to insist his checks were good, all her instincts were on alert.

"Louis said there were a slew of agent arrests in Paris," she'd said. "I think this man is a traitor."

"But HQ . . ." said the doctor.

"I know. But my gut tells me otherwise. And he keeps asking for me directly. I don't think I should be here for the meeting. I wish you weren't involved."

"I'm fine. But he'll be here any minute. You'll have to hide. I'll make up a lie."

"All right. Be sure to ask him about the Paris circuit. If he doesn't tell you about the arrests, we can be almost certain he's the rat."

They could hear the housekeeper open the door, and the tones of a male voice. Virginia ducked into the closet in the study just in time. Through the crack in the door, Virginia saw the betrayer's blue eyes and white, pasty skin as he entered. He blotted his sweating face with a hand-kerchief and peered around the room. His eyes found the dark space she inhabited, so she slid back, careful not to make a sound.

"The doctor sent me," he'd said, smooth and polite.

"It has been a long time," the doctor replied. "Come, sit."

"I thought Marie would be joining us?"

The man's piercing gaze returned to the closet where she stood, making it difficult for her to breathe. She hadn't had a reaction like that to someone in a long time.

"Not today," the doctor said.

"I didn't expect this," the man said. "I came a long way, and I don't know when I can return."

"She was needed elsewhere. Urgently so."

There was a quietly concealed fury in the man. Though he looked smooth and unruffled, his blazing eyes were lit with blue-white heat.

"How are the Paris circuits operating?" said the doctor.

Virginia held her breath, waiting for the man's reply.

"Well, in spite of constant danger."

Upon hearing the lie, Virginia began to tremble. She clenched her hands into fists, trying to contain her fury.

"But the money will help tremendously," the man continued. "It's hard to say how long they can hold up under such intense pressure."

The doctor stood abruptly.

"Come back next week," he said, with a strain in his voice. "I'll see what can be done by then."

"Thank you," the man said, feigning humble acceptance. "And please, ask Marie to be here then. I have specific questions I need to ask her."

THE EARLY-MORNING KNOCK pulls Virginia out of her memory.

Disoriented, heart pounding, she stands to open the door. Mimi steps into the room.

"Is she back?" asks Mimi.

Virginia shakes her head no.

"Lavi?" Virginia asks.

It's Mimi's turn to shake her head.

June 1. It's June, and the Allies haven't come.

"I'm taking the boy to Lavi today," says Mimi. "I'll tell him what's going on and try to persuade him to come back tonight."

Virginia nods, and watches them go. In truth, she's grateful. She needs the space and quiet to make plans.

After leaving Estelle's father—still at the window—with a tray of toast and a cup of café nationale, she pulls on her coat and boots, and heads outside for her chores. When she arrives at the goat stalls, the new babies suckle their mother. They've grown so much in the short time since their birth. How does the world keep spinning? She cleans out the pens, refills their food and water, and milks the goats that need it. After storing the milk in the larder, she heads to the barn. Estelle doesn't like her going, but Estelle might not be coming back. She needs to know if anyone is there.

The beauty of the June morning is balm to her weary soul. Mist rises and burns off in the welcome sun. The vines and flowers are rich in color—jewels glittering in the dew—their sweet fragrance perfuming the air.

The sacrament of the present moment.

The phrase comes to her mind. The nun from Lyon had told Virginia about a work by that name, written hundreds of years ago by a priest.

When Virginia was becoming overwhelmed by her tasks and fears, the nun consoled her with this idea of how sacred each moment of a life truly is if we view it with purpose, with love, with gratitude and mindfulness. Children understand the idea intuitively. Adults forget. The past and future are the devil's playground—the place he can torture us with regret and anxiety. The present is rarely a place of suffering.

Until it is.

Then we rise up to meet it or we fall.

When Virginia arrives at the barn, she knocks four times, peeks in her head, and says, "Where did I leave my milking stool?"

After mourning doves flutter and resettle in the rafters, only silence remains. She pushes open the creaky door the rest of the way and peers up to the loft. She walks in, gazing around her, noting the stove, the swept floor, the water pitcher, a milking stool. She finds a ladder, lays it against the loft, and climbs.

There's no one there.

She returns the ladder to its place, and sets out on a long walk, seeking a new drop field. Carrying on. Finding the sacrament of the present moment. By the time she returns to the house, it's midday.

Estelle's father is still in the window. His toast is stale. His coffee is cold. She takes the tray away, forcing down what the old man didn't touch so it isn't wasted. She brings him cheese, grapes, and water. He doesn't eat that, either.

"Monsieur, let me help you to the bathroom," she says.

He shakes his head.

"Let me help you to bed. You need rest."

He doesn't reply.

Virginia watches the sun make its progress through the blue all day. Evening brings quiet birdsong and lavender skies, and rising fear. Estelle still hasn't returned.

Lavi's arrival brings a wave of joy. When he comes in the room, they don't speak—words would break them—but Lavi wraps Virginia in a warm hug of apology and consolation that threatens to undo her.

Sophie arrives next. After hugs and greetings, she holds up her hand, now bare of the small silver engagement ring Louis put on it.

"I've found a contact at Fresnes," she says, her voice wavering. "Louis is alive. Weak, but still going. I gave the guard the ring and told him to tell Louis he can put it back on my hand when we're reunited."

Sophie is no longer able to hold back her crying. Mimi takes her in her arms, while Virginia rubs her back. She needs to find a way to persuade this girl to go back to London.

When the eight o'clock hour arrives, the sad, incomplete group makes the slow climb to Estelle's father's bedroom, where he still sits at the window. While Virginia and Lavi set up the radio, Estelle's father makes a wheezing sound. Virginia rushes to him. He gasps and clutches at his heart.

"What is it?" Virginia says, grasping his shoulders. "Are you all right?"

His eyes are glassy with tears. A sudden cry erupts from him. He points out the window. She turns to look.

"Estelle!"

They all cheer while Virginia hurries out of the room and down the stairs as quickly as she's able to meet her friend. When she bursts through the door, they rush to each other, embracing, laughing, talking over one another. They hurry up the stairs, and Estelle crosses the room to her father, knocking into him with her embrace.

The boy has to hush them for the broadcast. Lavi makes a waving motion at the radio as if it doesn't matter while Estelle tells them what happened.

"There was a convoy that held up the train. I was stuck in Chambon for the extra night with no way to get word to you. I'm so sorry for the worry I've caused."

"It doesn't matter," says Virginia.

"All that matters is that you're here," says her father.

"But the delay was good," says Estelle. "I have a contact for you, Diane. More than one. There are hundreds of Maquis, in formation, ready for orders. But they have nothing."

"Hush!" says the boy. "Personal messages are starting!"

They all grow quiet and huddle around the radio.

"Are you listening?" the announcer says. "Please, listen for personal messages."

The silence around them is rich and dark, like a fertile, well-composted soil. It's in this seasoned garden that the words drop like seeds one at a time and bring forth such sweetness, such a harvest of joy and hope, the likes of which each of them has never before experienced.

Finally—now—the night of June 1, 1944, they hear the words for which they've been longing. From London to France. Over the airwaves. The beginning of the end.

Les sanglots longs des violons de l'automne.

The long sobs of the violins of autumn.

Chapter 21

THOUGH EXCRUCIATING, THE waiting for the second stanza of the poem to announce D-Day's commencement is filled with energy and excitement, like a child's anticipation of Christmas. HQ orders Virginia to wait to travel to Chambon until after invasion. Eager though she is to fold Chambon into her network, her fondness for the people here and the work they have before them keeps her satisfied.

They spend their days assembling, cleaning, and loading Sten submachine guns. The weapons are simply and cheaply constructed, easy to use, and able to shoot either Allied or German magazines. The group prepares railway explosives and studies the maps and timetables of their targeted bridges and lines. Though the weather remains rotten, they come together each night, disappointed when they don't hear the words but also relieved in the small, secret places in their hearts. For they know, when it starts, the fires of France will grow into a mighty, terrible conflagration that will consume without discernment.

On the night of June 5, they gather around the radio holding hands.

How strange that we can feel one another's heartbeats in our palms, Virginia thinks.

It's not the fists alone that win the fight.

In these weeks, they've all become new. They are all strong fists. All fierce guts. Intelligent brains. Blazing, pounding, loving hearts.

Virginia imagines rooms like this in places all over the country. Little shelters before the storm. She imagines the faces of those she's loved and lost, and makes a silent wish for the safety of those who've survived, especially Louis. She longs for the redemption of the dead and for full, swift Allied triumph.

It's this night, holding heart-pounding hands, when their wait is rewarded. They hear the final words announcing D-Day.

Blessent mon coeur d'une langueur monotone.

My heart is drowned in the slow sound, languorous and long.

After the words, they are quiet, breathing heavily.

She wants to tell them she loves them—that they are putting her broken heart back together—but she can't speak over the lump in her throat.

The next day, June 6, the Nazi soldiers contract to their barracks and stations, leaving the streets empty of patrols while they learn of the arrival of 155,000 Allied troops at Normandy.

The banging of hammers rings from village to village, hanging notices for the inhabitants of the area:

THE HOUR HAS ARRIVED.
IT'S TIME TO RISE AND TO FIGHT.

That night, Virginia and a small team of Lavi and two of his men creep to a site along the railway linking Cosne with Sury-près-Léré. One of the men—the one she christened "the explosives expert"—works with another who looks especially lethal. He has the aura of one who has lost much and wants to take even more.

While Virginia stands guard, they prepare the explosives, warming and shaping the material in their hands, inserting the fuses, and running the wires to detonators placed farther along the track. On the first morning ride, when the train hits the detonators and passes over the main devices, the engineers will evacuate the locomotive before it tips off the fuses and explodes. Virginia and her group won't see it, but they'll be able to hear it loud and clear from a nearby safe house. Then they'll make like hell for the forest.

The night is so still, it's hard to imagine what rages on a few hundred kilometers from them. Hard to imagine the arrival of the Nazi panzer divisions coming from the south to meet it. Hard to imagine the bloodshed that will touch even this field. She savors the sacrament of the present moment and tries not to be anxious about what waits coiled in the dark.

When their task is complete, they hurry across the meadow to the safe house.

She doesn't know how any of them will sleep that night, but somehow they must have, because they are awoken at six in the morning by the blast. With wide smiles they look out the window to the horizon and see the black smoke rising.

THAT NIGHT, BACK in Estelle's garret, in her first wire to HQ after D-Day, Virginia reports on the success of her team and three others on the severing of the rail lines around Cosne. One Nazi nerve center amputated. Hundreds to go.

—Reports panzers on the move to reinforce Normandy bases. South to north. Delay them as much as possible.

—We're on it, Virginia taps.

—Keep skirmishes to a minimum. Sten guns no match for German artillery.

—Copied.

—Jed team for your Maquis will drop soon. Await date. You're needed elsewhere.

And Lavi and his men are in fine fighting shape, and the Jed team will have not only military officials but also a pianist. She will miss her people here, but she knows they can stand on their own. Her only hesitation is getting farther from Louis, but deep down she knows she must press on. He survived a Spanish prison for seven months. Like he told her, captured doesn't mean dead. Not today, anyway.

Virginia gives HQ the field coordinates for the Jed drop and signs off.

Knowing how badly her body needs rest, she takes a downer and allows it to pull a black curtain over her consciousness, where she sleeps a blessedly dreamless sleep.

Chapter 22

I N T H E D A Y S following, there's no rest to be had.

Estelle was smart to listen to the Nazi soldiers about gathering medical supplies, but it isn't them she's helping. It's the increasing numbers of downed Allied airmen appearing at her barn. They bring news of Normandy, of flying with over two thousand aircraft, and more than seven thousand boats, all transporting one hundred fifty-five thousand men who stormed ashore in tides turned red with blood, tides visible from the sky.

Virginia wonders when hell will reach them. They're only 280 kilometers—just 175 miles—southwest of the fighting. But she can't waste time watching the horizon. She coordinates supply movement and sabotage with the Maquis, gets messages out to neighboring networks through Sophie, and helps Estelle and her cousin take care of the airmen—the work that makes her feel most alive.

It has been nearly a week since D-Day, and Estelle's barn holds two injured pilots—one British and one American. Six others have passed through on their way to corral at a forest to wait for the Allies to reach them. The Brit sleeps, but the American has been chatting continually. He's stocky for a pilot, and grunts as he readjusts himself in the hay. He tells them he works with the OSS and was on his way back from a drop over Dijon when he got shot down. Virginia chastises him for giving away more information than he needed to, but she can't help but warm to him. He's sweet and friendly and refreshingly American. She was able to smuggle him some cigarettes and playing cards, so he's content as a clam.

"I'm no doctor," she says. "But it only seems like a knee sprain. You'll need to rest that leg, though, so you can get to the next stop."

"Do I ever have to leave?" he says in his sweet Southern drawl. "It's so nice and quiet here."

"At least you won't have to try to cross the Pyrenees in winter," says Estelle in English. "Like she did."

She nods to Virginia.

"I can't believe I'm with the legend," he says. "Diane. The pride and joy of two continents."

"Is Diane famous?" asks Estelle.

"Within our ranks she is," the pilot says.

"As if I needed another reason to hate the Gestapo," Virginia says. "They did me no favors calling me the Limping Lady. Everyone has been bugging me about my leg ever since."

"You're my idol."

"You're ridiculous," says Virginia. "While I appreciate your admiration, I must insist on discretion."

"Yes, sir," he says, saluting her.

She smiles in spite of herself.

A quick knock quiets them. Sophie peers around the door.

"There's more of you!" the pilot says. "I'm never leaving."

The look on Sophie's face wipes the smile off Virginia's.

"What is it?" Virginia says in French, standing. "Louis?"

"No."

Sophie steps forward, helping a man as he stumbles in. He falls to his hands and knees and vomits. Virginia and Estelle rush over and help Sophie carry him to a place he can lie down. Estelle covers the vomit with a pile of straw and uses a shovel to scoop it up and throw it outside the barn, before locking the door. The man is an American pilot, with "Murphy" stitched on his torn flight suit. He shakes so violently it's as if electric currents run through his body. He can't stop mumbling.

Virginia pulls a downer from her stash and feeds it to him. The trembling soon stops, but he doesn't close his eyes, only stares at the ceiling as though seeing a place not in this barn. He keeps squeezing his eyes shut and shaking his head, as if trying to shut out a terrible vision.

"You're safe," Virginia says, kneeling beside him and rubbing his arm.

Aside from a few cuts on his face, Murphy has no visible injury, but Virginia knows well the hidden injury of memory can be just as painful. After a long while he focuses on her face as if seeing her for the first time. He moves his cracked lips open and closed. Virginia reaches for the canteen and gives him a drink.

"Thank you," he says, draining it.

"Of course," she says. "Are you injured?"

He shakes his head.

"Can you say what pains you?"

He looks around at all of them, including the British pilot, who awoke in the commotion. The American hands Murphy a cigarette, but his hand shakes too badly for him to light it. Virginia takes the matches and helps him. Once he's had a long drag, he starts speaking.

"I got shot down a while ago. I've been trying to make my way home, but I can't seem to get anywhere." He starts crying, and it takes him some time to compose himself. "Sorry," he says.

"Don't apologize," Sophie says, kneeling on his other side and taking his hand. "What happened?"

He looks off in the distance again, his face so young while his eyes are old.

"I don't know if I should say this around ladies. I can't bear to think it myself."

"These girls aren't fragile," says the American. "You're in the company of great sp—"

Virginia cuts him off with a sharp look.

Murphy looks at the women before continuing.

"The road led me to a town called Oradour-sur-Glane, or what was left of it. It's destroyed."

"Allied bombs?" says the American.

Murphy shakes his head in the negative.

"It was the smell that hit me first. Burning bodies. Piles of 'em. Face-down in the dirt. Shot and burned. While I looked from the bodies to the buildings, I saw an old man standing by what used to be the church. He was mumbling and shaking. I went to him to see what happened and where the rest of the townspeople were, when I saw it."

He stops and looks at the women.

"Saw what?" asks Virginia.

His hands again quake, and it takes him great effort to compose himself.

"A crucified baby."

Sophie and Estelle gasp. Virginia swears under her breath.

"The rest of the townspeople were in the church. All the women and children herded, locked in, and set on fire. Shot if they tried to escape. Hundreds of 'em."

It's incomprehensible. Virginia almost can't make sense of the words.

"The old man was from the next village. He said the Milice told the Nazis one of their officers had been captured and killed by the Maquis. One officer. Six hundred souls and a . . . a baby for one Nazi officer. The old man said his village had heard music and shots and explosions all day. It sounded like a party."

"My God," says Estelle.

Virginia can't speak. Even with all she has seen, she can barely process this level of evil, an evil that not only tortures and kills but makes sport and entertainment of it. How can men become such monsters?

SHE'S AT HOME in the darkness. It's her ally. She imagines she's an owl, gliding through the black, unseen, while she pedals to the Maquis.

Virginia tries to imagine how she'll communicate this incomprehensible evil over Morse code to HQ. How can dots and dashes fully convey the horror? How will she speak it to Lavi? Will this knowledge cripple him from what he needs to do, knowing the danger he puts civilians in? Can she continue? Peasants on fence spikes. Women and children burned alive in a church.

A crucified baby.

Why did she refuse the L pill?

The full picture arrives in her mind, making it impossible for her to go on. She stops her bicycle and gets sick. Once she's wrung out, a quick scan of the landscape shows she's near enough to the safe house where they waited out the railway explosion to spend the rest of the night there, working through the aftershocks of this horror. Anyway, it's better she doesn't surprise the Maquis in the dark.

It's June 13. Twelve weeks since she arrived. Double the time she was supposed to live. There is no longer any pride at beating the odds, only the sick knowledge that death isn't yet interested in her. But it's there, always lurking, on the faces of the Nazis who searched Estelle's house, the shadow of the panzer divisions getting closer by the day, the Milice and the MPs.

At first light, she rides to the forest and locks her bicycle to a tree, walking the rest of the way. She smells real coffee and eggs the closer she gets. When she whistles, the explosives expert appears, places the board over the stream, and reaches for her hand as she crosses. She takes it, glad to have his warm, steady grip. She's so cold.

"What is it?" he says.

Unable to answer, she walks to the camp in silence. When Lavi sees her, he grins, but his face quickly becomes serious. When she tells him what happened at Oradour-sur-Glane, his face goes dark, and his exclamation is loud and swift. He overturns a table of maps, and kicks the leg, breaking it off. He picks it up and uses it to bash a chair to splinters. She watches him, feeling his rage, but still so cold she's unable to move freely. His men come over to try to stop him, but Virginia finds herself holding up her hands, urging others to give Lavi space. When he's through with his outburst, he runs his hands through his hair, catching his breath.

"Sabotage only" is the sole order she can muster before leaving them.

She takes the side roads on her return to Estelle's—head swiveling forward and back—and by the time she arrives, her shoulders and neck ache. Mimi greets her with shaking hands and a pale face.

"How did we get here?" Mimi says. "How does the world ever spin again after the likes of this war?"

There's no answer. Not for any of it.

In the passing days, Virginia heads to the solitary cottage for her transmissions to HQ. The women establish a centrally located cemetery with a nook under a bench where they may leave one another messages at appointed times. Through the messages in the passing days, Virginia learns the pilot Murphy has left the barn, but Sophie and the two other pilots stay on. Mimi tried to get to Cosne but spotted a column of troops marching from the barracks there and hastily made her exit. Lavilette's Maquis continue their sabotage work, blowing up two more important points on the railway lines. Most notably, they've begun to join forces with other Maquis units in the surrounding areas, bringing their numbers to over five hundred. They're eager for the expertise of the Jed team—the officers from France, Britain, and the US—when they drop, but they're holding strong.

The waiting and the isolation are making Virginia go mad. Eating is labor. She doesn't want to use downers in case she's needed, so she barely sleeps, and when she does, she's plagued with nightmares. The hours drag on without action.

But her waiting is finally rewarded. HQ lets her know to expect the Jed team who will take command of Lavilette's Maquis on the next full moon. Then they give her the order for which she's been waiting.

—It's time for you to make contact with Chambon.

VIRGINIA RISES, NAKED, from the claw-footed tub, where she's left a ring of dirt. It's the night before the trip, and she's allowed herself the luxury of a hot bath at Estelle's place to wash away the road dirt, the field soil, the gun grease, the layers of old-lady makeup. Her sweat and tears.

Her sins.

She hops to the table near where Cuthbert stands, and catches sight of herself in the long, thin, black-spotted washroom mirror. Skin over bone and lean muscle. Bruises from banging around in the dark. A scrape along the inside of her good leg from the bicycle. A calloused knee stump. Haunted eyes, flushed skin, wet hair.

In the candlelight, she's surprised, however, by the striking figure she cuts.

She drops her towel on the floor and runs her hand along her flat stomach, sees her breasts somehow remain full in spite of her hunger. She hasn't bled since she arrived—helpful in the field, but that can't be healthy for a woman in her thirties. Will she resume her cycle when all this is over, or will she stay an old woman?

You're still in there, she thinks. *But, for now, you must remain invisible.*

Chapter 23

FRESH LAYERS OF old-woman disguise applied, Virginia arrives with Estelle at the station at eleven thirty for the noon train. They picked a midday departure so all the rails wired with explosives overnight would have already gone off. They also want to allow enough time to buy tickets and endure the checkpoints, but not so much that they're waiting around under scrutiny.

At the station, engines exhale, Nazi soldiers shout, Milice patrol, travelers tremble, airplanes cause all of them to crouch low with every flyover. HQ won't allow the RAF to bomb them, but the Luftwaffe might. The engineer in charge is arguing with a Nazi officer about the blown line that forces them to reroute, adding hours to the travel times. Troublesome as it is, the Maquis are doing good work.

In case any rebels wired the rail during daylight, Virginia and Estelle make their way to the back of the train, but the seats are full. They have to return to the front, each car closer to the locomotive bringing a new wave of anxiety. Squeezing into the second car doesn't make their companions happy, but they've all long abandoned hopes of comfort.

An hour into the trip, Virginia thinks she might as well not have taken a bath last night. The compartment is sweltering, and she feels as if she will suffocate in her layers of clothing with packed money bags at her hips.

Since D-Day, the temperature in France has been rising, and she doesn't know if it's the coming solstice, the fires of war, or the gates to hell opening to engulf them all.

Progress is excruciatingly slow. Line changes, train changes, climbing upward into increasingly mountainous terrain. How does Estelle endure this trip so often? Thankfully, the closer they get to Chambon, the thinner the crowd. By the time they arrive at the station at Saint-Étienne and make their final change onto a little steam locomotive that looks like a blown-up child's toy, the evening light is soft, and the air is cool.

Climbing aboard, Virginia notices a number of single women traveling alone with groups of children. Each woman has the same alert yet haggard look. Each child, the same numb stare. Some children whimper, but none speak. The older ones sometimes console the younger, but not in all cases. She's disturbed to see one girl of about ten rocking herself from side to side, her head hitting the window with little bumps.

It's the flash of light on the silver plate around his neck that makes her sit up in her seat. A massive MP enters the compartment, silence falling over the travelers with his shadow. She dares a look at his face.

No. It can't be, she thinks.

Heart pounding, hands sweating, Virginia looks down and squeezes her eyes shut and open again, reassuring herself it's not him, but when she looks back up, it is.

Anton Haas.

He seems to have grown taller—he must be six foot five. He has a bandage wrapped around his head over his left eye, a sling around his left arm, and a crutch.

Dear God, he's spent so much time with her wanted poster. Will he make the connection?

Virginia slouches, pushes her glasses up her nose, and pulls her shawl up and over her forehead so it shadows her face. As they move away from the station, she uses the chugging of the train to regulate her breathing and wills her blood to become ice.

The women and children recoil as he limps by, metal necklace clanking against his silver buttons. The closer he gets to Estelle and Virginia, the harder Estelle squeezes Virginia's hand. She's able to extract her hand from Estelle's and to cross her arms over her chest. She can at least try to pretend they're not together. After a moment, Estelle slides slightly away from Virginia, understanding.

The MP takes the seat across the aisle and one forward from theirs, and drops heavily into it, lifting his leg with some effort to elevate it. His huge black boot blocks the aisle, and soon Virginia can feel him staring in her direction. She keeps her face turned away from his, toward the window.

How could she have such terrible luck? What is Haas doing here, alone, going to Chambon? Is there a convalescent center in the village? Or is this a ruse, and he's onto her? Has the betrayer somehow found her and communicated her new identity to him? Or was it Louis? Has he been tortured to reveal her whereabouts? No, he wouldn't. She's certain.

She thinks so, anyway.

"Open the window," he says in German.

Proud of how calm she has made herself in the face of such strain, she doesn't flinch. Not a flicker of understanding passes over her. From a few rows up, a little boy's head turns slightly before snapping forward. Virginia is glad the soldier stares at them so he didn't notice.

"Open the window," he says in French. "You."

He points at Virginia and then at the window across from him. She rises a little, keeping her face turned away from his, and obeys, letting in a rush of cool, sweet mountain air. He inhales deeply and leans his head back against his window.

"Merci," he says, closing his good eye.

She feels the smallest sliver of release. Unless he's a very good actor, he doesn't recognize her. She dares a look at him, and hatred rises in her.

You bastard, she thinks. *Damn you to hell. Not one of us has the luxury to breathe easily for a second, but you think you do. You, who helped destroy*

*my first network. If you knew who I was, you wouldn't close that eye. I could
kill you before the next stop. I could leave your body on the train and no one
would know.*

She reaches in her pocket and feels the garrote, the thin wire HQ gave
her in the last drop for her bag of tricks. It looks like a simple shoelace, but
it can suffocate a man in a minute flat.

Could she kill him? Estelle wouldn't ask questions. There'd be no better place. With so many travelers, no one could trace her, and with the
Germans now battling the Allies for their lives, she can't imagine they'd
investigate too deeply for one lame MP.

But the children. They're so close—just a few rows up. If any of them
saw the struggle, they would be traumatized.

The internal war is torture. As soon as she decides she'll do it, another
voice arises, cautioning her. By the time they reach the next station, she's
sick to realize she missed her chance. The rows between her and the children fill with even more passengers. The announcements and motion
awaken MP Haas, and he now spends more time with his eye open than
he does with it closed. Indecision prevented her from avenging her Lyon
network. She has again failed them.

At the last station before Chambon, there's an announcement that a
pine tree has fallen over the line ahead, and they can't continue. The MP
sits up, drops his leg from the seat with a grunt, and struggles to stand.
Virginia can't be sure because she keeps her head down, but she's almost
certain he stares at her. It seems to take him an eternity to gather his
things. When he finally does, everyone waits for him to disembark before
moving, and there's a collective release of breath as he's driven away in the
black Mercedes waiting for him.

She takes a few deep breaths to steady herself before they leave the
train.

Keep going.

It takes great effort to stand, but she manages to follow Estelle.

Along the road, farmers line up with horse-drawn carts, and one of the groups of children climbs aboard the wagon Estelle selects. The woman leading the group gives Estelle a nearly imperceptible nod.

The travelers bounce and bump over the rocky road. Cliffs and steep ledges rise on all sides, and birds slip in and out of tall pine clusters. Every time Virginia dares a glance at the mountains, she feels light-headed, so she concentrates on the rolling green fields, the changing sky, the gray stone farmhouses and their outbuildings.

The children.

She's never seen so many children. Peeking up from meadows and cottages, running over farmland to forests and along the banks of meandering streams. Tall, short, dark-haired, fair-haired, red-haired, feral, erudite, stoic, stubborn, scared. All varieties, in as great an abundance as the wildflowers. Once the silent travelers with them disembark at a building that looks like a school, Virginia can't help herself. She leans close to Estelle.

"I see there's only one thing to do in a remote mountain town," she whispers.

"What's that?" asks Estelle.

"Reproduce."

Estelle breaks into a grin.

It's nearly seven o'clock by the time they approach the main street in Chambon. They give the farmer a generous tip from Virginia's stash. When they climb down, Virginia spots the black Mercedes parked below the red-and-black swastika flag flying over a building across the street: the Hôtel du Lignon.

Of course, she thinks. *Just my luck. He's here.*

Thankfully, there's no sign of Haas among the Nazi soldiers who sit outside smoking at tables, listening to music like they're on holiday, their broken arms and blasted legs and bandages revealing this is, in fact, where they convalesce. Virginia finds it strange how cavalier they behave when their peers are getting cornered by the Allies in some of the bloodiest battles of the war to date. Are they just glad to have survived the fighting? Glad to be away from the bloodshed?

Estelle slips her arm through Virginia's and leads her to the Hôtel May to book a room. Once they're safely inside, the women drop their bags and fall backward on their respective beds.

"Do you want to tell me anything about that MP?" Estelle says.

"No," says Virginia.

I'll tell you once he's dead, she thinks.

"Then, a moment of rest before we find food," says Estelle.

"I won't argue with you. Are we meeting anyone tonight?"

"I'll leave a message with the proprietor of the hotel café. She can link us to our man: Auguste Bohny, head of the Secours Suisse—a children's relief organization. If he feels safe enough to meet with us, we'll go from there."

"If not?"

"I have confidence you'll find your way to the Maquis either way."

"Secours Suisse. What's the Swiss Red Cross doing in Chambon?"

"Oh, Diane, haven't you guessed?"

Virginia sits up and looks at Estelle.

"The children," Estelle says. She stands and walks to the window, wrapping her arms around herself. "The ghosts. Some on their way through to Switzerland. Some here to stay out the war, to see if their parents make it out alive. The residents here who shelter the children call them the 'Old Testaments.'"

Realization comes to completion in Virginia as Estelle says the words out loud.

"You must protect the region because the region protects Jewish children."

Virginia sits for a moment, allowing the clear purity of the knowledge to wash over her. It feels like her lungs open more with each new breath. She thinks of the little ones who have made their way here alone. The girl with the polka-dot scarf, the boy from Estelle's goat stall with the streak of white in his hair, the girl banging her head on the train window.

The women who escort them.

The peasants who shelter them.

She rises to join Estelle at the window and places her hand on Estelle's back. The swastika flag across the street flaps in the setting sun. Virginia wonders how her heart can feel so heavy and so lifted at the same time.

"How many?" Virginia asks.

Estelle looks at her with glassy eyes. She reaches for her friend's face, holding Virginia's cheeks with her hands. She says the precious word in a whisper.

"Thousands."

Chapter 24

THE MAN WITH the bow tie and glasses who meets them is so tall he has to stoop down when he walks through the café doorway. They exchange code phrases and answer one another's safety questions before ordering potato cakes and salads from the limited menu. When the waitress leaves them, Virginia leans toward Auguste.

"I need to meet the head of the Maquis here."

He studies her.

"As soon as possible," she says.

He nods but doesn't answer. He takes his time with each bite, savoring the food. She sees he doesn't want to talk here. It takes a great act of self-restraint to match his eating pace and keep herself still in her chair when she's ready to storm the forest, arrange the drops, drill the men, dig a moat around the village.

"We're five hundred and fifty kilometers from Switzerland," he finally says. "We have people here who take *copies* of the Old Testament there. But the trip is expensive."

"How expensive?" she asks.

"A thousand francs per copy."

A thousand francs per Jewish child to smuggle out of France. She opens a folder in her mind—Needs of Chambon—and files the information.

"How much to keep the ones who stay?" she asks.

"American Quakers and the Swiss Red Cross fund the copies we keep here."

Noted.

"If I need a good doctor in Chambon, I see Dr. Le Forestier," he says. "It's a shame there are so few supplies when he has to treat so many."

"How many patients does the doctor have?" she asks.

"Hundreds. Both children and men who have neglected their health needs for some time."

Based on the amount of boys and girls she's seen, their numbers likely far outnumber the Maquis to which he must refer. Her sails deflate. She needs an army of men if she's to ensure these children are kept safe.

"Perhaps you saw the cars parked with grass growing around their wheels," he says. "It's a shame there's no petrol. Benzol works, but it breaks down the canisters quickly. Bicycles are our legs, but the mountain roads wear our tires to nothing."

They're going to need an enormous amount of supplies in a short time. She hopes she can gather a decent reception squad.

The sound of squeaking brakes calls their attention to the street. From their table, she has a good view of the Nazi hospital across the way. She's on alert when she sees two lorries arrive. She and her companions watch as a small group of soldiers emerges from the hospital, standing at attention while the Kommandant inspects them. She catches bits of his biting comments from what appears to be a dressing-down of these men who would rather play cards with their boots up than return to the theater of war. The men can hardly be called men; they're largely baby-faced underlings—the bottom of the Nazi barrel—plucked from their mothers' houses as a last resort. No wonder they're glad to be at the hospital in a remote village. But their holiday is over. They're herded and loaded into the lorries like lambs for the slaughter. Once they're gone, Auguste again speaks.

"I'll come to your room at eleven o'clock."

Estelle whispers the room number. He nods, and then reaches for his ration coupon book. Virginia waves him away and glances around the café before providing the necessary payment for all of them. He bows to her and leaves them.

Back at the room, Virginia paces.

"Please," Estelle says. "You're making me nervous."

"We're wasting time. Why so late?"

"This is a more delicate operation than you're used to. Surely you understand the need for extra caution."

Virginia drops onto the bed and rubs her face.

"I know. I'm sorry," she says. "I'm at least encouraged by the hospital cleanout. I wonder how many Nazis are left?"

"Not many, I hope. And you saw the quality of what was here."

"Is that why the kids are able to exist up here? Because of child soldiers tired of war?"

"Maybe, in part," says Estelle. "But mostly it's the courage and love of the people in the region. The village hasn't been without its share of trouble, but they risk it, just the same."

"Tell me," Virginia says, sitting up to face her friend. "How was a village of presumably Christian men and women persuaded to take on Jewish children?"

"They're mostly Protestants. Huguenots. Years of ancestral Catholic oppression has made them sympathetic to others who are persecuted for their faith. And their pastor and his wife, André and Magda Trocmé, are its beating heart."

Virginia brings her hand to her own heart. She thinks of the kids she's seen picking flowers and following farmers and herding goats. Of Estelle and the children she has sheltered and escorted. Of the women on the train chaperoning Jewish children under the noses of Nazi soldiers. Of the risks these people take. These are the true heroes and heroines of this war.

"Are you all right?" Estelle asks.

Virginia smiles and closes her eyes, nodding.

"I'm getting there. I didn't know after that night in the barn, hearing about the reprisals. But this place? It's extraordinary. You are extraordinary."

"I'm not."

"You are. You might be restoring my faith in humanity."

Virginia stands and crosses to the window to watch the street. Eleven o'clock comes and goes. She resumes her pacing. The money bags at her hips are making her sweat. She lifts her skirts to readjust the packs, then drops them to smooth her clothing.

"How much will you give them?" says Estelle.

"That depends if we ever get to meet the commanding officer. But if we do, it will also depend on a test to see if he's trustworthy."

"What test?"

"HQ approved one hundred fifty thousand francs to hold the Maquis over until I'm here permanently. I have one hundred fifty-two thousand. When I give it to them, I'll ask them to count the money. If they tell of the discrepancy, I'll trust them. If they don't mention the extra two thousand, I'll take it all back and leave them to the dogs."

A knock startles them. Virginia crosses the room, and when she opens the door, Auguste is there with a tall young man with brown hair, large ears, and an eager look on his face, like a teenaged Jimmy Stewart. Is he even twenty years old? She can hardly believe one so young is the head of the area Maquis. She needs men, not boys. Once the door is closed, he holds out his hand to shake hers.

"Edmund Lebrat," he says.

"Diane."

"Edmund can introduce you to the man you need," says Auguste.

Though Virginia wants to pull out her hair over all the layers of people between her and the Maquis, she's at least glad this teenager isn't her main point of contact. And she admires the security precautions they've taken.

"Let's go," Virginia says. "We're wasting time."

VIRGINIA AND ESTELLE follow closely behind Edmund as they travel the dark roads and fields out of town. His stride is swift and steady, but she senses he makes unnecessary turns and twists, ensuring the women would not be able to find their way alone. A dense fog further obscures the route. He keeps an eye on the women but maintains a good pace. After a while, they arrive at a small farmhouse on a hill with a good view of the surrounding area. They walk around the rear, and Edmund hoots like an owl. At the back door, he knocks in a pattern. In a few moments the door opens, and they're admitted.

The kitchen is hardly a kitchen, more like a storage room. Racks of patched clothing hang beside a sewing table, where a slender woman works by candlelight. Worn shoes and boots line the wall like soldiers. The man who let them in is sharp and slight. His dark stare touches each of their faces. When he gets to Virginia, she removes the blue scarf she's wrapped over her hair and smooths it, standing to her full height and meeting his eyes. Something in his face changes.

"La Madone," he says with a grin.

The Madonna. She can't help but laugh at his impression. She holds out her hand to him and shakes it.

"Diane," she corrects.

He returns her strong grip.

"Code name Simon," he says. "Head of the Secret Army."

"Army?" she says. "What kind of numbers are we talking?"

"Two hundred at the ready. Double that if you can arm us."

That's a relief.

"Can they follow orders?" she says.

"What kind?"

"Sabotage."

"From whom?"

"Me."

He looks her over and gives a derisive laugh.

"We'll see about that," he says.

Edmund's head ping-pongs between the two of them. Estelle stands in the dark, silent as a shadow. The woman at the sewing machine never stops working.

"How about this," Virginia says. "They have a problem with me, they can continue on, empty-handed."

"Don't bristle," he says. "I'm only being honest. These boys are going to have difficulty taking orders from a woman. But your orders can go through me."

"I won't suffer delays because of pride. The truth is, you have nothing without what I can offer."

"I know."

"Good. Then make sure everyone I interact with also does."

He stares at her without answering.

"I need a washroom," she says.

He points to the hallway. She leaves them to get the money from her skirts. In the mirror, she sees that removing the bags takes quite a bit off her old-woman's frame. She looks around for something to pad her body. She tries stuffing in her blue shawl, but it's too thin. She stares at herself for a long moment. It will have to be all right.

When she returns, Simon whispers with the woman at the sewing machine. Edmund's eyes lower to Virginia's hips and back to her face, but when she drops the two money bags on the table, his attention shifts focus. She directs Simon and Edmund to open the bags. When they do, their eyes grow wide.

"One hundred fifty thousand francs," she says. "Approved for your use until I return for good and we start receiving drops. Count it."

The woman at the sewing machine rises and steps forward. She has lovely dark curled hair and a pleasant face, though she looks too thin for her frame.

"I'm Simon's wife. Code name Dolmazon. May I offer you water and a little bread while you wait?"

Virginia and Estelle follow Dolmazon through the maze of goods to the other end of the room, where there's a table with four chairs. Dolmazon pours water from a clay pitcher into two mugs and opens the bread box. There's very little inside.

"Just water for us," says Virginia.

Dolmazon looks relieved.

"You're a seamstress," says Virginia.

"In a way," says Dolmazon. "I'm in charge of outfitting our boys. So many are still of an age where they're outgrowing their clothes the moment they touch their backs. Even without proper nutrition. And the mountains are murder on the soles of their shoes. Thank goodness the winter is over. It's brutal here."

Virginia shudders at the thought.

"The only positive is how the snow closes the roads, keeping us sheltered. The thaw reopens them, bringing in the unwanted world."

"If it's any consolation," says Virginia, "if this works out, I'll be able to get more clothing and supplies for you."

"We'd be very grateful," says Dolmazon. "These clothes have been refurbished to death. They're all patched and pilled. And our medical needs are great. Dr. Le Forestier makes do, but I worry to think about when the Maquis are engaged in fighting. Even without war, boys find ways to get hurt."

"Indeed," says Virginia.

Though Virginia is not warm to Simon based on his first impression, Dolmazon seems like a strong, kind, and reliable woman, and the men are clearly in need. Virginia wants this partnership to work out—for the war and for the children. But if she doesn't trust their leader in small matters, she can't trust him with her life, let alone the lives of thousands. She's afraid to feel optimistic.

After a while, Edmund walks over to Virginia with Simon following. Looking sheepish, Edmund presents Virginia with a stack of bills.

"We counted twice, but you gave us two thousand too much," he says.

Virginia catches Estelle's eye, and the women grin at each other.

Chapter 25

A KNOCK BEFORE sunrise is never a good thing.

Back at her safe house in Sury-ès-Bois—exhausted from her travel to and from Chambon, and messaging with HQ—Virginia fell asleep last night in her clothes, without removing Cuthbert, so she's able to answer the door quickly.

The cadence of the tapping tells her Mimi's on the other side of it. A peek out the window confirms this, but also reveals Sophie. Virginia pulls them in and shuts the door behind them.

"Agent numbers at Fresnes are growing by the day," says Sophie. "They're being tortured, and there are rumors they'll be deported. My contact thinks we can get just one out. Maybe two with enough money."

"Louis won't leave his men," says Virginia.

"I told her," says Mimi. "She won't listen."

"I beg you," says Sophie. "You're my only hope."

Sophie is beginning to deteriorate. Her hair is unwashed. She wears no lipstick. Her polish is chipped, her nails dirty. Virginia takes Sophie's hands and leads her to the small table, where she pulls out a chair for Sophie to sit. Mimi joins her at the table while Virginia prepares a pot for tea.

"Please," Sophie says.

She cries and buries her face in her hands.

Virginia shares a look of pity with Mimi. Sophie has lost a husband.

The thought of her losing a fiancé makes Virginia sick. Further, Virginia feels a level of responsibility for Louis. She brought him into this clandestine life. His own actions brought consequences, but she has to try to help him at least one more time. What's the worst that can happen?

Capture. Imprisonment. Torture. Deportation. Murder.

She can almost hear Vera arguing with her.

But Virginia has already beaten the life-expectancy odds of her peers. She's had many successful drops. The Maquis of this region are effective, and their numbers are growing. She has confirmed the existence and size of Maquis groups in Chambon. God forbid she's arrested, another agent can go in her place.

Also, Chambon is not yet ready for her. When she left them, she charged them with procuring her at least two safe houses, and gathering coordinates for at least three drop fields. After the next full moon phase and the Jedburgh drop, once she's stationed in Chambon, there will be no more trips to Paris until after the liberation.

She feels the ever-present urge rising again—not just for herself this time, but for Louis, too—and knows she must make the most of every hour she's here.

The kettle whistles, silencing her musings. Virginia removes it from the burner and makes three teas from the last of the secret stash Vera sent her. She places each steaming cup before the women and looks into Mimi's eyes with a question.

Should I?

Mimi nods.

"Sophie," Virginia says.

The young woman lifts her head from her arms and looks up at Virginia. Mascara streaks down the sides of her face.

"Drink your tea," says Virginia. "Wash up. We have a trip to make."

MIMI INSISTS ON going. The boy will stay with Estelle.

"What if Estelle gets captured?" Virginia asks.

"He'll go to Estelle's cousin."

"What if the cousin is captured?"

"Then the nuns will take him. And if the nuns are captured, he will be in God's arms."

Virginia can't argue with that.

Mimi will serve as Virginia's travel escort. At Virginia's advice, Mimi dons a kerchief over her hair and scrubs her face dry and pale, trying to look more like an old woman. Sophie will pretend to be alone but will stay close. Finally, Virginia has a key to Estelle's safe-house apartment, should they need shelter.

Their mission: Arrive. Rendezvous. Hide. Rendezvous. Depart.

If they're able to make contact at Fresnes, and Louis and his team are alive, they need to find out how much bribe money it will cost to smuggle one or more out, if Louis would even be open to escaping without his team. Or—if deportation is imminent—when that might be and the route they'll likely take.

Sunup to sundown.

Just another day in the field.

Knowing she survived her last trip to Paris gives her confidence, but when they arrive at the train station, plans already need to adapt. They learn the lines aren't running because of Maquis sabotage, and they'll have to take a bus, which not only takes longer but doesn't leave for another hour and a half.

"We'll never be able to get back by curfew," says Mimi, just loud enough for Sophie to hear, where she stands in line behind them.

"Then we'll spend the night," says Virginia. "Do you still want to go?"

"Yes," Mimi says.

Sophie coughs twice, the signal they agreed upon for yes. No is a single cough.

They're the last ones sold bus tickets—lucky to have gotten three. When it's time to board, they join the end of the line. The MP stationed at the door to the bus is rough with Sophie. He demands to know why she's traveling at so dangerous a time.

"My cousin is sick. He may be dying."

"We're all dying," he says. He looks again at her ticket. "Fresnes. Your cousin isn't Resistance scum, is he? That's where all the terrorists are being sent. I keep asking for a posting at the prison there so I can shoot some. They're thinning the population by the day, you know? Food is scarce. Less mouths to feed."

Virginia can't see Sophie's face, but she can see that her shoulders are straight and proud. There's no heaving of breath. Her hands hang at her sides and they don't shake.

Good girl.

"Maybe I'll let you go if you promise me a dinner when you get back," he says, reaching for a lock of Sophie's hair. "After you bathe. I think you're pretty under there."

Virginia has never been gladder to be an old woman. She doesn't hear what Sophie says, but sees her board the bus. He barely gives Virginia and Mimi a second glance.

Invisible.

They climb aboard and see there are no seats left but those in the front rows. The smell of body odor is terrible. The passengers look as if they're on a death caravan. Virginia and Mimi take one seat, opening the window to let in the air. Sophie sits across the way, next to a toothless old man.

The trip takes five hours, but Virginia feels safer and more in control than if they'd ridden a train. There are no tracks that might explode, and they're low to the ground, close to the exit. Also, the Allies don't bomb buses because they're almost exclusively traveled by civilians.

The bus stop of their destination is across from a beautiful public garden: Le Parc de Sceaux. They allow Sophie to get ahead of them, and follow at a distance while she leads them onto the tree-lined trails, where long pools reflect the blue sky and lead to an elegant château. Defiling the gardens are the footsteps and shadows of Nazis escorting women on dates, officers and French collaborators stealing moments they don't deserve. Virginia wants to spit on their boots and high-heeled shoes, but she holds in her venom.

They pass a waterfall—its whoosh and spray a welcome coolness in the heat—and follow where Sophie has turned down a canopy-covered path. Virginia notices the slight pause and slip of the hand in the hedge, but no one else would. They continue to follow Sophie at a distance out to the street and to a row of terraced houses, where Sophie disappears in an alleyway. She uses the key she just snagged and opens a small shed. She pulls out three bicycles, locks the shed, and takes off. When the coast is clear, Virginia and Mimi take the two remaining bikes and follow the signs to where they know Fresnes waits.

About two kilometers away, the imposing prison looms over the street. Even larger than Cherche-Midi, the walls of Fresnes are higher and the gate is more formidable. Each of the bicycles has its own padlock, and the women take care to fasten them carefully next to Sophie's, which they see she has left at the stalls outside the café across the way. Taking separate tables, the women order, and they wait. Finally, after about an hour, a guard walks in, orders a café nationale, and takes a seat near Sophie. The bald man has a fierce face with gleaming black eyes and bad teeth. She can't imagine how a man with his looks could be an ally to anyone. He drinks quickly, and when he stands to leave, Sophie drops her napkin. He bends to pick it up, and places it on the table. Then he's gone.

Sophie gets up to leave, and Virginia and Mimi soon follow. Virginia now takes the lead on the bicycle and starts them on the route to Estelle's apartment. It takes them a little over an hour. Though Virginia's body is tired from travel, riding through the streets of Paris for what she knows will be the last time in a long while encourages her to be mindful of this time in the city of her heart. How grateful she is to have survived as long as she has. How badly she wants to be able to help Louis and, by extension, Sophie and Mimi. How happy she is to again get to see her old neighborhood.

The sacrament of the present moment.

When they arrive, they come around the back way, and Virginia and her partners lock their bicycles in the building's underground parking garage. Then they creep, one at a time, to the safety of the apartment. Sophie and Mimi collapse on the couch, while Virginia fetches three glasses of water.

"I'm so tired," says Sophie. "But I don't know how I'll sleep. I might go crazy waiting until tomorrow."

"I know," says Mimi. "It's agony."

"Especially because the guard won't get to the library until his lunch break," says Sophie. "So, it won't do us any good to arrive before noon. There's an astronomy book I'll need to check for his message."

"We've made it this far and this long," says Virginia, distributing the water. "And, unless we were found out and followed, presumably we'll make it another day. Day one hundred and one."

"Day one oh one?" says Mimi. "What's that?"

"It's how many days I've managed to live as a wireless operator in occupied France."

"Oh, that's something," says Sophie. "Pianists only average six weeks at this point."

"Six weeks?" says Mimi. "And they're still able to recruit you?"

"I can't call myself one," says Sophie. "I couldn't even manage a single transmission."

"Don't sell yourself short," says Virginia. "You've been invaluable to my network as a courier. I couldn't have gotten this far without you. Without either of you."

Sophie beams so brightly and relaxes so completely, Virginia feels both affection for her and shame for being so stingy with her praise. Mimi gives Virginia a smile of gratitude. Virginia turns away, walking to the window to look at her old building.

Virginia is about to tell the women about her old pension and Johnnie the griffin and a hundred sunrises on the balcony, but she's jarred to see the flowers are gone. Pots, petals, all of it. Disappeared. She hates to be superstitious, but it seems like a terrible omen. She drops to the windowsill and stares out in silence, feeling a shadow descend upon her mood.

Night falls fast. The women eat the hard-boiled eggs Mimi packed, and prepare to sleep. Virginia insists Mimi and Sophie share the bed, and she'll take the couch. She wants to be alone, to keep watch over the blacked-out city. Yet her memories torment her. And it's so much harder to keep hope alive for Louis in the middle of the night. She's certain that, even if given the chance, he'll never leave his partners. Their best hope, if he is alive, is intelligence from a guard on intercepting a departing train.

At some point, amid her fitful dozing, the paper with Louis's handwriting again comes to mind.

Found him. Home: 16th A. Rue Spontini. Work: Saint-Maur-des-Fossés.

The tempter's voice rises.

Saint-Maur is just a bike ride away.

She sits bolt upright on the couch.

You have the entire morning.

She checks the wall clock. It's five o'clock.

You won't get back to Paris for a long time. You can at least confirm Louis's intel on the betrayer.

Virginia stands and walks to the window. She sits on the sill and pulls her shawl tight around her arms. She can see ripples of gold on the Seine in the first light of dawn, and thinks, *One hundred and one.*

One hundred and one days.

One hundred and one Paris sunrises.

Watching the changing light in the sky, she roots herself to her seat and breathes deeply, stilling her heart and mind, and taking care to clear her thoughts. She leans her head back and dozes until the sound of church bells awakens her.

Is it a sign?

Clearheaded and openhearted, she decides. She checks her disguise in the mirror, finds a piece of paper, and scribbles a note to Sophie and Mimi.

I'll be back.

In the changing light, the streets begin to stir. Virginia keeps her stare on the pavement in front of the bicycle, lifting her eyes only to check signs. After almost an hour's ride, and a little before eight in the morning, she arrives at the church in Saint-Maur and locks up the bicycle. The sign says Mass is at eight thirty. From what she has observed with Mimi and the time spent with the nun from Lyon, confessions are often heard before services.

A bell tower rises over a crucifix, which hangs high over a bricked façade with a large, encircled stone cross at its heart. She passes through the doors, her step faltering as she walks under the chiseled words VENITE ADOREMUS. Come, let us worship.

Inside the church, the aroma of incense is potent. The ceiling is lofty—a dome rising over the altar with a resurrected Jesus presiding. Light slants in through the stained-glass windows, illuminating in red, blue, and green light the pews and the wooden chairs lining the perimeter of the space. An altar server lights candles, and the organist plays softly. Virginia's gaze finds a small queue of women in a dark corner, leading to the carved, wooden doors of the confessional. She takes her place at the end of the line. By appearances, she's the "oldest" one there.

Invisible.

As the women file in and out of the confessional, she recalls a conversation she once had with the nun in Lyon. They were close, so Virginia could ask her anything.

"I don't understand how telling my sins to a man who sins just as badly absolves me of my own," Virginia had said.

"The priest stands in for our Lord. He's a channel of the grace of forgiveness."

"Why can't I just think of things I'm sorry for?"

"Speaking them aloud to another is deliberate. It requires premeditation. It makes you more mindful of your sins and unburdens you. And the Lord gave his apostles the authority to bind or loose us from our sins."

Virginia doesn't know if she believes the nun's words, but she has thought about them many times since. Over the past few months, she's certainly experienced a release each time she's given voice to her burdens, but it's not easy to do. She'd learned the words to say in the confessional, but she'd never gone. Until now.

The church starts to fill. When her turn arrives, she glances around to make sure she's not being watched. In a smooth, silent motion, Virginia slides one of the wooden chairs away from the wall, slipping it under the knob of the priest's door. She enters her side of the confessional, taking her place at the kneeler. When she sees his profile through the screen, hatred rises in her like a fire.

The betrayer.

From this very confessional and that of the prison, *abbé* Robert Alesch has heard the sins of resistors and reported them to the Gestapo.

For money.

Using his power and position, he'd gained the trust of her Lyon network before feeding them to the wolves.

If she could, she would start his eternity in hell's furnace by burning him alive in the box, but that would be too kind, too quick. Better to draw out his sentence.

"Forgive me, Father," she says. "It has been a lifetime since my last confession."

She takes great care making her voice that of the elderly woman, speaking her French as perfectly as possible.

"Sister, what has kept you away for so long?"

His German-accented French still makes her skin crawl.

"I have a priest hatred," she says.

"Why?"

"Many friends have suffered at the hands of an evil one."

"One man does not represent the entire clergy."

"I can't help but judge the rest because of him."

"There is only one judge: the Lord. When we put ourselves in that place, we fall prey to the sin of pride."

"I have many sins. Pride is the least of them."

"Confess. Relieve your burden."

She takes a deep breath and pulls herself farther back into the shadows. The noise of the church fills outside the box.

"I want to murder this priest," she says.

"That is a grave sin."

"Not only do I want to murder him, but I go through the motions of how I will do it, how I will slit his soft, white throat while he sleeps."

"No."

"I know where he lives. Sometimes I stand outside his house, watching through the window. Once, when I was sure he was out, I picked his lock and wandered through his home."

A lie. In the confessional. But it's worth it to watch him squirm.

"It's full of fine things," she continues. "Why would a priest have such fine things?"

"I'm alarmed you would do such a thing," he says.

"But I think God wants me to kill him."

"God would never tell his daughter to murder a priest."

"But doesn't God say, 'Woe to those who lead my flock astray'? Doesn't he want justice where there's grave sin?"

"The Lord's hand is the only one that should administer that justice."

The noise of the congregation and music continues to rise outside the box.

"This priest betrays resistors to the Nazis for money," she says. "I hear he keeps a mistress. Maybe two. Can you imagine a priest like that?"

Abbé Alesch snaps his attention to her, peering through the screen with his white-blue eyes.

"I could kill you now, Robert Alesch," she says. "The music of the choir will drown out the sound of your struggle."

She hears him try the doorknob, and the small, weak whimper he makes when he realizes he's trapped.

"I know where you live," she says. "The sixteenth arrondissement, on the rue Spontini. I know what you've done. And I will be watching you until I decide to administer the justice you deserve."

He pulls back from her, as if slapped, and shakes the doorknob. Banging and pleading.

She leaves the confessional, ducking into the crowd filing in, and slipping out to the streets of Paris.

Invisible.

WHEN VIRGINIA STRIDES into the apartment, the hall mirror reveals her flushed skin and wide, alert eyes flashing behind her fake spectacles. She places her hands on her cheeks to cool them.

"You look like Diana, just in from the hunt," says Mimi.

You've no idea.

After taking several deep breaths to clear her mind, and drinking a large glass of water, Virginia helps the women tidy the rooms. She again leads them as they set out and, an hour later, they arrive at the library to wait for the guard. Sophie browses the shelves. Virginia and Mimi read the newspapers. It's now noon. They're taking the one thirty bus home. Time is running out.

At one o'clock, the guard from the café enters the library and heads to the section on astronomy, disappearing briefly in the stacks before reemerging and hurrying back out. Shortly afterward, Sophie emerges from the same aisle looking pale, the circles under her eyes more pronounced. She makes brief eye contact with the women and shakes her head before leaving the library. Virginia and Mimi wait only a beat before they follow.

When they're only a block away—Sophie just ahead of them—Virginia feels the hair on her neck rise. She glances over her shoulder, and the sight that greets her makes her draw in her breath. Mimi follows her look, and they see three Milice racing out of the library looking left and right until their stares find the women.

"Go!" says Virginia. They stand and pedal with all their might as the Milice race on foot, trying to catch them.

Sophie is stopped at the crosswalk ahead of them. Mimi calls to her, "Go!"

Sophie turns her head and sees the women pedaling swiftly toward her, the Milice on the chase. The men blow their whistles and yell, "Halt!" Sophie's eyes widen. She shoots forward the moment there's a break between vehicles. Virginia and Mimi follow, horns blaring as they weave in and out, racing along the road against traffic, until they get to the shed. Breathless, they stow the bikes, lock them, and hurry through alleyways back to the park. The whistles of the Milice tell them they're still in pursuit.

"Separate!" Sophie yells.

They don't want to leave her, but three women in a hurry together are more suspicious than one. Virginia and Mimi break off and rush to the station, barely able to breathe by the time they arrive at the ticket counter, and Virginia's knee stump feels as if it's on fire. The man selling passes regards the sweating, breathless women with narrow eyes, but when a pair of Milice on the hunt appear at the door, he moves fast, winking at Virginia and Mimi as they hurry back outside to the waiting bus.

They climb aboard, watching the park, praying to see Sophie's face. The time to go draws nearer, but Sophie still doesn't arrive. Travelers fill the bus. The Milice leave the station and head toward the park. Mimi looks at Virginia with panic in her eyes.

As the driver steps down and makes last call, a familiar man with a mustache enters the bus. He keeps his gaze down and slips past them and toward the back seats. Virginia turns to watch him more closely, but Mimi grabs her arm, calling her attention to the window.

Sophie!

She walks coolly inside to the ticket counter, buys her pass, and strides out to the bus, arriving just as an MP intercepts her, demanding her identification card. Virginia can't hear the exchange, but she can see Sophie's face, dark and beautiful under interrogation. Sophie points toward the park and makes a motion as if showing the height of someone. Then she holds up two fingers and points to the park again. The MP nods and leaves her, and she climbs aboard as if the whole chase never happened.

Chapter 26

AFTER THE ORDEAL, upon return, Sophie tells the women that even though the guard says deportation is imminent, Louis refuses to leave his men. And the guard knew neither the date of transport nor their destination.

"We knew to prepare for this," Virginia says.

"No," says Sophie.

"Sophie," says Mimi. "Louis is a good man. Of course he wouldn't leave his team."

"They've been together since Lyon," says Virginia. "They've been through hell and back. Brothers-in-arms."

"Then why did we try?" says Sophie.

"To know he was still alive," says Virginia.

"It was worth the off chance he'd take our offer," says Mimi. "And I'm heartened he was able to say no. If he were broken by torture, he'd have accepted."

Virginia is troubled to see Sophie's face go blank. There's no other description for it. It's as if her light goes out. Virginia has experienced the shock of loss. It's like she's watching herself after her father's death, after Emil's breakup, after the hunting accident, the war losses. She kneels at Sophie's side and takes her hand.

"You need to return to London," Virginia says.

Sophie shakes her head the slightest bit in the negative.

"You need rest," Virginia says. "You were magnificent in Paris, but you can't hold up under this level of strain much longer. It's too personal. The only hope now is that Louis survives through the liberation, and there's a good chance he will. Please, leave France. Take care of yourself. Give your fiancé a healthy woman to come home to when this war is over."

Sophie's eyes remain blank.

Virginia hopes Sophie heeds her words, but she can't force her. She leaves the women and heads outside, taking great gulps of fresh, cool air. It's heaven to walk outdoors at night without being cold. The air still hangs with the sweet smell of grass and the pungent odor of goats. The silver stars in the navy sky wink as if all is well. She stops at the top of a hill and stares up. She thinks of the night in Spain when Louis found her, after his escape.

AFTER VIRGINIA'S FIRST mission, Vera wouldn't allow Virginia to return to France. Vera tried to placate her with a posting in Madrid. As she had done in Lyon, Virginia was to secure safe houses for agents, resistors, and Allied airmen on the escape, while working undercover as a newspaper correspondent. It was a clear night in May when Virginia waited in a café for the arrival of three men. Her contact said they'd escaped via the Pyrenees months ago, landed in a Spanish prison, and now that they'd served their sentences, needed shelter and help arranging travel back to London. Those she'd harbored all had the same haggard look, the one she wore after surviving the mountain crossing. Though the weather was considerably kinder this time of year, she was watching for men with that look.

It was a Saturday night on the Gran Vía. Music poured out of bars, and Virginia was surprised to find she was a little drunk on Rioja Alta. It was hard to come by those days, but she'd had the money to ensure her glass refilled itself. It now sat empty, only the half-moon of her red lipstick staining its rim. She lifted her crossword puzzle book and used it to fan herself until her attention was drawn to the street. Three gorgeous flamenco dancers spilled out of a lively club and picked three men from the crowd. The dancers were dark red beauties, flames in the night, reflected in the glassy, hungry stares of the men they led in the dance. A crowd clapped around them, and, when it became clear one of the bystanders was a good dancer, the other couples faded away, leaving the two to finish the dance alone.

Spain was like nowhere Virginia had ever been. Ravaged from years of civil war, crawling with spies, embassies for Axis and Allied powers within walking distance of the others, Spain was the rope in an international tug-of-war. Yet the streets pulsed with vitality. Dancing, wine, music, bullfighting.

The Spanish understand the sacrament of the present moment, she'd thought. *They are stars. Comets blazing through the night, living while there's still life left.*

The dance ended, and the crowd cheered. She looked into her empty wineglass thinking how thirsty she was, but the beauty of the night sky over Madrid distracted her. She was so lost in her stargazing that it took her a moment to realize a shadow had fallen over her. The man from the dance gazed down at her as though she were the star.

"How long since you've had a boarder, Auntie?" he'd asked, grinning.

She'd recognize that voice anywhere, though the man inside the mess of dirt and hair was barely recognizable.

"It has been a long time, Nephew," she said.

His grin had grown even wider. He laughed and raised his eyes to the heavens. Music started again. He reached for her hand. She took it, and he pulled her into his arms and led her into the street, where they danced under the stars in Madrid.

GAZING AT THE sky, Virginia thinks, *How will I leave them?*

Her team watches together for the last time, awaiting the change in command, the arrival of the big guns. The officers and military men who will really make soldiers of these guerillas. The air is heavy with unspoken emotion, but they've worked together closely enough not to have to speak. Virginia dares a look at their brave, beautiful faces.

Lavilette and Mimi, dear to her as family.

Their son. How is it possible a ten-year-old child is with them, yet it's all right?

Five Maquis, including the explosives expert and the angry one.

The American and the British pilots from Estelle's barn.

Sophie, stubborn girl. Girl after her own heart.

Estelle, the sister she never had.

Estelle looks at her, and Virginia sees her friend's tears illuminated in the light of the full moon. Then, suddenly, Virginia feels a foreign sensation. A stinging in her own eyes. She doesn't realize she's crying until Estelle wipes the tears off her cheeks. Virginia sputters a laugh, and the tears fall harder. A deep feeling of tension releases itself in her. She takes the first good breath she's had in months.

Soon, the hum of the plane starts. They rise, separate, make a new formation, that of an L, a runway of light. These officers aren't being dropped; they're being landed. This will be even more dangerous for the pilot, but safer for the precious human cargo, and necessary to get the wounded airmen out of France.

What a miracle all this is.

The plane is soon visible. She flashes her light, and the pilot responds. The plane lowers, growing larger, louder, and closer. Her heart pounds as she scans the surrounding countryside. They're in a remote area, but not quite as far away from Cosne as they'd like to be. This field is the highest and flattest they were able to find.

The plane lands with a little bump and stops short. They descend upon it, helping the men unload containers of supplies as quickly as possible before loading on the two downed pilots from Estelle's barn to go back to London.

Virginia looks at Sophie and motions her head to the plane. Sophie refuses.

The American pilot kisses Virginia's cheek before they help him aboard. He keeps his hand pressed to the window as the plane turns to take off. It taxis, accelerates, and rises, just clearing the treetops, becoming tinier in the night before disappearing altogether.

The officers are introduced. The wagons are loaded. And just like that, Lavilette and the men are gone.

The women and the boy are all that's left.

The boy is the first to crush Virginia with a hug. He leaps into her arms and kisses her cheek.

"Diane," he says. "You were much better than we expected."

She smiles at him through her tears, and plants a kiss on his cheek.

"Colonel Lavilette," she says, "you also exceeded my expectations."

Mimi comes behind the boy and lifts him down so she can hug Virginia.

"You really were the answer to our prayers," Mimi says.

"No, you were the answer to mine. And I didn't even know I made them."

Mimi laughs through her tears.

Sophie waits for Virginia to motion her over.

"You're a heart, Sophie," says Virginia, taking her hands. "Hearts need love and care. You have far surpassed anything that was expected of you. When you're ready, go home and get well."

Sophie doesn't answer but wraps her arms around Virginia and cries on her shoulder.

Estelle is the last to stand before Virginia. The women hold each other for a long time.

"It's not good-bye," says Virginia. "I'll see you after the liberation."

Estelle nods, but her smile soon contorts into a sob, and Virginia again pulls her into an embrace.

But they can't stay out here all night, not with the danger so acute. With reluctance, the women and the boy climb on their bicycles and ride away from Virginia, disappearing into the night like spent stars.

Chapter 27

VIRGINIA'S DECISION TO travel alone to Chambon may have been foolish. The Cosne station is infested with Nazis. If the Milice arrive, she's in trouble.

All rail travel in the region had been suspended for days because of sabotage repairs. With warnings from HQ about increased raids and roundups of suspected Resistance members in the region, Virginia insisted her people stay away from her. After nearly a week of agonizing, self-imposed isolation, she's finally able to proceed, as trains are again operational.

Virginia had told HQ her travel times and changes so the RAF bombers wouldn't target her train, but when she arrives, the engine and times have been switched because of repairs. There's nothing to be done.

Seated at the wall with her two suitcases at her feet, blue shawl covering her hair, she watches and waits. There are considerable delays—it's a miracle there are rails left to ride—and she has been here for two long, hot, frightening hours. She watches the crowd with an eagle eye, aware of every person in the space, including the mustached man from the bus to Fresnes. The moment he entered the station, she remembered exactly where she first saw him. He was the man in the dinghy who took the weapons from the boy's wagon. Though one would assume the man is a resistor, she's unsettled by his presence. She'll need to get word to Mimi to watch out for him.

The man reads his newspaper with great production, like he wants her to think he doesn't see her. While it is standard to pretend not to know other resistors in public, she questions the coincidence of seeing him here again when she travels. Also, she knows by now how accurate her radar is for betrayers.

Will the train ever arrive?

In the small crowd entering the station doors, a young woman in a worn, pine-green dress stands out. She has large eyes, a dark braid, and full lips—a face of innocence that makes her look like an oversize doll. After she buys her ticket, she looks for a place to wait. Her eyes dart this way and that, and her forehead is creased with worry. Virginia thinks she must not be from Cosne, because she appears lost and frightened. Also, her clothing is even more provincial than that which is found here. The woman scans the crowd until her eyes find Virginia. She gasps with a quick laugh and moves quickly, taking the seat next to Virginia, knocking the wireless suitcase in the process.

"La Madone?" the woman says, breathless.

Virginia flinches.

"Diane?" the woman says. "Is it really you?"

Without looking at her, Virginia whispers, "How do you know me?"

"Simon sent me to find out when you were coming back to help us, but I wasn't getting anywhere. I thought the trip was wasted, but here you are. A miracle. La Madone!"

"Stop calling me that."

"I'm sorry. I'm so thrilled to see you. Are you coming to us?"

"I am. Trying, anyway. But the train."

"Yes. Delayed. I'm so happy I can travel with you."

Virginia can't believe her change in luck. She really shouldn't have embarked alone, but here is her own little miracle, a native Frenchwoman who can speak for her at the checkpoints.

"You're actually a great help to me," says Virginia. "My accent . . ."

"Oh, I know. Simon said how bad it was."

Virginia gives the young woman a stern look. The woman smiles sheepishly and shrugs her shoulders.

"I'm Danielle Le Forestier."

"The doctor?"

"No, I'm his wife. But I assist Roger where I can. When I'm not taking care of our two little sons, and our guest, that is."

Virginia no longer wants to speak with this woman. She keeps her lips pursed and continues to watch the travelers. When she notices that the mustached man no longer sits reading his newspaper, she looks at the doors. He walks out to the street, heading to where two Milice stand.

"Trouble," says Virginia.

The stationmaster is before them.

"Follow me. Now," he says.

Virginia knows this man is an ally. She stands and lifts her suitcases. Danielle offers to take one. Virginia passes her the suitcase with her personal belongings, keeping the wireless to herself. They walk in a hurry past the counter, down a poorly lit hallway, and to a room with a window facing the tracks. He closes the door behind them.

"There's been a roundup. A large one in this region. They're being taken to Vichy for interrogation."

He points down the track about a hundred yards to where the Milice unload a bus to a railcar, men and women tied to one another by ropes, stumbling as they try to navigate down and up steps.

Virginia rushes to the window, squinting her eyes, struggling to make out the faces, trying to convince herself that her people would have gotten word and hidden.

"Now, over there, do you see the man with the orange scarf around his neck?" he says, pointing about twenty yards from the station to a different track.

"Yes," says Virginia, forcing herself to pay attention even as she keeps scanning the line.

"When he puts that scarf in his pocket, leave through the back door at the end of the hallway, and meet him on the platform. When your train arrives, he'll see you get on safely."

"Will we be on the same train as the prisoners?"

"No. The boches commandeered that train. And yours was switched and held up because of line repairs."

"Do you know any of the captives?" she says.

"Not yet. I just got word. When I saw you, I knew you needed to leave immediately."

"Are we in danger?" says Danielle.

The man looks from Danielle to Virginia and departs in silence.

Virginia continues to try to see the prisoners' faces, but they're too far. The bus pulls away, and the train door is locked. She finds herself praying for her friends.

The sound of a commotion in the waiting area reaches them in the room. Virginia locks the door and pulls a wire from her pocket, passing it to Danielle.

"What's this?"

"A garrote. It looks like a shoelace. But if you wrap this around a neck, it will suffocate a man, even cutting through to the trachea if you pull hard enough. I have two."

Danielle's face contorts with revulsion. She pushes it away.

"No!"

"We might need to defend ourselves," says Virginia.

"I would never kill a man."

"It's war, Danielle."

Danielle stares at Virginia a moment, then nods her head. "So, you don't know about us villagers of Chambon?"

"Don't know what?"

"We're pacifists."

"What?"

"Our pastor, André Trocmé, says we're never to fight with guns and knives and dirty tricks. We fight the war with the weapons of the spirit."

"Are you joking?" Virginia says.

"I couldn't be more serious. Pastor Trocmé just got out of hiding and returned to us. He isn't happy about the growing numbers of the Maquis. Especially because some of the refugee boys have left the villagers who've sheltered them to join the Secret Army."

It's not the fists alone that win the fight.

"If you're a pacifist, why are you working with Simon to find me?" Virginia says.

"Well, I may be a pacifist myself, but my husband isn't. And I'm not a fool."

THE FOLLOWING MOMENTS are to Virginia like flashes from a camera.

The orange scarf in the pocket.

The swift boarding of the train.

The orange scarf shoved in her own pocket as she passes the engineer.

The Milice spilling out of the station as her train pulls away.

The mustached man scanning the windows, looking for the women.

Pulling back so they can't be seen.

Reaching in her pocket to touch her garrote for comfort.

Fingers touching the orange scarf.

Feeling the slip of paper folded in it.

Pulling it out and reading it.

MIMI ARRESTED.

Reading the words in Estelle's handwriting several times before they make sense.

Eating the paper.

Feeling it tear apart in her teeth and her saliva, scratching her throat as it slides down into the bile of her belly.

Pressing her face to the window as they pass the cattle car, eyes searching until she finds her.

Mimi.

The women locking eyes.

Mimi crying, her face bruised.

Virginia standing, pushing out of her car while people shout at her, Danielle begging her to sit.

Stepping out on the gangway, struggling to stay upright as the train gathers speed, leaving Mimi's train behind.

Fighting the urge to throw herself from the train.

Stumbling back to the car, numb.

Willing the ice to return to her heart.

Feeling it pump hot and fast in spite of her.

The train stopping in the middle of a field, travelers urged to get off and take cover because of the coming bombers.

Virginia staying on the train while Danielle and the passengers rush out, shrieking.

As bombers roar over, standing, clutching the ceiling bar, allowing her rage and despair to erupt.

Screaming.

With every engine that tears over, with every bomb that falls. Again and again.

Screaming.

WAR IS BLACK: blood on dirt, char on buildings, fuel puddles, rising smoke. After reading the paper, after watching the bombing, Virginia feels as if all the war black implodes into her heart, incinerating it, turning it to ash. In the absence of heart, the brain can take over.

Virginia cannot turn back, neither literally nor figuratively. The only way through is forward. She has beaten her own life expectancy in the field, so she will no longer count the days and the weeks. From this moment on, time will cease until the war is over.

Cold though it is, she forces herself to tuck the men, women, and children of Cosne away in a file folder in her mind. If she's to continue on, there's no other way. She imagines stamping MIA on the folder, closing it, and handing it to Vera.

PART THREE

La Madone

Chapter 28

AFTER MIMI'S ARREST, and the endless journey that miraculously continues to Chambon, Virginia is half out of her mind and desperate to be alone. She parts ways with Danielle, and is again met by Edmund, the one who looks like a young Jimmy Stewart.

She can't deny the fact that she resents these new people, these new faces, the new world she's supposed to inhabit. She wants her old world back. She wants to spend the rest of this war figuring out how to rescue Mimi and Louis and every other friend she's lost.

With every step she takes, she feels her blood pressure rising. Edmund gives her worried glances as she curses in the dark, and by the time they arrive at Simon's house, her temper explodes.

"I told you to find me at least two safe houses," she shouts. "Why am I here?"

"I didn't know if and when you were coming back," says Simon.

"I gave you my word," says Virginia.

"That means nothing to me. We waited. You didn't come. Like we've waited for years without anyone coming."

"I gave you one hundred fifty thousand francs. Did that mean nothing? What the hell did you do with it?"

Edmund steps forward. "I have an accounting of every franc spent. Food, supplies, fuel, medical."

Virginia snatches the paper, reading over the sloppy, boyish handwriting.

"We're happy to have you stay here at our farm," says Dolmazon.

"It's no trouble," says Simon.

"No trouble to have the head of the Maquis and the head of the Resistance circuit in one house? Why not gather all the section leaders and agents you can round up to make it easier for the bastards to grab us in one swoop?"

She crumples the paper in a ball, throws it on the floor, and strides to the window to look out into the twilight. Shadows grow. Tall trees loom. The silhouette of the mountains is new to her yet somehow familiar. Like the Pyrenees, this mountain place feels inhospitable. The air inside the house is choking her.

She thinks of her panic while following Mimi and her son to the forest the first day she met them. If only she had the boy's small hands to steady her. Is he at Estelle's now? Estelle's cousin's farm? With the nuns? Will Mimi survive, or will another child lose another parent in this godforsaken war?

Mimi, oh God.

Virginia pushes out the door, slamming it behind her, and stumbles toward the blackness. Even though it scares her, even though she doesn't know this place or these people, she walks toward it. Someone follows— Edmund, she thinks—but she holds up her hand to wave him away.

"A moment," she says.

She stumbles around a stone outbuilding to a barn and leans against the side of it, staring at the stars, struggling to catch her breath. She pulls off her phony glasses, tears off her shawl, and loosens her top buttons before she continues on toward the black forest. Her breath comes quick and shallow, and she feels so dizzy she staggers. A dead tree breaks her fall. She leans against it and again looks to the sky. The moon is a sliver above like it was the night of her escape from France.

"Los Pirineos."

The voice of the Spanish guide who led her is loud enough that it's in her ear.

Flashes like photographs come to her of the climb, of her bloody leg stump, of the frostbite beginning in the toes of her good foot, of the trouble breathing in the thin, thin air. Of opening her eyes on the other side only to have a gun pointed at her face. She shakes her head to clear the vision, but when she opens her eyes, there's still a gun pointed at her face.

It's a German Luger.

"You have three seconds to tell me who you are before I put a bullet through your forehead," he says in his raspy voice.

The words are uttered lightly, almost as if he's joking, though she's quite sure he isn't. In spite of the provenance of the gun, he's a Frenchman. For a brief, savage moment, she thinks, *Do it. End me.* But her survival instinct isn't obedient to her exhaustion.

"La Madone," she says.

She wants to take back the words the moment they fall from her lips.

The man's teeth flash white in the night, and he spins the Luger—cowboy-style—around his finger and slips it into his belt.

"Finally," he says. "It's a good thing you spoke quickly. Otherwise, I'd be in a fresh grave for killing you. Do you know how long we've been waiting for you? Follow me."

He starts walking to the forest, but she calls to him to stop.

"Wait, who are you? And why should I trust you?"

He turns back around to face her, grinning. With his dimpled chin, he has a face like a young Cary Grant.

"My apologies," he says. "I'm a Maquis commander. Code Name Bob."

"Don't you need to tell Simon where we're going?" she says.

"What is he, my mother?"

She laughs. It surprises her, the way laughter does in these circumstances. It makes her feel sane.

"Come," says Bob. "If he gets upset, I'll tell him you had to use the outhouse for a good, long while."

She puts on her glasses and gives him a reproving look but falls into step with him.

"I see you're a clown," she says.

"If you don't have your sense of humor in situations like this, you've got nothing."

"Wise words from one so young."

"I'm very old under this twenty-four-year-old skin. At least as old as the disguise you're wearing."

She doesn't reply, but follows him through deep forest paths, their boots crushing the pine, bringing the sweet, earthy smell to their noses. Up and down the rocky outcroppings they climb. He never slows his pace but simply, silently offers his arm to help her along twisted paths, his rough hands to help her up and down boulders. The last bit of path is steep, and he reaches back for her hand again, still holding it as she reaches the top. She gasps when she sees the sight below them.

Here, nestled in this rugged mountain forest, under an extraordinary night sky, is a perfect patchwork quilt of fields. Beautiful, soft, hidden, protected drop fields. The moon wanes, but Virginia can imagine what this will look like once it's full. The whole placid scene before her soothes her nerves and clears her head.

"Will these do for drops?" Bob says.

She nods.

"I'm sorry we didn't find you a place to sleep," he says. "But we had other priorities. We've never had a drop. We have nothing. It makes us single-minded."

"No, I understand. You've done well."

Though she could stand here all night under the stars, in the pines, breathing the sweet air, she knows she should get back to the others. She motions her head for him to lead but can't stop looking back over her shoulder. It's hard to believe such peace and serenity still exist in the world.

Chapter 29

I'S STRANGE SLIPPING into another new life. New safe houses. New terrain. New code phrases. New contacts. Since Virginia's arrival she hasn't seen Danielle Le Forestier. The little life she made with Estelle and Mimi is utterly gone. The life she had with the Lopinats could be a century ago. Everything before that feels like a dream.

She's already learning the rhythms of Chambon, the days anchored around the sound of the little engine that puffs up the mountain, arriving in the evening, when the light makes shadows of the travelers ushered off and hurried to the Hôtel May. The night that makes ghosts of them, while they're whisked away to haunt the cellars and barns and rooms of the farmers' modest dwellings.

To always remember her friend, Virginia wears the orange scarf that brought her news of Mimi's capture around her neck. It feels like hands squeezing her throat, but it's a good reminder of how near to danger she always is. And it is dangerous. Though she hasn't seen MP Haas since her arrival, he could still be in the hospital. In addition to that, the rutted roads are well traveled by Nazi lorries shuttling the wounded up the mountain and transporting the healed back down to return to the fighting. It's dizzying watching the flap of swastikas on the same streets where Jewish children from all over Europe, with forged Protestant identity papers, walk to and from boarding schools and day schools and scouting excursions, their only outward protection the little French Christian songs they've been taught. If she thinks about it too much, if she watches it too closely, it makes it hard for her to breathe. So, she looks away and tends to the things that she came here to do.

Edmund has found Virginia much-needed lodgings away from Simon. Aside from their incompatible personalities, as commanders and leaders, Virginia and Simon shouldn't stay together. The house where she'll reside until Edmund can find her a place of her own belongs to his cousin Léa. As they walk the long dirt driveway, seeing her limp, Edmund offers to take a suitcase. She gives him her clothing valise.

"Léa's husband is a German prisoner of war," says Edmund. "She looks after the farm and their two young children."

Virginia stops walking.

"Must every safe house have children?" she says.

"I'm afraid so. Aside from villager children, every home in the region has at least one copy of the Old Testament, if you know what I mean."

At least one Jewish child in every house.

Extraordinary.

Her observations support Edmund's assertion. Children are everywhere. In town, out of town. In fields, forests, and shops. In lines behind elderly men and women, proceeding along the streets.

"We teach them Christian prayers and take them to Temple Protestant for show, but they keep their holidays in secret. We only wish to protect them, not to erase their heritage."

"It's miraculous what you all do here," she says.

"It's what God asks of us. There's no other way."

If only that were true for the whole world, they would never have gotten to this. There is so much darkness, but seeing this living, breathing, thriving antidote to inhumanity is restoring her faith. They resume their walk, and Edmund continues educating her on her new contacts.

"I picked this safe house because it's centrally located and, more important, the maquisard staying here will be respectful of you, and help you in any way you need it."

"That's a relief."

Simon's open disdain for her, as a woman, and his general skepticism, are tiresome, and she's only been here a week. He has a military background and bristled when she told him how to divide up the boys for training. He told her plainly he doesn't believe she'll ever be able to get them weapons in this mountain region. She was so frustrated with him the last time they spoke that she said he didn't deserve them anyway.

"With me, Bob, and the man I'm about to introduce you to," says Edmund, "you'll have a core team. We can go between you, Simon, and the other Maquis forces, so you don't have to put up with them."

"They're going to need to swallow their pride and learn how to work with me."

He gives her a look that shows he doesn't know if that will ever happen.

"You'll like Léa," says Edmund, changing the subject. "She's housed countless refugees and Maquis. With the little food we have, she's a creative cook. She never asks questions, and her only rules are that no guns or swearing are allowed inside her house."

"No swearing?" Virginia says. "I don't know about this."

"I know it will be hard for you, but please, think of the children."

Remembering her profanity-laced arrival, she gives Edmund a grin. He blushes. Seeing the color in his large ears—his sweet, simple innocence—makes her affection rise. In the short time she's known him, he's already becoming dear to her, like a little brother to tease and boss. She finds that she's more at ease interacting with and recruiting young men for her network. The fact that they are single and unattached makes them good soldiers, though they are startlingly young. Most of the Maquis here are under twenty years of age, on the run since they turned seventeen, the age the Nazis conscript for compulsory work service. She's trying to keep all the boys straight in her mind by imagining the Hollywood actors who could play them in movies.

Like Cosne, her objective is to arm the Maquis so they can protect the region and conduct sabotage. Unlike Cosne, D-Day has already come, so as soon as she gets the weapons in their hands, they can get to work. There are greater numbers of Maquis in hiding here; they've been pushed to this remote location at the end of the line. Because it will take a while for the Allied forces to make it this far, these fighters might even be able to liberate the region themselves, including the city of Le Puy. It's the largest city nearby with a Nazi garrison.

Around a turn, the small stone house appears. Tidy barns fan out from it. Wildflowers wave in welcome along the walkways. Hens peck around the yard. In the distance, a woman urges a goat herd into their pen, while a young man rides a little boy on his shoulders like an airplane, a small girl laughing and chasing behind them. When the young man catches sight of Edmund, he calls out to him, places the boy on the ground, and he and the children come to greet them. The woman watches with her hand shielding her eyes from the sun as the children jump into Cousin Edmund's arms. When he puts them down, they stare at Virginia only for a moment before their mother calls them back to her.

Smart woman, Virginia thinks.

"Bonjour," says Edmund. "I have someone I know you'd like to meet."

"Diane?" the young man says.

He's soft-spoken and has heavily lashed, dark eyes. He looks like a very young Laurence Olivier.

"What a relief not to be called la Madone," she says.

"Edmund mentioned you don't like that name."

"Boys who can take orders—how refreshing."

He extends his hand. "Code name Dédé."

"Ah, and one smart enough to use a code name," she says, giving Edmund a stern look. "Good to meet you, Dédé."

"Dédé heads a Maquis group," says Edmund. "He used to be a *passeur*, but we need him here now."

"A passeur?"

"A guide. For the Old Testaments who need to be shelved in other places."

"I understand," says Virginia. "That's hard, brave work."

Dédé lowers his eyes.

"Dédé lives with my cousin," Edmund continues. "He helps around the farm when he isn't busy with us."

"So, you never sleep, either?" says Virginia.

"Never," Dédé says with a grin.

"Dédé can get you anything you need from the village shops," says Edmund. "Everyone loves him."

"Not the boches," says Dédé.

"No," says Edmund. "He may look gentle as a fawn, but he's ferocious as a lion."

"That's exactly what I like to hear," says Virginia.

They walk to the farm, where Edmund's cousin has shooed away her children and waits, regarding Virginia with curiosity. Léa wears a floral apron that looks funny with her farm boots. She has reddish hair parted down the middle, fair skin, and clear eyes.

"Diane," says Virginia, extending her hand.

"Welcome," says Léa. "I have a room for you on the second floor."

"I'm happy to stay in a barn," says Virginia.

"The barns are occupied, I'm afraid," says Léa. "By Dédé and a few others. But don't worry about us. You have other safe houses, yes?"

"We're working on that," says Edmund.

"Work faster," says Léa.

EDMUND LEAVES THEM that afternoon to keep searching for safe houses. The children are sent to bed early. Only Virginia, Léa, and Dédé are left around the dining table.

Virginia is ashamed of how quickly and how much she eats, but Edmund was right: Léa is a wonderful cook. Mushroom soufflé, salad greens drizzled in oil, and a golden liqueur over ice chips that tastes as fresh as the mountain air.

"Verveine du Velay," says Léa, pointing at the drink. "My husband used to get us bottles from Le Puy, until his capture."

"Don't waste anything so precious on me," says Virginia, pushing what's left in the glass toward her hostess. Léa slides it back.

"Not wasted. We don't normally eat like this, but you need strength."

You have no idea, Virginia thinks.

"Are you even allowed to drink?" she asks. "I hear this is a conservative place."

"We all have our little secrets," says Léa with a wink. "And your arrival is a special occasion. We've been waiting so long for you. Now we can celebrate."

"Decide if you want to celebrate me after the job here is done. I tend to leave a path of destruction in my wake."

"Destruction with a purpose," says Dédé. "You've armed and organized the Cosne Maquis, and a scout brought us news of their fine work cutting off transportation and communication lines in their region."

"Do you have news of any individuals? Any casualties or captures?"

"No specifics."

When Léa stands to clear the dishes, Virginia tries to help her.

"No," Léa says. "You two: Go, make plans. Leave the domestics to me. That's an order."

They thank her and head to the barn where Dédé resides. The sky is pink and orange in the fading light, and the air is full of frog song. Inside the barn, a corner has been swept clean. A straw mattress rests on a crudely built platform next to a lantern on an overturned bucket. Dédé closes the door, locks them in, and unearths a map he spreads on a table, holding down each end with a stone. He lights the lantern and hangs it on a hook above them. Virginia appreciates his security measures, and how he gets right to business.

"Simon and the other Maquis leaders in the Haute-Loire are working on setting up central command at the Château de Vaux," Dédé says, pointing to the location on the map. "All of us should eventually convene there. What do your commanders wish for us to accomplish?"

"Sabotage," she says. "Destroying strategic points on the rails, bridges, and tunnels, cutting off Le Puy."

He points to the most strategic places, and she begins to make a mental map to report to HQ. They discuss the need to keep one road from Le Puy open, not only for their men or the Allies to drive into the city, but to trap the Nazis if and when they try to retreat from the garrison there. Once they've selected the route they'll preserve—a road that runs low, with hills on either side that will allow the Maquis to have the high ground—she turns the focus to Chambon.

"In terms of protecting the town," she says, "once the Nazis are on retreat, we'll need to secure Chambon and the surrounding villages outward, ensuring they're swept clean."

"Can we kill any stragglers?"

"That depends. If they're retreating in large groups, no. You and your boys aren't yet armed for battle. But if any linger—especially on an individual level or in small groups—yes. As long as they can be eliminated without a trace. Then they'll simply be thought deserters."

"Can we kill the ones left at the hospital at Chambon?"

I wish, she thinks.

"Not yet," she says. "As they're rehabilitated, they're being transferred out. But once I get word that all the able-bodied Germans have been ordered to the garrison at Le Puy, any Nazis left you may either dispose of or take prisoner."

"Are you under Geneva protection?" he asks. "Because I'm not. Not as a guerilla. Not without a uniform. I don't think you are, either, as a uniformless woman. So, if we aren't protected upon capture, why are they?"

"That'll be for you and your boys to decide. What can you live with?"

"I'll tell you. I have no family left. My father died when I was a child. My mother was shipped out to a work camp as punishment for my Resistance activity. I escaped capture and found my way here. It's my fault she could be dead. The question for me is not if I can live with myself having hurt Nazis, but can I live with myself having not avenged my family and my country?"

She stares at Dédé a long moment. His dark-lashed eyes are black and fierce. He looks older in the shadows cast by the lantern light. She places her hands on the map.

"I can't bring back your mother," she says, "but I'm certain: You'll have your country back."

Chapter 30

I N T H E D R E A M, it's 1934, and her prosthetic leg had finally arrived. She'd held up the seven-pound bundle to the light.

"I'll name him Cuthbert," she'd said, much to the doctor's amusement.

"Dindy is so grateful," Virginia's mother said. "She can hardly wait to try it, once she's fully healed."

Virginia looked up from where the nurse had helped her pull on the sock that would cover her stump. Though there was still a bit of redness and swelling, she wouldn't wait another moment.

"Show me how to attach it," Virginia said to the doctor.

"There's no reason to rush this," said her mother. "You have nothing but time."

"You're wrong. I've lost time. I'm atrophying. I need to get back to work."

"Dear, I don't mean to be vulgar, but you don't have to work another day in your life."

"I *do* need to work," Virginia had said. "If I don't do something of use, I might as well die. I might as well have died in that hospital in Turkey."

Her mother's distress was clear on her furrowed brow and in her pinched mouth. Virginia tried to be gentle. She knew her mother almost lost her, but she couldn't keep her cloistered forever. Virginia passed the prosthetic to the nurse, hopped over to her mother, and knelt before her on the cold tile of the doctor's office. She took her hands.

"Mother, you must try to understand that I'll die without occupation. I have so much to offer—so many skills that I can use in the world. You see how restless I am. Besides, I've already written to the assistant secretary of state asking to be reinstated to a consular position."

Her mother cried out and tried to pull away her hands.

"Mother, please. Try to understand. Daddy would. He would have known that staying here is not what I'm made for."

Her mother succeeded in wresting her hands away from her daughter. Virginia stayed at her feet for a minute more before pulling herself to standing. She hopped back to the chair by the parallel bars and sat.

"Show me," she commanded.

The doctor handed the nurse the belt and averted his eyes while Virginia lifted her skirt to fasten it around her waist. Elastic straps connected to a corset encircling her thigh and attached to the top of the prosthetic. Once the nurse had all the belts connected and adjusted, Virginia pulled herself to standing.

"Mrs. Hall," the doctor said. "Forgive me for saying so, but you must see how important it is for Virginia to get back on the proverbial horse."

Her mother continued to stare out the window with her arms crossed over her chest.

"All right, my dear," the doctor said to Virginia. "Let your weight settle over both legs."

Virginia tried to shift her balance, but she couldn't. Her face flushed with heat. All the excitement, all the money, all the anticipation, and she felt as if she'd be sick. She tried not to look at her mother. What if she was right, and Virginia wasn't ready?

"You don't have to do this now, Virginia," said her mother.

Defiance rose in Virginia. Her mother only used her daughter's full name when she was angry with her. Virginia closed her eyes and tried to make her brain connect to the limb. She imagined nerves reaching out from her spine, down her leg, synapses that had been firing at dead ends in the knee for months suddenly finding something to ignite. She imagined the hollow limb electrified.

"Trust it," said the doctor. "It won't come off, and you can't hurt it. You can only hurt you."

Her heart pounded, her breath was short, her hands sweat on the metal parallel bars. Virginia willed calm, willed trust, and allowed her weight to shift.

Cuthbert held her.

She opened her eyes and looked down at the prosthetic, exhaling with a laugh.

"Do you feel balanced?" asked the doctor.

"I think so," she said, nearly breathless. "I do. Yes."

"Good. Now, holding the bars, flex the foot. Get a sense for how it moves."

It was so difficult to get a feel for something one could not feel. Panic again rose, but reconnecting to the rebellion of her mother's wishes gave Virginia the fuel to overcome it. She commanded her brain to understand what she was asking of it.

"When you're ready, holding the bars, you may try to walk forward."

The parallel bars ran about ten feet in front of her but somehow looked like a mile. She still didn't trust this leg. How could she? There were seventeen inches between what she could feel and the floor.

Brain to knee, knee to foot, foot to floor.

Step.

She allowed Cuthbert to lead, her full leg to follow. One step.

She gasped, elated.

Then she allowed the full leg to lead, Cuthbert to follow. Two.

Virginia stumbled on her third step but caught herself on the bars. The doctor grasped her arm.

"I'm all right," she said. "I feel like a baby, learning to walk again."

Four steps.

Her mother rose and stood at the end, smiling though her tears. Virginia took the last two steps without holding on and fell into her mother's arms.

IN SOME WAYS, it's like she's learning to walk again at each new field assignment. She's had practice and should feel most confident here, at her third stop, but she's plagued by several problems.

First, without news of Mimi and Louis, she feels divided and unable to fully move on from Cosne. She's been to the Hôtel May several times to check for messages from Estelle, but there's been nothing. Of course, Estelle would need to keep away, Virginia tells herself, but every time the train arrives, she can't help but watch for her friend. Virginia doesn't allow herself to imagine that any harm has come to Estelle. If she did, she doesn't know if she'd be able to carry on.

The second, deeply unsettling problem is that she has been seen by MP Haas. He has a room on the second floor of the hospital, where his window overlooks the main street. The bandage is off his left eye, and his puckered skin reveals he's likely blind in it. With his good eye, however, he spotted her while she was on her way out of the Hôtel May. Her shawl covered her head, but he'd still stared. From now on, she'll need to use the hotel's back entrance to stay out of his view.

The final problem has to do with Simon and his Maquis.

Virginia spends most of her time on the bicycle Dédé got for her, riding to and from Simon's Maquis groups in the region to her safe houses. Edmund found the perfect place for her: an old storage building and barn on the outskirts of town that the Salvation Army isn't using. Not only is Virginia able to keep her wireless equipment safely hidden in the barn, but the main building has many rooms, allowing the boys in her core team to stay over on the long planning nights. Virginia is still close enough to Léa for the good woman to bring her dinner, but far enough away from her children to keep them safe.

All day long Virginia rides from barn to town to forest to field, noting drop-site coordinates and Nazi movement and numbers, and trying to get to each Maquis group's commander to schedule training. But some commanders refuse to meet with a woman and, though Simon is the liaison, he often keeps her waiting so long she leaves cursing and unsatisfied. Not only is there unmasked disdain for her, but the political differences of the groups are causing infighting, especially with the communists, who are hated almost as much as the Nazis. There's mounting frustration that, even though Diane is here, there hasn't been a single drop. They've been waiting by their radios each night listening to the BBC for the code phrase *Les marguerites fleuriront ce soir*—the daisies will bloom at night—but there are no daisies in bloom, which means there are no weapons or supplies, which makes them resent her all the more.

Her core group of Bob, Edmund, and Dédé is her saving grace. They understand why planes might be tied up at the moment and how a fuller moon makes for better drops. They keep their boys in check and, because of their respectful meetings with Virginia, have come up with means of passive resistance in which the Maquis can satisfy their need for action without encouraging reprisals. She teaches them straight out of the SOE manual on tactics like transposing labels on mail, switching street signs, and more daring deeds like poking holes in the gas tanks of German trucks and unscrewing vital vehicle parts. These pranks frustrate the Nazis to no end but don't lead to reprisals the way overt resistance does, because they seem natural.

Unfortunately, Simon and some of his peers remain impatient and difficult, which brings out the worst in Virginia. After a particularly grueling day riding the bumpy mountain paths, her leg stump raw, her stomach empty, she heads to Simon and Dolmazon's farm for the nightly meeting. She's running late because her tire blew out on a sharp stone, sending her head over handlebars—shattering the lenses of her phony glasses—and she has to drag her bent bike the rest of the way.

When she walks in the door, the group cringes at her disheveled appearance. Dolmazon places a cup of water on the table, but Virginia doesn't take it. She marches up to Simon until she's close enough that he can smell her.

"Where were your boys?" she says.

"Excuse me?"

"Drop Company Four was supposed to report to Field D for training at fourteen hundred hours, and they never showed up."

He looks at his watch. "Criticism coming when you're an hour late?"

"I fell off my bicycle," she says through gritted teeth.

He takes in her torn skirts, her bloody cuts, and her bruises, seemingly unmoved.

"How can I order them to show up for training when we haven't had a single drop?" he says. "Not one. We have no weapons. The boys are running amok, desperate to ambush the Nazis at the hospital."

"I gave you the okay to allow them acts of passive resistance."

"Passive resistance—bah! That's stuff our grandmothers can do."

He looks her over with contempt and cuts her off when she's about to protest.

"I keep telling the boys, 'Wait until we get a drop,'" he says, "but no drop comes. Not last night, not the night before, the week before, the year before. We have nothing!"

"As if I haven't explained the situation a hundred times," she says. "Any night now the drops can happen. And once they start, they'll all be clustered around the full moon. So, all teams will need to be up to speed on procedure."

"You know I'm dealing with the Lost Boys here. Restless teenagers, half of them, itching for action. It's exhausting trying to keep their behavior in check. I can't police them every second, especially when they're getting nothing from you."

"They'll continue to get nothing if they don't learn how to signal a drop plane."

"Diane," says Dédé, placing his hand on her arm. "My boys are ready.

Bob's are, too. We can rotate back and forth if we have to. We're all willing to lose sleep every night to receive drops."

"I know you're willing, but you need to be fresh," says Virginia. "Once we have the supplies, your teams will be up all night wiring railways. Of course, that's if I can even communicate with headquarters."

"What's that mean?" says Edmund.

"The battery on my wireless is dying. My transmission cut out three times last night, and there's no power source in any of the barns."

Virginia unties the orange scarf at her neck—feels the spike of pain reminding her of Mimi's capture—and uses it to wipe her face. Seeing the old-lady makeup on it when she pulls away, she laughs bitterly.

I'm melting, she thinks. *The Wicked Witch of the West.*

Dédé hands her the glass of water, and she takes it, greedily finishing in one long drink and flinching when she slams it on the table. Her wrist and elbow ache from the fall.

"You need to get these cuts looked at," says Dolmazon.

Virginia waves her away and reties the scarf tightly on her throat.

"You must take care of yourself," says Dolmazon. "Simon, go fetch Dr. Le Forestier."

He gives Dolmazon a look of aggravation, but the reprimand on her face humbles him. Once he leaves, Dolmazon invites them all into the sitting room to wait for the BBC broadcast. The chair Virginia selects faces out toward the room, and she notices an adolescent boy peer down from the upstairs hallway.

A ghost.

"Our son," Dolmazon says, once he disappears. "Hope for the family name when so many of our kind have no more of that hope."

"Are you?"

"Jewish. Yes."

"Yet Simon called me 'La Madone'?"

"France is a Catholic country. La Madone is everywhere, including Marseille, where Simon comes from a prominent family."

Virginia holds up her hands.

"I know," says Dolmazon. "I shouldn't say too much. I only want you to know that if Simon seems a little harsher than you want him to be, you must understand all we've lost. All we have left to lose."

Virginia looks down at her lap, shame creeping in for judging Simon badly. How many people have called her too harsh? And she knows there is nothing she has suffered that can compare to that of the Jewish population of Europe.

"It still doesn't give him an excuse to make your job difficult," Dolmazon continues, "but I only explain so you understand."

"Thank you. That's helpful to know."

Dolmazon nods.

Bob lights a cigarette.

Dédé watches Virginia.

Edmund paces, seemingly working something out in his head. After a few moments, he stops.

"Is your broken bike in the yard?" he asks.

She nods, and he disappears.

In a short time, Simon walks into the room followed by a man of startling good looks. He's tall, and his dark hair is impeccably styled. His silver belt buckle gleams under his white shirt, rolled up at the sleeves and unbuttoned at the collar.

"Roger Le Forestier," he says, kneeling at her feet. "Honored to finally meet you."

Goodness, she thinks. *What a pretty pair the Le Forestiers make.*

"Danielle sends her best," he continues in his deep, smooth voice. "She said you were so brave on the trip."

"Danielle is very kind," Virginia says.

"Let me see your injuries," he says, holding out his hands.

She raises her right arm before him, and he takes it, gently squeezing and moving her joints from her wrist to her elbow to her shoulder. "I don't feel any breaks. Let's get you cleaned up and a little salve on the wounds to keep infection away. I'll leave you with some bandages for that wrist; it took the worst of the fall and you're lucky it didn't snap. You must be made of steel."

Hardly, she thinks.

Dolmazon fetches them water and a towel, and the doctor makes quick work of cleaning and wrapping her cuts.

"I'm afraid I don't have more bandages," he says, "or I'd also wrap that elbow. Try to keep it clean and dry."

"I've ordered ample medical supplies, if this drop ever comes through."

"I'd be most grateful."

When Roger leaves, and Edmund returns from the yard, they all re-settle around the radio.

Please, she thinks. *Let tonight be the night.*

She's exhausted by all the bickering, and the tension feels as terrible as it did in Cosne leading up to D-Day.

At the end of the broadcast, the personal messages are read, but there are no daisies in bloom. There will be no drop tonight.

Chapter 31

WHILE VIRGINIA STANDS arguing with Simon about his unruly Maquis, the door bursts open. Bob draws his gun and points it at the man with flashing eyes and a red face. It's Roger Le Forestier, and he looks utterly different from the way he did at their first meeting. He charges up to them.

"What is it, man?" says Simon, grasping Roger's arms.

Roger shakes off Simon's grip.

"You tell your roving band of terrorist pirates, I want that car back and I want it by nightfall, or I will personally report them to the Milice."

"What are you saying?"

"Your Maquis," he says, spitting the word, pointing his finger into Simon's chest, "told me to give them my car. The one I use for doctor visits from here to Le Puy. The one the Salvation Army needs for transport. When I refused, the asses pointed a gun at me and told me they'd shoot if I didn't hand it over. I put my hands up, one of them grabbed my keys, and they took the car. The car that was running on empty as it was!"

Simon utters a curse under his breath.

"Which ones?" says Dédé.

"Do you need to ask?" says Roger.

Virginia knows the group of which he speaks. There are three of them who've managed to find old guns, who strut around town like roosters, constantly having to be told to put their weapons away. The only thing keeping the Nazis at the hotel from pouncing are their infirmities, and the fact that most of the ones left are as young as the Maquis of the region. All except the one in the window.

Virginia gives Bob a long look. He nods at her and leaves them.

"I slave over them," Roger continues. "All hours of the day and night for no pay. These ridiculous boys who think they're men, stabbing their fingers with their stupid knife games, breaking limbs, endless infections."

"I'm sorry, Roger," says Simon. "Sometimes I feel like the father of hundreds of orphans more than a military leader."

"That isn't good enough. These boys are feral, and that makes them dangerous. We're so close, Simon. Don't let them jeopardize the fragile safety we have on the mountain."

"They'll be disciplined severely for this."

"Make sure that discipline doesn't require medical care, because I'm done with them."

Roger slams the barn door, leaving them in silence. Virginia doesn't look at Simon. She could see something like this coming. Anyone with eyes could. While Simon paces, Edmund touches Virginia's arm.

"Come," he says.

He leads her to the barn stall.

"This has nothing to do with that," Edmund says, "but I have the answer to your battery problem solved. Voilà!"

He pulls a tarp off a contraption. She's able to make out pieces of her broken bicycle, wood, and wires. When she sees it's all connected to her wireless, her face flushes.

"Why did you touch that?" she says.

"Don't get mad," he says, holding up his hands. "Just watch."

He hurries around to a stool, flips a few switches on her equipment, and uses his hands to work the bicycle pedals. In a moment, the light on the battery flickers to life.

"A generator," he says. "Now we don't need a new battery or a power source."

She exhales with a smile.

"Are you proud of me?" he asks.

"Yes, Edmund, I'm very proud of you. And grateful."

Their mutual enjoyment doesn't last long before the barn door again slams open. Three pimply, dirty, terrified young Maquis walk in with their hands in the air, followed by Bob, pointing his Luger at the head of the last one.

"On your knees," Bob says.

The boys obey, hands shaking.

"Do you know what we do to those who break our laws?" says Simon.

"We kill them," says Bob.

"We are technically not recognized yet as military," says Simon, "so we operate under our own rules. Those who disregard them will find the sword falls swift. Do you need to be reminded we are not anarchists?"

They shake their heads in the negative.

"Today, you boys will dig three graves," says Bob. "If the car isn't returned with a full tank of petrol by the time the sun sets, your bodies will be in them."

Virginia is glad to see this show of power. This is exactly the kind of discipline they need to keep order.

"Sir," says the one with red hair, "where are we to find petrol?"

"That isn't my problem," says Bob.

"And it better not be stolen from another of our allies," says Simon.

"But the only ones who have it are the boches," the redhead says.

"Good," says Bob. "Let them kill you for theft. Better your blood on their hands than mine."

ON THE WAY to Simon and Dolmazon's that evening, Virginia and her core team take the road by the Le Forestiers' place. The car is back in the driveway, so clean it shines in the light spilling out of the window, where they can see the family gathered for dinner. Danielle leans down to place a platter on the table where her two little boys sit with another child—a girl, maybe seven or eight years old. She reminds Virginia of her niece, Lorna. The family chatters like it's any other night, like they aren't sheltering a displaced Jewish orphan in wartime. As Danielle walks to the window to pull the drapes closed, Roger intercepts her, runs his hand down her braid, and kisses the side of her neck.

Uncomfortable witnessing the Le Forestiers' intimacy, Virginia resumes their walk.

"I didn't think the Maquis would be able to get the petrol," says Virginia.

Bob takes a long drag of his cigarette before dropping it to the ground and crushing it with his boot.

"I knew they could," he says. "You know the one with the red hair? The one who said only the boches had petrol?"

"Yes."

"We suspect he's an informer."

Virginia stops walking.

"Why don't you kill him now?"

"We're using him for the time being," says Dédé. "Giving him false leads to tell the boches. We'll dispose of him when we no longer need his services."

"I look forward to it," says Bob.

As the group resumes walking and crests the hill on the final climb to Simon's place, the sight of the moon is arresting. Though not quite full, it's enormous. It appears close enough to touch. The evening sky is clear and, though a strong wind blows, conditions are as favorable as they'll ever be.

Without a word, the group picks up their pace. They don't have to hear the phrase over the BBC to know the daisies will bloom tonight.

"I CAN'T BELIEVE it's happening," says Simon.

His face is ecstatic as he looks to the heavens, the moon lighting up his eyes.

Nestled between mountains and forests, the fields lay waiting in the glorious, shimmering, sweet summer night. Virginia has never seen such beauty. It makes her feel humbled and awed.

Her team waits: Simon and Dolmazon, Bob, Edmund, and Dédé and his boys, thirty well-disciplined, hardworking, fresh, eager young men. Their exemplary progress in training has led to their reward as the first drop team.

"It's like a dream," whispers Dolmazon.

Simon touches Virginia's arm.

"I'm sorry," he says. "For all the doubt. For all the trouble."

"Thank you," she says. "I understand. And I'm sorry for my sharp tongue."

He gives her a small smile before looking back at the sky.

Earlier that night in the broadcast, after the announcer gave the phrase, he repeated it two more times, alerting Virginia to the fact that they could expect not one plane of containers, but three. She's glad she had more holes dug on the field periphery. They'd used the exercise as discipline for the more unruly Maquis, but it turns out the holes will be needed.

When the droning sound starts and the shadows of the planes can be seen in the distance, she hushes all their happy whispers and instructs them to take their positions. She flashes the agreed-upon Morse letter signal R to the anonymous pilot, and soon the parachutes begin to drop. One after another. Dozens of them, dancing toward the ground. As the containers land with thuds on the earth, the group is careful to avoid getting smashed. She blows a kiss to the planes as they fly away, their dear shadows crossing the moon.

Chapter 32

THE EMPTY SHELVES of the weapons depot are now full. Machine guns. Ammo. Anti-tank grenades. Hand grenades that explode on impact—no need to pull a pin. Caltrops: spikes to throw on the road to pop German tires and make sitting ducks of them for ambush. Liberator pistols: One shot, kill the German, take his weapon. Manuals, in French, on everything from explosives wiring, to communications cutting, to hand-to-hand combat.

She looks at Dédé with skepticism when he introduces her to the sweet-faced kid he's installed as depot guard, gun nearly as tall as he is. When they leave the boy to his duty, Dédé chastises Virginia in his quiet way.

"You know as well as I do that looks can be deceiving," he says, eyes touching her leg and rising back to her face.

"Touché," she says.

Dédé knows about her hunting accident and Cuthbert. She had to tell him because she needed new screws to replace those that were rusting and wearing on her foot hinge. He'd been so awed—his admiration so much greater for her—she decided to take Bob and Edmund into her confidence. As she'd hoped, it proved to strengthen their bond. She's fascinated and thankful that what she used to take such pains to hide—that kept her from acceptance in the US Foreign Service and from intimate relationships, and that brings her an element of shame for exposing weakness—deepens their esteem for her.

She hasn't discussed her disguise with them, though her core group seems to understand she isn't an old woman. The gray dye is beginning to fade, and traces of her auburn hair are beginning to show at the roots. She knows she should add more gray, but she has no time. She's rarely alone and, if she is, she uses that time to sleep.

In the drop, Vera got a parcel through to her. In it were two women's field uniforms—one with trousers, one a skirt—in her size. Vera writes:

When the time comes, this is your armor. Geneva, etc.

Also, tied with a bow, was a shining new S-Phone. It will make field-to-plane communication a breeze, and she can use it to properly thank these brave pilots for their dangerous work. Finally, she was relieved to see the coded message telling her Sophie was making her escape. After the roundups, Sophie got word to HQ through a pianist and disappeared into Spain. Virginia dearly hopes Sophie makes it safely back to London.

Back at the Salvation Army house, Dolmazon works with the boys to fill the shelves with food, vitamins, clothing, and boots. A pile of parachutes is folded in the corner. On the drop night, when the Maquis began to bury them, Dolmazon insisted they stop. "I can use it all," she'd said. Now they were just taking up room. Dangerously so.

"A miracle," says Dolmazon, motioning to the supplies.

"No, simply a coordinated Allied effort," says Virginia.

"You're too modest. This is overwhelming."

"Perhaps you'd be less overwhelmed if you allowed the boys to bury the parachutes. It isn't safe having them here. If the wrong eyes see them, we'll have a situation."

"Don't worry," Dolmazon says. "Simon has a group who will take them to our farm tonight. I have a place to hide them."

"What are you using them for?"

Dolmazon smiles at her but doesn't answer.

THE LE FORESTIERS arrive in their car, draped in the Red Cross flag for protection. Virginia helps Danielle and Roger load it up with medical supplies: bandages, antiseptics, aspirin, thermometers, uppers, downers, and L pills.

"You keep this," Roger says, tossing her the bottle of cyanide. "I took an oath."

"I did, too," she says. "To myself. But I'll give it to Bob. If the Maquis don't want the pills, I'm sure he can put them to good use."

Roger laughs, and they continue the work, which lasts an hour and leaves them all hungry and tired. Happy with the return of his car, Roger never again brought up his outburst, and has disregarded his proclamation not to help the Maquis. When they finish loading the car, Danielle asks Virginia to come for dinner.

"You're very kind," Virginia says.

The little girl at the Le Forestiers' house who reminds Virginia of her niece comes to mind. It has been so long since Virginia has seen Lorna; will she even recognize "Aunt Dindy" when they're reunited? She thinks of how nice it would be to share a family meal around a dining table. But no, she must refuse.

"I'm sorry," Virginia says. "It still isn't safe."

Danielle sighs as Roger wraps his arm around his wife.

"Soon," he says. "Now that the boys are armed, the end is coming."

"I pray you're right," Danielle says.

The sudden sound of the cadence of shoes on cobblestones puts them on alert. They hurry around the car to where there's a good view of the street, where lines of children march like little soldiers. Small, tall, young, adolescent—rows and rows of them flow like rivers from the town out to the field that leads to the forest, singing, "Alouette, gentille alouette," all the way.

"What are they doing?" Virginia asks.

"We must have gotten a warning call," says Roger. "When the Nazis or the Milice go out on patrol, we have a system of telephone calls from village to village."

"The children are told it's time to pick mushrooms in the forest so they don't panic," says Danielle.

"Do they need armed guards?" asks Virginia.

"Already covered," says Roger. "See?"

Only because he pointed out the movement at the forest edge can she make out the camouflaged forms of the Maquis. They flank the forest border, looking like Boy Scouts out for a bit of exercise. Boy Scouts who know how to disarm, kill, and gut anyone who tries to harm the children, that is.

The Le Forestiers leave, but Virginia is unable to carry on as if nothing is happening. After watching the last of the children slip into the woods—their sweet voices fading away—she feels a terrible sense of unease. And soon, as warned, a truck of Milice patrols the village, slowly snaking through the streets, looking into doorways and windows. She stalks them, keeping watch until they finish their route. Only when the black Citroen grows smaller as it drives away from Chambon can Virginia breathe better, but the anxiety remains.

As she starts back for her safe house, she scans the side roads and buildings, turning on her route to avoid the Nazi hospital, swastika flag snapping in the wind. From behind the edge of the Hôtel May, she peers up at the second-floor window, and sees the pale face of the MP, his one-eyed gaze sweeping back and forth along the street like a searchlight.

Before he spots her, she ducks into an alley.

IT'S THEIR THIRD reception night in a row, and they're all sharing the handle of Beefeater gin Vera slipped in on the last drop. Virginia's grateful for it. She can't get the lingering unease of seeing the children herded like lambs to the forest out of her head, nor can she stop thinking of the MP in the window. Does Haas remember and recognize her? Though she's disguised, she can't change her bone structure or hide the limp.

"I wish we'd been in Lyon at the same time," Bob says, nudging her, pulling her from her thoughts. "We'd have raised hell together."

"What ended your mission there?" asks a maquisard.

"A car accident," Bob says. "Driving with no lights on sometimes leads to trouble."

"No surprise there," says Edmund.

The group shares a laugh. Bob loves to drive at breakneck speed in the dark, and he's terrible at it. The Maquis have succeeded in repairing and filling the tank of a small truck, and Virginia is trying to teach the boys to drive. But without much time—and her having so little patience—she often takes over the driving herself, especially with Bob.

"I wasn't driving," says Bob. "I didn't know how to at the time."

"So, no different from now," says Virginia.

The boys laugh. Bob ignores the jab.

"We were racing to a drop and hit a tree. I was knocked unconscious and taken to the hospital. It would have been all right if it weren't for those pesky guns the gendarme found on us."

"Oh my," says Virginia.

"Yes. From civilian hospital to prison hospital we went."

"How'd you get out of that?" asks Dédé.

"A cleaning woman. The boches had killed her son, so she helped me. She got me a rope and a cake we drugged that I shared with my guards. Once they were out, so was I."

"With a head injury?" says Virginia.

"Yes. I passed out a few times, but luckily it was in the forest, so I didn't wake up in any unwanted beds. Not that night, anyway."

Bawdy laughter titters among them.

Since the drops have started, the atmosphere has changed. The boys at large are behaving more respectfully toward her, and now that they're busy, they cause less trouble. There's the tension of anticipation of the coming sabotage and ambush missions, but it's laced with excitement. Now that the fires of her temper have been dulled, however, in the absence of blazing fury, she finds an undercurrent of sadness that some-

times threatens to pull her under. Attempting to distract herself, Virginia
continues the conversation.

"How'd you get out of France, after that?" she asks. He once made a
vague reference to being trained by the Intelligence Service in London at
some point but didn't elaborate.

"Out of France?" says Bob. "I never left France after I was dropped. I
hid and hiked my way to the Haute-Loire, where I joined these fine boys
of the Maquis. I've been here ever since."

He never left France after he was dropped, she thinks. *Yet I could.*

"What about you?" Bob says. "How did it end for you in Lyon?"

Sober, Virginia stands.

"Enough," she says. "We're going to be late."

THE DROP GOES well, the boys are efficient, and the whole operation
is over in less than an hour. Still, the sadness that has crept in lingers, and
Virginia is desperate for a good stretch of sleep before sabotage begins.
Before she leaves the boys, Bob hurries over to her with a letter marked
"Diane." She thanks him, and bicycles to her safe house.

Once Virginia puts on her nightgown and takes off her prosthetic, she
hops to bed with the letter. Though the address has been thoroughly blocked
out, she'd recognize her mother's Box Horn Farm stationery anywhere.

In the candlelight, through her tears, it's hard to read, but she savors
the words—the quality of which she has never received from her mother
until this night. How could her mother have known how desperately she
needed them?

Dearest Dindy,

I don't know where in the world you are, though I have an idea,
and that idea terrifies me. You're my only daughter. The one I
tried to restrain in bows and white dresses, whose knees were

always more bruised than her brother's. You are my rugged adventurer. Pirate, hunter, sailor, soldier. Yet also—somehow— scholar, linguist, actress, beauty. Lorna found the childhood picture of you with Daddy and your brother. It's the one with Daddy reading Robinson Crusoe *to you both but—while John sits politely paying attention—you straddle the arm of the chair like it's your horse, your face blurry because you couldn't sit still. It made me laugh to see it. I felt foolish for how that picture— that girl—used to vex me. How silly of me to try to tame you. How wrong.*

You are perfectly you, and I wouldn't change you for the world. For the world needs you, just as you are.

I pray every day that you come home to me when this war is over. Either way, I know I speak for your dear, late father and myself when I say how proud we are of you.

With love,
Mother

Chapter 33

HER MOTHER'S WORDS touch her deeply, and she gets her first restful night's sleep in a long time.

It's a good thing.

Sabotage begins tonight but, before they start, HQ ordered Virginia to take a day trip to check a report they've received that the German General Staff has left Lyon and is on its way to Le Puy. If this is true, it's a major development in favor of the Allies. She dares not hope too much for what it means for the imminent liberation of Lyon and the people of her old network.

Virginia wants to go to Le Puy by herself—old ladies on bicycles are still invisible—but Bob and Dédé insist one of them accompany her. Between the two of them, she's almost never alone, and knows how seriously they take her safety. If they were any other boys, they'd drive her crazy, but these two are like beloved little brothers.

"I'll go," says Dédé.

"No, I will," says Bob. "Your face is too young. I'm more weathered. I can dress up like an old man, and anyone who sees me with Diane will just imagine we're a nice old couple out for a pleasure ride in war-torn France."

"Are you sure you're up for a two-and-a-half-hour bike ride?" says Virginia. "I'm not stopping a hundred times along the way so you can smoke."

"Please," Bob says. "I'm a professional."

She rolls her eyes as he disappears into the storage barn to find suitable clothes. When he leaves, she checks her padding and her old-lady makeup in the mirror. Behind her, in the reflection, she sees Dédé light a cigarette and hop to sit on the table, legs hanging like a little boy. She has an urge to wrap him in a hug.

"It's best you stay back," she says. "You and the boys need to be fresh for tonight."

"And you don't?" says Dédé.

"I haven't slept since 1940; there's no sense in starting now."

She ties a kerchief around her hair to cover her auburn roots, and adds more powder and kohl to her face and hands. Dédé was able to find her a new pair of false glasses, so she's back to having lenses. Once she's satisfied with her disguise, she turns away from the mirror and notices the calendar hung on the wall. It's July 30. As if on instinct she mentally calculates her grim statistic.

One hundred thirty-two days.

"You should know," she says, attempting to keep her voice light, "I'm living on borrowed time. If I don't make it back, Edmund can take over my duties. He knows how to operate the wireless."

"What do you mean, 'living on borrowed time'?" says Dédé.

"I was only supposed to have lived six weeks as a wireless operator in occupied France."

"How many have you lasted?"

"Triple that. So, I expect to go any day now. Especially now that we're getting closer to forcing the Nazis' hand."

Bob emerges, cutting off the conversation. He looks like an old Frenchman, even finding a pipe for good measure. He hobbles to her and kisses her cheek.

"Come, *ma chére femme*," he says. "Let's go for a bike ride and find a haystack to tumble in the way we used to when we were young."

Virginia laughs, but Dédé's face is serious.

"I would prefer to go with Bob," he says.

"I'm not tumbling in any haystacks with you," says Bob.

Virginia walks over to Dédé and touches his arm.

"You're needed here," she says.

He gives her a small nod, but his face remains troubled.

Once she and Bob are on the road, he's all business. She keeps count of the Nazi lorries they pass, the directions they travel, the children—so many children—not just in Chambon, but in all the surrounding villages.

On the outskirts of Tence, Virginia stops her bike when she spots a girl with a polka-dot scarf—the girl from the bus ride she took with Estelle. The girl holds the hand of a smaller girl as they walk to a well in front of a quaint farmhouse. Her stride is strong, and her skin is flushed with good health. She has none of the fear on her face from that bus ride. Virginia is careful not to meet the girl's eyes so she doesn't shake anything loose inside her that might unsettle her. As Virginia rides away, she offers up a silent wish for the girl's safety and peace, and another for Sophie's, and Mimi's, and Louis's. It pains her that she can arm and train hundreds of Maquis, but she can't do anything to help her friends.

When Bob sees Virginia has fallen behind, he slows his pace.

"Everything all right?" he asks.

She nods, unable to find her voice from the lump in her throat.

He takes her at her word and again pulls ahead, continuing on the road to Le Puy.

The new bicycle Dédé found for Virginia is better than the first. It rides smoother and the seat is more comfortable, but even with the improvement, the ride is becoming brutal. Aside from the torture of mountain roads, the sun blazes forth, and—with a half hour left to go—they've drunk all the water in their canteens. Bob pulls off on a side road that leads downhill to the Loire River, but downhill means uphill on the way back.

Along the shaded banks, they find a fast-running stream, where they refill their canteens. Virginia wants to remove the sweaty stump sock that's chafing her knee, but that isn't possible. Instead, she slips an aspirin from her pocket and takes it. Seeing Bob rubbing his temples, she takes out another.

"What's this?" he asks.

"Aspirin. Does your head hurt?"

"Yes," he says. "It's throbbing."

"You get headaches a lot."

"Have you met the woman I have to work with?"

She smiles while he takes the aspirin and washes it down. When he does, she notices the flash of the revolver at his hip.

"You need to hide that better," she says.

"Yes, sir," he says, saluting.

She helps him tuck in his undershirt around it. Then they walk their bikes up the hill to continue the journey. After a short while they reach the Le Puy city limits, and she's impressed by the sight before her: miles of red roofs climbing the mountainous terrain to the peak where a grand statue of the Virgin overlooks it all.

"Now that's la Madone," Virginia says.

Bob looks to the huge Mary on the mountain. She's red as blood, golden tiara gleaming in the sun.

"Our Lady of Le Puy," says Bob. "Made from two hundred melted Russian cannons after their capture during the Crimean War. A woman of iron."

He raises his eyebrows at her and continues on the road that winds down the narrow streets bordered by brick walls and stone houses, right into the heart of town. German headquarters looms with swastikas flying. The streets crawl with Nazis and the Milice, who've assumed a larger role with patrols since D-Day, now that so many of the French gendarme have abandoned their posts and taken to the woods to join the Maquis.

Bob leads them to a café littered with Nazi soldiers. It's only slightly less intimidating than the one full of Milice across the way, but at least it's more likely Virginia's accent will go unnoticed.

In a short time, the loudspeaker issues a call for soldiers to report for exercises, and the café empties. The music of a German brass band plays while formations parade through the square. Bob leans close to her.

"Do you know what Dr. Le Forestier did when the boches in Chambon used to do this?"

"What?"

"He'd blare his car horn over the music."

"Roger did that?"

"Every day. They never could figure out who it was, especially when others in different places around the village would join in. All those cars sitting idle with nothing to run on were put to good use. Such a small act of subversion, yet strangely unsettling for the pigs. You could feel how uncomfortable it made them."

"It's not the fists alone that win the fight," she says.

"I'll drink to that," he says.

While they each sip their putrid café nationale, she thinks of Sophie, hoping for her safe arrival in London. Virginia is surprised how much she misses her. She was a good courier. Though, if she's honest, she knows it's more than that. For a moment, Virginia allows herself to dream of a time they could meet outside the strain of war.

At twelve fifteen, Bob leaves to check in with his contact at the bookshop. They've discussed the plan in detail, and if he isn't back at the table in fifteen minutes, she's to leave without him and return to the spot where they stopped on the Loire River. If he doesn't return there within a half hour, she's to start back for Chambon alone.

While he's gone, she uses a ration stub to order the only menu item available: foul, watery cabbage soup. Choking it down, she watches the town, taking note of the bank, the post office, and the prefecture. The atmosphere here feels charged. The people are hurried and nervous. The Milice are watchful. The Nazis, menacing.

Twelve twenty.

She locks the bicycles to the fence and rises to use the café restroom. There's a line inside, but she's desperate so she has to wait. She doesn't like how the hostess at the stand keeps looking at her. The woman appears to be in her twenties and is voluptuous and blonde. She's bright with the Nazi soldiers but less friendly with the townspeople.

You'll pay for that, Virginia thinks.

The woman's head turns sharply toward her as if she hears Virginia's thoughts.

Virginia fixes her stare on the washroom sign. The line still isn't moving, and the clock over the kitchen reads twelve twenty-eight.

Damn.

Pressure from her full bladder is painful, but she's out of time. Besides, she needs to get away from this woman.

She returns to the bikes, taking hers but refastening the lock on Bob's. He has a second key. She gives the square one last look for Bob before walking her bike to the street. She senses a change in the air, an increase in motion. Suddenly, dozens of black, shining Mercedes with Nazi flags flying race into town and park along the street at the prefecture.

My God. It's them, she thinks. *The German General Staff has been run out of Lyon.*

Struggling to keep her elation in check, she climbs on her bicycle and pedals around the square, taking mental pictures of what she sees. On the way out of Le Puy, she passes dozens more Nazi vehicles, and spots a convoy of soldiers parked in formation along the road leading north. None of the fools pay an old woman like her any mind.

Once out of their sight, pedaling with all her might, she turns off along the river path, drops her bike to the ground, and relieves herself behind a tree. Then, she hurries back to the path, gasping when she sees Bob already there. He leans against his bike, smoking.

"It's a good thing I waited here for you to finish," Bob says. "I would have scared the piss out of you."

She narrows her eyes at him.

"My contact told me the Lyon boches started arriving yesterday," he says. "He thinks they must find Le Puy a more strategic location for reinforcement."

"No way," says Virginia, a grin touching her lips. "Transportation from Lyon is far more efficient than from this region. It's the Resistance."

"What do you mean?"

"The Lyon Resistance has finally made Nazis there so miserable they're sending them packing. Starting with the bigwigs."

"I can't believe all this is finally happening."

"But that means the danger is higher than it's ever been," she says.

He nods. He's witnessed too much himself.

"We have to get to Simon as soon as possible," she says.

If the Secret Army is able to ambush German convoys, surround Le Puy, and cut off the Nazis from communicating with other cities, they'll be crippled. And then the Maquis can liberate the area.

"Come on," says Virginia, climbing on her bicycle.

Bob reaches for her, touching her arm.

"La Madone," he says.

She flashes a dark look at him and pulls her arm away.

"Don't be mad," he says. "When we call you la Madone, you must imagine the statue here. Not the quiet, vulnerable face of the Virgin in the stable but the conquering woman on the mountain."

It's rare for Bob to act so seriously, and she sees that he doesn't want her to make a joke or dismiss him, but she can't. She feels as if she'll choke from his admiration because she believes she's unworthy of it.

She wants to tell him she hasn't conquered anything, especially not the mountain. Those she crossed conquered her because she never should have left her people. Now she's stuck with the memory of them, and the new faces she's added, always dragging heavy behind her, suffering again and again in her nightmares. But how can she say these things aloud—to a subordinate—when she hates to even think them herself?

Chapter 34

BUZZING FROM THE uppers she took, eyes wide in the night, she stands guard with a machine gun, while Dédé and a group of his boys wire the tracks. They took the truck—lights out—all the way to Monistrol d'Allier to perform the cut. Her heart won't stop racing, but it isn't because of their activity. It's Simon and his team who are on her mind.

Once Simon received report of the convoys heading north, he decided his and Bob's teams would make their first ambush tonight. As Simon promised, once armed, their numbers grew from two to four hundred, and they add men by the hour. The Maquis are ready to start closing in on Le Puy.

Simon said they'd do one of two things. If grossly outnumbered by the Nazis, he'll place his snipers at various points along the road, firing shots from different types of weapons to make the Nazis think their numbers and artillery are stronger than they are.

"And if you aren't outnumbered?" she'd said.

"We'll attack."

As difficult as Virginia's relationship began with Simon, her respect for him has grown. He's decisive and has kept the best control he can in a near-impossible situation. He's organized and trained troops who not only had no weapons but didn't know if they'd ever get them. His impatience, stubbornness, and need to take charge cause friction with her because she shares the same attributes, not that she'd ever admit such a thing to him. She hopes desperately for their success.

"Psst."

Dédé waves her over.

"I'll take guard," he says. "Please, check us."

She passes him the machine gun and inspects the fifteen meters of track they've wired leading up to the tunnel on each side. The first will detonate when the morning freight train full of supplies for German forces passes into the tunnel. They'll blow the second on the other side after that, trapping the train and ensuring it can't continue. The second detonator wire extends about a hundred meters down a cliff, where they'll wait with the truck on the road. They'll ride like the wind once the sabotage is complete.

Hit and run.

Once they've cleaned up their materials, they have an hour to watch the sunrise. She smells the pine and the sweet smoke of their tobacco. The sky is still dark blue, but the stars have disappeared, and a rim of light peeks over the distant mountains. When the morning light brightens, Dédé pulls a paper out of his pocket, unfolds it, and holds it up to show her.

"*Les Étoiles*," she reads. "What's that?"

"A clandestine paper. Resistance writers publish essays, stories, poetry—small acts of subversion. I liked this poem, 'The Weapons of Pain,' by Paul Éluard. I want to read it to all of you."

One boy chuckles, like it's silly to read poetry. Dédé slaps him on the back of the head, silencing his insolence.

"I would love to hear it," says Virginia, glaring at the boy. He looks down at his hands in shame.

Dédé clears his throat. While he reads and the sun rises, their memories rise with it. All the young faces age before her. She feels the age in her own bones, the many pains and losses she has suffered, the catalog of the faces she has known, the missing, the dead, the beloved. He reads of warriors—reckless and true, passionate and sleepless. Their motivations.

What they represent. How every one of them—no matter how great or small—is the shadow of all of those fighting for the good in the world.

When he finishes, she looks to the sky and is startled by the light of the great sun that has appeared over the mountains. She feels tears on her face and looks around to see the sunlight reflected in the others' tears. They all let out embarrassed laughs.

"This poem is a spark," Dédé says. "Just think, little papers like this start the big blazes that win wars."

He folds it and tucks it in his pocket. After checking his watch, he stands and holds his hands down to Virginia, pulling her up with him. He motions for the others to rise, hands the keys to the truck to Virginia, and picks up the detonator.

The sound of the freight train starts faint but grows closer and louder, rumbling to a roar as it passes. The boys wait, wide-eyed. She tenses, ready to spring to action. Dédé counts down.

"Trois, deux, un . . ."

Nothing. Nothing.

Boom!

They feel the great blast under their feet, and rocks rain over the cliff, stinging them like bits of meteor shower. Dédé presses the detonator, setting off the second blast.

The boys whoop and holler, and Virginia orders them to the truck. She drives them as fast as she can toward the rising sun.

THEY SLEEP FOR several hours but awaken before noon to prepare the groups for the coming nights. They need to cut the rails at Langogne, Brassac, and Solignac, the telephone lines from Brioude to Le Puy, and the bridges at Montagnac, Brioude, and Lavoûte-sur-Loire. The largest railway bridge cut they'll need to make is at Chamalières, but they'll need to work up to that. It will require the most heavy and precise explosive placement to enact.

All day, Virginia watches the clock and the door, anxious to hear from

Simon and Bob. If the ambush was a success, the German convoy will have no option but to fall back to Le Puy, pushing the boches into the trap the Resistance forces are slowly, methodically setting. But she must prepare herself for the worst-case scenarios: heavy Maquis loss to Simon's and Bob's teams, and no advancement. And if the Maquis fail and are put on the run, the threat to Chambon and the region will rise.

By three o'clock in the afternoon, they still haven't heard from Simon or Bob. Dédé and Edmund pace and chew their fingernails. They want to get to their teams to prepare them for the night's sabotage, but they need to know what happened first. If they head to a region now swarming with Nazis, they'll be walking right into a trap.

When Virginia's nerves can't take another minute of sitting and waiting, she pulls on her shawl.

"I'll check in at the Hôtel May to see if there's been any news," she says.

Dédé jumps to join her.

"No," she says. "Please. I need to be alone."

She doesn't wait for his reply before heading out the door.

The bicycle ride in the mountain air is invigorating, and by the time she arrives at the heart of town, she feels steady. Taking the back entrance to the hotel to avoid the watchful stare of MP Haas, she weaves her way through the dark hallways. Just as she steps into the lobby, the phones at the front desk and in the café start ringing, slicing through the air with their shrill cries. The old woman at the front desk answers, and her face goes white. She hurries to the woman at the café, and both tell the waitress and maid to go and sound the alarm.

"What is it?" Virginia asks the woman at the front desk.

"A raid."

Virginia's hope crashes. Does this mean the Germans mowed through Simon's men?

"Is it the boches?" she says.

"I don't know. We were just warned to get the children to the forest.

Here, take this basket. Help the teachers escort them there safely to pick mushrooms."

Virginia doesn't want to endanger the children with her presence, but she can't tell the old woman, who has no knowledge of Virginia's role, nor will the woman take no for an answer.

"Don't look panicked," the woman calls as Virginia heads out the back door. "You mustn't let the children know you're afraid."

VIRGINIA TAKES THE alley to the nearest school, where summer lessons were just letting out, and is soon caught up in a swell of primary-aged children. Their teachers have bright smiles and lead the kids in song, the pace they set the only indication of trouble. Virginia falls back toward the rear of the line, where a teacher asks her to check the school to make sure they didn't miss anyone. Grateful for a task away from the children, Virginia passes off the basket, and hurries into the building.

The windows are open, allowing the sweet mountain breezes to sweep through the classrooms. Virginia climbs to the third floor, checking each level, opening closet doors and looking under desks, making sure the building is empty. The rooms are decorated with wildflower collages, and finger paintings, and sets of building blocks. French lesson books line the shelves, and cages squeak with field mice on wheels and baby bunnies drinking from water bottles. She notes the Bible story puppets and pictures are of the Garden of Eden, Noah's ark, David and Goliath—stories Jewish and Christian children have in common. In one of the classrooms, a photograph of a boy with haunted eyes is pinned to a corkboard, where little messages of kindness, scrawled in children's penmanship, surround his face.

My God, she thinks. *These teachers are giving these boys and girls so much more than instruction and shelter.*

Struggling to keep herself composed, Virginia hurries to join the group and nods to the teacher to show there are no kids left in the building. The lines of children parade into the forest, their gentle songs muted and swallowed as the understory folds around them. Three Maquis appear to keep watch.

She stays with them along the forest edge, guarding the children, alternating between feelings of affection for the people of Chambon, hatred of the Nazis, and terror over the fate of Simon and Bob's Maquis. After an hour that feels like a day, a woman from the village waves a kerchief along the meadows' edge, and one of the boys enters the woods to tell the teachers it's all clear.

Desperate for news of her boys, Virginia rushes back to town, finds her bicycle, and pedals as fast as her legs will push to her safe house, but there's no one waiting for her.

Chapter 35

SHE PACES, WATCHING the window, battling with horrid thoughts of those she has lost, from Lyon to the present. She thinks back before all went south in her first mission in Lyon, before the Nazis spilled into the unoccupied zone, when she and her people all lived and worked together in harmony. In spite of their vastly different situations, their fight against evil was their bond.

She recalls a sweet night when she and Louis and the prostitute and the old couple were able to sneak to the doctor's living quarters, above his office, and share a modest Christmas dinner. The prostitute had been able to buy them a goose on the black market, and the rest had pooled their resources to make baked sweet potatoes and even to buy a few bottles of wine. The old woman drank hers too quickly and got the hiccups, and the rest of them couldn't catch their breath from laughing.

She smiles, warmed by the memory of her little Lyon family and proud of herself for combatting her hourly battle against despair with good thoughts.

Suddenly, she hears a truck screech around the corner and come to a halt outside her place. She rushes out to meet it, thrilled to see Bob.

She learns his and Simon's teams ambushed the Germans, killing fourteen of them while suffering no casualties in their own ranks, and forcing the convoy back to Le Puy. As a result, hoping to boost German morale, the Milice attempted a raid on Chambon, but when they arrived in town, not a single suspicious child or resistor could be found. They left with lower morale than ever, and reportedly stank of fear, their positions as collaborators now clearly tenuous.

In the following nights, Virginia's teams successfully cut two railways and two bridges, and derail a train at a tunnel. The boys are starting to leave the forest to quarter at the nearby Château de Vaux, and Virginia helps Bob and another maquisard pack a crate of weapons and medical supplies for the storage closets there.

"We need to arrest the Milice in the area as soon as possible," says Virginia. "I don't want them threatening those children again. Do we have a place we can jail them?"

"The boys found an abandoned château at Pont de Mars. There's one road in, and its position allows a good view of the landscape. They're preparing it for prisoners now."

"Good. The moment it's ready, you also need to lock up the betrayer."

God knows how a betrayer can destroy a network.

"I don't know that we'll give him the courtesy of locking him up, la Madone."

They're startled when the door behind them bursts open. Bob pulls out his gun and stands in front of Virginia. When they see Danielle Le Forestier, Virginia places her hand on Bob's back. He lowers his gun.

"I'm sorry," says Danielle. "I wasn't thinking. Please, I need you to talk Roger out of this mission of madness."

"What do you mean?" asks Virginia.

"Two Maquis were arrested and taken to Le Puy. Roger's going to plead on their behalf."

"Which ones?" asks Bob.

"Two of the three who stole his car," says Danielle.

Bob's face darkens.

"What of the third?" asks Bob.

"He got away. That's how Roger heard of all this."

Based on the look Bob gives her, Virginia has the same awful thought that Bob has: the betrayer.

Bob and the other maquisard pull on their jackets, Virginia wraps her hair with her shawl, and the group follows Danielle to the Le Forestiers' house. As they arrive, Roger is securing the Red Cross sheet over the top of his car. The girl staying with them watches out the window, her eyes wide.

"We can't recommend you go to Le Puy," says Virginia. "Not at this time."

"It's all right," says Roger. "Since the incident with my car, these boys have gone above and beyond to help me and show they're sorry. I need to be there for them."

"Between skirmishes and the increase in Nazis at Le Puy, it isn't wise. Bob and I were just in town, and the German General Staff from Lyon has moved in. Tensions are extremely high."

"Please," says Danielle, clutching Roger's arms.

Roger looks down at his wife and takes her face in his hands. "My love, this is diplomatic and it's the right thing to do. These boys are orphans and patriots. I have to be there for them. Even if I can't get them out, they'll at least know they're cared for. It will be all right. I'm familiar to the Germans in Le Puy. They know I'm a doctor."

"Not the new ones," says Danielle.

"I'm going," says Roger.

"Then I'll go with you," says Bob. "For protection on the road."

"I will, too," says Virginia. "I need to keep HQ as up to date as possible."

Roger looks at his wife with his eyebrows up, seeking her blessing. With reluctance, she nods and reaches for him. He wraps her in his arms.

"Why were the Maquis arrested?" asks Bob.

"They were on an errand for me," says Roger, releasing his wife. "I had them running med supplies, but they apparently added a box of ammunition to the trunk. They got stopped at a checkpoint and searched. The maquisard that got away told me."

"Where is he?" asks Bob.

"Inside the house. He's pretty shaken up."

Virginia's heart begins to race. Her hands feel clammy.

"Danielle," says Virginia. "Where are the children?"

"Inside."

"Take them at once to the forest. *All* of them. For an hour."

"But—"

"Now."

Danielle looks from Virginia to Roger. He nods, and she obeys.

"Bob," Virginia says.

He follows Danielle. Once they're inside, Virginia takes Roger's arm, and whispers to him.

"Don't move or react," she whispers. "The maquisard in your house is a collaborator."

Roger flinches, trying to pull away from her, but she holds him fast.

"It's all right," she says. "Bob's getting him."

On cue, Bob emerges, his gun thrust into the back of the maquisard with the red hair. The young man walks stiff and straight. His face is white, and the underarms of his shirt are soaked with sweat rings. Bob opens the door to the back of the car and climbs in after the young man. The other maquisard gets in the other side. Virginia releases Roger and takes the passenger seat. In a moment, Roger climbs in the driver's seat, giving a dark look to all of them before starting the engine.

On the ride, the only sounds are the shaking, gasping breaths of the betrayer. By the smell, she thinks he wet himself. Virginia rolls down her window. Several kilometers outside the village, Bob asks Roger to pull over near a small thicket of pines bordering a cliff. Roger wordlessly obeys. The betrayer whimpers but still doesn't speak as Bob pulls him from the vehicle and walks him to the trees at gunpoint. Virginia watches the pines swallow them up. Several seconds later, she, Roger, and the other maquisard flinch when they hear the shot. Roger covers his mouth with a shaking hand and breathes heavily. Bob returns to the car alone, and they continue to Le Puy in silence.

Somewhere inside, Virginia knows she should have compassion for the misguided youth who was just executed, but she can't summon it. Not a drop. Has the war killed off her sensitivity, or has it sharpened her thirst for justice? Was that killing justice, or did it add to the scale heavy with humanity's sins in this war? Will there ever be enough good deeds to balance the sin?

They pass the lane that leads down to the river where she and Bob met after their day trip, and soon Our Lady of Le Puy is in view.

Roger wipes his face, and Virginia sees he has been crying. War is so much worse on the tenderhearted. Or maybe it isn't worse because they know how to love and to grieve and to atone instead of turning to stone the way she has.

"I'll go alone to the prison," Roger says. "We'll need someone to stay at the car."

"I'll guard it," says the maquisard with Bob.

"What's your name, son?" asks Roger.

"Leroi, sir."

"Thank you, Leroi."

"Diane and I will go to the bookshop," says Bob. "We'll be safe there, and we'll be able to get information from my contact."

"Good," says Roger. "I don't know how long this will take, but I hope not more than an hour. I want to get back to Chambon as quickly as possible. I promised Danielle I won't make any more trips until after the liberation."

"Understood," says Bob.

"If there are any problems," says Virginia, "meet at the turnoff we just passed for the river."

Roger agrees, and drives carefully on the narrow roads, finding a place to park just off the heart of town but with a good view of all the buildings. Knuckles white, he holds the steering wheel and closes his eyes, his lips moving in whispered prayer. When he finishes, he gives Virginia a small smile, nods at the boys in the back seat, and leaves them.

"Hide the guns under the seat," Bob instructs Leroi. "Take a chair at that café and order a cup of café nationale. You can see the bookshop, the prison, and the car from there. Be ready to spring at a moment's notice."

"Yes, sir."

The three of them get out of the car and start for their destinations. Virginia and Bob veer toward the bookshop, while Leroi heads to the café. Ahead of them, Virginia sees Roger speaking with the guard at the prison gate. When he's allowed entrance, she's overcome with nausea. She hopes the terrible feeling is only because of the circumstances, and not any premonition. Sensing Virginia's unease, Bob threads his arm through hers.

The bookshop off the main square is tiny and easily overlooked. Dark wood panels frame the doorway, and the window display is full of books about the region and France in general. It's a comfort to walk inside and inhale the scent of yellowed paper, linen spines, dust from many houses settled in the pages of the used tomes, and the warm, sweet tobacco of the pipe the old man at the register smokes. When the bell rings announcing their arrival, he looks up from the magnifying glass perched over the large text before him. His gaze lingers on Bob a heartbeat longer than it does on her, but quickly returns to the text.

She and Bob separate. He takes a lap that will bring him close to the bookseller, and she turns the other way, perusing the fiction shelves. She runs her fingers over the book spines, stopping when she sees the title: *La vie et les aventures surprenantes de Robinson Crusoé.* Smiling as she flips through the pages, she thinks of the doctor from Lyon, and the photograph of her father reading the book to her and her brother.

A fierce longing ignites in her to return to Box Horn Farm. To hug her mother. To use an indoor toilet and take a bath with hot, running water. To sleep in a comfortable bed. To eat unrationed food and drink wine until she's drunk. Or simply to visit a bookshop in a town without looking over her shoulder. To take a car ride through the mountains that doesn't include murder.

"That was my favorite when I was a boy," says Bob, coming up beside her.

"You're still a boy," she says. "It was my favorite, too. I was in a theater production of it at my school."

"You? Are there any female characters?"

"No, silly. I was Robinson."

"Why does that not surprise me?"

"It shouldn't. Now, who could you play? The ship's captain?"

"That's a good one. How about Dédé?" he says.

"My man Friday, poor kid."

They laugh, but Bob becomes serious.

"Do you think I'm a monster?" he says.

He stares out at the street, unable to meet her eyes.

"I can't answer that question," she says.

"That wasn't the absolution I was looking for."

"I told you, I'm not la Madone," she says, turning his face back to hers. "But there's no one I'd rather have at my side in war than you. And, for the safety of the children and for all of us, you did what you had to do."

He continues to stare at her until the noise of sirens takes their attention.

They look out the window and see the cars of the MPs racing past. Hurrying out to the street, they see a commotion near the bank. The MPs fan out, shoving guns in civilians' chests, kicking in doors, bashing windows out of the cars they search. There must have been a robbery. Unsettled, Bob and Virginia rush along the boulevard toward the café, but the sight that greets them stops them in their tracks.

Leroi has a rifle from one MP pointed at his forehead, while another searches Roger's car. Virginia utters a curse and pulls Bob into an alleyway, where they watch the terrible sight of the MP in the car holding up one of the guns. The MP with Leroi pulls his rifle back and uses the butt of it to strike Leroi in the face. He hits him so hard, Leroi's head swings to the side, blood shooting from his nose. He collapses on the ground, where he's kicked repeatedly.

Virginia holds Bob back, and they continue to watch the second wave of horror that greets them. Roger runs toward the MPs, begging them to stop.

"No," Bob hisses.

Roger pushes the MP kicking Leroi, and a shouting match ensues.

"Has Roger lost his mind?" says Virginia.

The MP exchanges angry words with Roger, while Roger tears the Red Cross flag off the vehicle and shakes in front of his face. The one searching the car shouts, holding up the gun from the back seat. Roger's face goes white. He doesn't fight when they slap him with handcuffs. Virginia can almost feel the blow when they punch Roger in the stomach and drag him and Leroi away. In the shadows, she leans her head back against the wall, trying to stay clearheaded and in the moment, but the memory yanks her out of time.

It's as if she's back in the Lyon doctor's office. Books and papers litter the floor, the furniture is overturned, the doctor has a black eye. As she falls to her knees, digging through piles to find *Robinson Crusoe*, he thrusts a poster at her. Her wanted poster.

"I told the Gestapo you were only a patient," he says. "I said I didn't know anything else about you. But they'll be back. They knew things. So many things."

"The priest. I told you!"

"I don't know anything about anyone. Not anymore. All I know is you must go."

"How can I leave?"

"Lyon is our home, not yours. You've done what you can."

"But there's more to be done."

"Not by you. Now, go!"

Disoriented by the vividness of the memory, it takes Virginia a moment to recognize Bob in her face.

"Diane!" he says. "We have to go. Now!"

He drags her several feet deeper into the alley before she comes to her senses and follows of her own accord.

Through the narrow streets they rush, weaving in and out of alleys and side roads, along bricks walls, up and down hills. They turn a corner, and Our Lady of Le Puy appears massive and imposing. Worried she'll be sick, Virginia pauses and puts her hands on her knees, but soon continues forward to catch up with Bob. They hurry until they're out of town, collapsing at the riverbank.

"How will we get back?" she says. "I can't run—not with my leg—especially not all the way to Chambon."

"There's a Maquis group a short distance away. They have a car. They can take us."

"We'll get stopped. I know it."

"There's a priest with them. He can put on his cassock and put the cross in the window to show he's on church business. He has forged travel papers."

"No," she says, feeling dizzy. "No priests."

Her vision blurs. She has a sudden image of Abbé Alesch looking on with ice-blue eyes. The frozen Pyrenees looming.

"Diane," Bob yells, grabbing her face. "Stay with me. He's a good man. It's all right. We'll get back to Chambon. But if there's to be any hope for Roger or the Maquis, we must go, now."

TRUE TO BOB'S word, the priest gets them safely to Chambon by nightfall. They drop Virginia in town to find the head of the Secours Suisse, Auguste Bohny, to see if he can help. With Auguste, she makes the terrible trip to the Le Forestiers' place to tell Danielle what happened. The woman is hysterical. At least the children are all in bed, so they don't know what's going on.

Virginia stays with Danielle, while Auguste leaves them to find Pastor Trocmé. Between Auguste's position as a Swiss representative, and Trocmé's ability to find common ground with just about anyone, Auguste assures Danielle they will bring Roger home. Virginia is not optimistic.

"I knew it," Danielle says over and over again.

"Stay strong," Virginia says. "Roger can easily say he didn't know about the gun. With Auguste and Pastor Trocmé vouching for him, there's a good chance he'll be all right."

Maybe if she says it, it will be so.

The strain of the day makes her feel like a frayed rope about to snap. She's glad when Pastor Trocmé arrives with his wife, Magda, and they take over care of Danielle. Virginia slips out and walks home, but the sight of the MP's face in the second-floor hospital window again makes her feel sick. She takes a side road so he can't see her and nearly collapses once she's at the Salvation Army house.

There, waiting for her, is Dédé. He wraps her with a blanket and shows her the meal Léa has left her, and a bottle of wine she has no idea how he procured. Edmund has already set up the wireless and waits for her. She leaves the food on the table, takes a long drink from the bottle, and starts the terrible transmission to HQ.

Chapter 36

VIRGINIA'S CORE TEAM is assembled at her place, discussing how they might rescue Roger, when they receive a knock at the door. Edmund admits Auguste Bohny. Auguste's face conveys the awful news before the words emerge.

"Roger Le Forestier has been sentenced to death."

Gasps and curses are uttered around Virginia. She keeps hold of her emotions.

"Pastor Trocmé is breaking the news to Danielle. Though I do not wish to convey his message to you, I must. Pastor Trocmé sends a stern reproof to the Maquis who brought firearms on the trip, reminding you that those who live by the sword will die by it."

The room is silent.

"If you'll excuse me," he says, putting on his hat and leaving them.

She's afraid to look at Bob, but she doesn't have to. He exits through the back door.

While the others fold in and console one another, she leaves to follow Bob. It takes her a while to find him, but the smell of his cigarette and the glowing ember at its tip lead her to where he sits on a boulder overlooking the valley. The sky is cloudy and gray, and the grass smells sweet from a rain shower that passed through earlier that day. She climbs the boulder and sits next to him.

"Don't say it isn't my fault," he says.

While he smokes, they stare out to the horizon in silence, gazing upon the stony Pic du Lizieux. She hears him sniffing and thinks he might be crying.

"Tell me what happened to you in the Pyrenees," he says.

"Why?"

"I need to hear it. We're so close to liberation, and I'm depleted. I'm sick over Roger." Bob's voice catches. "I need some kind of inspiration."

"How could you be inspired by a coward, running away with her tail between her legs?"

"Stop," he says, banging his fist onto his knee. "Stop calling yourself a coward."

Bob's coming undone, she thinks. His war sins, his guilt. It's cracking him to pieces. She knows how he feels.

"Why was it so bad?" he continues. "I need to understand."

"I guess it's because there's always something in me that feels bigger and stronger than human beings, but there's no way to feel more powerful than a mountain."

"That's not it, and you know it. Not all of it, anyway. Tell me the truth."

Here we are, she thinks.

In her last mission, this was the time the dominoes began to fall, and she fled. But she will not flee this time. No matter what happens.

Bob slips his arm through hers and draws her closer to his side. She allows herself to relax against him. She takes a deep breath.

"When we set out," she starts, "the night sky over the Pyrenees was crystal clear. But all I could see were my friends' faces. Klaus Barbie had begun capturing and torturing them, trying to break them to get my address, while an MP hunted me. They had been informed by a double agent. A priest."

Bob curses.

"You see why I didn't want the priest to drive us?" she says.

"Yes."

"And do you know that, as we speak, that very MP is in the hospital in Chambon?"

Bob flinches and starts to climb to his feet.

"Later," she says, holding his arm.

Once he settles, she continues her story.

"HQ had been urging me to return to London, but they finally ordered it. The Allies had crushed the Germans in North Africa. The Nazis were spilling into the unoccupied zone. My doctor friend told me the Gestapo were onto me. He showed me the wanted poster with my face. And in my panic, I fled. I fled France instead of staying. I left all my people to the dogs to save my own skin."

"You were ordered," says Bob.

"When have I ever let that sway me?"

He looks away from her because he knows it's true.

IT'S NOVEMBER OF 1942. There are three men who also found their way to the Pyrenees guide, two Frenchmen and a Belgian she's almost sure are fellow agents, but who keep as quiet about their situation as she does. Her last fifty-five thousand francs gets them the guide, rucksacks with canteens of water, meager food supplies, and heavy boots. She agrees to be the interpreter; she's the only Spanish speaker among the refugees.

Virginia passes out uppers, explaining to the guide that they'll help them stay awake and suppress their appetites. He waves it away, but the others take them.

Without ceremony, they begin.

The guide tells them the climb will be steepest on the French side. They are at six hundred meters, but they will peak at about three thousand. Though the Spanish side will be a more gradual descent, it will be harder. The air is thinner, and the snowdrifts are waist deep.

Virginia takes in this information and communicates it as soberly to the others as she's able. She has one sock for her stump and can't imagine what it will look like after this trip. A sudden, sharp longing to remain in France, to find a new identity and return to her people in Lyon, rushes at her. She has sent countless downed pilots and agents along this circuit, but now that she's the pawn in the game, she's shocked to find how unequal she feels to the task.

Aside from the guide, breath already comes hard and fast for them. Their guide is petite and light, sure-footed and fit. She wonders how many times he has done this. Will he be able to get them safely to the other side? Every time a dog howls or a searchlight flashes, they crouch low. There are border patrols they'll have to avoid on the ascent and descent. Snow they will have to survive at the peaks.

As the fragrance of crushed pine needles under their boots rises, a heavy, wet fog descends. The craggy, mossy rocks cause them to stumble. In spite of the protests of her fellow refugees, she situates herself last in the procession so they won't notice when her limp worsens. Soon great silver firs surround them on all sides, and they reach the snow. A dusting, two inches, four inches, a foot. In drifts, snow seeps into her boots, making her good foot feel as numb as her prosthetic.

A little voice in her mind jabs her.

You should have listened to Vera and left Lyon before the winter weather. Then you wouldn't have had this much snow to contend with. Your network wouldn't be in such danger.

Try as she might, she can't silence this hateful voice. It accompanies her on the sharp climb, along with the ghosts of her people.

Not ghosts, she tells herself. *They might not be dead.*

If that's true, why do they haunt you?

Struggling through many hours, they reach a summit and stop to catch their breath, but she can't. The air is too thin. It's like a fist around her throat. The coming winter has made a frozen, terrible beauty of the landscape. She wants to turn back. They are so alone in the wilderness. They drop their rucksacks, massaging their bleeding shoulders. The men struggle to breathe around her. The guide watches, unmoved. It takes every ounce of training she has to steady her heart and suppress her panic.

She's certain she'll die out here. Her frozen body will be passed by hundreds of others on their escape. She'll be stuck and stiff until the thaw, when she'll rot and slide down a cliff and get buried in the mud.

And she deserves it, for leaving her people.

She pulls the scarf off her neck, desperate for a breath. The man next to her bumps her arm, shoving a flask at her. She takes a greedy drink.

Eau-de-vie. The water of life.

Slowly, the sweet brandy begins to relax her, and soon—though not soon enough—she finds a way to breathe. Shallow gasps slip into her lungs, and her organs adjust, taking what they can from the air. As the wind picks up, the guide grows impatient. He resumes the hike.

Virginia had thought the climb would be the hard part, but the descent in the rushing, icy wind sends them through snowdrifts up to two feet deep. Balancing on the downward hike is excruciating, and because it's more gradual—because there are as many ascents as there are descents—they remain in the thin, impossible air for hours. As the sun rises, a cabin appears. Virginia thinks she's seeing things, but the guide motions for them to go in, and they all collapse.

"Sleep," he says.

As if on a hypnotist's command, they drop. It feels as if she has only just closed her eyes, when he pokes her awake and tells them to eat. While the men are occupied with the stale bread, she sits on her cot and inspects her stump under the smelly blanket. Her knee is bloody and blistered, and pus makes it stick to the sock. She quickly covers it, removes the blanket, and asks for another drink of brandy. Though she thinks she could stay on that cot in that crude cabin forever, the guide urges them to prepare for the next leg of the journey. Virginia passes out more uppers, and pulls on her rucksack, feeling the sting as its straps settle into the deep grooves on her shoulders. The pain on her stump is searing, but there's nothing to be done for it. They have so far to go.

As the hours pass, as the second day turns to evening and falls into night, nearly out of her mind with pain, Virginia continues to think she will die. She's become so numb from the cold, she can't feel anything about the fact of her death any longer, only that she hopes it comes soon. On and on they hike. Sudden ascents torture them; sharp descents are even worse. She thinks her good foot might have frostbite. She worries that it will have to be cut off, too.

It takes her some time to realize the wind has left, transporting the clouds, pulling back the curtain on a spectacular night sky. The guide stops them and points. Bewildered, she looks ahead and wonders why the stars are so low. Have they climbed above them?

"Una aldea," the guide whispers.

A village.

The lights aren't stars—they're houses.

"Village!" she says to the others. The guide shushes her.

The refugees reach for her, embracing. They laugh through their tears. The guide leads them, creeping, to a solitary cabin on a ridge. Inside, a beautiful young man and his pretty wife and their noisy, fat baby welcome them. There's a fire, warm bread, and a bottle of oloroso. Virginia asks for a sock, and the woman produces a pair made of soft, dry wool. But even these socks aren't as welcome a sight as the suitcase the man fetches, opens, and reveals that holds a wireless transceiver.

"¡Gloria a Dios!" says Virginia.

He strings up the wire and taps the message to HQ that the travelers are safe. The minutes of silence while they wait for the reply stretch on, endless, but then a response comes.

There's a great cheer all around as headquarters congratulates them. Virginia tells the wireless operator the code names in the group and then has him tap that, while the others are cooperative, Cuthbert has been troublesome. The response comes back quickly; the man reads the words aloud as the Morse code delivers them.

"If Cuthbert is trouble, eliminate him."

Virginia howls with laugher. Those around her don't understand, and she doesn't enlighten them.

The next morning, they arise to the aroma of eggs cooking and tea brewing and the baby fussing and babbling. They leave the beautiful people on the mountain with many thanks and blessings, complete their descent, pay the guide the balance, and head for safe houses to rest until their rendezvous at the train station for the five o'clock to Barcelona. When they reunite, they are strengthened and confident, but anxious for the journey to be over. None of them have papers, so they need to keep moving. She and the men sit on separate benches, watching the clock, willing the long hand to move faster.

It's here that her grief and guilt settle over her shoulders like a harness, tethering her as if on a rope over the mountain and all the way back to Lyon. Virginia has a physical ache for human comfort, but she knows that if her people are captured and in prisons or camps, they won't have it. She resolves that she won't, either. She will return to London to restore her strength and tell Vera everything she knows, and then Virginia will insist on returning to the field.

She closes her eyes, imagining all the ways she might return, but the train whistle stirs her to attention. She sits up fast, but when she opens her eyes, all the hope drains from her.

She stares down the barrel of a gun.

"SINCE WE DIDN'T have papers, the Spanish police arrested us," Virginia says. "A prostitute with tuberculosis was my salvation. When she got out of prison, she went to the American consulate to tell them who I was. They got me back to London."

"Incredible," Bob whispers.

"And in spite of all that, I don't feel as if I've conquered anything. Those mountains I crossed continue to conquer me. I don't feel like I've ever left them. I think I can't leave the mountains because I shouldn't have crossed them. I should never have left France to begin with. I abandoned my people because I was a coward."

"No," he says. "There's nothing cowardly in you."

"But you didn't leave when you were caught," she says. "You never left France. You joined the Maquis."

"France is my home, not yours. And I did leave Lyon. I left when I couldn't be of use any longer, and I found where I could be. If you had stayed in Lyon, you'd be dead. If you hadn't left, you wouldn't have learned the wireless. You wouldn't have been sent to us here. We'd have nothing without you."

She shakes her head no.

"You don't believe me," he says. "You think any old agent could help get us boys in shape? Any old agent could make us want to push ourselves to impress him? This from an agent wearing a fake leg called Herbert."

"Cuthbert."

"One who has been here since the beginning as a volunteer for a country she wasn't born in, willing to come back and fight to the death, even when she has a price on her head."

He jumps down from the boulder and looks up at her.

"Only la Madone could help us like this," says Bob. "And once we're liberated, when you stand there looking over the mountain you've helped conquer, I want you to take off this scarf at your neck and raise it in the air to me in surrender because I was right."

Chapter 37

T HE NIGHT TO blow the bridge at Chamalières, their final act of sabotage before the battles for Le Puy begin, has arrived. The train carrying Nazi troops and supplies is a night train on the last line left in the area for their transport. The Maquis have used a tremendous amount of explosive power on the bridge supports, and, if they calculated correctly, it should collapse, plunging the locomotive into the ravine below. It's a big job that will be followed by an attack on the German convoys scheduled to meet the train.

The train is running late—no surprise at this point—and they wait anxiously. The engineers have been warned. They'll slow down the locomotive on the approach to the bridge and jump into the field, abandoning ship, where medical care waits. The maquisard training to be a doctor, Serge, will see to any injury. If all goes according to plan, Virginia will use the truck to transport the engineers to a safe house, and then she'll return to Chambon to await news from the boys.

Simon positions himself next to Virginia so he can whisper to her.

"It's good to see you, Diane," he says.

She raises her hand to her forehead in salute.

"I confess, I had my men check you out thoroughly," he says. "Full reports are in, and you're very respected in international intelligence circles. That shut up any of your remaining antagonists pretty quick."

"Thank you," she says. "I know it's hard to take orders from an old lady."

"They have a hard time taking orders from an old man," he says, pointing to his thinning hair.

She smiles.

"HQ says you can expect Jedburgh teams soon," she says. "Not that you need them for leadership, but they'll help you fold into the Allied forces more easily once they reach us."

"I'm glad to hear it."

"Look," she says. "I want you to know what a fine job you've done readying these boys for war. All I had to do was find the guns to drop into their waiting hands."

"You understate your importance. But I thank you for your kind words."

They shake hands, and in a moment the rumbling starts. It's so loud and so close and so full of Germans and means so much, it fills her with dread. Closer and closer it gets, like the war arriving on her doorstep, like it has a hundred times before. There's no getting used to the feeling.

The screech of the brakes—metal on metal—hurts her ears. The engine door opens, and the two forms inside leap out and roll in the grass to where the medical team waits. Though waning, the moon is still bright and large, and shortly after the train passes in front of it, a mighty blast rises, shaking the earth and polluting the air with fire and smoke. They scramble to witness the twisting groan of iron and steel and the deep quaking of the ground as the train plunges into the gulf below.

Awed and a little shocked by their success, they pause only a moment to wish each other luck before separating.

ENGINEERS SAFELY DELIVERED—with minimal injury—to their safe house, Virginia proceeds back to Chambon. She isn't good at waiting, especially when she knows the boys are in such danger. All her groups are out on ambush missions, leaving her alone in the place that's usually bustling. She longs to wire HQ about the success of the bridge, but Edmund is out fighting somewhere in the night, so she has no one to pedal the generator.

She runs her hands along a liquor bottle some of her boys stole from the kitchen at the back of the Nazi hospital. More and more Nazis evacuate by the day—with rumors a full cleanout is imminent—leaving only the sickest men and their nurses. Will MP Haas remain? She feels the letters in the glass—JÄGERMEISTER—and pours herself a generous shot.

She soon hears a hooting sound followed by a soft knock, and lets in Dolmazon and her son. She feels guilty for not thinking of keeping them company while Simon was out fighting.

"I'm sorry to bother you," says Dolmazon. "I didn't know if you'd be here, but I need to keep busy."

"It's no bother," says Virginia. "Come in."

Dolmazon and her son have arms full of clothing on hangers.

"Can I pour you a glass of Jägermeister?" says Virginia. "I don't think I should drink alone."

"No," says Dolmazon, screwing up her face with distaste. "I'd never partake of German liquor, stolen or not."

"I understand."

The woman and her son take the clothing to the storage room, and Dolmazon returns holding a garment.

"I have something for you," says Dolmazon. "For later. If you . . . need something different to wear."

She holds up the dress. It's simple—a V-neck with a collar, rolled short sleeves, and a skirt, airy as a dandelion wisp. Though light and feminine, it has a military feel. Virginia reaches for it, running her hands along the cool white silk.

"Is this made from—?"

"Yes," says Dolmazon. "Parachute silk. United States issue."

"This is incredible. Now I know why you wouldn't let us bury them."

"I like to put everything to good use. Sometimes something can become so much more than what it was intended for."

The words touch Virginia. She's moved by the gift.

"I'll treasure it," she says. "Thank you."

She leaves to hang it in her wardrobe and returns to find Dolmazon pacing and the boy chewing his nails. She needs to find a way to keep their minds off the danger Simon is in. In answer, the bicycle pedals in the corner glint in the lamplight.

"I have a job for you," she says to the boy and his mother.

DÉDÉ COMES TO Virginia in the middle of the night. Dolmazon and her son are sleeping over, and, once Virginia lets Dolmazon know Simon is all right, she tends to Dédé's injuries. She pours him a shot of Jägermeister and lets him drink it before she uses tweezers to remove a line of shrapnel from his shoulder and chin.

"Your first time shaving, and you've cut yourself," she says.

A quick smile touches his face before disappearing. He exhales and leans his head back against the wall.

"How many boys did we lose?" she says.

"Twenty."

She pauses, allowing the word to pass through her.

"Who?" she asks.

While he recites their names, she thinks of all their young faces, their short lives ended. Candles snuffed.

"We underestimated their numbers," Dédé says. "Twelve lorries full of Nazis had the advantage over our boys on foot. Two of the lorries got through, but when Bob's team joined us with the bazooka, they blasted about one hundred and fifty boches to hell. The ones left thought we had more men and firepower than we did. They surrendered. Almost five hundred of them."

"That's incredible," she says.

His eyes meet hers, and they are dark and full of pain. She takes his hand.

"I know the losses are awful," she says. "But our boys died heroes."

"I know," Dédé says. "It's not just that."

She stares at him, waiting for more news.

"It's Roger. He was in one of the lorries that got past us. I saw him. We got a boche to spill that the prisoners are being sent to Montluc."

Montluc. Klaus Barbie's prison.

Virginia swallows, but her mouth is dry.

"The Allies are getting closer," says Virginia. "Once Lyon is liberated, Roger will go free."

Dédé's face relaxes a little. He wants to believe her. She wants to believe herself.

"Where are the German prisoners now?" she says. "Did Bob take them to the château at Pont de Mars?"

"Not yet. He corralled them in the forest under armed guard."

"What will he do with them?"

"That's why I'm here," he says. "Bob wanted me to ask you."

What to do with them? The United States military has rules for prisoners of war, as do the French. The Allied world has made conventions to ensure humane treatment in the end. She knows the answer she should give.

Finished pulling the metal out of his shoulder and chin, she douses the cuts with the rest of the liquor and bandages them where she can. Sitting on a stool across from him, she looks into his dark-lashed eyes.

Dédé. Sweet boy. Twenty-two years old, fighting in a war. Twenty of his boys—brothers he has lived with and trained and cared for—dead. No family. No home.

Roger. On his way to Klaus Barbie's prison.

She shudders.

"Tell Bob," she says, "their fate is in the hands of the boys who have been on the run for years. The young men who've had their families and homes and country destroyed. They're more qualified to make that decision than I am."

Chapter 38

H ERE'S THE LIST," says Bob.

He steps into the barn, where Dédé's team prepares to raid the Nazi hospital. They received a message from the old woman at the hotel that the boches were evacuating the last patients. Once they get the all clear, they'll sweep in to make sure there aren't Nazi soldiers left there or anywhere in Chambon.

The paper Bob hands Virginia has all the names and addresses of the suspected Milice from the region. They might not be able to help Roger, but they can ensure that every betrayer and collaborator from here to Le Puy is eliminated.

"Hunt, imprison, and interrogate them," says Virginia. "Shoot any who resist."

Bob nods, and leaves with his team.

Virginia ties the orange scarf at her neck and wraps the blue shawl over her hair. She checks the liberator pistol and tucks it in her belt.

"I think you should stay here," Dédé says.

"I didn't ask your opinion."

"HQ won't be pleased."

"What they don't know won't hurt them."

She won't be deterred. She needs to know MP Haas is gone or dead.

Every time she closes her eyes, she sees his thinning blond hair, his pale eye, and his translucent skin. She hates the way he looks at people in town as if they're his property, and the way he watches for her. If she and the Maquis are the shadow of the Resistance, he is the shadow of the Reich.

On the way to the hospital, angry storm clouds gather. The wind has been fierce, even blowing drops off target. They had to cross a forest for the last one, pulling massive containers out of trees and dragging them up cliffs. Thank goodness the men are so young and strong. In spite of looking old, she, too, is strong—thirty-eight years strong. The men love to see her hauling and climbing. On the last drop, while she gave the final, curse-laden yank freeing a container stuck in a thick hedge, one of Simon's Maquis—the young, Jewish man named Serge, whose studies to become an obstetrician are on hold because of the war—laughed and told her she could have birthed a baby. Then he proposed to her.

Absurd as it is, it feels good to be the object of adoration of hundreds of strapping young men. In spite of their rough start, they've grown to love her, and she them. But because of this, the stakes are high.

On the group's march through town, shopkeepers watch with interest, some pulling their curious daughters out of doorways and windows. Guns in the open, the Maquis grin and wink at the young women of town, on whom Virginia sees an interesting commonality. They wear silk shirts and skirts, in army green and white. It dawns on her that she's not the only one for whom Dolmazon has made parachute clothing.

It's not the fists alone that win the fight.

On the approach to the hospital, Virginia looks up to the window where the MP's face has been staring out, but he's no longer there. Why is she still so unsettled?

Dédé's men lead, kicking in the door and shouting as they surge into the hospital, up staircases, breaking in rooms, overturning furniture. Once inside, Virginia pulls out the liberator pistol, cocks it, and loads the cartridge. Tense and ready to shoot, she passes through the lobby and climbs the stairs to the second floor. Halfway up, she hears Dédé shout.

"Hands up!"

Two Maquis run into the room. She hears a groaning noise and looks around the corner.

The smell is the first thing to greet her, followed by the horrid sight of MP Haas and his infected leg. What's left of the putrid thing is black to the thighbone, green ooze covers his hip and pubic area, and flaking red skin rises up to his bare chest. The bed where he sweats and gasps is at an odd angle, facing away from the window, as if someone tried to move him but abandoned the task. The large, impressive uniform he once filled hangs on the wardrobe door—the silver of the neck plate flashing—while his body wastes away on threadbare sheets. She pulls the shawl off her head to cover her mouth and dismisses the gagging Maquis.

"You, too," she says to Dédé. "Leave me."

"I won't," he says, his gun still pointed at the monster, as if it could lift a hand to harm her. While she admires Dédé's dedication to her safety, she shows him she's armed and gives him a stern look. With reluctance, he obeys.

The sounds of the Maquis' boots and shouts can be heard echoing through the halls, moving away from her. Pointing her pistol at the MP, she crosses the room, exaggerating her limp, while keeping the gun trained on him. When she gets to the window, she opens it to let in some fresh air. She sits on the sill but keeps the gun aimed at the man.

"Here I am again, opening windows for you," she says in German.

His eyes widen.

"I know you," he says.

"You should. La dame qui boite."

He utters a curse.

"'Most dangerous of Allied spies,'" she continues. "If you weren't so stupid, you could have turned me in to Klaus Barbie. You'd have been decorated. Elevated. Rewarded. Maybe a fancy Nazi doctor could have fixed you."

He groans and drops his head back on the pillow.

"Why didn't your people take you?" she says.

"I told them I wanted to die here."

"What happened?" she says, nodding at what's left of his leg.

"A railway explosion. By terrorist scum."

She smiles.

"Was the war worth it, Herr Haas?"

He remains silent.

"Why wouldn't you let them amputate?" she says.

"And end up a *Krüppel*? I'd rather be dead."

The irony. She shakes her head.

"And you will be dead," she says. "Before the hour's up, by the smell of you."

Seeing his total impotence, she lowers her pistol, and turns her face to draw in a breath of fresh air. From his room, she can see the train station, the hotel, and the school, all the stops on the journeys of the Jewish children. She thinks of the sweetness of the classroom pets and Bible stories and corkboards celebrating these haunted little ones. It turns her stomach to look back at the MP rotting on the bed, knowing his proximity to that sweetness.

When her gaze returns to his gangrenous leg, she shudders to remember the hideous pain of her own infection. When the doctor in Turkey had asked her to choose her leg or her life, for a long time, and many times since, she's wondered if she chose correctly. The answer lies decomposing here before her.

Every day, every hour, in every interaction, we're given two options, and this man has been given the cup he chose. How many choices away from this thing in the bed is she? Three? Four? Fewer.

"Shoot me," he says, struggling to lift his head. "Put me out of my misery."

"Why not shoot yourself?" she says.

"They took my weapons."

"Running low on the front, I've heard."

He drops his head back on the pillow, grimacing from pain. Unmoved, she watches him struggle to readjust what's left of his body. When he regains his breath, he begs.

"Please. Kill me."

She thinks about it. On the train, she wished she had, but now she wonders: Would it free her from his haunting her, or forever link them? Would killing him be an act of mercy or vengeance? Does this man still have a chance at redemption before infection eats him alive?

She returns her gaze to the street and thinks of the lines of children singing "Alouette" on their trips to the forest. The MP has been able to see them come and go. Did he know what he was witnessing?

Virginia thinks of the orphan Danielle cares for alongside her own children, even now that Roger is gone. Of the girl in the polka-dot kerchief and the other children Estelle and dozens of women have escorted here and beyond, over the mountains to Switzerland. She thinks of Sophie and Mimi and Louis. The three musketeers. Her Lyon network that this man helped shatter. The mountain. Her leg. All she has lost flashes back to her like it's the end of her life.

But it isn't the end for her.

Vera told Virginia she had six weeks to live. All this time, Virginia thought it was a countdown to death, but maybe it was a countdown to new life.

Six weeks to *live*. To start living again.

To shed the past. To become tenderhearted. To love and to grieve and to atone instead of turning to stone.

Did Wild Bill know this mission would resurrect Virginia? Did Vera? Maybe.

She hates herself now for criticizing Sophie and Louis for holding a small place of love where they could meet, away from the war. Someday, Virginia hopes she's able to apologize to them.

She looks at the MP. The veins at his temples pulse on his skin that's coated in a slick sheen of sweat.

They crucified a baby.

Resolved, she stands.

If shooting him is mercy, there will be none of that here. She'd like to say it's because she isn't the Author of Life so she can't end it, but that's the belief of a Christian pacifist, which she is not. He'll be dead within hours, and she wishes for him to die slowly.

Leaning out the window, she tears the swastika off the pole, pulls it into the room, and drops it over the MP. Then she slams the window closed and drags his bed back to it while he groans and pleads.

"I hope you live," she says in his ear. "To see the raising of the tricolor."

She leaves the man writhing, dying slowly in the room.

Dédé waits for her in the hallway.

"You didn't kill him," he says.

"I didn't need to," she says. "He'll be dead by sundown."

On her way down the stairs she hears Dédé's voice say, "Yes, he will," followed by the gunshot.

BACK AT THE house, Virginia locks herself in her room and strips off the layers of elderly peasant clothing. She removes her glasses and scrubs her face and her hands, washing away the old woman. She unknots the bun and rolls her hair into a style becoming her true age. She pulls on the uniform Vera sent her—a khaki button-down slim-fitting shirt, pants, and knee-high boots perfectly suited to cover Cuthbert. She replaces the orange scarf at her neck with a tie but wraps the scarf at her wrist to keep the reminder.

Pausing at the mirror before she leaves, she takes in her flushed face, her shining eyes, her tanned skin, and her taut body.

There she is. No longer invisible.

She opens the door and walks down to meet her people.

PART FOUR

Virginia

Chapter 39

Bob is the first to see Virginia out of disguise.

When she enters the room, his cigarette dangles from his open mouth and falls on the floor. Dédé's eyes widen. Edmund blushes, his ears turning bright red. The rest of the assembled boys murmur, and someone whistles. Virginia doesn't address the reaction, only joins them at the planning table.

"Are your boys ready for all this?" she asks Dédé.

He looks at her as if he doesn't understand the words she speaks.

"Oh, come on," she says. "It was obvious, wasn't it?"

"No," Dédé says. "I mean, we knew, but we didn't *know*."

Though secretly pleased, she rolls her eyes and pretends to be exasperated.

"The only thing I'll say is to remind you that I'm your commander and you are my subordinates, and it's insubordinate to remark on the appearance of your commander, is that clear?"

They nod their heads and get to work.

Knowing the village is clean of Nazis and Milice, Virginia and the boys decide to move to the Château de Vaux, where Simon's men are headquartered, until Le Puy is liberated. The château is less than thirty kilometers from Le Puy, and there she'll have electrical power and a new wireless battery, so there's no need to pedal on an old bike in a barn to keep HQ informed and up to date.

Once they arrive at the château, they find so many Maquis groups have joined together that their numbers have swelled to a thousand, with over forty vehicles and enough artillery to make a small but formidable army. Recognized by General de Gaulle, they're now called the FFI: the French Forces of the Interior. From Allied drops, they're now uniformed and can stand proud: no longer thought of as terrorists, but as the soldiers they are.

HQ has asked that they hold at the château before the final push because of another "period of activity" commencing. They're overjoyed when Virginia is able to deliver the news that the Allies landed on the Mediterranean coast of France. Amid the roaring cheer of a thousand Frenchmen, Simon pushes through the crowds to where Virginia stands, and grasps her hands. Dolmazon soon finds them.

"Marseille," Dolmazon says through her tears. "Our beloved home will soon be out of their clutches."

Simon breaks down and embraces his wife.

In a few moments, Bob joins them.

"A scout just returned from Le Puy," he says. "The boches are frantically packing. They'll be moving out anytime now."

"And now that we've severed all those rails and roads, there's only one way out," says Dédé.

"We'll have them trapped," says Simon.

We've done it, Virginia thinks.

In moments, word spreads, maps hit tabletops, commanders are called. As they bend their heads together to plan, Virginia recedes into the shadows.

As she wanders the hallways, she notes what a strange building the château is. Its central structure was built centuries ago, while the more recent wing installed—still, a century ago—was grafted on with little regard for maintaining integrity of style or form. Inside, it's more harmonious, the rooms like a gothic lodge, a place men feel at home. A place she feels at home.

She climbs the long, spiral staircase to the window that looks out over the valley toward Le Puy. The road leading to the city is low, running like a river between hills and mountains and forests. The FFI will flank the enemy from all sides along the way. It won't be a simple fight—they're still outmatched and outnumbered—but they stand on the higher ground.

She has no doubt; they will be victorious.

SIMON ONCE SAID about the Maquis that he felt like the father of hundreds of orphans. She realizes she now feels like their mother. It occurs to her, if she'd married when her mother wanted her to, these boys are about the age her children might be. Further surprising, the thought doesn't distress her.

On her 152nd day in the field, before disembarking for the final push to Le Puy, they seek her. They are the Lost Boys—motherless waifs in need of love and reassurance before the final battle for the region. She kisses each of them on both cheeks, ending with Bob. She takes him by the lapels the way Vera took her all those months ago.

"Don't do anything foolish," she says. "This war doesn't need more martyrs."

She releases him and turns to the others.

"That goes for all of you," she says. "Make me proud."

"We are now le Corps Franc Diane," says Dédé. "Vive le Corps Franc Diane!"

Virginia laughs as the boys cheer and join their teams.

As the men leave on the march to battle, she watches the formation of the infantry units, flanked by commandeered trucks, led by a motorcycle scout. A once motley band of pirates is now an impressive army. It will be agony to wait for news from them, but she'll keep busy transmitting to HQ and helping Dolmazon and the village women prepare for the wounded.

The farther away the FFI get, the more they look like one being. Peasants, noblemen, young, old, Jewish, Gentile, all joined into one great shadow bearing down to conquer the enemy.

When the last man is out of sight, she thinks she can still hear the echo of their voices, shouts of "le Corps Franc Diane" dying out around her.

—As the Germans evacuated Le Puy, FFI closed in. 30 Germans killed, 6 wounded.

—FFI losses?

—5 FFI killed, 4 wounded.

—Copy.

—Germans asked for cease-fire to collect wounded. FFI said no, surrender in 15 minutes or get ambushed.

—Result?

—22 August 1944, Germans surrendered. FFI liberates Le Puy.

Chapter 40

POPPIES COVER THE cars parading down the main street in Chambon. "La Marseillaise" plays over the loudspeaker. Tricolors fly. Maquis wave and throw marguerites to the girls in parachute blouses and skirts. Children stand in the sunlight, out in the open, lining the parade route. Some clap and smile, others watch, dazed, wondering why they aren't being rushed to the forest to pick mushrooms.

Virginia wears the white silk dress Dolmazon made for her. Her friends in the village were all surprised and delighted to see her out of disguise. She stands with Léa and her children, Danielle and hers, and the girl Danielle keeps. Danielle's guest stands on tiptoe, jumping up and down, trying to get a better view. Virginia reaches down for her. The girl hesitates but then lets Virginia lift her. She wraps her slender arms around Virginia's shoulders, holding on, and stares at Virginia instead of the parade. It seems to take her great effort to speak.

"Is it true?" the girl whispers.

"Is what true?"

"Your leg?"

"Cuthbert? Yes, I'm afraid it is."

"Does it hurt?"

"Sometimes. But it doesn't keep me from doing anything. Except maybe ballet. But I never was one for tutus anyway."

The girl's face breaks into a grin.

"You look just like my niece," Virginia says. "How old are you? Seven? Eight?"

"Eleven."

It's heartbreaking to hear this tiny wisp of a child is much older than she looks. Malnutrition. Fear. Lives hidden in the shadows. Will this girl catch up? Will she ever outgrow her sad start in life? Will any of the hidden children?

Virginia swallows the lump in her throat and pulls a chocolate from her pocket.

Dédé got the chocolate from the surrender. The convoy at large had not only Germans but sixty families of Milice from Le Puy, terrified and hoping for protection from the Nazis, which they could no longer provide. They had trucks full of fine wines, bread, cheeses, and chocolates. The fools thought they'd continue to eat like kings when trapped like rats. The Maquis helped themselves to the supplies, distributing them to the starving villagers and their boarders from Le Puy to Tence to Chambon.

The girl unwraps the chocolate, eats it, and closes her eyes to savor it.

Returning her attention to the parade, Virginia sees three women, heads shaved, strung like cattle on a rope behind one of the Maquis trucks. They are suspected of fraternization with Nazis. Simon is eager to try all collaborators. The worst among them were shot without trial, but as recognized military, the FFI will need to be more orderly in dealing with the betrayers at large. It's a vulgar display, and Virginia doesn't want the child to see. She tries to distract her by pointing out the French flag flying over the Hôtel May.

The crowd is beginning to weigh on Virginia, so she places the girl back on her feet and excuses herself. Walking in the shadows of the cheering townspeople along the parade route, Virginia nods to Auguste Bohny, to Pastor and Madame Trocmé, to Dolmazon and her son. She waves to her boys on the floats and finds the ghosts in the crowd she has seen on her journey. The girl with the polka-dot scarf is here. So is the boy from Estelle's barn, with the white streak in his hair.

You're safe now, she thinks as she passes.

Safe as one can be in a world where a war like this was possible, where it still rages, but where the enemy is being beaten into submission one region at a time. The Allies are cleaning out Cannes, Nice, and Marseille, and the BBC has reported the liberation of Paris. Will Alesch be caught before she can get her hands on him?

The sound of the little locomotive that has been making runs to Chambon—the one line she ordered the Maquis not to cut so the Jewish children still had an escape route—startles her. She walks slowly toward it, shielding her eyes from the bright sun. When it comes to a stop, the door opens, and two women and a boy emerge. One of the women is flanked by the others, on either side, each supporting her as she hobbles along.

It takes a moment, but Virginia recognizes the gray hair of the older woman, then the dark eyes of the younger woman, and finally the spring in the step of the boy who has a face like Louis. For a moment, she thinks she must be dreaming, but when she sees the dagger the boy wears, she knows she isn't.

It's as if she's been fired from a cannon. She cries out, taking off toward them, moving as quickly as she's able, calling to them through her tears. The three stop, seeking the voice they know on the figure they do not.

"It's me!" Virginia says. "Diane!"

As each of them recognizes her, their faces break into grins, and when she reaches them, she nearly knocks them over with her embrace. The four of them laugh and cry and hug and talk over one another.

"Mimi," says Virginia. "I thought . . . You're all right."

"I will be," Mimi says, eyes wet with tears. She looks down at her son. "I am."

"My God, look at you," Estelle says to Virginia. "They already speak your name like you're legend. When they see you now, they'll be beside themselves."

"Please, you flatter me," Virginia says.

"Diane," the boy says, motioning up and down from her head to her toes, "now that's what we were expecting."

They break into fresh laughter and hugging, and Virginia helps Mimi find a bench. She can't imagine what tortures Mimi endured, nor does she want to. All that matters now is that she's here and alive. Estelle and Virginia sit on either side of Mimi. The boy asks if he can join the children along the parade route, and Mimi allows it. Once he's gone, Virginia stares at Mimi in wonder.

"I'm sorry," Virginia says. "I didn't know if I'd ever see you again."

"I know," says Mimi. "There were days I didn't think so."

"Is Lavi all right?" Virginia asks. "Has he seen you?"

"He has, my friend, but he's not well."

"Was he injured in any battles?"

"No, but he lost thirty-five men."

"I'm so sorry to hear it," says Virginia. She thinks of the angry man, and the explosives expert, and the tree they blew into the shape of a V.

"Do you have any news on Louis?" Virginia asks.

"The last we heard, he and hundreds of agents were deported to Germany, but we don't know precisely where."

Virginia shakes her head. The Allies are liberating France, but Nazi Germany still stands.

A movement on the platform draws Virginia's attention back to the train. A column of frail, pale people emerges, one at a time. They squint from the sunlight.

"Who are they?" asks Virginia.

"Jews from the camp at Drancy," says Estelle. "The last ghost train to Chambon."

"Oh, Estelle, how will they . . . ?"

Virginia can't finish the words.

"How will they learn to live again?" says Estelle. "Sometimes, all we have is to begin again. But that's a beautiful gift."

The people from the train look like skeletons, like walking ghosts. But they aren't ghosts; they are alive. They made it to the liberation.

The parade rounds the street to where they sit. Virginia feels someone staring at her and scans the vehicles until she finds the source. It's Bob. Grinning, he salutes her.

With the music playing and the crowd cheering and the tricolors moving in the breeze, Virginia stands, unwinds the orange scarf from her wrist, and waves it in the air.

Chapter 41

LIBERATION DOES NOT happen all at once. It's many small swells leading up to the crest of a wave breaking on the shore of freedom. Then it retreats and builds again, crashing over and over. And though the Haute-Loire is liberated, the war continues.

On August 31, they'd gotten a fright when a boy from town came running, crying out that tanks were coming. Hearing the distant rumble growing closer, Virginia's men armed and mobilized quickly, preparing a bazooka and tearing down the road in their trucks at breakneck speed to intercept it. When they saw the flag, they screeched to a halt. The tanks flew the tricolor, and when they reached the main street and started throwing gum and chocolates, there was another parade.

General de Lattre de Tassigny of the Free French Forces officially read the proclamation of liberation over the town of Le Chambon-sur-Lignon. The French liberated by the French. The townspeople laughed and cried, and then they watched in wonder when they spotted the African soldiers, the first people of color in the village. Virginia wondered if those men had volunteered for service or if they'd been conscripted. She couldn't imagine what their war looked like.

On September 2, Lyon was liberated. The demons who'd possessed that magnificent city of Virginia's first mission had been exorcised, cast back to hell with the Allies on their tails. How she longed to join the chase, to find and free Roger, to put the bullet into Klaus Barbie herself, to hunt Abbé Alesch.

The first of the Jedburgh drops in the region came too late to liberate, but having officers now to command the FFI frees Simon and many among his groups to join General de Lattre de Tassigny's ranks and head north. Upon learning Simon and his men left, hers grow even more restless, eager to join the fighting. She is, too, but HQ has asked her to receive one more Jedburgh drop in Chambon before leaving. The officers being sent to her specialize in arms and infantry, and with what they'll bring in the way of talents and funding, le Corps Franc Diane—as her men persist in calling themselves—will be able to form their own fighting unit.

Under the first full moon of September, Virginia and her men await the Jedburgh team of Hemon, Raphael, and the region's new wireless operator, Electrode. Because she knows her days here are numbered, Virginia is especially mindful of the gorgeous night views. The enchantment deepens when, far in the distance, from a farm somewhere on the plateau, the sound of a lonely violin reaches their ears, teasing out the strains of "Clair de lune." The music is hesitant and imperfect yet, somehow, all the more perfect because of it.

She knows she's needed elsewhere, but Chambon will always have a special place in her heart. HQ approved money from what the Jeds will bring to fund bankbooks for the orphans ages sixteen and under. Dolmazon will oversee the distribution and record keeping during the long process of finding their surviving families.

They get ahead of themselves, though. The war is far from over.

When the shadow of a plane appears in the far-off distance, it's clearly fighting the persistent winds. The team take their places and, as they shine lights to the sky—no sense in changing procedure now—she pulls out the S-Phone and calls the pilot. The connection crackles, even as he draws nearer, and she isn't able to make contact. To her frustration, the plane veers away from them. She curses as she sees the parachutes open far across the river, disappearing into the night.

"What do we do?" says Bob. "They have to be least thirty kilometers away."

"If the area weren't liberated, we'd have to find them," says Virginia. "But we're clear, so they'll just have to find us."

"Are you sure?"

Virginia gives Bob a look. He raises his hands in the air in surrender.

"They have our code names and phrase," she says. "If we're going to allow any of these men to join le Corps Franc Diane, they better prove they're resourceful. Come on."

VIRGINIA CAN'T SLEEP. First, she can't shake the face of the undernourished girl who stays with Danielle, who looks like her niece. What will become of the child if her parents are dead? Will she have distant family to raise her, or will she stay here, in Chambon? Will any of the ghosts? Also on her mind are the Jeds she abandoned. She doesn't feel guilty for not searching for them, but she doesn't want to wait days for their arrival. Restless, she and her men are anxious to be useful again to France. Blood is in the air, and they long to join the hunt.

As the first glimpse of the sunrise peers over the mountains, Virginia pulls on her uniform shirt and leaves it untucked over her dirty trousers. She doesn't bother to pin her hair and grabs her laundry before heading down to the hidden cove Dolmazon showed her. Protected by pines and beech trees, it's nestled in a secret swell of the river, and Virginia has been washing in its cool waters. Once there, she removes her uniform, her stump sock, and Cuthbert, and uses a walking stick for balance as she hops, leaving the stick on the riverbank before wading into the Lignon.

Born of melted snow at mountain peaks, the cold water is a shock on the skin. Once she adjusts to the temperature, she scrubs her laundry clean and hangs it on the bough over the water. Then she washes herself, taking time to enjoy the fragrance of the English tea rose soap Vera sent. The shafts of sunrise make a cathedral of the cove. Virginia floats on her back, staring up at the forest canopy and listening to the birdsong, wondering when she'll be able to do this at Box Horn Farm.

After a while, with great reluctance, she readies herself to leave. She's scheduled to meet Edmund for transmission at nine o'clock, and she can't be late. When he is, she never lets him hear the end of it.

She combs out her wet hair and lets it hang long and loose over her shoulders to dry, before toweling off her body, attaching Cuthbert, and dressing in the parachute frock Dolmazon made for her. It will be nice to wear on a summer day, while her uniforms dry. Nice to wear one last time before she resumes the fight.

It takes her a moment to realize the forest has become silent. The birds no longer sing. The hair on the back of her neck rises. She scans the understory, alert to any movement, but sees none. She pulls out the knife she packed in her laundry bag and quickly gathers her wet clothes.

Butterflies rise from the meadow as she walks back to the Salvation Army house, looking over her shoulder the whole way. Is her paranoia just that, or was someone there? Will she ever be able to stop watching her back?

By the time she returns and finishes hanging her laundry to dry, Edmund is in the barn waiting for her. Lacking power and needing to save her battery for when they take to the road, they've resumed transmission with Edmund's bicycle generator. He taps his wristwatch and gives her a look of reprimand.

"It's eight fifty-six, I'll have you know," she says.

"You once told me five minutes early is late."

"For a drop to receive humans," she says. "Not for transmission."

"Will you forgive me for insubordination when I give you this?"

He presents her with a plate of scrambled eggs, a warm croissant, and grape jam.

"A croissant!" she whispers. "How did Léa manage it?"

"Dédé gave her yeast and sugar from the boches' stores."

"Yes, you're forgiven," she says, devouring her breakfast, eating with her fingers and—much to Edmund's delight—feeling no shame at licking a blob of jam off the plate when she finishes.

They begin transmission, Virginia alerting HQ that they await the Jeds, who went off course in the drop. She says the conversation aloud to keep Edmund up to speed.

—Once they arrive, permission to prep men to head north? she taps.

—Denied. Must await Electrode drop.

—Why wasn't he dropped with the others?

—Equipment malfunction. Drop set for 8 September.

"Argh!" says Virginia. "We have to wait another three days before we can even begin to prepare to leave?"

"More time in this lovely mountain place," says Edmund.

"The men are getting restless."

"Not just the men," he mumbles.

She rolls her eyes and continues her transmission.

—Why not drop Electrode tonight?

—Bad weather in London. Also, need to prep more containers.

"More containers," she says aloud. "God, they're trying to kill me with inventory."

"More supplies are always good, right?" asks Edmund.

"Stop trying to look on the bright side," she snaps.

—Anything we can put in that drop to make you feel better? taps HQ.

"Sure," she says aloud. "I'll take a bottle of fine French wine, delivered by a handsome, roguish man to distract me from my woes."

"I'm shocked," says Edmund. "I've never heard you speak that way. You could have your pick from any of us under your command."

"I said, 'a *man*,' Edmund. Preferably one of shaving age."

He pushes her while she laughs at him, but a creak in the barn door causes them to stand on alert, guns drawn. They keep them pointed at the face peering around the corner.

"How long since you've had a farmhand?" he asks. His voice is deep, and his French is perfect.

They lower their guns, and Edmund motions with his head for the man at the door to walk in. He's slender, with dark hair, light eyes, and a five-o'clock shadow on his chiseled jaw. He wears civilian clothes that look worse for wear, but his skin is tanned and healthy. When his gaze meets Virginia's, he breaks into a grin, as if he's known her a long time.

"I can't help you with that bottle of wine, just yet," he says. "But I've been shaving for years."

Chapter 42

RECRUITED FOR THE OSS F Section, Hemon—the first Jedburgh to find them—was born and raised in France and lived in Paris with his family until he turned fourteen, when he moved to the United States. Though his family returned when he was eighteen, he elected to stay on in New York, a city he'd grown to love.

Raphael had followed shortly. He was equally spry and friendly, and Virginia was impressed by how quickly the two Jedburghs got to work, falling in with her men as effortlessly as if they'd been there all along. They'd been dropped with several containers, and helped find, unpack, and store them before the early afternoon.

"The American pilots need a few lessons from the RAF," says Virginia. "They keep going off target."

"Don't be too hard on 'em," says Hemon. "The RAF have had a few years' head start on operations."

"At least they sent us capable men. I like how you two work."

"Only the best and hardest working for Diane's network. You're legendary in intelligence circles, you know?"

"She certainly has a legendary temper," says Bob.

She punches Bob in the arm, and they enjoy a laugh while packing into the truck.

Léa has rooms prepared for the newcomers, and invites them to dinner, along with Virginia and her core team. On the way, Virginia drives them around town while Bob and Edmund regale Hemon and Raphael with their tales of treachery and adventure, pointing out the key places and players in the theater of their war. It's a relief to have English speakers in conversation when one has been used to thinking and talking in another language for so long. She teases Bob and Edmund for their poor English accents, which gives them all a good laugh.

When they arrive at Léa's, Virginia is pleased but sobered to see Danielle, her two boys, and their guest child. Danielle is pale and quiet but smiles briefly when she sees Virginia. She sits near where the children play tag with Dédé in the grass. After introductions, Hemon heads straight for the kitchen to help prepare dinner for fifteen.

"He's quite a cook," says Raphael. "That's the main reason I stick with him." Virginia smiles.

"How will there be enough?" he wonders aloud, looking at the group.

"It's loaves and fishes around here," says Léa. "I never have enough, but there are always leftovers."

After their game of tag, Dédé takes the children out in the barn to see the litter of Brittany puppies born five weeks ago. The brown-and-white pups tumble over one another, nibbling the clothes and fingers of the children, to their delight, providing a glorious distraction from the heaviness around them.

Virginia, Edmund, and Raphael help set the table and fetch ingredients from the cellar, all while Danielle sits pale and blank at the kitchen table. Hemon pours sun tea in a tall glass over chipped ice, adds honey and a mint leaf garnish, and brings it to Danielle. Virginia can't hear what he says to the woman when he kneels before her, only sees him take her hands, wrap them around the glass, and help her drink. It's such a small gesture of kindness, but it awakens Danielle. She smiles and assures him she can drink the rest on her own.

By the time the meal is ready, the sun is beginning its descent through the lavender sky. Two long tables are set outside, overlooking the meadow.

The children pick wildflowers and place them in preserve jars, and Bob hangs lanterns from the trees. Léa brings the bread, potato cakes, and salads, and Hemon, now wearing Léa's floral apron, follows carrying a gorgeous, fragrant rack of lamb.

After Edmund offers prayers, they dig in with relish. Conversation flits between them like fireflies. Praise for Hemon and Léa for the feast, praise to God the region is free of Nazis, praise to Virginia and her men for helping bring it about. Toast after toast, echoing in the twilight, allowing them all to forget the war, if only for an evening.

"I raise my glass to you," Virginia says, holding hers up to Léa and Danielle, two single mothers with homes and farms and children to care for, who may never again see their men. She doesn't say the words, but the group senses them. They raise their glasses and toast the women.

Danielle finally speaks.

"I still have hope," she says. "I'm determined to. Besides, I would know if Roger were gone, and I feel him stronger than ever. It's as if he's right here with me."

Hemon catches Virginia's eye from across the table. They have an entire conversation with that stare. A tug on her dress turns her attention to the little girl from Danielle's house.

"Will you take me to the puppies?" she says.

Now that the girl is speaking with more confidence, Virginia detects an accent in the child's French. Is it German? Austrian?

"I'd love to take you to the puppies," says Virginia. "As soon as I help get this table cleared."

"Go," says Hemon. "We've got it."

Virginia nods at him, then rises and takes the girl's hand. When they get to the barn, Virginia lifts the girl into the stall and climbs in after her.

"Sit here," Virginia says. "See which one picks you."

Three puppies nurse at their mama, but one gets distracted by the entrance of the humans. It tumbles over and rubs against the little girl's leg. Virginia picks it up and looks under its soft belly.

"It's a boy," she says. "What will you call him?"

"Parachute," the girl says.

Virginia bursts out with a laugh.

"Where did you get a name like that?"

"Papa Le Forestier always said the parachutes brought the good things to Chambon."

Virginia feels the sting of tears. She places the dog gently in the girl's lap to take the attention away from herself. Another puppy soon wanders over, and the girl tells Virginia to name it.

"I'll call this one Locomotive," says Virginia. "Loco, for short."

"Why?"

"Because I know the locomotive is what brings the good things to Chambon."

The girl looks at her for a long moment before a smile touches her lips. She looks back at the puppy, and starts to run her finger in circles, whipping it and its littermates into a frenzy.

Soon, the adults gather in the lantern-lit barn. Danielle climbs into the stall to join the children in playing with the puppies.

"I know I offered my extra rooms to Hemon and Raphael," Léa says, "but do you have space at your place, Diane? I think Danielle and her children should stay with me for a while."

"Of course," says Virginia. "That makes more sense anyway. Now that we're allowing the new arrivals to officially join le Corps Franc Diane."

Hemon and Raphael cheer as if they've won an award. Bob, Dédé, and Edmund slap them on their backs.

In case they don't get to see the women and children again, they take their time with good-byes. They'll be on the move any day now, and they don't know when they'll get back. As they climb in the truck and drive away from the farm, Virginia steals one last glance at Léa, Danielle, and the many little heads silhouetted against the last light in the sky. She presses her fingers to her lips and blows them a kiss. They raise their arms in farewell.

———————

AFTER SHOWING HEMON and Raphael to their rooms, Virginia tries to sleep, but she can't, not with these new men under her roof, and her worry about Roger and Louis.

Virginia is out of downers, so all that's left to do is walk. She pulls on Cuthbert, her uniform pants, and a button-down shirt, places a liberator pistol in her pocket, and goes quietly down the stairs, out of the house, and toward the cliff overlooking the Pic du Lizieux. When she gets to the boulder where she sat with Bob after Roger's capture, she climbs up on it, standing so she has the best view. She takes a deep breath, drawing in the pure air.

"You look like the Statue of Liberty up there."

She spins around on the rock, drawing her pistol. Hemon stands below her, his cigarette glowing in the darkness.

"You should be more careful," she says. "That's the second time I almost shot you."

"I can think of worse ways to die."

She grins at him while putting her gun back in its holster and motioning for him to join her on the rock.

"Wild Bill and Vera told us about all you've done," he says. "It would have been extraordinary for anyone—and I hope you don't mind me saying this—but when you add the leg, it makes it all the more fantastic. Cuthbert, that's what you call it, right?"

"Yes. Cuthbert. Nobody ever gets that silly name right."

As the stars move across the sky, Virginia and Hemon talk about a thousand things and nothing at all. It's easy being with him. She doesn't mind that he brings up her leg, and she tells him the whole story. He tells her about his deep love for his parents and sister, and how he can't wait to surprise them in Paris. When they try to figure out if they ever would have crossed paths while Virginia was a young university student, she's surprised to learn he's eight years younger than she is.

"Well," says Virginia. "We wouldn't have run into each other at a Josephine Baker show, since you were only twelve when I was twenty."

"I saw Josephine Baker dozens of times," he says. "Including when I was far too young for the burlesque. I even sent her a marriage proposal by mail."

Virginia smiles at him, remembering that night almost twenty years ago with her friend from her pension. He returns her smile, and stares at her a long time. She realizes their hands touch on the rock and looks down at where his rests on hers. When she returns her gaze to his, a lock of hair falls across her eyes. He reaches up to tuck it behind her ear.

"What's your real name?" he whispers.

His lips are millimeters away from the side of her neck, but he doesn't touch them to her skin. She can feel a buzzing between them, like an electrical current. She raises an eyebrow and shakes her head.

"I'll tell you mine," he says. "It's Paul Goillot."

"That suits you," she says.

"Thank you," he says. "Now yours. I won't tell a soul. I just want to know your name."

"You really want to know?"

"Yes."

"Why?"

"Because I want to start knowing *you*. The you behind the legend. I know she's in there."

"No," she says with a smile. "Not until the liberation."

"We're liberated!"

"Not the rest of France."

"But I already know you intimately."

"Please," she says, pulling away and climbing down from the rock. "A few days in a dusty barn hardly makes us intimate."

"No, I once came across a water nymph, swimming in a cove, and she almost made me lose my senses. Imagine when I found that nymph in the dusty barn."

She's glad for the darkness of night so he can't see her burning. She was right about someone watching her bathe, and that someone is sitting before her. Not only that, but he saw her completely naked—even without Cuthbert—and he didn't run away screaming. In fact, he's been running toward her ever since.

He jumps down from the rock and places his hands on her waist, pulling her close to him. He leans in as if he's going to kiss her, but again deflects up to whisper in her ear.

"Tell me your name."

She takes his face in her hands and holds his stare as long as she can bear it. Then she puts her lips close to his ear, where she pauses one second—two, three—before whispering, "No."

Chapter 43

IT HAS BECOME their game. He asks her name, she refuses. Even as they get down to business with the men, training them in weapons, packing trucks, ensuring they have enough arms, food, tents, and medical supplies to make a contained infantry unit, and waiting for the actual, final drop.

Electrode was promised on September 8, but weather prevents the drop until the eleventh. His arrival goes well and now that he's here, he can take over wireless transmission for the region, freeing Virginia to leave. They've received approval to set out, heading north toward the Swiss border. If they find FFI groups along the way to join, they may do so, or they will rendezvous with the Allied command center at Bourg to decide their futures.

Before the group leaves Chambon, many families join them in the good-byes. Le Corps Franc Diane is made of village boys, orphans, and Maquis, young men beloved by many. There are tears from parachute-blouse-wearing girls and admonitions from mothers—foster and real. There are baskets of food pressed into hands, puppies and children tumbling about, and prayers said over the convoy. One of the boys who has decided to stay in Chambon asks to snap a few pictures of the group, and Virginia agrees only if he promises to guard them with his life and never show another living soul. He takes a picture of her with the Jed team and Parachute the puppy. Then he asks for one more that he can join. Her Lost Boys line up on a porch, with her in the middle. They shout, "Le Corps Franc Diane," before the photograph is snapped.

Her emotions threatening to get the better of her, she issues a stern order for the boys to fall out. The sixteen of them climb into the two waiting lorries, and they wave good-bye until the last villager stops running.

Then all Virginia can see are the walls of rock rising, and the forests growing, closing their protective curtains around the miraculous village of Le Chambon-sur-Lignon, the place that helped bring her back to life.

THEY'RE QUICKLY SOBERED by all they pass on the long journey.

Rotting horse carcasses. Burned-out vehicles. Dead bodies. Shell-shocked refugees. Bombed towns. She can see in some of the boys of Chambon that they didn't bargain for this. They were unprepared for how sheltered they were on the mountain.

Now that it's mid-September, the nights are becoming cold in the high elevations through which they travel. Lack of sleep and food rationing make the boys bicker. She finds herself feeling more the mother than ever. And yet . . .

Paul.

Is it wrong she thinks of him as his real name instead of his code name?

Paul is always in the passenger seat when she drives. He's first to catch the fish and fastest to kill and skin the rabbits that he somehow transforms into delicacies over the open flames of their campfires. Each night, he sleeps with his tent outside hers, guarding it. Each morning, the first thing she sees is his arm poking through the opening, holding out a tin of hot tea. All the time he whispers, "What's your real name?" She continues to dodge the question.

The boys adore him. At thirty years old, and with Simon gone, Paul is the new father figure of the group. He teaches the younger ones to fish. He shows them how to make a tent out of a parachute. He's a patient instructor with shooting and weapons cleaning, and a tireless leader in physical exercises. He makes them talk about the bad things they see along the road, keeping them from pushing memories deep down to haunt them later.

They find no groups to join, so they continue on to Bourg. Fifty kilometers outside the city, they pop a tire on a shred of metal. The sun setting, they decide to push the truck off the road for the night behind a pair of twisted iron gates hanging askew from an arched entranceway. After hiding the truck under cut branches, they drive the other truck slowly, while the overflow of boys follows on foot. At the top of the driveway they stare with open mouths at the magnificent fountain standing dry and crumbling before the abandoned château.

The place has been decapitated, its highest turret shaved off by a bomb, the tower below black from having burned. But that's only one side of the château. Though the windows are blown out—pigeons fluttering in and out of them—and vines choke its doors, the beauty of the manor is still apparent.

The boys run toward the place as if it were an amusement park but are stopped by Virginia's stern command. Paul and Raphael cock their machine guns and lead with Bob and Dédé as the boys fall into orderly, armed formation, checking each room on each floor methodically and thoroughly. Virginia is last, slowly walking in and looking at the high ceilings, running her hands over the moth-eaten tapestries, touching the keys of an out-of-tune piano, lifting corners of sheets draped over furniture now thick with rodent nests and bird droppings. Frescoes line a grand hall where Virginia can almost hear the tinny, music box sound of a waltz. The art contains gorgeous renderings of religious legends—slayed dragons, men in the bellies of whales, and Mary crushing the head of a serpent.

"La Madone," says Bob, ducking away before Virginia can slap him.

A whoop from the staircase winding down to the cellar brings her back to the foyer, and in a few moments, Paul rises with his arms full of bottles.

"Finally, I'm the answer to all you asked for," he says. "A man who can shave, bearing fine French wine."

"I think she said a handsome, roguish man," teases Edmund.

"He'll do," Virginia says.

THEY'VE MADE A blazing fire in the enormous hearth. Serge knows how to play the piano and bangs out song after out-of-tune song, while the boys sing, and smoke, and drink, and take turns dancing Virginia around the room. Each new set of hands that take her makes her long more for the strong hands of the man sitting next to Serge at the piano. Paul's neck strains as he throws his head back and sings. He stops only to take swigs from the bottles being passed or to grin at her around the cigarette between his teeth.

While she dances with Bob, then Dédé, then Edmund, then this boy and that boy, she turns her eyes continually to Paul, where he never takes his eyes from her but stubbornly refuses to dance. After hours, tired of waiting, she marches over to him and holds out her hands. He takes one and kisses it but remains seated.

"Well?" she says.

"I don't dance," he says, still holding her hand. He presses it to his pounding heart.

"What, too macho?" she says. "You only hunt and fish and shoot guns?"

"In part."

"What's the other part?"

He stands, moving her hand so it rests on his side, and leans to whisper in her ear.

"I only dance with women whose names I know."

She narrows her eyes at him.

"Then I guess you won't be dancing with me," she says.

He doesn't smile anymore. He looks at her like a wolf who wants to eat her, a look that makes her shiver. She takes her hand from his waist and turns her back on him, finding Bob, who's all too happy to spin her around without knowing her true name.

Soon, the boys begin to yawn. She tells them to drink the water in their canteens and corral their sleeping bags around the fireplace, and Paul says he'll take first watch. The rest negotiate second and third watch. When they finally settle, she's hit with a sudden melancholy that crashes over her like a wave.

They'll be at the Allied command center tomorrow and—though they haven't discussed it—because they didn't find any Maquis groups to join along the way, the boys will be folded into the French army. Paul and Raphael can join the Allies, but, as a woman, she cannot. The war will continue, and she might never see any of them again. She's angry with herself for letting down her guard, for playing this game that can't sustain itself.

A little drunk and burdened by the knowledge of what the future holds, she leaves the room and starts for the staircase. She'll seek out a room with a bed and maybe a pipe that will cough up some water with which to wash. When she reaches the top, she hears a voice.

"Where are you going?" says Paul. "I can't watch over you if you don't stay with us."

I can't watch over you.

The words pierce her. How foolish she was to indulge in feelings of love during war. How foolish to allow the ice around her heart to thaw, leaving it vulnerable to injury.

"I didn't need watching the four years of this war prior to meeting you," she says. "I don't need it now."

She doesn't wait for his reply, leaving him alone at the bottom of the stairs.

Chapter 44

THE ALLIED COMMAND center bustles with activity. British, French, American, Canadian. Men darting to and fro, organizing and reorganizing, sending le Corps Franc Diane from one tent to the next. She can imagine what they think seeing her group: a hungover, ragtag band of boys with a limping woman, and two cheap vehicles—one with a spare tire the size of a bicycle wheel—that had seemed loaded with supplies in Chambon but now look like street peddlers' wagons.

We liberated the Haute-Loire, she wants to say. *Do you understand how courageous these boys are?*

But there's too much noise and motion, and the end comes much faster than she anticipated.

While they take careful inventory of the weapons they must turn over, Raphael and Paul meet with French and American colonels. They return with sober faces.

"The boys have two choices," says Raphael. "One, go home to Chambon. For those of you seventeen and under, that's your only choice."

"I thought seventeen-year-olds could join," says a boy.

"Only with parental consent."

The boy looks down at his boots.

"There's no shame in returning home," says Raphael. "You can act as gendarme and continue protecting the village. And since the vehicles are from the region, they'll even allow you to take them back."

Edmund and some of the boys from the village look at one another in silent consultation.

"The other choice?" says Bob.

"Enlist with the French Ninth Colonial Infantry Division, and join the fighting," says Raphael. "For now, I'm going to work as a liaison for those who choose that route, reporting back to HQ through military communications."

The group starts to talk to one another, negotiating, seeking advice, deciding on their futures. In a short time, they've sorted themselves out. Bob is the first to look at her.

"What will happen to Diane?" he says.

She has been thinking about this the whole time.

"I'm going to Paris," she says. "I have friends there, and I'll be able to wire HQ to update them on what we've seen and find out where my next mission is."

And search for Alesch, she thinks.

It has just dawned on the boys that this is the end of the line with her, and some of them look like they're going to cry. Not wanting to waste any more time and desperate to keep herself together, she pulls swarms of them into hugs, and kisses each of their heads, wishing each young man good luck in his future endeavors.

"We'll reunite when the war is over," says Serge. "Under the moon in Chambon. We'll toast the swift, wondrous career of the illustrious le Corps Franc Diane."

This brings smiles to all of their faces.

The boys begin to fall away, leaving Edmund, Dédé, and Bob.

"Are you sure you want to join the big boys?" she asks.

"We couldn't be better prepared for it," says Bob.

Edmund steps forward to receive her first hug.

"Thank you," Virginia says, "For sharing your village and your family with me. And for making that brilliant generator."

She kisses him on both red cheeks and dismisses him to face Dédé. His eyelashes are wet, and he can't meet her eyes.

"My man Friday," she says. "You never called me la Madone, but you always made me feel as powerful as Our Lady of Le Puy. You took my abuse and my incessant demands, and always exceeded what I asked of you. I will miss you forever, and I pray we meet again after the war."

She kisses both of his wet cheeks and dismisses him. She's unable to hold herself together before Bob. He wraps her in a bear hug and rocks her back and forth while they both cry, pulling apart to wipe each other's faces and laugh and wish each other well.

"I'm not going to say good-bye," she says. "You, I *know* I'll see again."

With that, they're gone.

As she watches her men go, she feels a tap on her shoulder.

Paul.

"Aren't you going to be late?" she asks. "Raphael is already preparing to move on."

"Late for what? Paris?"

"Excuse me?"

"Paris. Isn't that where you said you're going? I was dropped to serve you. As the sole remaining member of le Corps Franc Diane, I intend to see my mission through."

THEY BUY THE truck with the small spare off the boys headed for home, and drive back to the château, where they'll stay the night before heading to Paris.

In the afternoon sun, they find a grand bedroom, and beat the mattress free of dust, and cover it with parachute sheets. They build a fire in the fireplace, and Paul cooks them a dinner of roasted pigeon, paired with more bottles of wine from the cellar, and they talk about their childhoods and their jobs and all their old loves and heartaches. They discuss how they can't wait to see the tricolor again flying over Paris, their most beloved city. To sip real coffee in a café. To hear the bells of Notre-Dame. To watch the sunrise over the Seine.

When they finish dinner, they heat and haul buckets of water to the enormous bathtub that overlooks the miles of rolling green hills and valleys, and in the setting sun, they pause to look at each other.

"You can go first," Paul says.

As he turns to leave, she reaches for his arm. He stands before her, face dark with longing.

She reaches down and slowly unrolls his sleeves, brushing his forearms with her fingers along the way. Then she lifts her hands to his neck and unbuttons his shirt. Once it's open, she slides her fingertips along his collarbones and down his arms, so the shirt drops to the floor.

She holds out her arms, and he slowly unbuttons and sheds her shirt, running his rough hands along her hips, and kissing her along the shoulders. His breath coming fast, he stares at her a moment before burying his head in her neck.

The time he's taking is excruciating.

She slides her fingers down his back and around to his stomach, but when they reach his pants, he grabs her hands and pulls back.

"I don't even know your name," he says.

She pulls him to her, pressing herself into his chest, reaching up to feel the softness of his buzzed hair, and running her lips along his earlobe. She gives him a little nibble before whispering to him.

"My name is Virginia Hall."

His tongue in her mouth is a shock. It's like oxygen.

They forget the bath, moving toward the bed, where they fall into each other. He forces her to slow down, kissing along her neck, whispering her name all the way.

"Virginia," he says into her hair, her shoulders, her lips, her stomach.

He removes her bra, but when he moves to unbutton her pants, she stiffens.

"What is it?" he says.

"I . . ."

"I've seen you. All of you," he says. "And you are perfect."

She's still, weighing his words, letting them burrow into her until she believes him. When she does, she allows him to remove her pants. She shows him how to remove the garter holding her sock. She teaches him how to detach her prosthetic, and he sets it on the floor next to the bed as casually as if it were a boot. He finishes undressing and slides onto his back, pulling her on top of him.

And all through the long night he never stops whispering, "Virginia."

Chapter 45

T HE LATTICED CAFÉ windows filter the London light at an enchanting slant. Dust motes play in the air. Virginia spots Vera in her corner booth, smoking, moving her gaze between the newspaper in front of her and the café. Her eyes light up when she sees Virginia.

"Still smoking," Virginia says, sliding in the booth.

Vera shrugs and holds out a pink container of Passing Clouds cigarettes.

"No, thanks," says Virginia. "You know I don't like to be dependent upon anything."

A flash of a smile flickers across Vera's face before she stubs out her cigarette in the near-overflowing ashtray. She turns her attention to her handbag, where she searches for her folding knife. Vera opens it and runs the blade along the pencil tip, slicing away wood and making a sharp point, curled shavings littering the tablecloth. A waiter joins them.

"The usual?" he says.

"Thank you," they each say.

Vera starts the crossword puzzle while she fires her questions.

"How is Cuthbert?"

"Stubbornly operative."

"Tell me about war. What surprised you?"

"Human capacity for evil."

"What about yourself?"

"Endurance."

As Vera completes the puzzle, the waiter arrives, placing two steaming, gravy-soaked plates of roast and potatoes before them. The women don't waste time chatting, making quick work of devouring their feast. When they finish, Virginia asks the questions.

"New destination?"

Vera scans the room. She leans closer to Virginia.

"Austria."

"Can Hemon join me?"

"Though I strongly oppose wartime attachments, yes. He'll slip right into your cover."

"Are you going to finally tell me?"

"Tell you what?"

"Why it was so important you send me to Chambon?"

"You know exactly why Chambon was important."

"Yes, but not why it was so important to *you*."

Vera stares at Virginia a long moment before speaking.

"In spite of your success, the war continues," says Vera.

"I'm aware of that," says Virginia.

"And though I'm sure you've divulged more than you should have to certain agents in the field, in no way do I wish to compromise my safety or that of others by giving you more information than you require."

"Understood."

The waiter returns and whispers in Vera's ear. She reaches in her handbag, places the ration cards on the table—which he whisks away—and erases random letters on the crossword. When she finishes, she drops the pencil back in her handbag.

"Forgive me," Vera says. "I must go. Wild Bill and I will see you and Hemon for the full briefing tomorrow at eight o'clock."

Vera nods and leaves her. Virginia watches her go, noting the pointed glance she gives the waiter. Virginia waits until Vera leaves before sliding the crossword so she can read the missing letters.

O. L. D.

Old what?

T. E. S. T. A. M. E. N. T.

Her heartbeat quickens. She grabs the crossword, shoves it into her pocketbook, and hurries out into the street to look for Vera. In the distance, she sees Vera's blue hat and glossy black hair. She rushes to catch her. When she finally does, she grabs Vera's arm and stops her.

"Please," says Vera. "We shouldn't be seen carrying on in public."

"Of course, I only—"

"You only what?"

"The missing letters. You."

"Yes."

"Now I know."

"Now you know. Does it change anything?"

"Yes," says Virginia. "You see, I had a thing I hid because I thought it would make others pity me. And I know it's very different from your secret but, as it turns out, sometimes the things we hide make others admire us all the more for what we do. As I now admire you all the more for what you do."

Vera's eyes glass over. She looks to the sky and blinks twice, dismissing the tears as she does her agents from her office.

"Eight o'clock tomorrow?" Vera says.

"Yes."

"We have a lot to accomplish in a small time."

"I know."

"And I probably don't have to remind you, but, for a wireless operator, at this stage of the war . . ."

Far away the bells of Saint Paul's ring and Big Ben chimes the hour and traffic honks around them.

And Paul waits back at her flat for her. And when the war is over, they'll sail across the ocean together so she can see her family.

"Are you listening to me?" asks Vera.

"Yes, I know," says Virginia. "I'll have six weeks to live."

Epilogue

May 1948
PARIS

A S THE SUN rises over Paris, the full moon lingers low on the horizon, dark and light sharing the same sky.

The morning train from Lyon arrives, and the sleepy crowd makes its way onto the platform. Wafts of freshly brewed coffee and warm croissants drift from cafés, the aromas perking up the travelers.

A woman disembarks. She has the day to herself before her rendezvous that evening, so she takes a long walk, passing under the French flags that line the streets and pausing to smell the tiny bunches of lily of the valley from a vendor's cart. Not far from the École libre des sciences politiques, she stops to look up at a balcony, spilling over with flowers. She bows to the building, and to another across the street, before continuing on to the Cour de justice.

When she arrives at the imposing, columned structure, a mass of people climb the stairs. She drapes a shawl over her head and folds in with them. It's already standing room only in the courtroom. Familiar forms take seats behind the prosecutor while she tucks herself deep into the crowd. In a short time, the doors that admit the lawyers and the defendant open, and in he walks.

Proud and haughty. Doughy white skin. Ice-blue eyes. The papers have been covering Robert Alesch's story, detailing his hideous war crimes, the mistresses he kept, and the wealth he accumulated from turning over Resistance members to the Nazis for money. Once the resistors were arrested, Alesch would break into their apartments and steal their belongings, including thousands of francs' worth of furniture, art, and jewels.

The judges and jury enter, and the trial begins.

The hours fall away at double speed as witness after witness—including members of the German intelligence service, the Abwehr—testifies against the vile man. A priest from Alesch's archdiocese says that though Alesch had been defrocked, he forged a letter from the archbishop of Paris to get work as a prison chaplain in Brussels after the war. A woman takes the stand and details how she trusted the priest and even confessed to him, only to have her people dragged away and tortured by Klaus Barbie one by one. Her testimony is followed by that of a doctor's. They both recounted how the priest infiltrated the network, and how they ended up imprisoned in death camps, though they were lucky to get out with their lives. They are like shining beacons of light on the stand, setting the courtroom ablaze with their charges.

The final witness takes the stand. A member of the French intelligence service gives the last, damning evidence, noting how the extensive reports of an American agent—who will remain invisible because of continued intelligence work—were crucial to Alesch's capture.

After the long day, jury deliberations begin. The crowd stands, stretches, and drifts into the hallway. The woman relocates to sit at the end of the row, behind Alesch, where she'll be able to see his profile. On her way, she makes brief eye contact with those who took the stand, their eyes twinkling in recognition. In almost no time, the judges proceed in, the crowd returns, and all are instructed to rise.

"Members of the jury, do you have a verdict?" a judge says.

"We do."

"What say you?"

"In the case of Robert Alesch, charged with intelligence dealings with the enemy, theft of personal property, and war crimes, we find the defendant guilty on all charges."

In the rising din of the crowd, the woman struggles to contain her emotion. The gavel is banged. Alesch hisses in anger in his lawyer's ear.

"For these crimes," the judge announces, "Robert Alesch is sentenced to death by firing squad."

The woman closes her eyes and takes a deep breath. When she opens them, Alesch is jerked to standing and handcuffed. His piercing blue eyes scan the crowd until they land on hers. His gaze nearly passes hers but tracks back. She holds his stare until she's sure he knows whom he sees.

Once he's gone, she recedes with the tide of the crowd onto the street, where the evening light softens the air, and the world glows, and the setting sun turns the Seine to a river of gold beneath the lavender sky.

As the bells of Notre-Dame ring for vespers, and the streetlamps light, the woman removes her shawl and makes her way to the café. As she nears it, she smiles at the sight of the silhouette in the window of the one who has been waiting for her.

Since the moment her father revealed Paris to her like a gift on a grand stage, lit by the sunrise, she has loved this city. In the crowd around her, she can almost see the faces of those she has lost slipping quietly away into the shadows to rest. She can see how Paris has come back to life in spite of what the war inflicted upon it.

Now, she may do the same.

Afterword

I AM A writer of fiction and not a biographer. While I follow historical record as closely as possible, I'm also willing to alter dates and details to serve the story. I have included a selected bibliography of suggested nonfiction titles for those who wish to read more on the fascinating and inspiring lives touched on in this novel.

A secret agent and intelligence officer of the highest caliber, Virginia Hall Goillot made for an elusive subject. In many cases, I was able to pin her down, but she and her networks also covered their tracks far too well for me to discover everything I wished to know. The Lopinats, for example, are a mystery. Also, the peasants I've named "the three musketeers" were nameless and faceless in history; it was up to me to animate them.

It feels like a grave sin but, because of the huge amount of people in Virginia's networks, I had to combine and simplify characters when possible. For example, there were so many male Lebrats (Edmund, Maurice, George, Samuel, Pierre . . .) that I chose Edmund to represent his family. That decision was made based on a powerful painting I was able to view at the CIA Museum's art gallery called *Les marguerites fleuriront ce soir* (the daisies will bloom at night), by Jeffrey W. Bass. It features Virginia and Edmund transmitting from a barn, using Edmund's bicycle generator invention.

For the sake of simplicity, I made the following decisions. If there are two safe houses mentioned in a region, there were likely double that number. If there was one train ride mentioned, there were likely triple that. Code phrases were abundant and changed often; I kept them as similar as possible. Finally, the B2 transceiver did not quite operate using the text-message style of communication portrayed in the book. For purposes of story I've simplified a complex process. My guides at the CIA Museum assured me it is not an easy or common process, and wireless operators were *not* common people of ordinary intelligence.

In terms of character, I could find very little about Estelle, so I wrote her and her family to fit my story. The MP, Anton Haas, is also a fictional composite of the Nazis who hunted Virginia. Danielle Le Forestier did not go to Cosne to fetch Virginia. That job was done by Jacqueline Decourdemanche (one of the village forgers) and Eric Barbezat (an electrician and bookshop owner). Because they did not come up again in the novel, I replaced them with one who did. I also never delved deeper into the passeurs—guides and escorts for the Jewish children to Chambon and the surrounding regions—but they deserve their own stories.

While the following scenes are within the realm of possibility, I can't prove them. It is unclear whether Virginia accompanied Mimi and Sophie on their visit to Paris, Bob to Le Puy, or Roger to Le Puy when he was arrested. There are conflicting reports about precisely when—before or during her mission—Virginia found out she was destined for Chambon. Finally, I don't know if Virginia went to confession with Robert Alesch, but numerous sources claim he betrayed from the confessional, that Virginia helped hunt him, and that Virginia made several trips to Paris during her second mission, so it is plausible. I don't know that Virginia was in the crowd for his sentencing, but it was certainly possible given that her passport had her in France at the time.

During the war, Virginia was awarded the MBE (Member of the Order of the British Empire). After the war, Virginia became the only civilian woman ever to be awarded the United States Distinguished Service Cross. In the name of keeping her identity secret so she could continue clandestine work, she refused a ceremony with President Truman, instead receiving the DSC in the privacy of "Wild Bill" Donovan's Washington, DC, office with only her mother in attendance.

Virginia became one of the first women in the newly minted CIA, where she worked until her mandatory retirement in 1966. She and Paul Goillot married in 1950 and lived in a beautiful château-style home in Barnesville, Maryland, where they enjoyed gardening, cooking, crossword puzzles, and their French poodles. Virginia died in 1982, followed by Paul in 1987. They are buried together at the Hall family plot in Druid Ridge Cemetery, just outside of Baltimore.

In telling this story, my goal was to illuminate the extraordinary courage of Virginia Hall, those in her network, and the villagers of Le Chambon-sur-Lignon and the surrounding region. Many of these people wished to keep their secrets, but now that so many have died, this novel is my prayer for those brave men, women, and children of World War II. I hope they'll forgive me for bringing their stories to light.

What Became of
Virginia's Networks?

AFTER THEIR ARREST, Louis (Marcel Leccia) and his team (Élisée Allard and Pierre Geelen)—along with Hector (Maurice Southgate) and a large number of agents—were deported to Buchenwald. In September, the Nazis began calling up and executing groups of them. I'm devastated to report that on September 10, 1944, Louis and his fellow agents were murdered. Because Hector was in the sick ward, he escaped the fate twenty SOE agents met, and survived through the liberation of the camp in April of 1945.

The doctor from Virginia's first network, Jean Rousset, survived Buchenwald. He hid patient files from the Nazis and was able to turn them in to the proper authorities after the war to bring countless Nazis to justice. The prostitute from Lyon, Germaine Guérin, also survived, but I was unable to find the identity or the fate of the nun from Virginia's first network. Rousset and Guérin both helped bring down the notorious Robert Alesch.

Sophie (Odette Wilen) survived her escape over the Pyrenees. Her guide, Santiago Strugo Garay, was so taken with her, he found her in London after the war. They fell in love and married, eventually moving to Buenos Aires and having two children. Sophie/Odette died in September of 2015 at the age of ninety-six.

In spite of the arrest and torture of Mimi (Marie Vessereau), and heavy losses to the Maquis group led by Lavilette (Fernand Vessereau), the couple survived the war. They had several children but, due to the abundance of characters, only one son—"the boy" (Gérard)—is mentioned in this book. At the age of ten, Gérard was awarded the Croix de Guerre for transporting weapons and supplies in his wagon for the Resistance. His parents were also given the Croix de Guerre, among other honors. Lavilette/Fernand died in 1961 at the age of fifty-five, but Mimi/Marie lived until 2018, when she died at the age of one hundred six.

Bob (Lieutenant Raoul Le Boulicaut) was reported to have joined the Free French's Ninth Colonial Division for the remainder of the war, and the French Intelligence Agency after it. Sadly, in February of 1946, he died shortly after checking into a Paris hospital at the age of twenty-five, likely from complications as a result of head injuries from his accident.

Most devastating was the fate of Dr. Roger Le Forestier, which came on August 20, 1944, when Klaus Barbie had Roger and 120 prisoners sent from Montluc to an abandoned house just outside Lyon. They were handcuffed in pairs, sent to the top floor of the house in groups, and shot. When the top floor was filled with bodies, the groups were sent to the floor below it, and finally to the ground floor. In order to destroy their identities, Barbie had the bodies covered in phosphorus and burned. Four days later, Montluc Prison was liberated.

Danielle Le Forestier didn't find out about Roger's murder until six weeks had passed. Inspecting what could be salvaged of the bodies, she came across Roger's distinctive belt buckle. A widow at the age of twenty-three, Danielle was left to raise her five- and three-year-old sons alone.

Happily, Simon (Pierre Fayol) and his wife, Dolmazon (Marianne), Désiré "Dédé" Zurbach, Estelle, Léa and Edmund Lebrat, and Serge Nelken survived their wartime ordeals.

I was especially fascinated by the complicated, singular, and private Vera Atkins. It isn't clear if she remained in contact with Virginia throughout their lives, but I'd like to think she did. Vera spent the years following the war seeking information for the families of every missing and deceased agent in her employ. She conducted hours of interviews of Nazis, which were used extensively as evidence in the Nuremberg trials, and she worked for UNESCO. An often criticized and controversial figure, she retreated to her cottage in Winchelsea in 1961, and led a somewhat reclusive life until her death in 2000 at the age of ninety-two. It is thought Miss Moneypenny of James Bond fame (author Ian Fleming was in the SOE) was modeled after Vera. Upon her death, even many of those who were close to her did not know she was Jewish.

Acknowledgments

This book was the most difficult I've ever written, and I am grateful to the many people who supported and helped me along the way.

To Virginia's niece, Lorna Catling, for the hours of wonderful conversation about her formidable, remarkable aunt Dindy; I treasure the time we spent together.

To my agent, Kevan Lyon, whose patience and enthusiasm have inspired new levels of my gratitude and admiration.

To my editor, Amanda Bergeron, whose instincts, cheerleading, and vision have made this story so much stronger.

To the entire team at Berkley—Claire Zion, Craig Burke, Lauren Burnstein, Jin Yu, Jeanne-Marie Hudson, Sareer Khader, Angelina Krahn, Michelle Kasper, and Emily Osborne—for their continued support of and belief in me and my work.

To Lee Woodruff, for the research books and the encouragement.

To Kristina McMorris, Devon Mish, Kelly McMullen, Frank and Sheri Damico, Dorie Thompson, Donna Triolo, Richard and Patricia Robuck, and my father, Robert Shephard, for endless moral support.

To Jim Rudnick, Ed Weihs, and Donna Cole, for sharing personal, informative, and earnest reflections on combat, duty, trauma, and its aftermath.

To Suzi Dixon and Suzanne Hartigan, whose frank, personal stories of amputation and prosthetics were so helpful to my understanding of Virginia.

To Alyson Richman and Pam Jenoff, for their insights into Jewish faith, families, and survivors of World War II.

To my "great-uncle Jack" (Francis J. Macauley III), for his tireless promotion of my books up and down Florida's Clearwater Beach.

To Michel and Candace de Messieres, the current inhabitants of Virginia and Paul's residence in Barnesville, Maryland, for so kindly opening their home and land to me.

To the knowledgeable staff of the National Archives in Washington, DC, for helping me navigate those thick files.

To the Special Collections Research Center at the University of Michigan Library, for sending digital copies of correspondence between Virginia Hall and Dr. Margaret L. Rossiter, author of *Women in the Resistance*.

To the magnificent and impressive men and women of the CIA; taking the tour of the museum was an honor I'll never forget.

To my husband, Scott, and our three sons: I wasn't easy to live with during the writing of this book, and I am grateful for their love, cheerleading, and willingness to eat dinners out.

And finally, to God, for His abundant grace and for leading me to Virginia.

Selected Bibliography

Atwood, Kathryn J. *Women Heroes of WWII: 26 Stories of Espionage, Sabotage, Resistance, and Rescue.* Chicago: Chicago Review Press, 2011.

Binney, Marcus. *The Women Who Lived for Danger: The Agents of the Special Operations Executive.* New York: William Morrow, 2002.

Buckmaster, Maurice. *They Fought Alone: The True Story of SOE's Agents in Wartime France.* London: Biteback Publishing, 1958.

Churchill, Peter. *Of Their Own Choice.* London: Hodder and Stoughton, 1952.

Escott, Beryl E. *The Heroines of SOE: F Section—Britain's Secret Women in France.* Gloucestershire: History Press, 2010.

Foot, M. R. D. *SOE in France: An Account of the Work of the British Special Operations Executive in France, 1940–1944.* London: Her Majesty's Stationery Office, 1966.

Grose, Peter. *A Good Place to Hide: How One French Village Saved Thousands of Lives During World War II.* New York: Pegasus Books, 2015.

Helm, Sarah. *A Life in Secrets: Vera Atkins and the Missing Agents of WWII.* New York: Nan A. Talese, 2006.

McIntosh, Elizabeth P. *Sisterhood of Spies: The Women of the OSS*. Annapolis: Naval Institute Press, 1998.

O'Donnell, Patrick K. *Operatives, Spies, and Saboteurs: The Unknown Story of WWII's OSS*. New York: Citadel Press, 2004.

Pearson, Judith L. *The Wolves at the Door: The True Story of America's Greatest Female Spy*. Guilford, CT: Lyons Press, 2005.

Purnell, Sonia. *A Woman of No Importance: The Untold Story of the American Spy Who Helped Win World War II*. New York: Viking, 2019.

Rossiter, Margaret L. *Women in the Resistance*. New York: Praeger, 1986.

Ruby, Marcel. *F Section, SOE: The Buckmaster Network*. London: Leo Cooper, 1988.

Stevenson, William. *Spymistress: The True Story of the Greatest Female Secret Agent of World War II*. New York: Arcade, 2007.

THE
INVISIBLE
WOMAN

Erika Robuck

A Conversation
with Erika Robuck

Q. Your previous novels are about American literary figures. What inspired you to write *The Invisible Woman*? How did you find Virginia Hall?

A. I don't want to get too fanciful, but I believe my subjects find me. I try to "write what I know" as much as possible. This means I'm always looking for extraordinary people from the past who come from places familiar to me, or to whom I feel a personal connection for one reason or another. Virginia was a fellow Marylander. The places she grew up and went to school, the waterways and hiking trails she frequented, her workplace and retirement sanctuary are all familiar to me. I understand the soil where she was grown.

On the practical side, when I was working on another wife-of-famous-male-writer book, an editor said, "Why not write about a woman who is special in her own right?" That stopped me in my tracks.

Around that time, Virginia entered my radar in a way I can't pinpoint, and she's been haunting me ever since. Virginia is not only a remarkable woman from history who grew up on my stomping grounds, but she is so extraordinary—in her own right—she could launch a subgenre of husband-of-famous-woman books.

Q. Finding information about a subject engaged in clandestine work for most of her life must have been a challenge. How did you go about doing the research?
A. It was a challenge, and Virginia was as elusive in death as she was in life.

My research process begins with inspiration and trying to walk in the footsteps of my subjects whenever possible. With three school-age sons, getting to France in person was not feasible. I'm thankful for YouTube, Google Maps, and my treadmill, which allows me to virtually walk, run, and hike all over the world.

The family land where Virginia spent her childhood summers, Box Horn Farm, is in Parkton, Maryland, north of Baltimore. The property has been sold and parceled, and the house razed, but I was able to find the approximate location of it using old land surveys. I spent many hours meandering along the trails where Virginia used to hunt, and I found the stream where she swam and canoed.

Virginia's niece, Lorna Catling, is a treasure. She welcomed me into her Baltimore home—not far from where Virginia attended school—and shared boxes of photographs and artifacts with me. Over many lunches, Lorna regaled me with tales of her formidable "Aunt Dindy." I'm happy to call Lorna a friend.

The home where Virginia and Paul lived while she was in the CIA and until their deaths is located in Barnesville, Maryland. The current owners of the house were kind enough to not only answer my strange letter asking questions about the property, but even invite me there to explore the beautiful château-style home, the kennels, and the grounds. I could feel Virginia there with me every step of the way, and even snapped a picture near the kennels that housed her French poodles that has a significant orb.

I applied as a researcher to visit the museum at the CIA headquarters in McLean, Virginia, and was thrilled to be granted access. Several officers escorted me through the exhibits, featuring artifacts from the OSS (including Virginia's Distinguished Service Cross, her passport, and a wireless transceiver), tricks of the trade (including those rat "letterboxes"), and finally that gorgeous painting by Jeffrey W. Bass. The experience was a true honor.

The National Archives in College Park, Maryland, have comprehensive files on Virginia Hall and the OSS in general, and I was able to read Virginia's reports on her war activities, her evaluations, and the letters associated with her Distinguished Service Cross.

Once I'm back at my desk, I read everything I can get my hands on—biographies, letters, articles, etc. I included many of the most helpful works in the selected bibliography. The most recent biography, *A Woman of No Importance*, wasn't published until I'd already written my novel, but I greatly enjoyed it and highly recommend it. The book that most informed my characterization of Virginia and the time and place I decided to set the novel was a French book, *Le Chambon-sur-Lignon sous l'occupation: Les résistances locales, l'aide interalliée, l'action de Virginia Hall (O.S.S.)*, by Pierre "Simon" Fayol. Because my French is very poor, I had to painstakingly type the text into Google. Though I'm sure much was lost in the translation, the obvious tension of Virginia's interactions with the Maquis of the Haute-Loire and the detailed coverage of Maquis operations in that region were invaluable to my understanding of Virginia's role there.

Once Penguin acquired my novel, I finally made the drive to Druid Ridge Cemetery in Pikesville, Maryland, where Virginia is buried. There's a family plot with a large stone labeled *Hall*, but

Virginia's modest grave is next to her dear husband's and labeled, simply, *Virginia H. Goillot*. With no special plaque or marker, Virginia Hall, the secret agent, remains invisible.

Q. What particular challenges did you face when writing the novel and, specifically, about a woman as complicated as Virginia Hall?
A. The hardest feedback to receive—and I got it from several people—and execute while remaining faithful to the character was that I needed to make Virginia more likable.

When I asked Lorna to describe her aunt, Lorna said Virginia was "intimidating and scary-smart." Virginia's landing partner on her third mission, Aramis, did not think highly of Virginia because of how she cut him off from the network. Pierre "Simon" Fayol had a contentious relationship with her. Quite frankly, no one ever described Virginia as "likable."

The fact remains, however, because this is a novel, the protagonist has to be someone the reader aligns with, sympathizes with, and wishes to succeed. My editor, Amanda Bergeron, brilliantly suggested giving the reader a look at young Virginia in a prologue. This would serve to show not only Virginia before the war and all its losses—not only before the amputation—but also the early days of Virginia's love affair with Paris. I think this ended up being the perfect introduction to a complicated woman and, with the epilogue, helped to frame the book in a satisfying way.

Q. Virginia had three missions in World War II Europe. How did you choose this time period?
A. This novel was the most difficult and unruly book I've ever written, and there were many, many drafts and restarts. (I can almost see Virginia smirking at me with an "of course, what did you expect?" look on her face.)

In the first version, I wove Virginia's story with that of a fictional female Iraq War veteran and amputee who inherits the property at Box Horn Farm without knowing to whom it used to belong. It soon became clear to me that Virginia's story was too big to be half of a multiperiod novel.

I started over and began writing Virginia's story woven into the stories of Vera Atkins and another female SOE agent. After about a hundred pages, I felt Virginia's impatience. "Focus!" she seemed to say. "This is about *me*."

So, I started over at the beginning of the war, when Virginia was in the French ambulance service, and then wrote through her first mission in Lyon, with the Pyrenees crossing at the climax. After I completed that, I realized it was all background for the story I needed to tell: the second mission. I needed to explore the question: Why did Virginia return to occupied France with a price on her head?

I believe Virginia needed me to work out her survivor guilt and PTS. She wanted recognition for and redemption of the everyday people of France and those from her networks, and justice for the betrayer. It was time to reveal the stories of the people of Le Chambon-sur-Lignon, their care for Jewish refugees, the coordinated Allied and Resistance effort to liberate the region, the beginning of the restoration of France, and Virginia's own identity. It took me a long time to understand, but once I finally did, it was as if a missing lightbulb in a string was found and replaced, and the whole circuit came to life.

Q. The novel largely deals with war. Why did you choose to include the early days of Virginia and Paul's love story?
A. First, I included it because it was true. Also, it overlapped with the end of Virginia's mission and provided such relief from the intensity and isolation that it gave Virginia—and by extension, the reader—space to exhale at the end of a very dark journey. Finally, in our inter-

views, Lorna always came back to their love story. Lorna had great affection for Uncle Paul and felt he was a softening force in Virginia's life—a true complement to her aunt. I wanted to honor him and the love he and Virginia shared.

Q. When you wrote about Ernest Hemingway in *Hemingway's Girl* and Zelda Fitzgerald in *Call Me Zelda*, there was suddenly a boom in books on the subjects. Now Virginia Hall—and female spies of World War II in general—seems to have taken hold in other works of fiction and nonfiction, and in film. What do you make of this phenomenon?

A. I believe in the power of the collective unconscious, the interconnectedness of all of us through space and time. I believe these people from the past—these real people—reach out to us for recognition. Like ghosts, some seem unsettled and need redemption. Artists tuned into that space seem to pick up on the same frequencies. It's a beautiful thing.

Q. What might we expect to see from you next?

A. I'll continue to write stories about women so remarkable on their own they could launch a subgenre of husband-of-famous-woman books.

Questions for Discussion

1. What most moved you reading *The Invisible Woman*? Which character will stay with you the longest?

2. Identity is a central theme in *The Invisible Woman*. Discuss how Virginia changes as she moves through each part of her journey—from Artemis to Diane to la Madone to Virginia.

3. Virginia's life would have been extraordinary on its own, but adding the fact that she had a prosthetic leg takes it to another level. Discuss what most struck you about her condition and how it made her more vulnerable in some ways and stronger in others.

4. In wartime, to advance their causes, soldiers, spies, and resistors sometimes engage in unsavory practices or behaviors that would be considered immoral under normal circumstances. Which of Virginia's or her associates' actions disturbed you? Did the ends justify the means?

5. Even decades after the war, Virginia Hall would not grant interviews. Not only was she still operative in the CIA, but she said she'd seen too many people die for talking. Similarly, the villagers of Le Chambon-sur-Lignon did not wish for any special recognition. They thought they were simply doing their Christian duty. Discuss whether you think Virginia and the villagers would give their blessing to this book and other works about their contributions to the war.

6. In Robuck's research on Virginia's personality changes over the years, and in speaking with veterans of war, post-traumatic stress rose as a central theme. Though contemporary understanding has greatly evolved since Virginia's time, it's still a major problem. Discuss how PTS—its effects and instances of healing—is shown in the novel.

7. What roles do the statue of Our Lady of Le Puy and references to la Madone play in the novel? Why do you think Robuck included them?

8. The women in the novel are very different from one another, but all show their own kinds of strength. Discuss the women most important to the story and how they contributed to the Resistance in their own ways.

9. At the beginning of the novel, reinforcing SOE/OSS training, Vera Atkins directs Virginia not to get attached to those in her network. How does Virginia obey and disobey this order? How does this help and hinder her efforts on both a personal and a global level?

10. What will you take away from having read *The Invisible Woman*? What aspects will resonate and linger for you?

Photo by Catsh Photography LLC

ERIKA ROBUCK is the national bestselling author of *Receive Me Falling, Hemingway's Girl, Call Me Zelda, Fallen Beauty,* and *The House of Hawthorne.* She is a contributor to the anthology *Grand Central: Original Stories of Postwar Love and Reunion* and to the *Writer's Digest* essay collection *Author in Progress.* Robuck lives in Annapolis, Maryland, with her husband and three sons.

CONNECT ONLINE

ErikaRobuck.com
 ErikaRobuck
 ErikaRobuck

Ready to find
your next great read?

Let us help.

Visit prh.com/nextread

Penguin
Random
House